KT-479-264

Aberdeenshire

COUNCIL

Aberdeenshire Libraries
www.aberdeenshire.gov.uk/libraries

27 Nov. '18   2 7 MAY 2019   0 4 APR 2020

28 DEC 2018   ABERDEENSHIRE   19 JAN 2022
                LIBRARIES

4.1.19   1 4 SEP 2019

                         1 0 JAN 2023
            WITHDRAWN
2 9 JAN 20   FROM LIBRARY
             2 4 OCT 2019

1 5 FEB 2019

                2 9 NOV 2019

- 2 MAR 2018   1 2 FEB 2020

- 1 APR 2019   1 2 FEB 2020

            ABERDEENSHIRE
            LIBRARIES

            1 8 MAR 2020

            WITHDRAWN
            FROM LIBRARY 8 DEC 2021

way ... perfect to enjoy in the afternoon' **Jane Linfoot**

Aberdeenshire

3234952

Also by Heidi Swain

The Cherry Tree Café
Summer at Skylark Farm
Mince Pies and Mistletoe at the Christmas Market
Coming Home to Cuckoo Cottage
Sleigh Rides and Silver Bells at the Christmas Fair
Sunshine and Sweet Peas in Nightingale Square

Snowflakes and Cinnamon Swirls at The Winter Wonderland

Heidi Swain

SIMON &
SCHUSTER

London · New York · Sydney · Toronto · New Delhi

A CBS COMPANY

First published in Great Britain by Simon & Schuster UK Ltd, 2018
A CBS COMPANY

Copyright © Heidi-Jo Swain, 2018

The right of Heidi-Jo Swain to be identified as author
of this work has been asserted in accordance with the
Copyright, Designs and Patents Act, 1988.

1 3 5 7 9 10 8 6 4 2

Simon & Schuster UK Ltd
1st Floor
222 Gray's Inn Road
London WC1X 8HB

Simon & Schuster Australia, Sydney
Simon & Schuster India, New Delhi

www.simonandschuster.co.uk
www.simonandschuster.com.au
www.simonandschuster.co.in

A CIP catalogue record for this book
is available from the British Library

Paperback ISBN: 978-1-4711-7436-0
eBook ISBN: 978-1-4711-7437-7
Audio ISBN: 978-1-4711-7478-0

This book is a work of fiction. Names, characters, places and
incidents are either a product of the author's imagination or are
used fictitiously. Any resemblance to actual people living or
dead, events or locales is entirely coincidental.

Typeset in Bembo by M Rules
Printed and bound by CPI Group (UK) Ltd, Croydon, CR0 4YY

Simon & Schuster UK Ltd are committed to sourcing paper
that is made from wood grown in sustainable forests and support the Forest
Stewardship Council, the leading international forest certification organisation.
Our books displaying the FSC logo are printed on FSC certified paper.

To Diane
Passionate, inspiring and occasionally hilarious,
She also happens to be my mum

Snowflakes
and
Cinnamon Swirls
at
The Winter Wonderland

Chapter 1

As I descended the stairs to the Wynthorpe Hall kitchen, the vacuum cleaner bumping along behind me, I couldn't help but think about how eerily quiet the place seemed. As a rule, lunchtime was a bit of a free-for-all as the family, which included us staff, made a beeline for a place around the table to feast on whatever delicious fare the hall cook, Dorothy, had spent the morning preparing. I reasoned that the unusual silence would likely have something to do with Anna, something she had arranged, and I decided to play along with whatever my well-meaning friend had dreamt up. Though I was, for once, itching to get back to town.

I had barely opened the door an inch before a rousing chorus of 'Here Comes the Bride' erupted. The vacuum was whisked from my grasp and the sounds of popping corks and party poppers filled the air.

'You twits,' I laughed, as Anna pulled me into a

suffocating hug. 'Tonight is just my engagement party, not my wedding day!'

'We know that, Hayley,' she said, squeezing me tighter, 'this is just a little taster of what we'll have lined up for you here at the hall when the big day finally dawns.'

Anna had certainly pulled out all the stops. I knew there would be no one better to take on the roles of wedding planner and chief bridesmaid.

'And when can we expect to see the handsome groom-to-be?' asked Angus, handing me a champagne-filled crystal flute. 'I take it the scorching scaffolder will be coming to pick you up?'

Angus Connelly, the eccentric gent who was married to Catherine, the hall owner, had certainly found a fitting nickname for my fiancé.

Gavin Garford, aka The Scorching Scaffolder, had been practically everyone's crush when I was at high school, and the subsequent years – combined with his job erecting and dismantling scaffolding – had played their part in turning a teenage tearaway into a fine specimen of manhood.

Gavin and his workmates had been called to Wynthorpe Hall earlier in the year to construct a scaffold tower that we all hoped would keep Angus safe while he worked at a height. Gavin had wasted no time in asking me out, and the whirlwind romance that led up to his autumn proposal certainly lived up to the steamy fantasies I'd had about him as a teenager.

'I'm afraid not,' I sighed, gently clinking my glass against

Anna's. 'He's working at the other side of Peterborough today and won't be back until late this afternoon.'

'Wouldn't his boss let him take the day off?' Jamie frowned. 'There must be loads still to check over at the pub.'

Clearly Jamie – Angus and Catherine's youngest son, and heir to the hall – wasn't particularly impressed by my beau's absence.

'We're both well aware of that,' I responded with a cheeky grin, 'but some of us don't have a grand family hall to live in. We have to work all the hours god sends to save up ridiculous deposits just to buy poky flats in town.'

'Still no news on the affordable housing front?' asked Mick, the hall handyman, who also lived on-site.

'Not a word,' I sighed. 'At this rate we'll be drawing our pensions before the council even approve the plans.'

'You know you're always welcome here,' said Catherine, kindly. 'We would be more than happy to accommodate you and Gavin if it meant you could secure your own home sooner.'

Catherine had been offering me a room ever since my final year at school when I'd found myself pregnant and was abandoned by my parents when they couldn't stand the shame. At the time, my nan had been working as a cleaner at the hall, and her untimely death, along with my miscarriage, had ensured my education had never been properly finished. I had gone home soon after Nan's funeral, but I gratefully took over her job. I loved working with the antiques, paintings and curios and had become something of a self-taught expert in historical conservation.

'Thank you, Catherine,' I smiled at my kind-hearted employer, 'I do know and, as always, I appreciate your generous offer—'

'But you're not going to accept it,' Jamie cut in.

'And be constantly on-hand to pick up your pants, Jamie Connelly?' I batted back as Anna giggled and Dorothy tutted. 'I don't think so.'

Washing the family's clothes had never been part of my job description, but teasing Jamie about his slack habits with the laundry bin was far easier than explaining why I needed to be at home; Mum and I may have had our differences in the past, but I couldn't leave her defenceless against Dad and his belligerent temper. I knew the time for me to move on would come at some point, but not just yet.

'And besides,' I cunningly added, 'we'll be into November next week. You'll no doubt be too busy planning for Christmas and packed to the rafters with more family and friends than you'll know what to do with, won't you?'

Moving the conversation on to Christmas was a masterstroke on my part. The mere mention of it had Angus bobbing up and down in his seat. I focused my attention on devouring Dorothy's delicious sandwiches to soak up the fizz, barely listening to the ideas Angus was rattling off, until the words 'Winter Wonderland' were spoken and I looked up to see Catherine's face fall.

'Absolutely not,' she said sternly.

'But—'

'No, Angus,' she said again. 'We're going to be stretched to our limit as it is, what with the addition of the Christmas tree competition *and* the party on top of the usual sleigh rides.'

'What Christmas tree competition?' I asked, pushing my plate away.

'Have you not been listening at all?' tutted Anna with a smile. 'We're hosting the tree-decorating competition this year because the church has so many December weddings booked that they haven't got room for all the trees amongst the pews.'

'It's going to be spectacular,' Angus joined in. Clearly, he could already picture it. 'There were almost thirty trees last year, all decorated by a different community group. The one from the hardware store was a triumph, covered in mini tools and DIY materials. I thought it was the best by far.'

'What with that and the party to raise funds for the charity,' Catherine was quick to remind her husband, 'I hardly think we'll have the time or the manpower to establish this Winter Wonderland you've dreamt up.'

'But as you just reminded us, Mum, we do already have the sleigh,' said Jamie, catching his father's eye, 'and none of what Dad has in mind would encroach on the hall. Just a couple of extra tweaks outside and we could be in business.'

'We could have a snow machine,' said Angus, wistfully.

'Are you joining ranks with your father, Jamie?' asked Anna.

She sounded as surprised as the rest of us were no doubt feeling.

'Well,' Jamie swallowed, 'the charity is going to be closed

throughout December so we could use the space in the courtyard, and we'll have an extra pair of hands on-site to help out by then. A very *practical* pair of hands.'

Anna and Catherine raised their eyebrows in perfect synchronicity and I thought it was just as well that the charity, which supported bereaved children and young adults, was going to be closed if such extravagant festive plans were afoot.

'I'm not siding with him exactly,' Jamie mumbled. 'I just don't think it would be all that tricky to set up, that's all.'

That was as good as a green light to Angus, and I could already tell that a manic few weeks lay ahead. I might have drawn the focus away from my refusal of Catherine's offer but, in the process, I'd opened up one heck of a can of tinsel-toting worms.

'So, who does this extra pair of hands belong to then?' asked Molly, who had suddenly appeared in the doorway, her wild pre-Raphaelite hair framing her pretty face.

Molly, with her white witch tendencies, had a spooky knack for popping up out of nowhere. She always looked to me as if she floated on a cushion of air, not setting her feet on solid ground like the rest of us mere mortals.

'Is it someone who is going to be passing through or someone who is staying for good?'

'Since when did anyone get away with passing through?' laughed Mick, as he pointed first at himself, then me, Dorothy and finally, Anna.

We had all arrived at the hall on the understanding that we wouldn't stay long, but that wasn't how things worked here. Once Catherine, Angus, the dogs and the hall had found their way into our hearts, we were hooked – for good.

'That's true,' Molly laughed, claiming the seat next to me and giving me an incense-scented hug. 'I just wanted to pop in to wish you good luck for tonight, Hayley, in case I don't get a chance later.'

'Thanks, Molly,' I smiled, squeezing her back.

I appreciated the fact that she had left the cosy confines of her cottage in the woods, but I really didn't need luck. It had been Molly herself who had read my tarot cards in the spring and had told me love would feature dramatically in my life before the end of the year. I admit I had been dismissive at the time, but then Gavin had turned up in his too-tight vest and set my heart pounding. Sure, he had a reputation, but who didn't? As far as I could tell, he was the person Molly had predicted, and his timing couldn't have been more perfect.

'So, who's coming to stay?' Molly asked again.

'A pal of mine,' explained Jamie. 'Someone I've known for ages and worked with out in Africa. He's visited here before, too, but that was years ago. He's agreed to take on the outdoor activities we offer at the centre, as well as adding a few more of his own design.'

'I thought you were in charge of all that, Mick?'

'I have been,' he said, 'but I'm not getting any younger and this chap has other skills Jamie can put to good use.'

'You aren't being put out to grass are you?' I teased.

'No,' he said, 'of course not. I just want to get back into the garden. The students from the horticultural college coming out every week have made a massive difference, and Catherine and I think now's the time to think about a proper renovation.'

He sounded needled that I had suggested he was on the wind-down to retirement, so I winked to show I was only teasing.

'You don't change, do you, missy?' He tutted, shaking his head. 'I hope with a wedding to plan you'll soon be more interested in your own goings-on than everyone else's.'

I laughed at that.

'I wouldn't hold your breath,' I told him. 'And on the topic of other people's business, does this pal of yours bring some tragic baggage with him, Jamie?' It was an unwritten rule – more of an assumption now – that everyone who turned up at the hall had some heartbreak they needed to heal from. We all had a sob story to tell.

'More to the point: when is he coming and where is he going to be staying? I'll need to get cracking if I have rooms to prepare.'

'He'll be with us by the end of next month,' Jamie explained, 'and he's moving into the gatekeeper's cottage, so if you could give it an airing, that would be great.'

I noticed he hadn't responded about his friend's baggage, but I didn't quiz him further. I was sure it would all come out at some point. It always did, whether we wanted it to or not.

'I'll set a fire going first thing tomorrow,' I told him, 'and I'll open the windows to get the air moving, that way the weather won't have a chance to take hold and make it feel damp.'

'And in the meantime, Hayley,' said Anna, pushing back her chair, 'we need to get you to town so you can prepare for your engagement party tonight. Are you ready?'

'As I'll ever be,' I smiled, taking a deep breath as I prepared to meet my fate.

Chapter 2

'I'm home!' I called out as I shoved the back door open with my shoulder, slammed it shut again and dumped my bag on the table. 'You still haven't fixed the door, then?'

I didn't shout out the bit about the door. My dad and his moods were always tricky to gauge when you didn't have eyes on him. These days, his temper came down to how well he'd fared playing the online gambling sites he favoured.

'But I'm not going to be here long!' I added, reaching for the kettle and checking the clock. 'I want to make sure everything's set up at the pub before I start thinking about what to wear.'

Anna, Molly and I had been on a shopping trip to Norwich to pick out outfits for the party, but I still wasn't convinced that the rather demure dress we'd settled on was really right for me. I was more of a tight top and skinny jeans kind of girl.

'But what about my dinner?' came Dad's gruff voice.

'Evelyn's laying on a buffet,' I reminded him, 'there'll be plenty to eat. Where's Mum?'

'She said she was going straight up to the home after she'd finished at school.'

Dad didn't work. I could barely remember him leaving the house during daylight hours to go anywhere other than the pub or the bookies, but Mum had always managed to hold down a variety of jobs. School cleaner, dinner lady – or midday supervisor as they were now called – and nursing home housekeeping assistant, was the current combination.

Living at home with the Hurren family was nothing like being at work with the Connellys, but I managed to juggle the two contrasting parts of my life. Most of the time.

As much as I longed to take up Catherine's kind offer, I knew Mum would be lost without me acting as the buffer that she needed when Dad had been on a bender and gambled away his beer money.

'Are you going to sort me out some dinner, then, or what?' Dad barked.

'I just told you there's going to be a buffet.'

'Titchy sandwiches and those stinking devilled eggs Evelyn keeps churning out?' he moaned. 'I'm going to need something more substantial than that to see me through the night.'

Given his tone, I'd say the casinos hadn't played in his favour. I had a cursory look in the fridge, flicked the kettle off again and reached into my bag for my purse.

'I'll nip down to the chippy,' I said, resignedly, knowing

11

I'd have to shelve my trip to The Mermaid. 'They should have the fryers on by now.'

'Make mine a large cod,' Dad called back.

I took my annoyance out on the dodgy back door and headed up the road into town.

'Large cod, large chips and a couple of bread rolls, please Sharon,' I requested as I rifled through my purse to see if I could cobble together enough change. The Connelly family paid well, but stretching out my wages to accommodate an appetite as large as my father's wasn't always easy.

'I can't believe you've got room in those jeans to squeeze that lot in,' said a familiar voice close to my ear. 'And I thought you were cutting back on carbs until we've been up the aisle?'

'What are you doing here?' I laughed, spinning round and finding myself face to face with a wall of firm chest. 'I thought you were supposed to be working late this afternoon?'

'I wanted to surprise you.' Gavin grinned, pinning me with his piercing blue gaze before planting a passionate kiss on my lips in full view of everyone.

'And you made a detour to the chippy because ...?'

'I wanted to pick up some dinner for your dad,' he cut in. 'You know as well as I do that if he hasn't got his belly full he'll be a miserable sod all night, and I'm not having him spoil our party because the sandwiches are too small.'

That was typical Gavin. He was always coming up with

things to smooth the way in the Hurren household. We'd barely started dating before he'd worked out that fresh flowers were the way to Mum's heart, while Dad was always happier to see him when he turned up with a pack of lagers tucked under his arm.

'Are you still meeting the lads for pre-drinks?' I asked, keeping my tone light as I started counting out change.

I was none too impressed with the idea, but Gavin's mates had insisted that, if they were losing their leader, then they were going to send him off in style. I had tried to suggest that sort of thing would be best saved for the stag night they were already planning in Dublin, but they hadn't listened.

'Nope,' said Gavin, handing a crisp twenty pound note over to Sharon, who couldn't resist batting her lashes at him even though she knew he was well and truly spoken for.

'Seriously?' I frowned.

'Seriously,' he grinned. 'I told them I'm going to be with you right from the off tonight. My place is next to you now, Hayley.'

'Mum?' I called when I arrived back and found her coat flung over the back of a chair.

'I'll be down in a minute.'

I grabbed two plates and set about filling one and adding a handful of chips and the extra bread roll to the other.

'I thought you were at work,' I stated when she finally came in.

'They let me finish early,' she told me, rolling her eyes

when she spotted the plates. 'Did you remind him there's going to be a buffet?'

'Of course,' I said, 'but this one's for you. Just don't let him see it.'

'Thanks, love.' She smiled gratefully. 'I haven't had a bite since breakfast.'

'Guess who I bumped into in the chippy.'

'Who?'

'Gavin,' I grinned. 'He's finished early as well. He's just popped to the shop so he'll be here in a minute.'

'Well, I should think so,' said Mum as she began packing the buttered roll with chips. 'This is going to be a night to remember.'

I didn't get a single word of thanks from my father when I presented him with his early extra dinner on a tray and plonked it on his lap.

'You were gone a while,' he snapped, waving me out of the way of the television.

'You're welcome.'

'They're skimping on the chips again,' he grumbled, when he finally looked at his plate. 'And what am I supposed to do with one tiny roll?'

One thing The Codfather never did was skimp on portion sizes, but I wasn't going to correct him or let him know that I'd given some to Mum, who had been working her backside off long before he had even rolled out of bed.

'Gavin will be here in a minute,' I said instead. 'He's got off work early and gone to get you some beers.'

'You've landed on your feet with that one, girl,' Dad muttered, sounding slightly mollified. 'He could have had any woman he wanted in this town – though I suppose he still can.'

I ignored his final comment. I may have heard rumours about the occasional indiscretion, but given that they came from one of Gavin's ex-girlfriends I chose not to believe them.

'So, you want to make sure you don't do anything to mess things up.'

'No danger of that,' said my fine fiancé as he popped his head into the room and passed me the chilled cans. 'Your Hayley's one in a million, Mr Hurren. You could say I'm the one who's landed right side up,' he added with a wink in my direction.

'Yes, well,' said Dad as he pulled the tab on his first lager of the day, 'I don't know about that, but after the business with that art teacher back in school, I'm just grateful to get her off our hands.'

'Talking of your old art teacher,' said Gavin as he made himself comfortable on the bed to watch me get dried and dressed after my bath, 'have you done any more drawing this week?'

When Gavin and I had first got together, his mates had only remembered me for my notorious year eleven reputation, whereas my scorching scaffolder had asked about my talent with a paintbrush.

'Your work was phenomenal,' he had said, sounding

genuinely awed. 'You won the end of year show three years on the bounce, didn't you? You must be even better now.'

I was flattered that he remembered, but I didn't tell him I'd packed my paints away along with my memories of those final few weeks at school before the summer holidays had even started.

'Are you seriously telling us that you can remember her etchings,' teased Gavin's so-called friends, 'but you can't remember her getting knocked up by a teacher old enough to be her father?'

I had shrugged off their spiteful comments and Gavin soon shut them up when we properly started going out, but he wouldn't let me forget what I was missing out on.

In an unguarded moment I had told him that, for as long as I could remember, I had been happiest when sketching, designing and painting, and how I once had plans to study art after my GCSEs and dreamt of making it to art college after that. He said it was a shame things hadn't worked out that way, but just because life had taught me a few harsh lessons, there was no reason to deny myself the pleasure of picking up a paintbrush again.

Once he knew how I felt, he wouldn't let the subject go, and one wet Sunday afternoon he helped me dig out my easel from the loft and I hadn't looked back since. Not that I had told anyone else about it. Not even Anna.

'I've managed a couple of rough drawings,' I told Gavin now, blocking out all thoughts of the art teacher whose timely desertion had left me with little more than blank pages and an incredibly guilty conscience. 'And I finished the one of the dogs curled up in front of the Aga.'

Floss and Suki, the Wynthorpe Hall pooches, were perfect sitters. They could snooze for hours as long as their bellies were full. I had made some quick preliminary sketches when I was on my own with them, and I took a couple of snaps on my phone to work from in private after that.

'Can I see them?'

'Maybe later,' I said, nodding at the clock on the nightstand. 'We really need to get on.'

'Are you two nearly ready?' Mum hollered up the stairs the second I'd finished my sentence. 'It wouldn't hurt to get there early and check everything's set up.'

'We'll be going in a minute!' I called back, pulling my new dress over my head and turning around so Gavin could help with the zip.

I still wasn't convinced it was the right thing to wear, but I was out of time.

'The sooner we get our own place the better,' he muttered.

'I know,' I said, twisting around to scrutinise my reflection and wondering whether to go for heels or flats. 'Catherine offered us a room up at the hall again today.'

'That little cottage would be better.'

'Gatekeeper's, you mean?'

'That's the one,' Gavin smiled. 'That would be the perfect little love nest for a newly engaged couple.'

'That it would,' I agreed, 'but it's already taken. Or it will be soon.'

Gavin didn't say anything.

'We'll be all right squeezed in here together though, won't we?' I asked, wrapping my arms around his neck and thinking about how romantic it was going to be to wake up next to him every morning. 'I've heard that two can live as cheaply as one.'

'Not with someone like your father draining our resources.'

'There is that,' I sighed, the idyll quickly being replaced by an image of my father sprawled out on the sofa, devouring his body weight in peanuts, 'but I can't face leaving Mum.'

'I know you can't,' Gavin sighed, 'but it's got to happen sometime.'

'Just not yet,' I said, kissing him lightly on the lips.

'All right,' he smiled, holding me at arm's length and nodding in approval as he took in my new dress. 'And I don't suppose it really matters where we are, does it? As long as we're together.'

'Exactly,' I agreed.

'I love you, Hayley Hurren-soon-to-be-Garford,' he laughed.

'And I love you, too.' I laughed back.

Chapter 3

I had made a point of asking Catherine and Angus not to come up to town for the party. I knew it was going to end up being a raucous affair and not their sort of celebration at all. After initially shrugging off my concerns and insisting that missing out wouldn't be right, Catherine sensed my discomfiture and agreed to stay away, but she made me promise that Gavin and I would join her and Angus for dinner at the hall the following week. The rest of the clan were coming, but none of them were going to be able to make it until the evening was in full swing.

'Anna and I have a conference call at seven,' Jamie had told me earlier in the day, 'but we'll be along with Molly the second it's over.'

'It's fine,' I had told him, because I didn't mind at all. Running the charity had proved to be full-on, and regular working hours had flown out of the window for my friends.

'There's no rush,' I reassured him. 'I wouldn't put it past Jim to call for a lock-in, so there'll be plenty of time to toast the happy couple.'

'Dorothy and I will look in together,' Mick had later explained when we were on our own. 'It's a shame Gavin couldn't pick you up from work today. The pair of you should be getting ready and arriving together. I'm still annoyed that he thinks it's acceptable to put a drinking session with his mates before you.'

Like me, Mick had heard the rumours about Gavin so he, more than anyone else at the hall, was aware of the wide boy reputation Gavin had earned for himself during the last few years. I still hadn't managed to convince him that my fiancé had turned over a new leaf, but I hoped the fact that Gavin had decided to put me before pre-drinks would settle some of his fears.

As I walked into town with Gavin on my arm, him sober as a judge and with eyes only for me, I couldn't help wishing that Mick could be there to see it for himself.

The Mermaid, beautifully dressed for the occasion and with a fire burning merrily in the grate, looked both warm and welcoming, in spite of the underlying whiff of egg.

'Evening, you two,' said Jim, rushing round from behind the bar to relieve us of our coats. 'Is this all right for the pair of you?'

'It's perfect,' I told him. 'Thank you, Jim. I know how much work you and Evelyn have put into all this.'

'And look at the size of these sandwiches,' laughed Gavin,

pointing at a platter packed with sarnies large enough to satisfy even my father's perpetually rumbling guts.

'They were the wife's idea,' chuckled Jim. 'She reckoned some of the guests might not appreciate the delicate light bites some of us more refined folk favour.'

We all laughed and I moved further along the table before turning to admire the exquisite banner that was hanging above the bar.

'Where did that come from?' I asked.

'Lizzie at the Cherry Tree Café,' Jim beamed. 'She dropped it off earlier. Do you like it?'

The intricately painted artwork stretched from one side of the bar to the other and had mine and Gavin's names cleverly entwined.

'It's absolutely gorgeous,' I sniffed, as hot tears pricked the back of my eyes. 'I wasn't expecting anything as pretty as this.'

Gavin came and stood next to me again. He picked up my hand and kissed it.

'If you weren't so secretive about your talents,' he whispered in my ear, 'you could have made something like that yourself.'

I knew he was right, but I couldn't have bettered Lizzie's efforts. I was just about to say as much when the pub door was thrown open and Jemma, the Cherry Tree Café owner, reversed in, carrying what looked like a huge cake box.

'I'm sorry I'm late!' she shouted. 'It's been manic today. Customers are already asking about the Christmas menu and festive afternoon teas, so we've been completely snowed under.'

She carefully passed the box over to Jim and whipped off her coat.

'No pun intended,' she added, with a smile as she abandoned the coat and took the box back again. 'Seriously, though,' she gushed, 'I can't believe Christmas is almost here. It only feels like five minutes since we were packing the decorations up from last year. Now,' she added, turning to me and Gavin and sounding slightly calmer as she took a breath, 'where would you like it?'

I couldn't answer her because I didn't know what *it* was.

'Evelyn has left a space in the middle,' said Jim, stepping in. 'Pride of place, right near the front.'

I felt a bit of a spare part just standing there, but I had no idea what was going on. I looked at Gavin and he pulled me closer. Given the smug expression he was wearing, I guessed he knew exactly what was happening.

'I hope you like it, Hayley,' said Jemma, reverently lifting the lid to reveal the prettiest engagement cake I had ever seen. It was decorated in much the same style as Lizzie's banner and looked almost too good to eat. 'Gavin wanted it to be a surprise, although, to be honest, I thought he would have let the cat out of the bag by now.'

'Oh,' I gasped, squeezing my arms tighter around Gavin's waist as she carefully arranged the cake in the gap among the cocktail sausages and other things on sticks. 'It's beautiful!'

'I had a feeling you'd like it,' said Gavin, proudly.

'I love it,' I told him.

Jemma let out a sigh of relief and stood back to admire her handiwork. I hadn't been expecting a bespoke cake and felt thrilled that Gavin had gone to the trouble of sorting one out. The style and decorations were perfect and, again, I couldn't wait to sing my fiancé's praises to Mick. If this gesture didn't quash his concerns that my betrothed was still a bit of a playboy at heart, then nothing would.

'Do you mind if I give you the bill now?' Jemma continued, retrieving her coat and pulling out an envelope from the pocket. 'I know I'll forget later and you said you wanted to pay straightaway, didn't you, Gavin?'

'I did,' he nodded, whipping the envelope out of sight before I had a chance to look at it. 'I'll call around to the café first thing tomorrow to settle up. And the same goes for the buffet bill, Jim,' he added.

I looked back at the table and tried to do a quick calculation of what the total amount we'd be shelling out for the evening would be. It was doubtless going to make a fair dent in our meagre savings.

'Hey now, don't look so worried,' Gavin told me as I let out a long sigh. 'It's all in hand.'

Jemma and Jim moved a discreet distance away.

'But this lot won't come cheap, will it?' I frowned, biting my lip. 'And we've only just started saving—'

'Hey,' cut in Gavin, as he stuffed Jemma's envelope deeper into his pocket. 'Listen here, Hayley. We can always earn more money, can't we?'

'I guess,' I shrugged.

'But tonight,' he said, reaching for my hands, 'celebrating our engagement, well, this is a one-off.'

He was right.

'And I want it to be special,' he smiled. 'I want this to be a night we'll never forget.'

'Of course,' I smiled back as I heard the pub door open and our guests begin to arrive. 'So do I.'

I was amazed to discover that Mum had managed to get Dad off the sofa, into a clean shirt and out of the house with what appeared to be minimal fuss.

'I'll go and collect the buffet bill from Jim now,' said Gavin, kissing my cheek as he let me go. 'Why don't you find your parents somewhere to sit?'

'Hayley, I wasn't sure about that dress,' said Mum, looking me up and down as we bagged her and Dad a table. 'I didn't think it would suit you, but, actually, it fits the new you very well.'

'The new me?' I questioned, trying not to feel too taken aback by such an overt compliment about my outfit. 'What do you mean by that?'

'She means you've gone soft,' said Dad bluntly.

'That's not what I mean at all,' tutted Mum, shaking her head.

I looked at her and raised my eyebrows.

'Well, I suppose it sort of is,' she shrugged. 'Since that girl Anna arrived on the scene, you've been changing.'

Not all that long ago I would have jumped on that

suggestion and stamped it out, but Mum was right. Having watched Anna and Jamie fall in love and seeing for myself first-hand how a relationship could grow into a solid partnership, I had dropped my defences low enough to allow love into my own life. For years I had stuck to my 'guys are for fun' mantra, but now I was engaged to Gavin and had somehow secured a fairy-tale romance for myself. Maybe I hadn't gone soft as my dad had suggested, I'd just grown up.

'Well, I hope I've changed for the better,' I began to say, but Dad cut me off.

'You want to be careful,' he warned, 'you're getting ideas above your station, still working at that place. You need to remember, girl, you're one of us, not one of them.'

God help me, I thought, but I didn't say it. It wasn't all that long ago that Mum would have agreed with him, but I wasn't the only one who'd changed; her attitude towards Wynthorpe Hall and the family who lived there had too.

'I've told you before,' Dad droned on, making for the bar, 'you're lucky to have found a man willing to marry you after what you did at school. You want to keep hold of him, not scare him off by putting on airs and graces.'

'Ignore him,' hissed Mum, sensing I was about to retaliate. 'Don't give him the satisfaction of a row. Not tonight. He's only saying all this to wind you up. You know how he loves to make a scene.'

She was right, of course. I bit back my blunt retort and took a few deep breaths instead. The new Hayley might have been slightly softer around the edges but where my dad was concerned, the old version was still poised to strike when provoked.

'Have you lost that fella of yours already?' quizzed my auntie Jenny when she spotted Mum and me sitting alone at the table. 'That's not a very good start, Hayley, is it?'

'He's gone to talk to Jim,' I told her, looking across to where he had been standing by the bar.

There was no sign of him now, though, and the place was starting to fill up.

'Never mind her,' said Dad, dismissing me and handing Auntie Jenny half a pint of Guinness, which was her favourite tipple. 'It's a free bar for the first hour, Jen. Make the most of it.'

'It isn't free, Dad,' I tutted. 'Gavin and I are picking up the tab.'

'Same thing,' he shrugged.

'Yes,' I snapped, 'I suppose it is, but bear in mind that, the more that gets drunk, the more we have to shell out, which means less in the family pot for the next few weeks.'

It took a few seconds for the penny to drop, but he got there in the end and looked as if he bitterly regretted going around telling everyone to drink up because it was on the house.

'Here he is!' shouted my aunt, before Dad had a chance to start snatching back glasses, 'my fabulous nephew-in-law to be!'

She sounded as if she'd downed more than half a pint.

'Looks like someone's pre-drinks got out of hand,'

Gavin whispered, making me giggle as he came and stood next to me.

'And talking of pre-drinks,' I said, nodding over to where half a dozen of his mates had just fallen through the pub door. 'Go and have a word, will you?' I begged. 'I don't want them getting out of hand.'

'I'll try,' he promised, 'but I won't get far if they're still in a mood about me dumping them.'

'Silly sods,' I tutted. 'Tell them we're not at school any-more. We're grown-ups now.'

A noisy cheer went up as Gavin joined his gang, which left me thinking that, at least if they'd filled up on vodka shots at home, they wouldn't be adding quite so much to our bar bill.

Having to eventually pay for their own drinks didn't stop our guests enjoying the evening and, a couple of hours later, the party was in full swing, and the noise level had risen sharply along with the number of empty glasses. I looked around at the merry crowd, but there was still no sign of the Wynthorpe crew. I guessed Jamie and Anna's conference call was taking longer than expected, but I hoped Mick and Dorothy would be along soon.

'Isn't it about time you said a few words and cut this lovely cake?' said Mum leaning on the table to admire Jemma's skill with a piping bag. 'Where's Gavin?'

I hadn't seen as much of him since his mates arrived, and guessed he was probably outside having one of the crafty cig-arettes he had promised me he could live without, and which would save us a small fortune if he could. Or he might have been talking to his parents who had, unsurprisingly, taken a table as far away from mine as was humanly possible.

'I'll go and find him,' I told Mum firmly, 'when you've promised me you won't have any more to drink.'

She was beginning to look a little worse for wear and I knew from years of experience that if there was one thing guaranteed to kick off a Hurren domestic, it was an excess of alcohol. Dad already looked well on his way to being drunk, and if Mum headed the same way I knew Gavin and I were going to spend the night acting as referees rather than snuggled under the duvet planning what to include on our wedding list.

'I'll just have one more glass,' Mum hiccupped, 'to toast you and Gavin.'

I looked at her and narrowed my eyes. I supposed I could hardly deny her that. Not that long ago, she wouldn't have been bothered about toasting my future happiness at all. I had worked hard to repair some of the damage my teenage transgressions had caused, and the new me wasn't about to let old arguments flare up again.

'OK,' I relented, 'I'll go and find Gavin, but don't you drink another sip until we're cutting the cake.'

'All right,' she nodded, plonking down her half-empty wine glass. 'Not another drop will pass my lips until you've cracked open the champagne.'

'Now who's putting on airs and graces!' I laughed, mimicking my dad. 'Champagne indeed. You'll have Prosecco and like it!'

Gavin wasn't out front having a cigarette and he wasn't in the pub garden, either, so that only left one place. I squeezed my way past the well-wishers and through the door that led down the corridor to the loos. I was just about to walk in when I hit a brick wall.

Well, not a brick wall, exactly, but a pretty solid barrier nonetheless.

'Shit,' said the wall, catching me by the top of my arms as I ricocheted back almost as far as the bar. 'I'm so sorry. Did I stand on you?'

'No,' I said, pulling myself free and catching my breath. 'Not quite.'

My eyes travelled slowly from what I could now see was a torso, up to a chest that was as broad as it was firm, and finally came to rest on a face: rugged, frowning and bearded. I didn't recognise the brown and brooding eyes as local. Someone of this stature wouldn't be easy to forget, but there was something vaguely familiar about him nonetheless. I couldn't help thinking he looked like a strong-man competitor; a Canadian lumberjack or something. The red and black checked shirt he was wearing readily supported the stereotype.

'I'm really sorry,' the man-wall apologised, 'I didn't expect . . .'

'Someone to be on the other side of the door?'

'You do know this is the gents, don't you?' he said, pointing at the sign as I tried to get around him.

'Yes,' I said, 'I do know.'

'Well, I wouldn't go in if I were you,' he said, still not letting me pass. 'I'd give it a minute or two at least.'

'Nice,' I said, wrinkling my nose.

'No,' he said, a blush blooming beneath the beard, 'that's not what I meant. There's a couple in one of the cubicles. I think you had better leave them to it.'

I knew it couldn't possibly be Gavin, but, for some reason, I felt duty-bound to make absolutely sure.

'It's all right,' I told the lumberjack. 'I'll be really quiet. Whoever it is in there won't hear a squeak out of me.'

'Fair enough,' he shrugged, finally letting me through as he headed back to the bar.

I tiptoed inside and held my breath as I waited for a sound to prove that it wasn't my devoted fiancé on the other side of the door. My heart was pounding in my chest and I was sure the couple in the cubicle were going to hear me before I heard them. After what felt like minutes rather than seconds, there was a shallow panting, followed by a gasp and then a husky moan.

'Gavin, oh god, Gavin . . .'

As the shock hit home and the sharp tang of bile forced its way to the back of my throat I realised it was Sharon, that cow, from the chip shop. I'd recognise her dulcet tones anywhere, even in the throes of quickie passion in the pub.

'We better make this a good one,' Gavin groaned in response to whatever she was doing. I clapped my hands over my mouth to stop myself crying out, but for a very different reason to Sharon the slag. 'This is my last chance for a bit extra, so give it all you've got, girl.'

What a charmer. I was going to knock his block off once I'd ripped down the cubicle door.

'You said that the weekend after you proposed to her,' Sharon panted.

I could hear the amusement in her tone and thought I was going to be sick. That was the final straw.

'Gavin!' I bawled, hammering hard on the door with my balled-up fist. 'You bastard!'

My battle cry was met with stunned silence, and part of me wanted to peer over the top of the door to take a snapshot of their faces.

'I'm leaving now,' I said more calmly, 'don't forget to pick up the bar bill from Jim. You can pay for that, the buffet and the cake at the same time.'

I couldn't believe how cool and in-control I sounded. I certainly didn't feel it.

'But I'll need your signature to access the savings account,' came Gavin's pathetic voice through the door. 'I don't think I can get to the money without you.'

I couldn't believe that was the only thing he had to say to me. The old Hayley, the one Mum had reminded me about earlier, who was now reserved solely for retaliating against my dad, would have ripped the door from its hinges and then done the same to him. The air would have been blue with expletives, hair would have been pulled and clothes would have been flushed, assuming the pair had any time to remove them.

But I wasn't that person anymore; the person who would

retaliate, make Gavin look a fool and announce Sharon as a whore to everyone in earshot. That person no longer had a place here, and the new model who had stepped in to fill her shoes was heading for hurt, heartbreak and humiliation if she didn't act fast.

I left them to their special moment, slipped unseen behind the bar, grabbed my coat and bag and walked out without a word.

Chapter 4

The crisp autumn air slapped me hard in the face as I set off, desperate to put as much distance between myself and the pub as I could in the shortest time possible. As I stuffed my arms into the sleeves of my coat, I felt my phone vibrate in my pocket.

I ignored it.

I had no intention of going back and listening to Gavin's pathetic justification for having his sausage battered by the chippy girl on what was supposed to be our special night, but I couldn't walk the streets all night, either.

Relenting, I pulled out my phone so I could scroll through my contacts and decide who to call in my moment of need. However, it wasn't Gavin who had been ringing me. According to the log, he hadn't been in touch at all, but I had a fair few missed calls from the hall and half a dozen text messages from Anna explaining why she and the others hadn't made it to the party yet.

Mick was dealing with a flat battery on the Land Rover, and the planned conference call was taking far longer than expected, thanks to the ropey rural internet connection. I thanked my lucky stars that efficient wireless still wasn't a thing at Wynthorpe. I don't think I could have coped with Anna and Dorothy's kind words, and Jamie and Mick's wrath, had they witnessed my humiliation first-hand.

Shivering, I pulled my coat tighter around me and stepped off the kerb thinking I could grab a taxi at the market square and go to the hall. Just until I'd decided what to do next.

A piercing blast from a horn brought me back to the present far faster than the fresh air, and I leapt back up on to the pavement, my heart heaving in my chest as I shielded my eyes against the dazzling headlights as a truck screamed to a halt next to me.

'You again!' called a man's voice from the driver's side. 'You're the girl from the pub, aren't you? I'm not apologising this time. You stepped straight out in front of me.'

'Sorry,' I relented, knowing I'd had a very lucky escape.

The wheels on the lumberjack's truck could have squashed me as flat as a pancake without feeling a thing. Suddenly, I found I wasn't shivering anymore.

'I didn't see you,' I said feebly, my voice wobbling a little, no doubt from the shock.

'You are all right, though?'

'Yes,' I said, breathing out. 'Yes, I'm fine.'

I felt far warmer than I had been just a few seconds

before, that was certain. The effect a decent dose of adrenalin could have on a person's nervous system was amazing.

'Well, if you're sure?'

'I am.'

'In that case,' he said, leaning further across the seat, 'you don't happen to know the way to Wynthorpe Hall, do you?'

'Yes,' I told him, reaching for the truck door handle. 'You're in luck. I happen to be heading that way myself.'

I heaved myself into the passenger seat, dumped my bag in the footwell and secured my seatbelt.

'All right?' I asked, when he didn't say anything.

'I don't know,' he frowned. 'Do you normally jump into strangers' trucks?'

I still wasn't convinced this guy was a stranger. He might not have been a local, but I knew him from somewhere. Hopefully not a wanted poster.

'It'd be pretty bad luck if I turned out to be an axe-wielding murderer or something, wouldn't it?' he went on, confirming we were on the same wavelength.

'Oh, believe me,' I told him with a sniff, 'the way my luck's going tonight, nothing would surprise me.'

'Fair enough,' he shrugged, putting the truck back into gear as I pointed out the way he needed to go.

'So, tell me,' I said, keen to establish that he really wasn't an axe-wielding murderer before we had gone too far out of town, 'why do you need to get to Wynthorpe Hall?'

'I'm going to work there,' he explained. 'My mate Jamie Connelly has offered me a job.'

'You're the new outdoor activities guy,' I nodded as the penny dropped. 'Jamie's pal from his time working on the African kids' project.'

'That's me,' he confirmed, 'although we knew each other long before Africa.'

So, if he was taking charge of the woods, along with their maintenance and management, then he *was* a lumberjack of sorts. I awarded myself ten out of ten for my shrewd observation and thought back over what little Jamie had said about him.

'I'm Gabriel,' he said, 'but my friends call me Gabe.'

I suddenly felt a little less sure that my decision to hitch a ride with this guy was a good one. Jamie had said his friend had been to the hall before, but if that were the case, surely he'd know how to get there already, wouldn't he? Had I unwittingly just fallen into the clutches of an impostor?

'I can't wait to see Catherine and Angus again,' he went on when I didn't say anything. 'It's years since I've visited – getting on for a decade – and I didn't drive then, which is why I can't remember the way.'

That was music to my ears. There was no satnav in sight and finding your way around the Fen droves and lanes, which were sketchily signposted at best, wasn't easy in the cold light of day, but at night would be nigh on impossible if you didn't already know the area.

'I did write to Jamie to say I was going to be arriving early so I hope he's expecting me.'

'Couldn't you have rung the hall?' I suggested, 'or sent a text? The internet is pretty rubbish, but messages mostly get through all right.'

I was certain Jamie wasn't expecting him yet, given what he'd said earlier, and annoyingly, I hadn't had a chance to get Gatekeeper's sorted out yet.

'I've been travelling around,' he shrugged. 'And I don't have a mobile.'

'What?'

'I don't have a phone.'

'Really?'

'Really,' he said, laughing when he caught sight of my shocked expression. 'So, I popped a letter in the post just before I began to make my way back across the globe and hoped for the best.'

'Well,' I told him, 'I'm fairly certain your letter never arrived and, consequently, your accommodation isn't quite ready yet.'

'And how do you know that?'

'Because I'm the hall housekeeper,' I told him proudly. 'The cottage was supposed to be aired and warmed through before you arrived. You'll just have to make the best of it for tonight, but I can at least bring your linen and towels over from the hall.'

I didn't much like that he was moving into somewhere I hadn't given the once over. Had he been staying in the hall, that would have been fine, but the cottage hadn't been lived in for months.

'Are you Hayley by any chance?' he frowned.

'Yes,' I said, feeling even more shocked than when he announced he had no mobile. 'But how do you know that?'

'I remember you,' he said, narrowing his eyes. 'You were staying at the hall the last time I visited, but you were too young to be working then, surely?'

I didn't answer. He had obviously been a visitor around the time I parted company with school.

'You look different,' he said.

'The passing of time has that sort of impact,' I told him shortly. 'You need to turn left here.'

We drove a little further in silence. It was typical that the only person Jamie had appointed to work for the charity already had an insight into my beginnings at the hall. I supposed there was no chance I would ever wipe my slate clean if I chose to stay put rather than move miles away from my past, and now I had the added humiliation of what Gavin had done on top of everything else. Perhaps I should take a leaf out of Anna, Jamie and this chap's books and spend some time away in pastures new.

'What did you say your name was, again?' I asked, when I realised I hadn't really been paying attention the first time he told me.

'Gabriel,' he said, clearing his throat. 'Or Gabe, for short.'

'Like the angel?'

'Just like the angel,' he smiled.

There was a certain irony that he had landed in my life just when I needed rescuing, even if he had lit me up with his truck headlights rather than a celestial beam from above.

'And just in time for Christmas,' I said.

'Yes,' he nodded, 'I suppose I am.'

'Well, I hope you'll be very happy at the hall,' I told him. 'We're a pretty easy-going bunch . . .'

Out of the corner of my eye, something on the back seat began to move around and take shape. It was growing, filling the space and I was all set to leap out of the truck and run back to town.

'Shit,' I gasped, 'what the hell is that?'

'It's all right,' said Gabe softly, 'don't panic. It's just my dog.'

'That's not a dog,' I croaked, curling in on myself. 'It's a fricking giant.'

'You're almost right,' Gabe laughed. 'He's an Irish wolfhound.'

The dog's wiry grey head slowly appeared and he rested it on the back of the seat between us, staring out through the windscreen into the unlit Fenland darkness. He didn't take any notice of me. Thankfully.

'His name's Bran.'

'Bran?' I repeated, but not too loudly in case the beast heard me.

'After the giant ancient god.'

'Oh yeah, of course . . .' Molly was going to absolutely love this guy and his hound the size of a Shetland pony. 'Have you had him long?'

I couldn't imagine an Irish wolfhound was an ideal travelling companion. It wasn't as if you could fit him in your backpack or pop him in your pocket. He'd be able to swallow Suki, the hall's diminutive chihuahua, without her even touching the sides.

'Three days,' said Gabe, twisting around to give the dog's head a friendly rub.

Bran took absolutely no notice at all.

'Three days?'

'I took him off a bloke in a pub.'

'*Took* him?'

'I won't bore you with the details,' Gabe said darkly. 'Let's just say the bloke was a knob and he needed relieving of this poor chap.'

'You'll never get him into Gatekeeper's Cottage,' I said aloud. 'More to the point, *you'll* never get into Gatekeeper's Cottage.'

The place really was tiny and this pair were supersized and then some.

'We'll be fine,' Gabe shrugged. 'I travel light.'

With a dog the size of a baby elephant in the back, I wasn't so sure about that.

'Anyway,' he went on. 'Talking of knobs in pubs. I have to ask: did you know that couple back in the gents?'

I swallowed and looked out of the window. I could feel Bran's warm breath on my neck as I thought about how I could answer Gabe's question.

There was nothing else for it. I took a deep breath and

began to reattach my emotional armour. I was going to have to ask the old Hayley for some help to get me through this.

The impenetrable forcefield fitted me as snugly as Ironman's suit and I actually felt better for pulling it back on. Perhaps I should never have hung it up in the first place. Had I kept all of my sass and swag in situ, my relationship with Gavin would have halted at amazing sex rather than escalating to something serious.

'He was my fiancé,' I began, my eyes swivelling from the non-existent view back to Gabe. 'Sorry. No. Wait. My *ex*-fiancé.'

I could do this. I felt fine. I wasn't so sure about my chauffeur, though.

'Oh my god, Hayley,' he yelped, almost making Bran move, but not quite. 'Shit. I'm so sorry.'

'It's fine,' I told him with a smile, 'I was only in it for the jewellery.'

I waved the tiny diamond vaguely in his direction thinking thank goodness that wasn't true because I definitely would have drawn the short straw.

Gabe looked at me, his expression suggesting he didn't believe a word.

'I mean it,' I told him. 'That mortifying little scene back there has no doubt saved me a whole heap of heartache. Better to have seen him for what he is at the engagement party rather than the wedding reception, right?'

'Well, I guess . . .'

I dreaded to think what Mick was going to say. Having

heard the rumours for himself – including the one about the lap dancer during a particularly infamous stag weekend – he was bound to feel almost as angry as I did.

'Give it a couple of weeks and I daresay I'll be thinking I've had a lucky escape,' I said, perhaps a little too brightly. 'Good riddance—'

'To bad rubbish,' Gabe cut in.

'Exactly,' I said, flashing him a smile. 'So please don't waste time worrying about me, because I'm fine. You need to turn left again here.'

Chapter 5

Predictably, the Fen bush telegraph had been in full swing since I'd walked out of the pub. It turned out that Jim had been keeping a close eye on proceedings and, having seen me leave, had then found Gavin and dragged him out of the gents and back to the bar with his trousers around his ankles.

Anna, pale and wide-eyed, with Jamie at her side, enlightened me about all of this before I was even properly out of Gabe's truck.

'Jim phoned here in a right state,' she said, her tone a mix of anger and shock, 'and as Mick had just managed to get the Land Rover battery sorted, he headed off to find you.'

'But I didn't need finding,' I said, rubbing her back to calm her down. 'I had my guardian angel on standby.'

Gabe looked over at me and winked before releasing Bran from the confines of the back seat. His unexpected appearance had really saved the day, as well as what little dignity I had left.

'But are you really all right?' Jamie frowned.

'Yes,' I swallowed, with a nod to Gabe, 'I've been well looked after.'

'Gabe!' shouted Jamie, only just realising who I was referring to. He rushed around and pulled his pal into a heartfelt man-hug. 'I might have known you'd be on-hand to rescue a damsel in distress.'

I wasn't sure I would have assigned myself that particular label, especially now the old Hayley was back out of her box, but I was willing to let him off – for now.

'But what on earth are you doing here so early?' Jamie continued. 'And who is this?' he said gesturing to Bran.

'You didn't get my letter, then?' Gabe asked, after introducing his canine friend.

'Letter?' Jamie frowned, roughly rubbing the dog's ginormous head.

'Hayley didn't think it had been delivered.'

'Come on,' said Anna, taking me tenderly by the hand and leading me back to the hall. 'Let's leave them to it while you fill us in on what's happened.'

'*Us*?' I asked doubtfully.

I wasn't sure I was up to a full inquisition.

'Just Molly and Dorothy,' she elaborated. 'We've been worried sick ever since Jim called.'

'Hayley!' Jamie called after us before we had moved all that far.

'Yeah?'

'Are you absolutely sure you feel all right?'

'Yes,' I swallowed, clearing my throat. 'I'm OK. You boys can go into town and castrate him tomorrow.'

He gave me the double thumbs up and turned back to Gabe.

'Catherine and Angus went up to bed ages ago,' Anna carried on. 'We didn't think we should wake them until we had all the facts and you were home safe and sound.'

'There's no point waking them at all,' I told her. 'What's done is done.'

Once inside, Molly enveloped me in another incense-scented hug, and Dorothy went into cocoa-and-crumpet overdrive.

'So,' she said, once she'd made sure we all had something to eat and drink, irrespective of whether we wanted it or not. 'What on earth happened?'

'Jim's phone call was a little on the confusing side,' frowned Anna.

I warmed my hands around the mug and took a deep breath. I knew there was no point in explaining only what had happened at the party. The other rumours, which I had tried so hard to ignore, were bound to make their way out to the hall eventually, so rather than pretending they didn't exist, I thought I'd get it over with all at once.

'Well,' I said, 'as you know, Gavin and I have – *had* – been dating since the spring. But according to local gossip, he's managed to sleep with at least one other woman during that time, and tonight, in the gents' loos at the pub, he decided to go for the double. In fact, given what I had the misfortune of overhearing, I now know it wasn't the first time he'd been with this woman since we'd got together, either.'

My three friends sat in silence and I reached for the chocolate spread.

For a few seconds, I entertained the idea that Gavin's need to slake his sexual thirst elsewhere was because I didn't know how to satisfy him, but I quickly banished that thought. This was Gavin's problem, not some failing on my part. Had I been less convinced of that I probably would have fallen completely apart, undone by what I would have imagined was my own inadequacy. But I knew what I was doing in the bedroom department.

'Well, I for one ...' Anna eventually began before stopping herself.

Her furious expression suggested that perhaps the rumours had reached further than the edges of the town after all, but she couldn't quite bring herself to tell me.

'How long have you known about these rumours, Hayley?' Molly asked.

I couldn't be sure if she had heard them before or not.

'For a while,' I sighed. 'Although, until tonight, I'd tried to convince myself it was all just idle gossip.'

'But it isn't,' said Anna bitterly. 'Is it?'

'Nope,' I said. 'Afraid not. The lap dancer came first – no pun intended. I found that out courtesy of the Facebook page his mate created to share the more sordid details of his stag do. I thought it was just silly boys' banter at the time, but after what I heard tonight, I'm certain it was true.'

Dorothy tutted and blew her nose noisily on the cotton hanky she always carried in her apron pocket.

'Why didn't you tell us?' She sniffed. 'And more to the point, why did you put up with it?'

'Love?' asked Anna.

'Yes,' I sighed, 'I was in love. You know as well as I do that I'd fallen for him, hook, line and sinker. I had hoped he was the dramatic love Molly had predicted and, in a way, I suppose he was.'

Truth be told, I couldn't believe my luck when he'd hung back at the hall that day to ask me out. The fittest guy in Wynbridge had shown an interest in *me* and I was flattered. I had fallen headfirst out of three-month flings and straight into what I thought was a committed relationship. Dad had never stopped reminding me how lucky I was to have landed someone like Gavin, given my reputation, and I had believed him. I had clung to my good fortune and waved goodbye to rational common sense.

'And we thought he felt the same way about you,' Molly said severely. 'The way he carried on, we thought he worshipped the ground you walked on.'

I had thought that myself. He had made me feel Disney-princess worthy. The clever, cunning sod.

'I never would have encouraged you to go out with him if I'd known,' said Anna. 'I had no idea what sort of man he really is, until . . .'

I knew she was going to say until she'd heard the rumours but I didn't want her blaming herself so I stopped her.

'You can't blame yourself,' I told her firmly. 'I was the one who started up with him. I was the one who believed he had grown out of playing the field and was ready to settle down.'

Given that he'd whisked me away for a romantic weekend by the sea with the sole intention of proposing, and had slipped a diamond on my finger under the light of the full moon, it was hardly surprising that I had believed him when he looked deep into my eyes and told me he wanted to commit.

Had he worked out by then exactly when his cock-wandering cut-off point would be? I wondered. *Probably not.*

Faced with the cold, hard facts, I daresay he was as addicted to having risky sex in public places as my father was to his online roulette wheel.

'I suppose,' I carried on. 'I suppose I imagined that my relationship with Gavin was destined to be as wonderful as yours and Jamie's, Anna. I'd watched the pair of you together and made the mistake of thinking I was heading for the same place. I just ended up trusting the wrong bloke to make the journey with, that's all.'

Anna blinked away her tears and I leant across the table and squeezed her hand. It wasn't her fault that I had tried to re-create something for myself that she had so successfully managed. Perhaps my father was right, perhaps given my reputation, the terrible things I had allowed to happen in the past were destined to dog me for ever. This time I'd been well and truly bitten on the backside.

'Better luck next time, hey?' said Jamie as he, Gabe and

Mick, who had been called home before he had a chance to fell my ex-fiancé, filed in, catching the tail-end of the conversation.

'No way,' I said firmly, releasing Anna's hand and sitting up straighter. 'That's me done. I'm not setting myself up to be some bloke's doormat again.'

'We aren't all like that,' said Gabe.

'Well, I've been publicly chewed up and spat out now,' I snapped. 'So, I'd be an idiot to risk it happening again, wouldn't I?'

'Sorry,' he said, his shoulders hunched. 'I didn't mean—'

'No,' I sighed, 'I'm sorry. I know not all men are cock-wombles, I just seem to have an uncanny knack of attracting the ones who are. Thank you for the lift, by the way, and thank you, Mick, for rushing to town to look for me.'

'No problem,' he shrugged.

I knew, had he found me, it would have been an awkward drive back to the hall. Mick was a man of few words when it came to affairs of the heart, but I was sure he would have found it nigh on impossible not to mention the concerns he had always had about Gavin.

'And who on earth is this?' gasped Molly, when she spotted Bran loitering behind his new master.

The next few minutes were swallowed up with introductions and explanations. It was a welcome interruption from the evening's embarrassing drama, which had changed the course of my future.

I took another look at my phone. Still nothing from Gavin.

Was that because he really didn't care about what he'd done, or because Jim and his pals had strung him up, naked and tarred, to the nearest tree?

'It was pandemonium back at the pub,' said Mick, shaking his head. 'By the time I got there, Jim had pretty much thrown everyone out on to the street.'

'Oh dear,' I said, trying not to imagine how difficult my next trip into town was going to be. With such a rumpus going on, there wouldn't be a single Wynbridge resident who didn't know what had happened. 'Evelyn won't like that, will she? The bar takings will be down.'

'Actually,' said Mick, rubbing his stubbly chin, 'she seemed to be all for it.'

'Really?'

'Yeah, she was pelting one lot with what looked like eggs.'

I let out a snort of laughter.

'Hard-boiled,' Mick went on, encouraged by my reaction.

'I'm going to take Gabe over to the cottage and get the wood burner going,' said Jamie, wiping tears of laughter from his face as he reached for the keys which hung on the rack with all the others next to the Aga.

'In that case,' I said, standing up, 'I'll go and grab the towels and linen.'

'I'll do it,' said Dorothy. 'You stay where you are. We need to decide what we're going to do with you tonight before you start worrying about making up beds for anyone else.'

Part of me felt duty bound to go home and explain to Mum what had happened, but Anna's suggestion was too enticing to turn down. She decided that, given everything I'd been through, I deserved one night of cosseting in the Rose Room, at the very least. This was the prettiest bedroom in the hall, complete with a luxurious en suite, and when she first came to stay, it had been hers. Hanging from the bed were drapes made from the same fabric as the curtains, and the little sofa in front of the open fire gave the room a sophisticated yet cosy finish. The old Hayley would have said it was almost worth catching Gavin mid-shag for a night nestled under its eaves.

'I'm so so sorry this has happened,' said Molly, kissing me lightly on the cheek.

'I was going to say you could have gazed into your crystal ball and warned me,' I joked, 'but then I realised that, actually, you sort of had. That last tarot reading you did for me said love was going to feature dramatically in my life this year, didn't it?'

'Yes,' she said, sounding wary, 'but this isn't quite the interpretation I had in mind when I read the cards.'

'Me neither,' I swallowed.

'Do you think you'll give him another chance?' she surprised me by asking.

'Well, he did say to the girl he was with tonight that this was going to be the last time.'

'Hayley!' gasped Anna. 'You wouldn't really go back to him now, would you?' The outrage in her face almost made me laugh out loud.

'Not after something like this,' joined in Molly, wrinkling

her pretty nose in disgust. 'And at your engagement party! You wouldn't want to be with a man who thinks it's all right to treat you this way simply because you hadn't stood up in church yet, would you?'

'Calm down, you silly pair,' scolded Dorothy, who had realised I was only teasing, 'at this rate you'll wake Catherine and Angus.'

'Sorry,' they said together.

'Not five minutes ago you heard Hayley say that she was eschewing all men, didn't you?'

The pair nodded and came quietly around the table to escort me upstairs.

'I bet that if I'd gone through with it, I'd have found Gavin in the vestry on our wedding day giving it one last go with one of the bridesmaids,' I told them as they led me up to the Rose Room with the promise of a muscle-unclenching bath.

'Hey!' said Anna. 'I was hoping to be one of your bridesmaids.'

'And me,' joined in Molly. 'And believe me, I wouldn't go near Gavin with his longest scaffolding pole.'

'Well, never mind,' I muttered, stifling a yawn. 'I'm sure I can find other uses for the pair of you.'

'Maybe,' Anna suggested, 'Molly has a spell somewhere that will make his thing . . .'

'Don't even go there,' cut in my craft-loving friend. 'Revenge is never as sweet as you imagine it will be.'

Chapter 6

I was up early the next morning, rifling through the boxes of belongings that Catherine had recently let me move into the hall attic. The plan was for Gavin to move in with me and my parents after our engagement party, so I'd decided to have a good clear-out and rearrange things in my small bedroom to make space.

What a wasted effort that had been.

At least I now had access to my former uniform of tight tops and skinny jeans. If I was serious about reviving the old me, then I was going to need an outfit to match.

I found myself drawn to my school art folder, which I promptly hid under the bed in the Rose Room. For some reason I wanted to keep it close.

It was interesting to look through everything I had only recently moved out of my life to make room for Gavin to move into it. I hated the thought of heading back to my depleted room in town, but I knew I had no choice. I was going to have to brazen the embarrassment out, but at least I still had my most recent sketchbooks there to keep me company.

'My darling girl,' said Angus, when I returned to the kitchen to put the attic keys back on their assigned hook.

'Dorothy has told us,' said Catherine, shaking her head.

'Needless to say, I won't be hiring from his firm anymore,' said Angus.

'But what about your discount?' I smiled.

'That man can shove his discount up his . . .'

'Angus,' cut in Catherine, colour flooding her face. 'I don't think we need to resort to profanities, especially when there are far more pressing matters to resolve.'

'Quite right,' he said, winking at me. 'Sorry, Hayley.'

'It's fine,' I told him. 'I almost resorted to blasphemy myself.'

Catherine looked at me and shook her head. 'You sound remarkably chipper given the circumstances.'

'Yes, I suppose I do,' I said, biting my lip as I thought about everything that had happened in the past twenty-four hours. 'But, it won't last. I need to return this today for a start. That'll wipe the smile off my face, won't it?'

I slipped the ring off my finger and placed it on the table. Angus picked it up and scrutinised it.

'You know,' he frowned, 'I'm fairly certain this isn't the ring that Gavin—'

'Angus!'

'You're fairly certain that this isn't the ring that Gavin, what?' I asked, ignoring Catherine's interruption.

'Oh, it's nothing, my dear,' he faltered. 'My mistake.'

I looked first at him and raised my eyebrows and then at Catherine.

'It's all right,' I said, sitting back and folding my arms. 'I can wait.'

Catherine shook her head and Angus's face began to colour.

'Sometimes,' she said, 'I wonder what I'm going to do with you, Angus Connelly.'

'I'm sorry,' said Angus, 'sometimes I speak without thinking.'

'*Sometimes?*' Catherine snorted, making Floss, the springer spaniel, jump in her sleep. 'Well, go on,' she carried on. 'You might as well spill the rest of the beans now.'

Angus picked up the ring again.

'The week before Gavin took you away to propose,' he sighed, 'he came to see me and asked if there was any possibility that I would make him a short-term, but fairly substantial, loan, so he could buy you the engagement ring of your dreams.'

This was news to me. Shocking news. I didn't have an engagement ring of my dreams.

'Please don't tell me you gave him the money,' I croaked.

'I did,' said Angus, 'but this wasn't the ring he showed me on his phone. The one he said you were hankering after was far bigger than this.'

'And I daresay a damn sight more expensive,' I added. 'Angus, I never had a hankering for any ring. Until Gavin went down on one knee on that beach I had no idea that he was going to propose, and we had certainly never discussed rings of any kind.'

Seems I wasn't the only one who had been played by the scorching scaffolder with the mesmerising blue eyes. This explained the crisp note he had used to pay for Dad's fish and chips and his blasé attitude towards the bill for the party. He was using Angus's loan as flash money to try to impress me. There was no way I was going to sign any dotted line and let him access our savings now.

'I promise I will pay you back every penny he took,' I said, holding my head high.

'You will not,' said Catherine. 'Angus gave that money to Gavin and Gavin will be paying it back.'

I had no idea how she imagined that was going to happen, but she sounded too stern to challenge.

'Well,' I said, 'in that case, you keep the ring. I know it isn't anywhere near as valuable as the other one, but I don't want it in my sight. You can sell it and get a little of the money back.'

Angus laid his napkin over it, hiding it from view.

'Right,' I said, tearing my eyes away and trying not to think about the future I'd lost. Not that the one I had been hoping for had ever really existed. 'I suppose I better make a start. I'm going to work on the upstairs landings today, is that all right?'

I wanted to keep as busy as possible until I had to go home.

'No, it isn't all right,' Catherine tutted, 'of course it isn't. Sit down, for goodness sake. We have things to discuss.'

'And you haven't had a bite of breakfast yet,' added Angus, passing me a plate.

'Mick reckons your mum has been trying to get hold of you,' exclaimed Dorothy as she came bustling through, no doubt prompted by her telepathic skills that could pinpoint the exact moment the last crumb was eaten or the teapot was down to its last cup. 'She's rung here half a dozen times apparently but no one picked up, so in the end she left a message.'

I felt even worse about not filling her in on what had happened now.

'I'll text her in a bit,' I sighed.

I knew she must be feeling gutted about Gavin. He'd really managed to find her sweet spot with all those flowers. Dad, on the other hand, would no doubt be blaming me for everything. He'd see Gavin's philandering as a failure on my part rather than my ex's inability to keep his fly buttoned. What a mess.

I wished Dorothy wouldn't keep piling bacon on to my plate. All this family talk and the thought of heading back to town was making me feel bilious.

'There's no need to speak to her,' said Catherine quietly. 'Not yet anyway.'

'Why not?'

I knew it was going to be excruciating for a while, but I'd faced it out once before and had come through it almost unscathed. I could do it again.

'I really don't know how best to put this, Hayley,'

Catherine shocked me by saying. 'But, judging by the message she left, your mother doesn't want you to call home, and I think she would prefer it if you didn't go back just yet, either.'

'*What?*'

She must have been listening to Dad and decided it was easier to side with him. All the effort I'd made to rebuild those bridges had amounted to nothing. All that hard work had been ripped apart again, and this time it wasn't even my fault.

'So, what am I supposed to do then?' I demanded, throwing up my hands in despair and giving in to my frustration.

'I think you should move in here,' Catherine said simply. 'I think you should pack up in town and move into Wynthorpe Hall.'

Chapter 7

Catherine was insistent that I shouldn't do any work that day and, for the first time ever, I found that my heart wasn't pounding in joy at the thought of the few hours of vacuuming that usually formed a large part of my daily routine. But I wasn't up for sitting about and twiddling my thumbs either.

I cleared the breakfast dishes from the table and loaded the dishwasher before grabbing my jacket and phone and heading outdoors. Anna, Jamie and Mick were already busy at work in the stable block, which was the charity's headquarters, and I didn't much fancy the trek through the woods to see Molly.

I had barely decided how I was going to spend my morning when I walked into what must have been one of the few mobile signal hotspots and my pocket began to vibrate at breakneck speed. By the time I reached Catherine's little summerhouse in the garden, a whole host of text and voice-mail messages were jamming up my inbox.

This time they were all from Gavin, and ranged from

conciliatory and apologetic to frustrated and strained, ending up borderline aggressive and confrontational.

Listened to and read chronologically, I could pinpoint when his guilt gave way to annoyance about the fact I hadn't given in and gone back, and then the exact moment that he'd decided he could blame me for everything.

If I had ever harboured the belief that we could have worked things out – not that I had, of course – then the bullshit backed up on my phone would have certainly knocked that idea out of the park. I deleted every message, both written and verbal, and decided, for the sake of my sanity, not to log in to Facebook.

'Anyone home?' I shouted as I found myself walking up the path leading to Gatekeeper's Cottage.

The front door was open, but there was no sign of either Gabe or his hound. I was just about to head back to the hall when the strangled sound of someone singing – badly and with abandon – met my ears.

'Gabe?'

There was still no let-up in the din so I followed the noise around the side of the cottage to the little garden.

'Oh my . . .'

The sight before me was wholly unexpected and stopped me dead in my tracks.

Had it not been for the dreadful rendition of the Foo Fighters' 'Learn to Fly', I might have given in to a slight swoon, but the racket was just enough to keep me on my feet.

Stripped to the waist, the lumberjack of Wynthorpe Hall

was doing what lumberjacks do best: chopping logs. But not just any old logs. These were logs of magnificent girth and length, and Gabe was laying waste to them as if they were made out of cotton wool *and* he was doing it the old-fashioned way. My eyes travelled across the contours of his broad shoulders and down his muscular back before coming to rest on his mighty thighs.

I had no idea why he was operating shirtless, but, along with the absence of clothing and machinery, I observed there was no sign of feathery wings, either, so perhaps my rescuing angel had a devilish streak.

I had just begun to allow my imagination to run with that idea when I felt something cold and wet nudge its way into my jacket pocket, and I let out an ear-splitting shriek.

'Bran!' Gabe called, spinning round and catching me red-handed, or should that have been red-faced?

The dog didn't move from my side and I rubbed his wiry head, my eyes now trained on Gabe's heaving chest.

'Hey, Hayley!' he shouted, ripping the buds from his ears and dropping his voice a few thousand octaves. 'Sorry, I didn't hear you. Have you been there long?'

He thrust the head of the axe into the stump he had been using as a base and picked up his shirt.

'Long enough to hear you murdering the Foo's finest,' I grinned.

'Oh,' he said, grimacing in embarrassment.

'It's just as well you have a body sent straight from the gods, Gabriel,' I teased, 'because you can't sing for toffee.'

He shook his head as if he couldn't believe I would be so cheeky, but this was me at my best again and he was going to have to get used to it if he planned to stick around.

'Can I offer you a coffee?' he asked. 'To make up for the assault on your eardrums.'

'Thanks,' I nodded, 'coffee would be good.'

I had always thought Gatekeeper's Cottage was a little on the tiny side, but the addition of Gabe and a wolfhound made it feel positively Lilliputian. I sat myself at the kitchen table to avoid taking up too much space and watched how my host expertly avoided the low beams and doorframes.

'When you're as tall as I am,' he said, after I congratulated him on his ducking prowess, 'you walk practically everywhere under cover with a stoop. Although, the ceiling at the top of the stairs caught me an absolute cracker this morning,' he added, rubbing the top of his head.

I was almost tempted to ask if it needed my attention, but I wasn't sure I would be able to control myself should my fingers become entwined in his thick, dark hair.

'So ... about just now in the garden,' he went on, biting his lip.

'The singing, you mean?'

'No,' he blushed. 'Not the singing. It's hot work chopping logs and I didn't think anyone would be about this early in the day. That's why I had my shirt off.'

'Oh,' I said teasingly. 'I see. I thought you were just trying to cheer me up after what happened last night.'

'You're dreadful, you are,' he tutted.

It was good to know he really did have the measure of me – the real me – already.

'Well, the folk around here are all early risers,' I told him. 'So, if there's anything you want to do without being seen or heard you'd best get it done *very* early.'

'I'll keep that in mind,' he said earnestly.

'And the log store outside the hall kitchen door is packed with dry and chopped logs, but if the desire to head out into the autumn air and start swinging your axe takes over, then that's fine by me. You might want to watch out for Dorothy, though. She'll be all aflutter.'

We both laughed and drank our coffee.

'About last night,' Gabe began before the silence became awkward, although I wished he wouldn't. 'Are you sure you're OK?'

'I'm fine,' I shrugged. 'Like I said, better to have realised it now than when I'm wearing white and clutching a catering bill for feeding the masses.'

Gabe didn't look convinced, and Bran, huffing, ambled over and sat close to my chair, his head resting heavily on my lap.

'In case you were wondering,' said Gabe, with a nod to his dog. 'We don't believe you.'

'Well, it's true,' I swallowed. 'I'm back in my old clothes today and I'm ready to embrace the old me.'

'What's wrong with the new you?' Gabe asked, reaching for the coffee pot to refill our mugs. 'I thought she looked rather lovely last night.'

'Too soft,' I sniffed, ignoring the compliment, 'the old me has served me well in the past so I'm sticking with her.'

'Perhaps you could have some sort of amalgamation,' Gabe suggested. 'A happy union of the two?'

'Maybe,' I said. 'We'll see.'

'You know, Hayley,' he said softly. 'Everything in life that we go through, good or bad, changes us. The happy times and the sad times leave a mark.'

'I do know that.'

'And it's up to us to decide how those marks are going to scar us. Are they going to be something we go out of our way to hide, ignore and shut out, or are they something we learn to live with and accept? If we keep pushing the bad bits down and packing them away, then one day they'll burst out and it will be far harder to deal with.'

I looked at him over the rim of my mug. He sounded very much like a man who was speaking from experience, but of course he was. No one landed at Wynthorpe Hall without a tale to tell.

'You sound as if you know what you're talking about,' I said.

'Yeah, I know my stuff, and I'll be the first to admit that I need to learn to practise what I preach.' He said sadly. 'We all have baggage, Hayley.'

'Yeah, you can say that again,' I agreed. 'So, are you going to unzip?'

'Sorry?'

'Your baggage,' I said, leaning forward. 'Are you going to tell me about your scars?'

'No way,' he said, pushing back his chair and standing up. 'Uh, I mean . . . No need. It's all been unpacked, although I'm sure I do still have lessons to learn. No unburdening necessary, though.'

'Well, I have to warn you,' I said, joining him at the sink. 'No one keeps secrets round here. It all comes out in the end.'

Lunch that day was far lovelier than it should have been, given the circumstances, and it was good to see Gabe and Bran slip seamlessly into place, even if they did take up twice as much room as everyone else.

Both Floss and Suki had fallen head over heels for Bran and lolled at the gigantic dog's feet trying to catch his attention. He bore it all with good humour and eventually the three of them settled down, Bran sprawling in front of the Aga and the other two draped around him.

'So,' said Mick, 'are we definitely all set to collect your things from town tomorrow, Hayley?'

'Yep,' I confirmed.

Catherine's earlier suggestion, combined with Gabe's timely words of wisdom, had set me thinking and I had decided to just go for it. I was going to head home – whether Mum liked it or not – pack up the rest of my things and move into the hall.

'And the earlier we go, the less fuss there'll be. Mum will have gone to work and Dad will still be in bed. I don't want to have to see either of them.'

'And what about Gavin?' Anna asked.

'What about him?'

'Well, don't you need to talk to him?'

'About what?'

'Everything that's happened,' she said, colouring slightly.

'He knows where to find me,' I shrugged. 'But, to be honest, there's nothing to say. We were engaged, now we're not. I was shown the light just in the nick of time.'

'I'm sure you feel more strongly about it than that,' Anna began.

'I'm sure she does too,' said Gabe quickly, 'but perhaps sitting around the lunch table in the company of a relative stranger isn't the place she feels like talking about it.'

Anna looked rather taken aback.

'Sorry,' she said. 'I didn't think.'

'And I didn't mean to sound so rude,' Gabe quickly added.

'It's fine,' I told them both. 'I know you're all worried about me, but, please, don't fuss.'

'Have you got enough boxes?' Angus asked, thankfully pulling the conversation back to the practicalities. 'There are plenty stacked in the woodshed if you need some more.'

'Dorothy has given me enough, but thank you, Angus,' I smiled, 'you've reminded me that I need to show Gabe where to go to store the log pile for the cottage.'

Gabe looked at me and shook his head as I began humming his favourite Foo Fighters track.

'Right,' said Jamie, rushing in and dumping a pile of manila folders on the side before taking his place at the table. 'I have good, bad and good news.'

I felt bad for not noticing that he'd been missing from his usual seat, but these days there were so many people around the table it was easy to lose track.

'Well,' he went on, 'when I say good, bad and good news, I suppose that depends on how you feel about what I'm going to say.'

Catherine was already looking a little apprehensive, whereas Angus favoured a far more optimistic expression.

'Out with it, then,' tutted Dorothy as she handed him a plate.

'OK,' he said, taking a breath and then a bite of sandwich as he marshalled his thoughts. 'The first bit of good news is about the kids who were coming to stay with us next month.'

'The two sisters and their younger brother?' asked Anna.

'Yes,' Jamie confirmed. 'They were our only booking for November and, as you all know, we'd already decided to close for December, unless an emergency were to come up.'

'Were these the little mites who lost their parents in that car accident?' asked Mick.

A hush fell around the table. All of the children and teens who had been to stay at the hall had been through terrible things, but these three had really tugged at our heartstrings. They hadn't lost just one parent, but both, and in the most horrific of circumstances.

'I thought we'd decided to make them a priority,' frowned Anna.

'We had,' said Jamie again, his face splitting into a grin.

'And they'll still be coming to us at some point, but not just yet, because, as of next week, their adoption will be official and they're moving, all together, into a new home.'

This was the best possible outcome imaginable and we toasted both the children and their new family.

'I'd say that was better than good news,' said Anna, drying her eyes on her napkin.

She was right about that.

'So, what's the bad?' Angus asked.

'Twofold,' said Jamie. 'But the second bit of bad leads on to the last bit of good.'

'Oh, just spit it out so I can get it all straight in my head,' said Dorothy. 'I can't keep track, here!'

'I had a phone call from Christopher this morning.'

'If you remember,' said Catherine, addressing Gabe, 'he's our eldest.'

Gabe nodded.

'I'm sorry to say,' Jamie continued, 'that he, Cass and the boys won't be coming to us for Christmas this year.'

'I had a feeling they wouldn't,' said Catherine, sounding disappointed. 'But I understand that Cass wants to spend one year with her own family before the boys are too big.'

She sounded far more gracious about the situation than Angus looked. Jamie ploughed on before his father had a chance to say anything.

'So,' said Jamie, 'tracking back to work, and this isn't ideal but as we have no bookings for either November or December now, I think we should close. Keep the admin side running, obviously, but I think we should use the time for planning for next year, and . . .'

'And what?' frowned Catherine.

'Well,' Jamie swallowed as his father began to beam. 'I was thinking that, as you told me earlier we're going to have the lovely Hayley on-site full-time now as well as Gabe, this will mean two extra pairs of hands instead of one.'

'Go on.'

'And so, I was wondering,' said Jamie in a rush, 'if we'd have time to give this Winter Wonderland idea of Dad's some proper thought.'

'Did you now?'

'It'll keep Hayley occupied and stop her brooding.'

'Don't rope me into this,' I cut in as Jamie gave me a theatrical wink.

'And if we had some activities set up in the woods, it would give Gabe an opportunity to get to know the place and have a practice run before he heads up the outdoor operations with the kids in the New Year.'

Gabe leant forward in his seat and called down the table to me.

'Help me out here,' he pleaded in a mock-whisper. 'Who am I supposed to be siding with on this one?'

We all began to laugh and Catherine shook her head.

'Let's have a meeting about it after bonfire night is out of the way,' she said. 'But I'll only think about it if you come back to me with proper plans. *Proper* plans, Angus,' she reiterated, 'not the usual back of an envelope variety.'

'But that will mean we have a week less to set things up than if we get going right away,' said Angus in dismay.

'That's as maybe,' said Catherine with finality, 'but with the tree competition and the party and this already sounding far more complicated than anything we've ever hosted before, I'm not prepared to compromise on the planning. If it's all worked out properly, it will come together far quicker than something you've cobbled together during an afternoon in your man cave.'

'But—' he began.

'I don't think you'll get a fairer offer than that, Mr Connelly,' Gabe cut in.

He might not have been willing to let me unpack his baggage just yet, but I think it was more than obvious to everyone sitting around the Wynthorpe kitchen table that Gabe was the king of compromise and one highly skilled negotiator.

Chapter 8

My second night in the lovely Rose Room was every bit as lacking in R&R as the first, even though Dorothy had gone to the trouble of making me one of her, usually unfailing, mugs of soothing, sweet Horlicks. Every time I found myself teetering on the precipice and about to fall asleep, my tempestuous thoughts dragged me back and left me tossing and turning and wrapping myself even more tightly in the high-thread-count sheets.

Not content with just mulling over my own problems, I found myself dissecting snatches of the conversation I had overheard between Jamie and Gabe after lunch. It was Jamie's concerned tone that first attracted my attention and his words quickly ensured my curiosity was well and truly piqued.

'Are you absolutely sure you're up to doing this, Gabe?' he had asked.

Initially, I had thought there was some hiccup with him helping out with my impending move. If that were the case, he needn't worry, because I was fairly certain that if push came to shove, Mick and I would be able to manage it between us. Most of my things were in the Wynthorpe attics already. However, it quickly became obvious that wasn't what he was getting at at all.

'Yes, mate,' Gabe responded sounding resolute. 'I told you, I can handle it. Otherwise I wouldn't have said yes, would I?'

'Because this job isn't for the faint-hearted,' Jamie continued. 'It's been a steep learning curve, even for me, and even after everything I dealt with out in Africa.'

'I know,' Gabe sighed. 'You said.'

'And those kids we were talking about over lunch, they're just the tip of the iceberg, and I would hate to—'

'I know exactly what you would hate to do,' Gabe cut in. He was beginning to sound frustrated. 'You've told me a hundred times, at least.'

I couldn't help but wonder what it was they had been talking about. Surely if Jamie had doubts about his friend's ability to do the job, he wouldn't have offered it to him in the first place? The children who benefited from the charity needed stability, routine and the reassurance that, if they needed to return to us, they would come back to the team they had already bonded with. If Jamie didn't think that Gabe could offer that then I was fairly certain he wouldn't have asked him to join the workforce at all.

'I can do this,' said Gabe, sounding calmer again and, if anything, even more determined. 'I need to do it for myself as much as the kids. I know what they need. I can help them.'

This exchange obviously had something to do with the baggage Gabe insisted upon keeping zipped. As curious as I was to know the finer details, eavesdropping was underhand and I decided it was time to draw a line under my listening-in.

'Have you two finished clearing those dishes yet?' I called through from the kitchen.

My timely prod stemmed the chat and got them back on task, but it didn't stop me from wondering during the wee small hours what it had all been about.

'Right!' said Mick, clapping his hands together at the kitchen table the next morning. 'Are we all ready for this then?'

'Have you made a list, Hayley?' Dorothy asked, shoving a pen and shopping pad under my nose, 'because I reckon that, after today, you won't want to go back again, will you? This is your one chance to get everything out.'

'The truck's all set,' said Gabe, marching in, 'and Bran's going to stay here. He takes up too much space to be involved in Operation Rescue.'

'Operation Rescue?' I frowned.

My friends might have been excited that I was finally joining them under the Wynthorpe roof, but I was still trying to get my head around the fact that Mum had asked me to stay away.

'And have you thought about what you're going to say to Gavin if you bump into him?' asked Anna.

They had obviously all been chatting in my absence and

had planned the trip into town with military precision, factoring in every possible scenario.

'Guys,' I said, holding up my hands. 'As much as I appreciate your help, there's really no need for all this fuss. Everything's going to be swift and simple: Mum will be at work, Dad's too lazy to get out of his bed, Gavin will have long been on-site, and I've already moved more stuff here than I've left behind. An SAS-style manoeuvre is really not required.'

'Yeah, I've heard that before,' said Mick, no doubt harking back to his time in the armed forces. 'We leave in precisely ten minutes.'

'Good luck,' said Anna, squeezing my shoulder and kissing my cheek. 'I know Catherine and Angus have been asking you to do this for ever and I really believe that now's the perfect time for you to start living life for yourself, Hayley.'

She seemed to have forgotten that my hand was being somewhat forced into taking the independent route.

'I suppose it will be convenient to be more on-hand for work,' I shrugged, making light of the positive spin she was trying to put on the situation. 'The vacuum cleaner will never be far from sight if I'm living here, will it?'

'That's not what I meant and you know it,' she said, adamantly shaking her head, before adding in a whispered undertone, 'Besides, Molly reckons something amazing is going to come charging over the horizon for you very soon.'

'Yes, well,' I smiled ruefully, 'she also reckoned love was

going to feature in my life this year, didn't she? I'm not so sure about our friend's interpretation of the tarot anymore.'

'She said it would feature *dramatically*,' Anna reminded me with a nudge. 'You can't say she was wrong about that.'

'That's true,' I relented, 'but my guess is the only thing set to charge over my horizon is my father's wrath, which will be heading straight for me when he realises I'm no longer going to be on-hand to sub his trips to the pub.'

Anna's brow creased in concern and I wondered what else my two friends had been saying about me when I was out of earshot.

'We want only good things for you,' she said, echoing what I had heard Molly say to other people. 'Because we love you,' she added with a swallow.

'Now, don't start all that,' I told her sternly. 'The old Hayley is back, remember? Keep saying things like that and you'll have me blubbing and turning soft again.'

My heart sank when I opened the back door and spotted Mum's coat and bag in its allotted place, flung over a kitchen chair. I don't know why she had a table and chairs in the kitchen; she rarely ate at it and Dad never did. It had been a tray in front of the TV for as long as I could remember.

I'd left Mick and Gabe parked in the truck outside, insisting that I needed to get the lay of the land before we put Operation Rescue into practice. If there were words to be had, I would rather they were done out of everyone else's earshot, and the fact that Mum hadn't gone into work warned me that words were imminent.

'Hayley!' she called furtively from one of the other rooms. 'Is that you?'

I took a deep breath, pulled back my shoulders and checked my impenetrable superpower suit was still in situ.

'Yep,' I said, bracing myself for impact. 'It's me.'

'What are you doing here?' she muttered, racing through to the kitchen and closing the door behind her. 'Did you not get my message?'

'Of course I did,' I hissed. 'That's why I've come.'

'What?'

'You've obviously sided with Dad over what's happened,' I sniffed, trying not to think about how hard I'd worked to repair my relationship with her, 'and so I've decided to move out. I'm moving up to the hall.'

Her hands were shaking as she reached for a cigarette and lit it.

'But what about Gavin?' she asked.

'What about him?'

'He told me he's prepared to forgive you for going off with some random fella and that he's going to mend his ways.'

'And you believe him?'

She took a long drag on her cigarette.

'My god!' I burst out, not caring whether I roused the snoring beast above or not. 'I can't believe this. I can't believe that you think I'd just go off with some stranger to get my own back, or that I should just accept what Gavin has been up to and carry on like nothing happened!'

She shook her head and stubbed out her cigarette.

'I don't think that,' she said, pointing at the ceiling to remind me to keep my voice down.

'What?' I frowned, lowering my voice.

'I couldn't say so in the message because your father blundered in,' she said, 'and I didn't ring you again because I thought that if you believed I'd sided with him then you'd stay away and save yourself an ear bashing.'

'So, you don't think I should take Gavin back?'

'And have him treat you little better than your father treats me?' she said bitterly. 'Certainly not!'

'And what about moving out?' I asked, trying to take in what she was saying. 'Do you think I should?'

'Oh, I do,' she told me. 'I want you to do that more than anything.'

'But I don't understand,' I frowned. 'You won't be able to cope living here on your own with Dad. You need me here. I'm the go-between, remember?'

'Exactly,' she said, 'and if you're here then I'll never find the strength to leave and even if I did, how could I go knowing I was leaving *you* here with him?'

'Are you saying that you want me to go, so that you can go?'

'That's about the size of it,' she said, lighting another cigarette.

I couldn't believe it.

'I've wasted the best part of twenty years siding with your father just to keep the peace,' she said severely. 'I've ruined my relationship with you because of him and I've never stood up for myself. Until now.'

'You haven't ruined our relationship, Mum,' I swallowed.

She nodded but didn't comment.

'So, what will you do?' I asked. 'Have you thought it all through?'

'Not yet,' she said, 'but I'm starting to. I began mulling it all over when we got back from the party and he started slagging you off for leaving.'

'Good on you, Mum,' I interrupted. I didn't want to hear any more about what had been said. 'It's about time!'

She looked almost excited. Now her decision had been made, a weight had been lifted and I knew that, when the time came, she wouldn't have any regrets about going.

'I better get on,' she said, jumping up and grabbing her coat and bag. 'I'm going to need the best references I can get if I want another job. Don't tell anyone about this, will you, Hayley?'

'Of course not.'

I knew we couldn't risk word getting back to Dad.

'And don't worry about me, love,' she said, opening the back door before I had time to say anything. 'I'm going to be fine. I'll be in touch.'

Needless to say, I didn't speak to my father who was still snoring in bed despite the raised words Mum and I had earlier, and with Mick and Gabe waiting outside to ferry what little I wanted to take to the truck, I was packed and done in no time.

'If you aren't in a rush,' I said to my removal team after I had tossed my key on the table and slammed the ill-fitting door for what I guessed would be the last time, 'I have just one more thing I need to do.'

'Hayley,' said Evelyn, when I popped my head around the pub's back door. 'Come on in.'

I was rather pleased I had turned up ahead of opening time. I didn't have quite enough swagger to manage a walk through the bar just yet.

'Jim's in the cellar,' she told me, 'he'll be up in a minute. Come in and have a coffee.'

'I don't want to put you to any trouble,' I told her.

Evelyn wasn't known around Wynbridge for her hearty hospitality, even though she was the landlady of the most popular pub in town.

'It's no bother,' she told me. 'I'm in the middle of making one for us.'

'I've come to settle up,' I told her and Jim a few minutes later as we sat in the empty bar. With no access to our savings, I knew Gavin wouldn't have done it, even if he did have some money left from Angus's loan. 'I want to pay for the buffet and any damage you may have incurred ejecting certain punters from the premises.'

Jim shook his head.

'There was no damage,' he told me. 'Unless you count the dent I gave to Gavin's ego as I bumped him out of the gents and into the bar.'

'And I don't think we can put a price on that,' winked Evelyn.

I knew it wasn't funny, especially given the situation, but I couldn't stop the laughter escaping my lips as I imagined my pathetic Prince Charming being frog-marched into the bar with his jeans around his knees.

'But the buffet,' I insisted, 'and the cake?'

'The buffet is on me,' said Evelyn. 'It was a timely reminder of why I stopped serving eggs. The kitchen still stinks.'

I didn't mention that I had heard that she'd launched most of them, which no doubt accounted for the lingering pong.

'But there was a lot of food,' I tried again.

'And it all got eaten,' Jim told me. 'It's all done. Forget it.'

'Well, thank you,' I said. 'Thank you, both. It was hardly how I expected the evening to end.'

'You're better off without him,' Jim blurted out. 'I did try to tell you.'

'Indeed, you did,' I agreed, thinking back to the quiet word he'd had with me all those months ago, when Gavin and I came in together for a drink.

Like Mick, Jim had warned me that my date had a reputation, but I had shrugged it off.

'I for one have never liked the lad,' put in Evelyn. 'And not just because of his reputation. You mark my words,' she told me, 'if you'd married him you'd have ended up just like your mother.'

I shuddered at the thought.

'Evelyn!' scolded Jim.

'No,' I said, 'she's right. Perish the thought.'

I thought of the struggle Mum would now face. Finding

another job to make ends meet wasn't going to be easy. She didn't drive and I hadn't thought to ask if she was planning to stay in the area. Part of me hoped she wouldn't. A completely fresh start out of Dad's reach would be the best thing for her.

'Thank you, both, for being so understanding,' I said, finishing my coffee. 'I'd better head off. I need to go and settle up with Jemma.'

'Oh,' said Jim, shifting in his seat, 'about the cake.'

'Don't tell me you've paid for that as well?'

'Had to,' he shrugged.

'What?' This really was too much. There was no need for him to have done that.

'After he'd shoved Gavin's face in it,' Evelyn tutted, 'he didn't have much choice, did he? He all but obliterated the frosting.'

I decided there was no answer to that and, promising that I would come back and brave a proper drink at the pub soon, I left.

I had just emerged when Gavin's van screeched into the market square and shuddered to a halt, drawing curious glances from the traders.

'Hayley! Wait up!'

I ignored him.

'Wait!' he called again as I tried to spot where Gabe had parked. 'We need to talk.'

'No,' I said, pulling free as he caught up with me and made a grab for my hand, 'we don't. What could we possibly have to say to each other, and anyway, how did you know I was here?'

'Your neighbour Tracey called me. She said you were moving your stuff out. I've just been round to yours. What's going on?'

I didn't bother asking why my pretty neighbour had my ex's number.

'I'm moving to Wynthorpe Hall.'

'But what about us?'

'There is no *us*, you idiot,' I all but screeched. 'Have you already forgotten what you did, Gavin? Have you forgotten the messages you left on my phone?'

'I was upset,' he said, his tone suggesting that I should have factored his feelings into the equation. 'I was angry.'

'But you had no right to be,' I tried to tell him, 'you were the one in the wrong and yet you blamed me! Surely I should be the one to have first dibs on feeling upset and angry.'

'I found out you'd been seen going off with some other bloke,' he said, 'I was pissed off.'

'What?' That was no doubt the moment that kicked off the change of tone in his texts. 'But you were the one who had been seen with your knob ...' I began, but then stopped myself.

'Look,' he said, 'can we forget about that, just for a second.'

'Believe me,' I told him, 'I would love to.'

'I thought,' he said, fixing me with the blue gaze I had once found so beguiling, 'that if I left you alone, once you'd calmed down and got your own back with this other guy, then we'd be able to work things out.'

He really didn't know me at all.

'So, let me get this straight: you fired off those texts in a fit of temper after you assumed I had gone off with some other bloke as payback, and now you're thinking we can put it behind us, go to the vicar and set a date?'

For the first time since he'd jumped out of his van, the idiot looked slightly less sure of himself.

'Is that not what you want?' he still had the audacity to ask. 'I'm willing to forgive and forget if you are.'

I didn't have the impetus to try to tell him that I'd done nothing wrong; that I didn't need his absolution because I hadn't committed a crime.

'No, Gavin,' I said, simply, instead. 'That isn't what I want. Our engagement is off, our relationship is over.'

I was amazed that he could look so surprised. Did the fool really expect me to commit to spending the rest of my life with him in light of everything he'd done? He chewed his lip for a second as a steely glaze crept over his eyes.

'In that case, I'll need the ring back,' he said gruffly, thrusting his hands into his work trouser pockets and rocking back on his heels.

'I haven't got it,' I told him, showing him my fingers, which were devoid of any adornment.

'But I'm still paying for it,' he moaned. 'I'm going to have to flog it and put the money towards the repayments.'

'Hang on,' I said. 'You had a more than generous loan from Angus to buy that ring so how come you're making repayments?'

He didn't answer.

'What did you do with the money he gave you?' I demanded.

'That's none of your business now,' he snapped, 'but I'll need that ring.'

'I haven't got it,' I said again, thrusting out my chin.

'Well, you'd better get it,' he said, darting forward and making a grab for my wrist.

I was about to jump back when he was suddenly knocked to the ground.

'What the hell?' I heard him squawk, face down on the pavement with Gabe's hand around the back of his head.

'Sorry, mate,' said Gabe, pulling him up roughly by the scruff of his neck. 'I wasn't watching where I was going. No harm done, is there?'

Apparently, Gabe the guardian angel could slip unseen into any situation. It was quite a party trick for someone his size.

'No,' said Gavin, brushing down his trousers, and glaring at Gabe, 'no harm done.'

'Hayley!' called Mick. 'Are you ready?'

'Yep,' I called back. 'On my way.'

As I walked over to the truck with Gabe hot on my heels, I could feel Gavin's gaze burning into the back of my head.

'Hopefully that'll be the end of it,' said Mick, opening the door so I could climb in.

'Hopefully,' I said back, but I wasn't so sure.

Chapter 9

I tried my best to hide it, but I wasn't feeling quite my usual self by the time we arrived back at the hall. The shock of Mum's announcement had finally taken its toll. Even though, for as long as I could remember, I had been miserable living at home and should have been thanking my lucky stars that I had somewhere as wonderful as Wynthorpe Hall to move to, I suddenly felt afraid.

What if I couldn't fit in living here full-time? What if I ended up driving the Connellys crackers? Ever since my nan had first introduced me to the family, the offer of a room had been my safety net, but now that I had jumped into it I was terrified of messing it up.

'You all right, love?' asked Mick as we got out of the car. 'You didn't say much on the way back and you're looking a bit peaky.'

'I'm fine,' I told him, 'just a bit tired.'

'We'll unload this lot,' insisted Gabe with a nod to my

hastily packed boxes. 'Why don't you go and have a minute to yourself?'

Ordinarily I would have shrugged off their concern. I would have hoisted up my jeans and got stuck in to help lugging what needed shifting, but my legs felt like lead and it was all I could do to make it up the stairs. My head had barely hit the pillow before I was sound asleep.

When I finally woke and caught sight of the time, I was shocked to discover I had slept most of the day away, and I remembered an occasion when Anna had done exactly the same in this very bed. It wasn't all that long after she had first arrived at the hall and I had teased her about leaving us to do all the work. As far as I could recall, her life had started to change dramatically very soon after that.

I stretched my arms over my head and wondered if my own life was about to veer off on some exciting new path, or whether I would go stir crazy – or just drive everyone else that way – by Christmas. Living and working in the same place might not turn out to be the idyll I had once imagined, but it was too late to worry about that now. I needed to be here for Mum's sake as well as my own, and it was time to take a leaf out of my friends' books and put a positive spin on my change of address and newly single status.

Deep down, I was still amazed that I had found the strength not to give in and cling on to what Gavin was offering. As my father had so often reminded me during those last few months, I was lucky anyone had shown any interest in me. But, in spite of the constant recaps, I had somehow managed to scrape together enough self-worth to work out that, if that meant sharing my life with someone who thought they could get away with treating me with such little respect, then I really was better off alone, thank you very much.

For the moment, I set aside the niggling thought that reminded me how I, myself, had once treated someone I thought so highly of with even less respect than Gavin had treated me.

I knew I would have to deal with that at some point in the future, but not now.

For now, I would concentrate on mending my poor heart. After all, I might not have the perfect partner like Anna and Jamie had found in each other, but I had my health, a home, a job I enjoyed and I was surrounded by folk who loved me. I would just have to wait and see if they still felt the same way a few weeks down the line. And who cared if I was the talk of the town again? I just wouldn't go back to town.

The hall was deserted when I went downstairs, but Dorothy had kindly left a note accompanying a covered lunch tray loaded with triangular sandwiches and a thick wedge of her moist carrot cake. I devoured the lot then set off into the woods, determined to ask Molly what she had told Anna was poised to charge over my horizon.

As usual, I let myself in through the back door of her cottage, drinking in the heavily incense-fragranced air as half a dozen wind chimes announced my arrival. I was just about to shout out my usual greeting when the sound of voices alerted me to the fact she already had company. I reached for the handle again, hoping I could slip out without setting the chimes back off, but it was too late.

'Hayley?' Molly's voice drifted through the room. 'I'm in the front.'

'I'll come back,' I called. 'It's no problem.'

'No, it's all right,' she insisted. 'We're almost done in here.'

Reluctantly, I slipped through the rainbow-patterned curtain, which separated the kitchen from the little sitting room, and felt the warmth from the fire and more than a dozen candles envelop me. Nestled in the heart of the Wynthorpe woods, Molly's cottage was always a little on the dark side, but the curtains were already shut today and it really could have been any time of day or night. There had been numerous times in the past when I had lost track of the hour having crossed this particular threshold. The heady atmosphere always made me feel sleepy and lethargic.

I took another step into the room and was surprised to find Gabe sitting next to Molly on the shawl-covered sofa, and Bran stretched out in front of the flames.

'Well,' I said, 'hello, you two. Don't you look cosy?'

There was a note of irritation in my voice, but I couldn't understand why.

'What are you up to?' I asked, trying to make amends. 'It's dark enough in here for a séance.'

For a split second the air felt full of electricity and I regretted my flippant tone as well as the suspicious one that had preceded it.

'Really?' Gabe asked Molly, as if I hadn't interrupted. 'Are you sure?'

Whatever it was that she had said to him, he didn't look at all convinced by the answer. In fact, he looked stunned.

'Absolutely,' she nodded, sweeping together her tarot cards which had been set out on the little table in front of her. 'One hundred per cent.'

Gabe still didn't look entirely swayed, but he didn't say anything else.

'Not straightaway,' Molly continued, 'but soon. Sooner than you might think anyway.'

The pair of them looked at me and I began to feel like the proverbial third wheel.

'I'm going to go,' I said, backing towards the curtain. 'You two are clearly in the middle of something. I'll come back.'

'No,' said Gabe, jumping up. 'I'll go. I need to finish unpacking, and Jamie will be expecting me over at the stables in a while. I'm also hoping to start getting a feel for the woods today so I'll meander back.'

'Sure?'

'One hundred per cent,' said Molly again, before Gabe could answer.

'Come on, Bran,' said Gabe, clicking his fingers in the gargantuan dog's direction. 'Come on, lad.'

Bran didn't budge. He didn't even open one eye.

'He can stay,' smiled Molly. 'I don't mind. Perhaps Hayley could bring him with her back up to the hall later.'

'Would that be OK?' Gabe asked me, pinning me with his dark stare.

'I'll do my best,' I told him, 'but if he won't budge for you, then I can't promise he'll listen to me.'

'All right,' said Gabe, ducking under the doorframe. 'If he doesn't walk back with you, I'll come and collect him later, but only if you're sure, Molly?'

'One hundred per cent,' I said dreamily, mimicking our friend.

I was relieved to see Gabe crack a smile. He had been looking far too serious when I arrived.

'Are you feeling any better?' he asked me as Molly leant over Bran to stoke the fire.

'Much,' I told him, 'and thank you for your help earlier. With the boxes *and* the idiot ex.'

'No problem,' he shrugged. 'I'm sure you're more than capable of looking after yourself, but—'

'Everyone needs a helping hand now and again,' said Molly.

'Exactly,' said Gabe.

'Exactly,' I agreed.

As Molly followed Gabe through to the kitchen to ensure he left the cottage without concussion, I stole a quick glance at the tarot card on the top of the stack. It, and the few under it, had formed part of the formation that had been on the table when I arrived. I had no idea if they had anything to do with Gabe, or if Molly had been looking at them before he arrived, but the presence of the 'death' card was interesting for whoever it had popped up for.

I'd had enough readings with my friend to know this

particular card was not to be feared, but signified major change, new opportunities and transformation. If it showed up for me right now, I would be more than happy.

'Do you want a drink?' Molly called through from the kitchen.

'That depends on what you've got?'

I had learned never to accept something Molly was offering without questioning its origin or contents.

'Tea,' she offered. 'Made from Typhoo tea bags.'

'Yes, please,' I replied, 'that would be lovely. And just one sugar. I'm cutting down.'

I listened to her bustling about in her tiny kitchen and my eyes strayed back to Bran.

'You're a bit like me, aren't you, lad?' I muttered. 'You don't like doing what you're told either.'

He opened an eye, then took the longest time stretching out his lanky, lengthy frame before ambling over and sitting on my feet.

'I knew you weren't asleep,' I told him. 'I could see you were shamming.'

'He's a beauty, isn't he?' said Molly as she appeared with two mugs and a plate of biscuits.

'He is,' I said, running my hand down his back as far as I could reach. 'Did Gabe tell you he took him from some bloke in a pub?'

'I was talking about Gabe,' Molly laughed. 'Not Bran.'

'And there was me thinking you only had eyes for Archie,' I said, taking one of the mugs.

I was surprised to see two bright dots of colour light up her cheeks at the mention of the middle Connelly brother and decided not to tease her further. Not all that long ago I would have capitalised on her vulnerability, so perhaps there was more of the new, kinder version of myself left hanging around than I realised.

'So,' I said instead, 'what did Gabe want? It all felt pretty intense in here when I first arrived.'

Molly took her time munching her way through a biscuit.

'You aren't going to tell me, are you?' I laughed. 'I swear to all your goddesses, Molly, you know more secrets around here than the Wynbridge vicar!'

Molly shrugged and grinned.

'And which particular wind blew you to my door this afternoon?' she asked. 'Have you come for a chat, a reading, do you want your tea leaves read or were you just looking for company?'

'You used tea bags,' I reminded her. 'My cup is completely devoid of leaves, which I seriously hope isn't some kind of elaborate metaphor to describe my future.'

'Of course it isn't,' she gasped. 'Your future is bright, but you must have the courage and faith to grasp it.'

'Am I allowed to mourn the loss of my relationship with Gavin first?'

'No,' she said, sounding surprisingly unsympathetic. 'I don't think you need to go to the bother of digging out your black veil over this one.'

'That's not the attitude you had when Gavin and I headed

off to sunny Hunstanton the weekend he proposed,' I reminded her. 'You couldn't wait to wave us off in his van. You were all smiles then!'

'But I didn't know the truth then, did I? Anna might have heard the rumours, but she never mentioned them to me. I had no idea that Gavin was messing about behind your back.' Then she added before I had the chance, 'And don't start on how I should have gazed into my crystal ball and seen it coming. You know that's not how it works.'

I looked at the orb resting above the fireplace and wondered how it did work. I'd never really understood how anyone could see anything beyond their own reflection in a ball of glass.

'So, why didn't you have it out with him after you got wind of that first rumour?' Molly asked. 'I know Anna reckons it was because you loved him, and I'm sure you did, but that's not the whole story, is it?'

I drank a mouthful of the tea, which tasted surprisingly normal for a brew concocted under Molly's roof.

'Do you really want the truth?' I asked.

'Yes, please.'

I took a deep breath and ran my free hand down Bran's back again.

'The truth is,' I swallowed. 'Well, the truth is ...'

'Go on,' she encouraged gently.

'Back in the spring,' I told her, 'when the weather first began to change, I started to feel lonely. Every day I saw Anna and Jamie falling more and more in love and it just threw into sharp contrast how alone I was. Don't get me wrong,' I quickly added. 'I wasn't jealous of them, I just hoped that one day I would have the chance to experience what they had. I didn't want to be on my own anymore. I wanted to have someone look at me the way that Jamie looked at Anna, and then along came Gavin.'

'And you thought that he was the one?' she asked. 'You thought that he could be the guy to fill the void and build a future with?'

'Yes,' I shrugged, 'I thought it was time to stop fooling around, give a relationship longer than a few weeks and see what happened.'

'But why, out of all the blokes who have hung around you like bees round honey during the last couple of years, was he the one you decided to let in?' She frowned. 'Like I asked a minute ago, why didn't you tackle him after that first rumour broke?'

Suddenly our cosy chat had veered off down a path that was heading in a far more serious direction.

'Well,' I told her, 'I thought we were a perfect match, didn't I? Plenty of people had told me that he had a reputation to rival Casanova, but I also knew I still had a reputation myself, even though I'd lived a fairly blameless life for almost a decade.'

Molly nodded but didn't say anything.

'My parents, Dad especially, were always going on about how lucky I was to have a man, especially one as popular and good looking as Gavin, show interest in me, and I believed them. Who else was going to hitch their wagon to a girl who had had a fling with her teacher and ended up pregnant to boot?'

I felt my face begin to burn and knew there had been no need to say that last bit out loud. Molly knew the deal without me having to reiterate it.

'And as you've told me on more than one occasion,' I went on, 'the heart wants what the heart wants. I fell in love with him.' I shrugged. 'I believed in him, and us. I really thought that he was the one.'

The one who was good enough for a girl like me at least.

'I'm so sorry,' Molly whispered.

'Me too,' I told her. 'I know we all make mistakes,' I went on, thinking how unnecessary it had been to restate the embellished details of my past, 'but Gavin's public humiliation was unforgivable. I've had enough of being the town joke.'

There were tears in Molly's eyes when I looked at her. The softened model of me would have probably succumbed to a long and loud wail at that point, but the reprised me was dry-eyed and determined. Perhaps a part of me even thought I deserved what had happened.

'Don't look like that, Molly,' I told her. 'I'm fine.'

She didn't look so sure.

'I'm back to my old self,' I said brightly. 'Sassy, full of swag and sworn off men.'

'Really?'

'Well, for a year or so at least,' I confirmed. 'If a no-strings hunk shows up after that, then maybe, *maybe*, I'll force myself to take him on. But, in the meantime, I'm going no further than a mild flirtation.'

'But you said you want what Anna and Jamie have got?'

'*Wanted*,' I said with emphasis, to make sure she understood I meant the past tense. 'It was what I *wanted*. I gave it a shot and it was a disaster so I'm washing my hands of the whole idea. In fact,' I went on, 'I'm rather hoping you're going to tell me about this great thing you told Anna you saw galloping in my direction, because I could sure use something other than a man to get stuck into right now.'

Chapter 10

In spite of my pleading, Molly refused to go into specifics.

'It's Samhain in a couple of days,' she reminded me instead. 'The start of a brand-new cycle and I would advise you to throw yourself wholeheartedly into whatever comes your way after Hallowe'en. Remember, Hayley, it's your responsibility to make the most of every new opportunity that presents itself.'

'Well, I've already made a start with that, haven't I?' I reminded her. 'I moved out of town today and into the hall.'

'And that is a great start,' Molly agreed, 'but I'm fairly certain there's going to be even more on offer to you in the next few weeks than a change of address.'

'Are you talking about getting stuck into helping with the Winter Wonderland that Angus has been scheming about, by any chance?'

'Perhaps,' said Molly, staring dreamily into the fire. 'I mean, anything that requires babysitting Angus tends to focus the attention and stop one dwelling on other things, doesn't it?'

I could tell I was beginning to lose her. Once she started flame-watching you could be fairly certain you weren't going to get any more sense out of her.

'Right,' I said, putting my mug on the table next to the tarot pack. 'I'm going to head back.'

'Already?' she blinked, her eyes returning to me. 'You've only just arrived.'

'I know,' I said, 'but if I sit here much longer I'll nod off, and I've already lost half the day catching up on my sleep.'

Walking through the woods, I felt a definite nip in the air, which, I was sure, seemed all the more intense having left Molly's warm fireside. I wrapped my jacket tighter around myself and set off with Bran sticking close to my side and the crisp autumn leaves crunching underfoot. We hadn't gone far before the dog stopped dead in his tracks, his nose twitching in a completely different direction to the one leading to the hall. I hoped he hadn't caught the scent of a rabbit or anything else he might fancy tearing off after. My little legs would be no match for his lengthy strides, and I didn't want to lose him.

'Come on, Bran,' I encouraged, using my most persuasive tone. 'We need to go this way, mate.'

He didn't budge.

'Bran,' I said again, this time in the sing-song voice that always worked a treat on Suki. 'Come on.'

Ignoring me completely, he set off along his preferred path

leaving me no option but to follow. With no lead or collar to cling to, I was powerless to do anything other than cross my fingers and keep him in sight.

'If I'd known you were going to lead me astray,' I called after him, as a soft breeze began to stir the branches and the birds fell silent, 'I would have left you at Molly's.'

He quickened his pace as we headed deeper into the woods, and my chest began to heave as I struggled to keep up with him. Just when I was beginning to think I was heading for trouble, he let out a deep bark and tore off around a corner and completely out of view.

'Bran!' I called. 'Wait!'

I gave chase as fast as I could, wearing wellies that were slightly too large.

'It's all right!' a voice called back just seconds later. 'I've got him.'

I bowled into the clearing and found Gabe standing in front of the woods' very own Wishing Tree with Bran on his back legs, his front paws on his master's shoulders.

'You bugger,' I puffed, bending to cradle the stitch in my side as the dog wagged his tail and looked incredibly pleased with himself. 'I thought I'd lost you.'

'He must have known I was here,' said Gabe, gazing at Bran's smile in bewilderment as he patted his sides and gave him a rub. 'Do you know, I reckon there's something a bit funny about this dog.'

'Oh yeah,' I said, finally straightening back up. 'He's hilarious.'

Bran dropped back to all fours and padded over to me, his pink tongue lolling.

'You should have your own stand-up act, boy,' I told him. 'You'd make an absolute fortune.'

The gentle tinkling and rustling of the numerous flags, keys, letters and trinkets that adorned the tree drew our attention and I went and stood next to Gabe.

'Do you know what this is?' I asked him. I sometimes forgot that not everyone was familiar with the folklore.

'Yes,' he said, clearing his throat. 'It's a Wishing Tree, isn't it?'

'That's right. Molly says the breeze is always here because it carries away the wishes,' I explained. 'Even on the stillest summer afternoon, there's always some movement.'

Gabe nodded and I thought of the things I had added to the tree myself. I hadn't had any luck with wish-fulfilment so far, but I wasn't going to give up on the magic my wood-dwelling friend insisted existed here just yet.

'Have you ever made a wish here?' Gabe asked.

'Just one or two,' I swallowed, trying not to look too hard at the tree for fear of spotting my own tokens.

They might have only been inanimate objects, but everyone who added something to the tree's broad branches packed their offerings with silent prayers and the deepest desires they carried in their hearts. This was not the place that folk came to ask for a lottery win. This clearing and this tree offered something far more precious than anything money could buy.

Peace, understanding, the fulfilment of a hard-worked-for goal and good health were far more highly valued here than pounds and pence.

'Do you want to make a wish?' I asked Gabe, to stop myself dwelling on the words I myself had whispered on more than one occasion. 'I'll help you if you like,' I added, rifling through my pockets for something he could add to the tree.

'No,' he said quickly, 'thank you, but not today.'

I waited to see if he was going to explain why. I might not have been the most patient person in the world, but I had learned that if you didn't automatically rush into filling the silences in a conversation, then quite often the other person would, and in the process, would share far more than they meant to. I had no desire to try to trick Gabe into revealing his secrets, but his zipped-up baggage and the look on his face when I turned up at Molly's, had led me to believe that he might, perhaps, need a shoulder to lean on that didn't belong to his humungous hound.

'Perhaps I might one day,' he carried on, 'but, between you and me, right now I'm still chasing a wish that can't possibly come true, so it wouldn't be fair to ask the tree, or the universe, for something it could never give me.'

I had no intention of launching into a rousing 'nothing is impossible' speech because I knew for myself that some things simply weren't possible. When I had my miscarriage, I had spent months wishing it hadn't happened, wishing that I could turn the clock back and perhaps find a way to stop it, praying that I could bite back some of the things I had said. But there are some things in life that aren't meant to be altered, they were meant to happen, even though they ripped your very soul in two, and there was little point in pretending otherwise to either Gabe or myself.

'Shall we head back then?' I suggested. 'I reckon it must be time for tea by now.'

Gabe pulled back the sleeve of his jumper to look at his watch.

'Crikey,' he tutted, 'it's far later than I realised. Do you know the way back from here?'

'Like the back of my hand.'

During our walk back through the woods, Gabe explained about the sort of work Jamie had asked him to take on at the hall.

'Basically, it's going to be Forest School meets Ray Mears, with some very subtle counselling and lots of opportunities for informal chats thrown in for good measure,' he told me. 'Plenty of campfires, den building, sleeping out under the stars and woodland crafting. That sort of thing.'

In some ways it sounded similar to what Mick had been offering, but with extra nurture sessions as the added ingredient.

'I want to get the kids to connect with nature,' Gabe said enthusiastically, 'and get them talking in a different environment. Four walls and a table are all very well, but not all kids can open up in a formal setting. A friendly chat while gathering wood for the camp will suit some far better.'

I could understand that. I had experienced first-hand the well-meaning head bobs, concerned knitted brows and unwavering eye contact that could make a kid clam up. The baking sessions Dorothy had offered some of the kids had proved far more productive than the prescribed appointments, and not just because of the tasty results that came out of the Aga at the end of them.

'Oh, wow,' gasped Gabe. 'Would you look at that?'

The conversation I had overheard in the kitchen had just popped back into my head and I was just about to ask Gabe what qualified him to do the job, but hearing the rapture in his voice I decided I'd ask another day.

'Not bad, is it?' I smiled, following his line of sight to the biggest oak tree the Wynthorpe estate had to offer.

'Not bad!' He laughed, rushing forward and spreading his hands over the bark. 'Not bad! However old is it?'

'No idea,' I shrugged, as my eyes scanned its mighty heights.

The ground beneath the tree was littered with leaves and there were still a few acorns that had escaped the squirrels' attention. I bent to scoop a couple of the seeds up. They were still in their cups and the acorns themselves felt smooth in my fingers. I handed one to Gabe and put the other one in my pocket. Something I hadn't done for years.

'I wouldn't have put you down as a tree hugger,' I told him, 'having witnessed first-hand the way you laid waste to those logs back at the cottage.'

I felt my face redden a little as I remembered the sight

of Gabe stripped to the waist swinging his axe, the defined muscles in his back and shoulders flexed and taut.

'Well, I am,' he grinned. 'I'm a fully paid-up tree hugger, I'm afraid, Hayley, but that doesn't mean that I'm not prepared to make use of every bit of a tree once it has seen out its time.'

He was resourceful as well as respectful, then – two traits I could get onboard with.

'Here,' he said, reaching out and catching my arm.

'No way,' I said, taking a step back. 'You're not roping me in. Molly's the girl for you if this is what you're into.'

'Come on,' he insisted, trying to edge me closer to the twisted trunk. 'How will you know you don't like it if you've never tried?'

'Yeah, right,' I laughed, 'that's what all the boys say.' But I gave in anyway and stepped within reach again.

'You're incorrigible,' Gabe laughed back. 'Do you know that?'

'Of course I do. It's what I'm famous for around here.'

Amongst other things, but this wasn't the moment to get into that.

Gabe shook his head.

'Here,' he said, taking my hand in his before placing it flat on the trunk of the tree. 'Can you feel that?'

The palm of his hand felt warm pressed against the back of mine. I could feel something, but I wasn't sure it had anything to do with the tree.

'Can you feel how smooth it is?'

'Uh-huh,' I nodded, looking everywhere except at him.

'This big fella is slowing down for the winter,' he carried on. 'Getting ready for the long rest. Something we should all be thinking about, really.'

'With an Angus on the loose in the run-up to Christmas,' I said huskily, 'there's no chance of that.'

Gabe didn't comment, but slid his palm gently along the length of my fingers, and when I finally dared to look at him, he was staring down at me.

'We should get back,' I whispered, shocked by the intimacy in his touch. 'Dorothy will be wondering where we've got to.'

'OK,' he breathed, moving his hand away, but not taking his eyes off mine. 'Sorry.'

The skin on the back of my hand felt cold without the pressure of his and I put it in my jacket pocket, turning over the smooth little acorn as, with Bran at our heels, we walked the rest of the way in companionable silence.

'At last,' tutted Dorothy when we eventually entered the kitchen. 'I'd all but given up on you three.'

'We were in the woods,' said Gabe.

Anna's head snapped up from the paperwork she was looking through, her eyes flicking between Gabe and me.

'Bran got away from me when I was walking back from Molly's,' I quickly added.

The last thing I wanted was Anna thinking we had set out on a walk together. If I gave her even just a second, she'd start putting two and two together and coming up with the wrong answer, but if I wasn't careful, my paranoia would lead her to the wrong conclusion anyway.

'I'm beginning to think he has super-human powers, this one,' Gabe went on, rubbing Bran under the chin. 'He ran away from Hayley and came straight for me. Goodness knows how he knew where I was.'

'So, Bran led you straight to Gabe did he, Hayley?'

I busied myself taking off my jacket and hanging it over the back of a chair. Had she really forgotten that I had literally just ducked out of the shortest engagement ever known in these parts and was nursing a broken heart?

'He did, didn't he?' Gabe laughed, completely oblivious to what she was implying, assuming, of course, that I wasn't reading too much into it.

Just in the nick of time, Catherine came into the kitchen and saved me from protesting too much.

'How did you get on in town this morning?' she asked. 'I hope it wasn't all too traumatic for you, my dear.'

Gabe and I took our seats around the table with the others. I explained how Mum had been there and a little of what she had said, along with the update from the pub and details of what I hoped was to be my final encounter with Gavin.

'You really are an angel, then,' Anna said to Gabe once I had told them about how he'd tackled Gavin. 'Even if your approach is a little unorthodox.'

'Unorthodox or not, it was no less than Gavin deserved,' Angus shocked me by saying.

'Are you sure you haven't got wings under that jumper, Gabe?' Anna went on and everyone laughed.

'I promise,' he said, laughing at the sentiment. 'Hayley can vouch for that.'

'Can she now?' tutted Dorothy.

'Yep,' I said, thinking it best to brazen it out, 'I can confirm there's not so much as a feather in sight. There are some mighty fine muscles and a pair of powerful shoulders, but no feathers.'

Now it was Gabe's turn to flush red.

'Well, I think that's quite enough of that,' said Dorothy, fanning herself with the tea towel. 'Now, who wants more cake?'

'I'll have a slice please,' I answered. 'I'm going to need some extra calories inside me to lug my stuff upstairs.'

'Oh, yes, now I'm pleased you've mentioned your things,' said Catherine. 'Because I wanted to talk to you about the Rose Room, Hayley.'

I hoped she wasn't going to offer it to me on a permanent basis. As pretty as it was, for some reason I couldn't relax in it. It didn't feel right for me, somehow.

'How are you settling in?' asked Anna. 'I loved staying in it. In fact, now I know how slapdash Jamie is with bed-making and filling the laundry basket, I sometimes wish I hadn't moved out of it.'

'Hey!' pouted Jamie. 'I'm not that bad.'

'Are you happy to stay in there, Hayley?' Catherine asked.

'If that's where you'd like me to stay,' I smiled diplomatically.

The last thing I wanted to do was come across as ungrateful, and turning down the prettiest room in the hall would have been a sure-fire way of doing so.

'That isn't quite what I was asking,' Catherine said gently.

'Well,' I said, shifting a little in my seat, 'as it's the most popular bedroom here, I was thinking perhaps it would be better if it was kept for guests and family. It's so lovely and I know it's Cass's favourite.'

'You do know that we think of you as family, don't you?' Angus frowned.

'Of course,' I said quickly, 'but I'd be perfectly happy in another room.'

'What about where I suggested?' Dorothy said to Catherine.

She had finally taken her seat at the table, but was poised to spring back up should anyone look even remotely in need of further sustenance.

Catherine nodded.

'How would you fancy moving across to be next to me at the far end of the hall?' Dorothy asked. 'You could have the bedroom at the other side of the sitting room I use and we could keep each other company in the evenings.'

Dorothy's room was at the opposite end of the hall to the family rooms and had a cosy nook to relax in adjoining it. There was another bedroom on the opposite side of her little snug and it had always struck me as a comfortable spot.

'Are you sure you could put up with me in such close proximity?' I asked, only half joking. 'We're talking twenty-four-seven here, Dorothy.'

'I know that,' she tutted.

'The question should be,' grinned Mick, 'can you put up with Dorothy? She has pretty appalling taste when it comes to music and movie nights, you know.'

'Hey, hey.' Dorothy retaliated. 'I'll have you know there's nothing better than a little Tom Cruise to brighten up a bleak winter evening. I happen to do a word-perfect rendition of "Danger Zone" from *Top Gun*.'

I wasn't sure what I was letting myself in for, but it couldn't be worse than being at home listening to my father's snores rattling the roof night after night, could it?

'That's settled then,' said Catherine decisively. 'Leave your boxes where they are tonight, have one last sleep in the Rose Room and tomorrow you can air out and dress your new space with whatever takes your fancy from the attic.'

With such an exciting prospect on the horizon, I already knew I was in for another sleepless night.

Later that evening, as I lay tossing and turning, I wondered what Gavin would have made of my new abode. However, that wasn't the only thing on my mind. I could still feel Gabe's caress long after he had removed the palm of his hand from the back of mine.

Chapter 11

The next morning, after an unusually early breakfast, Dorothy and I walked practically the entire length of the hall from the kitchen to get to my new living quarters. I had to decide how I wanted to dress them, given that Catherine had allowed me to choose from the treasure trove in the attic rooms.

'All of this can be rearranged,' Dorothy insisted as she opened the door to the sitting room that we would be sharing. 'I'm sure we can switch things around so they suit us both.'

'It's perfect just the way it is,' I told her. 'There's plenty of space for my few bits and pieces, but, my goodness, I'd forgotten how big your TV is!'

I shouldn't have forgotten, given the way the delivery guys had puffed after they had finished lugging the gigantic box up innumerable flights of stairs. Still, Dorothy had rewarded them with a hearty lunch to make amends for their aching backs and had sent them on their way with slices of cake wrapped in parchment to see them through the rest of the day.

'As you know, I'm not one for turning out in the evenings, now,' Dorothy reminded me, 'but a screen this size is as good as going to the cinema, and no one minds if you pause the action to make another cup of tea.'

I shook my head and smiled. There couldn't be many pensioners with the same passion for films as my new roommate. I hoped she wasn't going to keep me awake all night with her super-duper surround-sound system. That *would* be as bad as Dad snoring.

'And this will be you,' she said, opening the door to the bedroom that was on the opposite side of the sitting room to hers. 'I've already opened the window, so it's nicely aired. In fact, I think we'll shut that now.'

The room was freezing, but fresh, and I took my time looking around the almost empty space. There was an old-fashioned metal bedframe, which Dorothy told me was Victorian, but the mattress was practically new and barely slept on.

'There's a really nice view from here,' she said with a nod to the window, which overlooked the gardens at the rear of the hall and had a sill deep enough to sit on, 'and the seat lifts up so you can store any bits and pieces that you don't want on display.'

I peered inside wondering if it was large enough to stash away the art folder, which was currently hidden under the bed in the Rose Room. The sooner that was properly away from prying eyes, the better. I looked out across the gardens and, in spite of my insistence that I was turning off my heart from hereon in, it began to thump away in my chest. The fact that Gabe had just come into view had nothing to do with it. The fluttering was all about the realisation that this could be the perfect spot to sketch from, should I decide to carry on.

I quickly stepped away from the window and set about exploring the two deep cupboards on either side of the fireplace, one of which had a hanging rail. There was no other furniture in the room and the wooden floorboards made it sound hollow, but thick curtains and a rug would soon solve that problem.

'So,' asked Dorothy, biting her lip. 'What do you think? I know it's not a patch on the Rose Room, but—'

'It's perfect,' I told her.

'Well, it will be when you've decided how to decorate it.' She smiled. 'And the heating is pretty efficient up here so you'll be nice and cosy.'

I nodded. I still couldn't believe that this was where I was going to be living. All these years Catherine and Angus had been asking me to move in, but I had stuck it out at home, and for what? Had I made the break sooner, Mum might have found the courage to move on a lifetime ago, but I knew there was little point in thinking like that.

It was finally going to happen for her now and I was lucky to have another family waiting in the wings to welcome me into their home. And at least I could say I had been a dutiful daughter. I might have made a complete mess of my schooling and what happened after it, but I had done my best to make amends and pay my way in the years that followed.

'You deserve this,' said Dorothy, as she crossed the room and rubbed my arm. 'It's about time you started living your own life, my darling. It's time you got out from under your father's thumb.'

I opened my mouth to explain just how grateful I was to have the opportunity to do so, but she carried on.

'It's high time you stopped blaming yourself for everything that happened in the past, Hayley. You need to leave it all behind.'

I knew she was right, but there was still one thing from the past that was holding me back. I would have to face it soon, but not quite yet. I didn't want anything to spoil today, not even thoughts of my shattered heart.

'You made the right decision choosing not to put up with that Gavin,' she told me. 'He wasn't good enough for you, my girl.'

I couldn't help but smile. Dorothy had demoted the once scorching scaffolder to 'that Gavin' the second she'd discovered what he had been up to.

'I know you're not going to get over him in a hurry, but please don't let his abhorrent behaviour be the excuse for shutting down your heart.'

'I'm not shutting down my heart,' I told her. 'I'm just hanging the "out to lunch" sign up for a while. Give me a few months and it'll be back in business.'

'But for what, exactly?' She frowned.

'Fun and frolics,' I shrugged, my eyes straying back to the window where I could still see Gabe walking in the garden. 'I won't be looking for anything heavy again. I'm not cut out for it.'

'What you're suggesting doesn't sound like it has anything to do with your heart to me.'

'Well, perhaps it doesn't,' I shrugged again.

'Please don't let everything that's happened stop you falling in love again,' Dorothy sniffed, as I heard footsteps in the corridor outside.

'Dorothy,' I told her with a small smile. 'I know you mean well, but I have no intention of falling in love again. It hurts too much when it goes wrong. Why would I set myself up for this sort of suffering all over again?'

'Don't say that,' she said. 'You can't assume things will go wrong.'

'Look,' I told her, wishing she didn't look so sad. 'I'm fine. I promise, I'm perfectly happy as I am, so please don't go crying over me and please,' I added, giving her a hug, '*please* let's not have deep and meaningful conversations every five minutes because, if we do, we'll never have any fun up here.'

She nodded and kissed my hair, then moved to the window to dry her eyes as Anna and Molly bounded into the room. They looked more like two excited teenagers who'd been downing WKD behind the village hall than sensible, grown-up women.

'What's got into the pair of you?' I asked.

I couldn't pinpoint why exactly, but I felt suspicious seeing them with such a spring in their step so early in the day.

Molly opened her mouth to say something, but Anna elbowed her in the ribs and got in first.

'Nothing,' she shrugged. 'We're just excited to help you get sorted in here, that's all.'

I could always tell when she was lying.

Dorothy had swiftly recovered from her unusually emotional moment and showed me the bathroom across the corridor, which we would also be sharing. 'If you find what you want up in the attic rooms, Hayley,' she said, 'I'll draft the menfolk in to help shift it after lunch.'

'I'm sure we'll be able to manage,' I told her. 'But thank you.'

'Don't be so stubborn,' said Anna. 'It will be quicker if everyone helps.'

She was right, of course, but the Hayley I was attempting to reprise – the smart-talking sassy one – had never been very good at accepting help. I needed to remember that it was only my heart that I was ringfencing. Accepting an offer of help didn't necessarily mean that I was going soft again.

'And you think about what I said,' Dorothy told me pointedly before she went back to the kitchen.

'What was that all about?' asked Molly as soon as Dorothy was out of earshot.

'And I thought you could read minds,' I tutted, striding by and heading up to the attics.

We squeezed our way past Dolores, the stuffed brown bear, which Catherine refused to have on display down in the hall, and into the rooms that were packed with all the things I wanted to put in my new quarters.

'Do you have a theme in mind?' asked Anna, as we looked along the corridor where Catherine had attempted, in spite of Angus's efforts to throw the system into chaos, to keep things packed away in alphabetical order. 'Or a colour?'

'And are you keeping the bedframe?' joined in Molly. 'Or is it too girlie?'

'Yes, yes, yes and no,' I told them with a smile.

'Oh well,' laughed Anna, 'that should save some time, then.'

My two friends had been rather taken aback as I began making a pile of things to carry down to my room next to Dolores.

'This isn't what I was expecting at all,' said Anna, shaking her head as I added another cushion to the three I'd already found.

'Me neither,' agreed Molly, as she tucked her untameable hair behind her ears for the hundredth time that morning and inspected the three framed rose prints I had just set out.

'Why not?' I asked, standing back up and smoothing out the kinks in my spine.

'Well . . .' Anna began.

'It's all a bit pink,' Molly cut in.

She was right. It *was* all a bit pink. From the Laura Ashley vintage curtains to the silky-soft hand-sewn eiderdown, it was all a bit pink and a bit flowery.

'I've never had you down as someone who likes this kind of pretty, pastel stuff,' said Anna. 'I thought this was all more my taste than yours.'

'Good,' I laughed out loud, making them both jump. 'Because do you know what? I can't think of anything worse than being predictable. I'm rather chuffed I've surprised you both and you're just jealous, Anna, because you have to share a room with Jamie, who litters the floors with his dirty laundry and wouldn't let this sort of stuff anywhere near your room.'

'So, have you picked this lot out to annoy me or because it's what you really want?' She grinned.

I didn't have a chance to answer.

'How are you getting on?'

It was Catherine.

'I see the moths still haven't got to Dolores, then,' she went on, skirting her way around the bear she had feared since childhood but couldn't bring herself to part with. 'Aha,' she smiled when she spotted what I had picked out, completely ruining my unpredictable reputation. 'I had a feeling you might go for this lot.'

'Is that all right?'

'Of course it is,' she told me. 'It should never have been packed away, but there's no point dwelling on that now.'

'Thank you, Catherine.'

'Now, come on. Dorothy is about to ring the gong for lunch and after that we'll see to getting this lot shifted.'

Anna and Molly were looking more puzzled than ever, but I didn't explain that Catherine had once used these pretty furnishings to dress another room to tempt me to take up residence in the hall. I had longed to move in back then, but family loyalty had stopped me. The beautiful room I had spent literally years dreaming about was finally going to be mine.

'Just your stuff in the Rose Room to shift now, then,' said Mick, brushing down his trousers as he straightened up after helping me position the rug between the bed and the fireplace.

'Yep,' I said, looking about me in excitement, 'then we can call it a day.'

'And is this how you hoped it would look?'

I cast my eyes over the pretty, pastel haven we had created. This was one longed-for wish that I had found the courage to make come true without the assistance of the tree in the woods.

'Yes,' I said, sighing with pleasure, 'it is.'

'That's good then.'

'Although,' I added, 'I was hoping Anna and Molly would be here to see it all come together. Do you know where they've disappeared to?'

'The Rose Room,' he said. 'They said they'd go and get the rest of your stuff while we were putting the rug down.'

I rushed from the room, my excitement forgotten as I hoped neither of them had thought to look under the bed.

'Is everything all right?' Mick called after me.

As it turned out, no, everything was not all right.

I could hear the pair chattering excitedly even before I had entered the room. I burst in to find them huddled together on the bed with my now-empty folder, its contents spread across the bed being scrutinised.

'What have you got there?' I asked, thinking that if I played dumb then perhaps they wouldn't associate the work with me at all.

'When we came up here to find you earlier, Suki dived under the bed,' began Molly, 'and tugged this out.'

I wasn't sure I believed her. The plucky little dog might have had a heart and attitude to match a bull mastiff, but her physical strength was chihuahua all the way, and the packed folder would have been far too heavy for her to heave out.

'Crikey,' was all I could manage.

'Why didn't you tell us?' asked Anna, her head still bent over one of the sketchbooks.

'Tell you what?'

'About this, of course,' said Molly, her eyes shining with excitement as she pointed at the piles of sketches and paintings. 'We waited all morning for you to mention it but you didn't say a word.'

'But I didn't know anything about it,' I replied. 'Someone must have hidden it there.'

'And you didn't spot it when you were vacuuming?' Anna tutted. 'Shame on you, Hayley Hurren. I had you down as a housekeeper who hoovered under the beds, not swept things under the carpet.'

I chewed my lip but didn't bite back. One thing I could never tolerate was having my work ethic criticised. Anna knew that and was purposely trying to get a rise out of me.

'Do you think it's been there long?' asked Molly, kicking off what was clearly a well-rehearsed little speech.

'Not all that long,' said Anna. 'I'd say no more than a few days.'

'Really?'

Even though I knew they meant no harm, my hands were beginning to sweat and my heart was beating so loudly I was sure one of them was going to hear it.

'Well, never mind about all that,' I said, in a vain attempt to try to throw them off. 'Come and see how the room looks. Mick and I have hung the curtains and laid the rug and you wouldn't recognise it. It's gorgeous.'

Neither of them was listening to me, as Molly's next question confirmed.

'So, what makes you say that, Anna?'

She was grinning now.

'Because I know for a fact,' Anna replied, finally tearing her eyes from the bed to look into mine, 'that Hayley put this folder here.'

'What?' Molly gasped in fake shock.

'What are you talking about?' I snapped.

'HH,' Anna announced, holding up one of the drawings

and pointing to my initials, which I had added in the bottom right-hand corner. 'Hayley Hurren.'

'Well I never,' said Molly, shaking her head.

'These are Hayley's drawings and sketches,' Anna carried on.

'Oh my,' whispered Molly in faux surprise. 'Did you do these, Hayley? Did you really do all of this?'

The game was up.

'Yes,' I said, dumping myself down opposite the pair of them, 'I did. You both obviously know I did.'

'But why didn't you ever tell us you had this amazing talent?' Molly asked.

She'd dropped her act and sounded rather hurt now, but I was sure she had secrets she had chosen not to share, even with her nearest and dearest.

'All this time we've been friends,' Anna added, her tone reflecting Molly's, 'and you've never said a word.'

'Well, I'm sorry, all right,' I snapped defensively. 'And anyway, it doesn't matter because it isn't something I do anymore. I packed all this away when I left school and I've barely thought about it since.'

That was by far the biggest lie I'd told in a long time. I might have set it all aside when I left school, but the guilt wrapped around it, coupled with the addictive urge to draw, had ensured I never enjoyed more than a few days when it wasn't on my mind.

'I don't believe you,' said Anna.

'It's true,' I shrugged, 'but you can believe what you want.'

'I know you're lying.'

'Come on, guys,' cut in Molly, 'let's not fall out. I'm sure Hayley had her reasons for stopping.'

'Thank you, Molly,' I nodded. 'I did.'

'But it's such a waste,' Anna went on relentlessly, 'and you know it is, Hayley. You have a phenomenal talent—'

'*Had*,' I corrected.

'*Have*,' she said again, reaching under the pile of loose sheets.

'What's that?' frowned Molly.

Clearly she and Anna hadn't discussed this bit.

'Proof that Hayley's telling porkies,' she said. 'Proof that she still has this amazing talent, along with the desire to use it.'

I couldn't deny the evidence in front of my eyes. She had found, and was now flicking through, the sketchbook that I had started to fill after Gavin had unwittingly re-lit the little torch, which had then gone on to burn so bright that I could no longer ignore its glare and had picked up a pencil again and again.

'These are places in the hall,' said Molly, pointing out various features, 'and these are spots in the garden, aren't they?'

'Yes,' I sighed, 'yes, they are.'

'So why did you say you didn't do this anymore?' Anna demanded. 'Everything in this book is dated from the beginning of summer.'

'Look,' I told her, 'the first guy to crush my creativity, having spent every lesson during my high school years encouraging it, was my art teacher, and then along came

Gavin, my cheating ex-fiancé, who said I should start again and then tainted my hard work with his humiliation.'

I carried on trying to use the ill-assorted men in my life and their treatment of me to justify my reasons for stopping, and gently released the sketchbook from Anna's hands before packing everything away again. The pair listened without interruption until I had finished zipping up the folder. I was surprised to discover that I wasn't quite as sure as I had been previously that all that was a valid reason for giving up something I loved so much, but obviously I couldn't tell Anna that. I just wanted her to forget it all and not make a fuss.

'You need to stop thinking about all that,' Anna told me.

The words died in her throat as she realised she was making it sound as if it were the easiest thing in the world to do; that I should just get over myself and move on.

'Sorry,' she said, 'I didn't mean to sound so flippant.'

'It's OK,' I shrugged.

It was impossible to be angry with someone who had your best interests at heart. Molly didn't say anything, but I could tell by the faraway look in her eye and the way she was twisting a strand of her wild and wispy hair around her fingers that she was mulling it all over.

Chapter 12

I made my friends promise that they wouldn't breathe a word to anyone else about the secret they had discovered, and then I stashed the folder away in the cubby hole beneath the window seat in my new bedroom. Throwing myself into my work was a sure-fire way to forget all about it and, having had a couple of days of not doing much at all, there was plenty for me to get stuck into.

By the time the first week of November was rolling by, I was feeling much more like my old self. I had purposely left my phone switched off, had bypassed all social media and was settled in my new space. I was sleeping better than I had in the Rose Room, but I couldn't help wondering how Mum was getting on in her quest to find herself a new life away from my father, and possibly Wynbridge. I did think about getting in touch with her, but I didn't want to risk doing or saying anything which might put her off or, worse still, stop her going altogether.

I also began to wonder how the pair had coped with the many adolescent trick-or-treaters who descended every Halloween and wreaked havoc on our estate. These weren't the cute youngsters escorted by parents in their quest for cheap candy, but a hardcore group who, bored with life in a small rural town, had to be told harsh words and threatened with phone calls to the police before they would abandon the quest to egg every door in sight and disband.

I smiled to myself as the vision of Evelyn launching dev-illed eggs popped into my head, and I wondered how much longer it would be before the sharpest edges of Gavin's public humiliation would be smoothed away and I would be able to smile at some of his antics, too. No doubt that would take time, but I'd get there in the end. This particular Hurren had the knack of being able to laugh at herself. It had formed a key part of my defence stratagem over the years.

'What's so funny?' Jamie asked as he passed me on the galleried landing and spotted my smile.

'Nothing,' I shrugged, expertly twitching my feather duster, which formed part of my work-kit, along the bannis-ter. 'You know me, I'm just happy in my work.'

'Fair enough,' he nodded, carrying on towards the top of the stairs. 'Oh,' he added, turning back, 'before I forget, we'll be leaving at about four this afternoon.'

'For what?'

'The fireworks in town, of course. You haven't forgotten, have you?'

I had forgotten, actually. Living and working at the hall,

time had already started to merge and I was losing track of my days. If I wasn't careful I would end up forgoing my usual Sunday duvet day to carry on with the cleaning. That said, a single whiff of Dorothy's legendary roasts would be enough to remind me what day it was.

'No,' I called down the stairs as Jamie carried on making his descent, 'I haven't forgotten,' I lied.

The Wynbridge fireworks display didn't launch from the town centre, but from a generous farmer's field on the out-skirts of town, which, apparently, because of the proximity of the river, wasn't much good for either growing or graz-ing. There was always an enormous bonfire to accompany the impressive display, as well as a hog roast and cider from nearby Skylark Farm, and a couple of stalls selling glow sticks and sweets to further stimulate the already wired kids.

I could only remember one year when I hadn't put in an appearance, and the Wynthorpe clan – Molly included – were always in attendance. Even Angus agreed that letting off fireworks at the hall, which would send Floss cowering and diving for cover, would be selfish and irresponsible, and he happily travelled further afield to satisfy his desire to indulge in the delights that erupted every 5th of November in Guy Fawkes' name.

'I'm really sorry,' I told Dorothy after lunch when I had taken to my bed, 'but I'm not going to be able to make it tonight. My head's absolutely thumping.'

'You do look a little flushed,' she frowned, pressing the

back of her hand to my head. 'But then, so would I if I was in bed, fully clothed, having just eaten a hot meal.'

I pushed the eiderdown back and sat up feeling annoyed at having been caught out and ashamed that I had tried to trick her.

'I just can't face it this year,' I croaked, 'it's too soon.'

'Well, there's no shame in that,' she frowned, 'but why lie about it?'

'Because I don't hide away from anything, do I?' I snapped. 'And I don't want anyone, especially Gavin, thinking that I'm hurting so much that it's stopping me from living my life.'

'But you *are* living your life,' Dorothy reminded me. 'You've left home and moved in here for a start. That's a huge step.'

'I know.'

'You need to stop being so hard on yourself, missy,' she told me, sounding stern. 'If you don't want to come to the fireworks, then don't come.'

'But I don't want everyone else to think—'

'You need to stop worrying about what everyone else thinks, Hayley. Try doing something for yourself for a change. Try that on for size and see how it fits.'

'Well, I'm fairly certain my father would say that moving here was a pretty selfish move and that's worked out OK, for me at least.'

'Exactly,' Dorothy agreed, 'and you should think of that brave move as your first step over the starting line.'

'What do you mean?'

'What I mean,' she said firmly, 'is that you mustn't stop now that you've started. You've spent far too many years living your life and doing things a certain way because you were trying to please parents you could never satisfy no matter what you did.'

She had a point.

'If you don't want to come tonight,' she went on, 'then that's entirely up to you. Spend the evening doing something you want to do instead. Take a bath, watch a film, finish my jigsaw, start a new hobby or perhaps pick up an old one.'

My ears pricked up at the mention of an 'old hobby' and I hoped Anna and Molly hadn't broken their promise to keep quiet about my skills with a pencil and paper.

'And in the meantime,' she said, 'I'll just tell the others you're giving tonight a miss. Simple as that.'

'Thank you, Dorothy.'

'You aren't the only one staying put,' she said, heading for the door. 'Gabe has already said that he won't be coming either.'

The hall was disconcertingly quiet once everyone had gone, and I realised that I wasn't used to being there on my own, especially after dark. I knew the place like the back of my hand, but that didn't stop it feeling a little spooky once it was devoid of the Connelly clan.

The living and breathing ones, anyway.

As a rule, the ghost stories about the obligatory 'grey lady', who somehow haunted every property in the UK over a hundred years old, didn't enter my head, but even the dogs were a little restless down in the kitchen and I decided that it would be a lovely idea to share the dinner Dorothy had prepared for me with Gabe over at his place.

'Hayley,' he said, taking a step back as I brushed past him and into Gatekeeper's Cottage, my arms weighed down with the insulated bag full of food, and Floss and Suki trailing close behind, 'oh, OK. Hi. Come on in.'

'Thanks,' I puffed dumping the bag and pushing Floss's inquisitive nose in the opposite direction. 'I wondered if you fancied sharing my dinner?'

'All right,' he nodded, 'thanks. I'll just get dressed.'

'Why is it,' I said, because it would have been impossible not to comment on his post-shower state of undress, 'that you are always half naked when I turn up here?'

'Beats me,' he shrugged, taking the smaller of the two towels, which was wrapped around his shoulders, and rubbing his dark hair until it stood up in all directions. 'But if you'd been just thirty seconds earlier you'd have caught me completely in the buff.'

'Damn,' I laughed as I pulled off my coat, 'I need to work on my timing.'

'I'll be two minutes,' he laughed back as he headed up the stairs.

'So,' said Gabe after we had finished eating dinner on our laps and the dogs had finally settled in a heap in front of the little wood burner, 'how come you haven't gone with the others? You don't strike me as the type to turn down a party.'

'I just didn't fancy it this year,' I sniffed. 'I don't usually miss it, but I didn't much feel like lurking about in the shadows.'

'Were you worried about bumping into Gavin?'

'Head straight for the heart of the matter, why don't you?'

'Sorry,' he smiled, looking anything but. 'But I wouldn't have had you down as the sort of girl who'd let a guy like him off the hook, Hayley. I don't mean that I would expect you to be bad-mouthing him all over town or anything, but I am surprised that you've been keeping your head down and avoiding the place completely.'

'I haven't been avoiding it,' I snapped back. 'I just haven't needed to go in for anything, that's all, and if you knew the whole story then you'd know . . .'

I stopped myself before I really put my foot in it and revealed too much. As far as I was aware, Gabe had no idea about the blemishes that blighted my past and I wanted to keep it that way. He had already been party to way too much of my dismal private life since his arrival and I had no intention of furnishing him further.

What happened when I was at school, coupled with the few chaotic weeks that followed, had shaped so much of my adult life and I wanted to leave all of that behind now. I was hopeful that my friendship with Gabe could develop without being subjected to full disclosure. After all, even he had admitted that there were things in his own life that he would rather keep under wraps, so it felt fitting that we would take our acquaintanceship forward based on a mutual respect that didn't involve delving into each other's pasts.

'Never mind,' I muttered.

'But it's a shame you didn't go,' he said, taking my plate and stacking it on top of his. 'You could have supplied one hell of a guy for the bonfire.'

'What?'

'Just think of the satisfaction you could have got from burning an effigy of your scorching scaffolder.'

I could picture it in my mind's eye. The flames licking around the straw-stuffed Adonis, complete with tight vest and empty wallet.

'Who told you Angus called him that?' I asked Gabe.

'Angus did,' he smiled. 'And if I were Gavin and I knew what was good for me, I wouldn't be heading back here to collect any poles that might have been left behind.'

I thought about the loan my kind employer was never likely to see repaid. No wonder he was hacked off.

'And before you start thinking it,' Gabe added, 'Angus isn't worried about the money.'

Clearly Gabe was aware of more than I realised.

'He's far more upset about *you* than his bank balance.'

Dear Angus. He'd hardly said a word about it all to me, but I could tell from the set of his jaw whenever Gavin was mentioned, which wasn't often, in my presence, anyway, that he was mortified on my behalf.

'He's a real sweetheart,' I sighed. 'I'm very lucky to have him and Catherine in my life.'

'We all are,' said Gabe softly as he topped up my glass of cider.

'Anyway,' I said, taking a swig and turning the tables. 'How come you haven't gone to town either?'

'I didn't want to leave Bran,' he said with a nod to the pile of dogs after a second or two had ticked by. 'I wasn't sure if you could hear any fireworks from here and, obviously, I have no idea how he would react to them, so I didn't want to risk it.'

'That's fair enough,' I shrugged, but I wasn't sure I believed him entirely.

A melancholy edge had crept into his tone and there was a faraway look in his eye, which suggested to me that his absence from the party was not all down to his desire to cosset his colossal dog.

'Anyway,' I went on, determined to pull him out of his dipped mood before it really took hold, 'I don't see why it should just be the others having all the fun. I nabbed these from Angus's secret stash before I came over,' I said, waving a massive handful of supersized sparklers. 'Come on. I'll go halves with you. We'll leave the dogs in here.'

Gabe and I stood in the cottage garden, chilled by the crisp evening breeze with the stars shining above us, and drew – sometimes rude – shapes in the air.

It didn't take long for Gabe to get caught up in the moment, and we laughed until our sides hurt. I don't know which of us started the descent into silly primary school humour, but it didn't matter. In those few minutes we were conspirators, laughing in the darkness and letting off steam that we both clearly needed to be rid of.

'God, I love the smell of these,' I shouted, inhaling the acrid tang.

'That'll be the mix of chemicals they're made up from,' said Gabe knowledgeably. 'Most likely the saltpetre.'

'Oh, will it now?' I laughed.

'Last ones,' he declared, handing one of the pair to me and lighting it from his.

I spun around waving my arm madly up and down, trying to beat the burn out, but Gabe stood quite still and it wasn't until his sparks were almost at an end that I realised he was spelling out a word, possibly a name, over and over again.

'What are you writing?' I asked, interrupting his concentration. 'That looked like a name to me. You haven't got a secret lover stashed away somewhere, have you Gabe? You aren't hankering after someone you've left behind on the other side of the world?'

So caught up in the fun I had completely forgotten about my former desire to base our friendship on the mutual 'no prying' foundation, but I needn't have worried. Gabe obviously wasn't in the mood to share.

'How about another drink?' I suggested when he didn't answer and I realised that my nosiness was poised to undo all the effort I had put towards restoring his good humour.

'And some music,' he smiled, shoving the now-defunct sparklers into a bucket of water. 'Let's have a song.'

*

Ray Lamontagne was Gabe's last artist of choice for the evening and as 'Trouble' struck up, he swept me into his arms and spun me around until I was almost giddy.

The sound of Gabe belting out that he'd been saved was too much for the dogs, and the three of them slunk off into the kitchen freeing up more floorspace for us to twirl around in. However, given the amount of cider we'd drunk, I wasn't sure twirling was a good idea, but apparently there was no stopping us and, just for a moment, I let myself relax into Gabe's embrace.

The closer he held me, however, the less amusing the lyrics began to sound, and the less drunk I began to feel, but he didn't seem to notice. The comforting feel of his firm body pressed close to mine, coupled with the woody scent of his aftershave and his freshly washed hair, was beginning to do funny things to my insides.

In spite of my very best efforts to shut down my heart and its desire to love and be loved, it was suddenly determined to have its own way. I was shocked to realise that lust wasn't the only thing on the menu.

'Gabe,' I muttered, trying to push him away, before my feelings ran away with me. 'I really should be making a move.'

'You are making moves,' he said, pulling me back into him. 'Great moves.'

'Not that sort of move, you idiot,' I said, laughing again because he sounded so serious.

'You should laugh all the time,' he said, stopping mid-twirl and looking down at me. 'You have a great laugh.'

'Do I?' I swallowed.

Where were these unexpected emotions welling up from? They were unfounded and unwanted and I quickly put them down to my drink-induced state.

'You do.'

'Well, so do you.'

'You don't have to say that,' he sighed, 'because I know it's not that great. It's been out of practice for a while.'

'Has it?' I breathed. 'Why?'

'It's had its reasons,' he said non-committally, before twirling me again, faster this time, 'but you've woken it up again, Hayley. I really can't remember the last time I laughed so much. It's been a great evening.'

The alcohol had certainly played its part in breaking down some of Gabe's barriers, but he was right, we had more than made the most of missing out on the fireworks in town.

'It has been a great evening,' I agreed, because it had.

Truth be told, I didn't think I wanted it to end. I would have been quite happy for it to carry on upstairs and run long into the wee small hours. So much for telling Dorothy I was going to wait before looking out for some no-strings fun, but I knew I couldn't act on my instincts. Spending the night with Gabe could well end up ruining a relationship with not only a work colleague, but now a very near neighbour as well. I needed to sober up and draw a line under proceedings sharpish.

'But now I really have to go,' I said, placing a hand on Gabe's firm chest to try to push him away.

'How about a goodnight kiss first?' he asked, running a finger lightly down my cheek. 'Just to make the evening really perfect.'

It was on the tip of my tongue to suggest a small one, one that couldn't last more than three seconds, when my jeans pocket started to vibrate.

'It's my phone,' I said pulling away properly this time.

'Well, that's a relief,' Gabe grinned.

I looked at the screen. It was a text from Gavin. Talk about timing.

'Anything important?' Gabe asked.

'Nothing that can't wait,' I told him, stuffing the phone back in my pocket without reading the message. 'But I really must go. It's late. The others will be back and I didn't leave a note.'

'That'll be a no to the goodnight kiss, then,' Gabe sighed, reluctantly helping me into my coat.

'Oh, I wouldn't say that,' I said shakily, stretching up to peck him chastely on the cheek. 'How about that?'

'That'll be fine,' he grinned. 'For now.'

Chapter 13

As luck would have it, the others weren't back from town and I managed to sneak up the many stairs and into bed before I heard the cars pulling into the courtyard. In spite of my spinning vision, which was made far worse when I closed my eyes, I thankfully drifted off to sleep and woke early the next morning with the classic 'tongue too large for mouth' hangover and a hundred 'what the hell is going on' questions thumping through my head.

'Are you all right, love?' asked Dorothy as I stumbled through our sitting room, across the corridor and into the bathroom. 'You look a bit peaky.'

'I'm fine, Dorothy, thanks,' I told her, despite feeling anything but. The sound of my voice hammered loudly in my head. 'I'll be down as soon as I've had a shower.'

The hot water streaming down my body felt like a harsh pummelling, which was quite something as the hall wasn't famous for its water pressure, and I stood under it, trying to wash away the muddled emotions that had stuck with me right from the instant Gabe had held me in his arms.

For one mad moment I had thought I was falling in love, but I wasn't, was I? The way I felt when I was with Gabe was nothing like I'd felt when I was with Gavin, so it couldn't possibly be the real thing. Damn and blast the Somerville clan and their infamous Skylark cider. One of these days it really would be someone's undoing, and then they'd be sorry!

'Don't forget Angus has organised the Christmas planning meeting for this morning,' Dorothy called through to me as she bustled about, efficient as ever, getting ready to start her day.

'He hasn't wasted any time, has he?' I muttered, pulling open the bathroom door as I secured my towel.

'Nope,' Dorothy replied, rushing to hand me a small glass of water and two painkillers. 'You looked like you might need these.'

I guessed she was thinking that, perhaps, I really did have a headache yesterday after all. I decided not to correct her. I had no intention of telling anyone that I had spent fireworks night drinking my own body weight in fermented apple juice and playing with fire.

'Thanks,' I said, gratefully swallowing the pills down. The chalky tablets and the taste of the water almost sent them back up again, but I fought down the desire to hurl and handed back the glass. 'I bet Catherine was hoping he'd forget all about her suggestion to talk about his latest festive scheme after bonfire night was out of the way.'

'I happen to know that's exactly what she was hoping,' Dorothy tutted. 'But there was never really going to be any chance of that, was there?'

'Nope.'

'Everyone knows we're going to be busy enough as it is, what with hosting the tree competition *and* the party.'

'Everyone except Angus, that is,' I reminded her as she headed off to the kitchen.

We had been beyond busy with various events over the Christmas period once before, but that hadn't stopped Angus making the month of December even more of an occasion, and I was in no doubt that the already-packed calendar wouldn't stop him this time around, either, especially given that Jamie had sounded in favour of whatever it was his dad was planning. As far as I was concerned, the Winter Wonderland Angus had been dreaming up was already a done deal.

I walked into the kitchen at exactly the same moment Gabe arrived with the insulated bag I had used to ferry dinner over to his cottage. Dorothy whisked it out of his hand, the dishes clanking inside as she gave me a knowing look, but thankfully didn't comment.

So much for keeping my cider-and-sparkler-filled evening under wraps.

'Hey, Hayley,' said Gabe hoarsely. His gravelly tone sounded about as good as I looked, in spite of the valiant efforts of my make-up bag. 'Can I have a quick word?'

'Of course,' I said, steering him back towards the door and ignoring the fact that the eagle-eyed housekeeper was locked on to our every move. 'Let's talk outside, shall we?'

It was a bitter morning and the wind was keen so we ducked – literally in Gabe's case – into the log store, where I was certain we wouldn't be overheard. For some reason, I found it impossible to look him in the eye so I fiddled about with the kindling bags.

'About last night . . .' he began, rubbing his hands through his beard.

'I had a great time,' I cut in. 'At least, I think I did. To tell you the truth, it's all a bit hazy.'

'We did have a great time,' Gabe chuckled. 'If the number of empty cider bottles littering the cottage kitchen this morning are to be believed, then we had a fantastic time.'

We both laughed and I gingerly shook my head. It was hardly any wonder I felt so groggy. I was going to have to dig out my ear plugs before I even thought about switching on the vacuum cleaner, and god help Gabe if he had to fire up the chainsaw.

'So, what's up?'

Something obviously was and I wanted to deal with it and get back to the kitchen as quickly as possible. Not because I was uncomfortable alone in Gabe's company, but because it was so bloody cold.

'Well,' he awkwardly began, 'it's about how the evening ended.'

'Disappointingly' was the first word that sprang to mind,

but I swiftly kicked the term into touch and replaced it with 'sensibly'.

'Oh,' I said, 'do you mean the kiss?'

The colour began to rush to Gabe's face, as well as my own, and I knew the only way to keep a handle on what was happening was to brazen it out.

'I can't say it was one of my finest,' I hurried on, 'but given that we barely know each other—'

Gabe cleared his throat and the words died in my mouth.

'I'm sorry, Gabe,' I told him, knowing that I had gone too far and that it wasn't his fault that he'd prematurely kickstarted my heart. If indeed that was what was going on. 'I keep forgetting that you don't know me that well.' I rambled on. 'I'm well-known around here for using humour in awkward situations so you'll have to forgive me if I sound flippant or flirtatious. It's just the way I am.'

That was perfectly true and I expected my explanatory speech, which I had tried to inject with a sprinkling of unrehearsed humour, to turn the corners of Gabe's luscious, full lips a little in the right direction at least, but he looked no happier at all.

'And you don't know me that well either,' he sighed, burying his hands deep in his trouser pockets. 'Amongst other things, I'm feeling embarrassed, Hayley.'

'What?' I laughed, before realising that wasn't the reaction he was hoping for. 'Why?' I added, more seriously. 'What on earth have you got to feel embarrassed about?'

'Well, the fact that I even asked you for a kiss, for a start,' he blurted out. 'That's not the kind of bloke I am. I think the copious amounts of cider we consumed lowered my inhibitions a little too far.'

There had been a moment, as I recalled, when I was happy to wonder what might have happened had they been lowered even further.

'I might, thanks to the assistance of an unprecedented amount of alcohol,' he continued, 'have come across as being too up for a laugh, and willing to indulge in considerably more than a bit of banter.'

'And where was the harm in that?' I cut in, trying to lighten his load. 'Nothing happened, did it?' I added. 'We survived to flirt another day.'

Whatever was wrong with him? He sounded as if he was feeling guilty for having a few minutes of unguarded fun. Was having a bit of a giggle something he really should have been feeling so bad about? Had he known of the maelstrom I was currently trying to manage, he would have considered himself to have gotten off very lightly indeed.

'But I should never have asked you to kiss me,' he carried on. 'That was taking things a long way too far. I was too drunk to realise it at the time, but I took advantage of the situation and I'm sorry. I don't go in for casual relationships,' he went on, turning redder with every word. 'Not that I'm suggesting we would have had a casual relationship.'

'A one-night stand, you mean?'

'You're not helping, Hayley.'

'Sorry.'

'Especially since you've just come straight out of a serious relationship and I'm—'

'Gabe,' I said, louder than I meant to, especially given the precarious pain in my head, and before he had a chance to explain further. 'You need to lighten up, my friend.'

'Do I?' He didn't sound so sure.

'Yes,' I laughed. 'We had a great evening, we laughed, we enjoyed each other's company, we got more drunk than either of us have probably been in a very long time, and the night ended with a one-second peck on the cheek.'

I was trying to convince my heart as well as his head that that was all that had happened.

'I guess,' he said, scratching the back of his neck. 'I suppose I am getting it a bit out of proportion. It could have been worse, couldn't it?'

'Believe me,' I told him. 'It could have been a *lot* worse.'

Had I slept with him, I really could have fallen for him, and then where would we have ended up? I might have opted to let him and everyone else think that I was going back to being some good-time girl. I might have even believed it myself for a few days, but, truth be told, I wasn't sure that was the right course now. Listening to Gabe tell me he wasn't a fan of no-strings fun was music to my currently painful ears. A melody I was very happy to hear, but what if I ended up liking him more than he liked me?

I could think of many things in life that would be worse than a committed relationship with the angel currently floating in front of me, but given his dogged determination to backtrack and apologise for the little that had happened between us, I didn't think he felt the same about me.

'It's just that I really like you, Hayley,' he then completely floored me by saying, knocking my theory for six.

'And I really like you,' I swallowed.

The words were out before I could check them. They'd burst out of me like some sort of involuntary reflex.

'Morning, guys! Are you all set for the meeting?'

'Molly?'

'Hey,' she grinned, her face appearing around the door-frame. 'What are you doing in here?'

'Checking we're going to have enough wood to see us through the winter, of course,' I shot back.

I felt Gabe's eyes snap back to me, but I didn't take mine from Molly's flushed face.

'OK,' she said, accepting every word, as she rubbed her mitten-clad hands together, 'I'll see you inside. It's freezing out here.'

The second she disappeared Gabe had thankfully started to laugh rather than quiz me on what I meant by saying those four loaded words straight back to him.

'You didn't miss a beat,' he gasped. 'I would have still been struggling for a plausible response.'

'Well,' I said, nonchalantly tossing my hair, 'it's not my first time. I've had years of perfecting how not to crack under pressure when asked awkward questions.'

'You're really something,' he smiled.

'We had better go back in,' I said, 'before Miss Molly Motormouth sets tongues wagging.'

It wasn't until we had joined the others around the table and I found Gabe's gaze still lingering on mine that I began to wonder what exactly he had meant when he said *'I really like you.'* Was he sitting there now wondering what I had meant by saying the same thing back?

Was he saying to me, I really like you as a cider-swigging buddy or, if he didn't do casual, as a potential proper partner, or, actually, nothing like that at all? And why was my heart so keen for me to entertain the idea that I would be up for more than a one-off so soon after I had allegedly sworn off serious relationships for good? That wasn't what was expected of the old Hayley at all, was it?

'OK,' boomed Angus from his position at the head of the table, 'now that we're all out of the woodshed . . .'

'I hope you didn't see anything nasty in there, Hayley?' said Jamie with a suggestive wink, which made Anna snigger.

I glared at Molly who mouthed 'sorry' and stared back down into her coffee.

'Now that we're all here,' said Catherine calmly, 'I suppose we'd better hear what it is you think you have in store for us this Christmas, Angus.'

As the plans for the potential Winter Wonderland weekend began to unfold, I set Gabe's admission aside and stole a glance at my friends around the table. Jamie was looking every bit as excited as his eccentric, fun-loving father, and

Anna, I noticed, was wearing the same slightly exasperated expression as Catherine.

It turned out that giving the guys time to plan and prepare hadn't worked in Catherine's favour at all because, with Jamie on-board, almost no detail had been left to chance.

'So, what we're thinking is . . .' said Angus.

'As long as everyone else is in agreement of course,' added Jamie, with a hopeful smile.

'That we could host a Winter Wonderland here on the fifteenth and sixteenth of December.'

'That will give us just about enough time to get everything properly set up and in place.'

'And it won't clash with the switch-on or the tree auction and bake sale in town.'

'Or the party here.'

'But it will tie in with the decoration competition and give visitors more to enjoy when they come to admire and judge the trees.'

You had to hand it to them, they sounded like a well-oiled double act. It was obvious they'd spent a lot of time thinking this through as well as rehearsing their speech. It was all political-party smooth.

'And what *exactly* is it that you have in mind for the visitors to enjoy?' Catherine asked.

I couldn't help thinking there was a note of resignation in her tone and wondered if her husband and son had picked up on it too. If that was the case, there'd be no stopping them.

'Well,' said Angus, 'there would be the usual sleigh rides, of course. They've always been popular.'

'And I could offer refreshments,' said Dorothy, before Angus had a chance to say another word. 'I was going to do mince pies and mulled wine for the folk who come to view the trees anyway, but if there'll be more going on then I'm sure I could come up with something a little more exciting than that.'

She sounded well and truly caught up in it all already.

'Thank you, Dorothy,' said Catherine diplomatically. 'Let's not get too ahead of ourselves. What were you going to suggest, Jamie?'

'Well, we've been talking about making proper use of the woods,' said Jamie, 'creating some sort of trail for people to follow, with activities and things to look at as everyone goes around.'

I remembered Jamie had mentioned making use of Gabe's skills when Christmas cropped up in conversation a while back.

'What sort of activities?' the man himself now asked. He sounded as intrigued as Dorothy was excited.

Clearly, we'd lost another one to the cause. I was going to have to keep my wits about me, otherwise I would end up getting roped into doing something as well.

'Some sort of hands-on session for families to take part in together,' Jamie explained. 'Perhaps they could make something out of wood from kits that we could put together ahead of time. Something with a festive theme, maybe?'

'Like when we made the bird boxes in the summer, you mean?' asked Mick. 'That worked very well.'

'Yes, anything along those lines would be good,' Jamie nodded, 'only with a Christmas twist, of course.'

'I like the sound of that,' Gabe nodded. 'In fact, leave it with me, guys. I think I might have just the thing.'

'And I've been thinking about hiring in a couple of reindeer,' said Angus.

This suggestion was met with stunned silence. Surely, he wasn't being serious?

'Or a snow machine,' he added a little more meekly. 'Perhaps we could have a snow machine on standby, just in case we don't get the real thing.'

'I like the sound of reindeer,' said Molly dreamily.

You could always rely on her to go with the most bizarre option available.

'And to end the trail,' Jamie rushed on, keen to move away from the idea of Rudolph and his pals, 'we could set up some sort of grotto with Santa inside to hand out gifts.'

'You could put the reindeer in an enclosure next to it,' suggested Molly.

'So, let me get this straight,' said Catherine, looking up from the notepad she had been busily scribbling on. 'Angus, Jamie, Mick and Gabe, you four would be in charge of the woodland trail and all of its associated activities, Anna and I will be organising the party, and Dorothy, of course, will be in the kitchen.'

'Yes,' said Jamie and Angus together.

'And I'll help the vicar with the Christmas tree competition,' Molly generously offered.

It always surprised me how well our pagan friend got on with the local vicar, but I don't suppose it should have, really.

'So, if we do decide to go ahead—' Catherine continued.

'And I really think we should,' Angus enthusiastically cut in, 'and the sooner the better because we won't have long . . .'

Jamie put a hand on his father's arm and subtly shook his head to silence him. The younger Connelly knew that the next couple of minutes were make-or-break as far as the plan was concerned.

'That just leaves you, Hayley,' Catherine carried on as if she hadn't been interrupted at all.

Everyone turned to look at me.

'Oh, don't worry about me,' I smiled. 'I'm sure with all the extra comings and goings there'll be plenty of cleaning for me to keep on top of. I'll just be the girl Friday, floating between jobs and helping out where I can.'

I didn't really fancy committing to more than that. If Angus had his way, I'd no doubt be dressed up as one of Santa's elves, sporting stripy tights – perish the thought – and keeping control of the crowds as they queued to see the Big Man.

And there would be queues. You could guarantee it.

Everyone from miles around would want to come and see what the Connelly family had to offer this Christmas.

'You could help me if you like,' said Gabe. 'I'll need a guinea pig to help me work on the kits I have in mind.

They'll need to be the right balance of practical and simple. Something impressive that can be easily put together in the great outdoors, and suitable for all ages. You could help me with the test runs.'

I wasn't sure whether he thought he was being helpful or not, but I didn't think more time alone with him was a particularly good idea, and there was no way I was going to get roped into chopping logs and hammering nails in the freezing woods. The thought of playing chief elf was bad enough, but at least it would leave my manicure in one piece. I might have been developing a soft spot for the hall's resident angel, but I had my limits.

'Honestly,' I said, raising my eyebrows, 'thanks, but I'm fine. I'm not much of an outdoorsy type. You'd be far better off asking Molly to help you with all that.'

'Oh, yes, please,' said Molly.

'Fair enough,' Gabe shrugged. 'It was just a thought.'

Was that a note of disappointment in his tone or was my mind still hanging on to the implications behind the 'I really like you', comment? Given the curious look Anna was giving Gabe, she clearly thought something was amiss, too.

'And we'll need a map, of course,' Angus announced.

'A what?' asked Anna, thankfully distracted from Gabe's slumped shoulders.

'A map.'

'What for?'

'To go with the trail,' Jamie explained. 'We thought a map would add to the fun. We could have little markers dotted along the trail, highlighting certain woodland features and reminding visitors to look out for things as they go around.'

'And little ink pads and stamps to brand the map to prove that you've been the whole way around and seen everything,' added Angus.

'There'd be a small prize at the end for completed trail maps, which could be handed out at Santa's grotto,' Jamie cut in, scribbling furiously on his own notepad.

By a sleigh–bell–toting elf, no doubt. I crossed my arms and tried to look invisible.

'So, as well as having a festive trip out to the countryside, folk would learn something about the woods, the trees and the creatures and birds that live there,' said Gabe, sounding slightly more cheery. 'I like the sound of that. I really like the sound of that.'

'We thought we could design the map to tie in with some posters and flyers,' Angus enthused, 'along with an advert in the local paper, perhaps even a spot on the radio.'

He was getting carried away again. Catherine looked at him sternly and held up her hand to stop his excitement.

'But none of this is going to come cheap, Angus,' she reminded him. 'You'll have to cost it out very carefully. If it's overpriced no one will come, but if we charge too little it could end up costing us a fortune.'

'Don't worry, Mum,' said Jamie, 'I'm looking into all that.'

'And who is going to do the drawing?' she carried on. The financial implications of the ambitious project had clearly made her jittery, and rightly so. 'We can't have it looking like something the local nursery cobbled together, can we?'

I sat stock-still ignoring the look that had just passed between Molly and Anna.

'We have plenty of things on-site that we can utilise, including our wonderfully skilled team,' Jamie told his mother, 'and I've even approached a couple of local companies about supplying bits and pieces in return for a mention in the advertising.'

Catherine looked somewhat appeased by her son's sensible approach and understanding of the situation. Angus was more of a make-it-up-as-you-go-along type, but, thankfully, Jamie had the business acumen to back up his decisions.

'Not catering companies?' asked Dorothy sounding aghast. 'You aren't hiring in caterers, surely?'

'No,' Jamie smiled, 'not catering companies. Unless the Cherry Tree ladies would like to help out, or, perhaps, Amber and Jake from Skylark Farm.'

'Well yes,' Dorothy sniffed, 'that's fine, that's different.'

'I'm talking more along the lines of someone to lend us a shed or summerhouse, which we could decorate as Santa's grotto,' Jamie continued. 'A tarpaulin to hang and turn into a temporary workshop among the trees in the woods for Gabe, in case the weather goes feral. That sort of thing.'

'But I suppose we could use the summerhouse in the fern garden for Santa,' Catherine tentatively suggested. 'The little garden would make a lovely grotto, wouldn't it?'

Well, well, well. They'd done it. They'd sucked her in,

but actually, the fern garden would be perfect. With the aid of Angus's longed-for snow machine and some twinkling lights, the little walled space would make a wonderful finale to a walk through the woods, but I wasn't sure there would be room for reindeer. Perhaps Catherine's offer of her beloved little spot was cannier than I initially gave her credit for.

'But that doesn't solve the issue of finding an artist for the map, does it?' said Anna, staring straight at me.

'No,' said Jamie throwing down his pencil, 'no it doesn't, and that could end up being the really pricey bit. That could be the stumbling block because we want it to look really special. I'm going to speak to Lizzie Dixon. She might know someone who could do it.'

'Mates rates are what we need,' said Angus, tapping the side of his head.

He looked just like Winnie the Pooh when he was having a good long think about something.

'Hayley could do it,' piped up Molly.

Did she really just say that?

'Oh, yes,' said Anna, using her very best why-didn't-I-think-of-that tone. 'You could do it, couldn't you, Hayley?'

Traitors. The two of them, masquerading as friends, sitting right opposite me.

'Do you draw, Hayley?' Gabe asked.

It was an innocent enough question. There was absolutely no way on earth that he could have known that. No one at the hall, aside from the dynamic duo, knew of my passion for pencil and paper, or that I had been hoping to keep it that way.

'She has been known to do the odd doodle,' Anna answered on my behalf, smiling wickedly.

'Has she?' asked Catherine as everyone's eyes turned to me.

'Well, I never,' said Angus, sounding more Tigger than Pooh.

'I had no idea,' said Mick.

'None of us did,' added Dorothy.

'She has a whole folder of stuff upstairs,' said Molly, the words rushing out as she dropped me well and truly in it. 'She's amazing.'

'I don't suppose there's any chance we could have a look, is there?' asked Jamie, his eyes shining with the same excitement as his father's. 'You might just be able to create exactly what we need.'

Chapter 14

Angus enthusiastically elected himself as the person most appropriate to scrutinise my artistic skills and followed me up to my room to look through the folder I had hoped to keep hidden in the cubby hole under the window. Had I been worried that my unpredictable feelings for Gabe were poised to take centre stage, I needn't have, because they weren't going to get the chance to dominate my imagination for a good while yet.

'Well,' he chuckled as we went, 'this is all a turn up for the books.'

I didn't say anything.

'All these years we've known you, Hayley, and we've never once seen you with a pencil or a paintbrush in your hand. Although, now that I think of it, your grandmother was always telling us that you were keen on art when you were at school, and that she thought you had a real talent.'

'Was she always telling you that?' I gasped, spinning

around and almost knocking him back down the stairs. 'Did she really think that?'

Neither of my parents had ever shown even the slightest interest in my sketchbooks when I used to sit drawing while they were immersed in the soaps. Not that I went out of my way to show them what I had been up to, of course, but I was rather taken aback that my nan had been so aware of what I was doing.

She wasn't what you'd call an artistic type, and I never really thought my efforts would have been of any interest to her. I had foolishly lumped her in with the rest of the family when it came to certain things, but, given all the love and help she gave me when I needed her most, I shouldn't have. I shouldn't have assumed that she was the same any more than I should have presumed Mum would never find the courage to change her course.

'She did,' Angus nodded. 'She was very proud of you, you know.'

'Yes,' I whispered, swallowing down the lump in my throat. 'That, I did know.'

I didn't let myself think about her all that often, but her voice, telling me how brave she thought I was, was still as clear as a bell in my head.

'She was a wonderful woman,' Angus sighed, 'occasionally fierce,' he added with another chuckle, no doubt remembering all the times she had scolded him for messing up her hard work, 'but always fair.'

She had certainly been a formidable woman with strong,

traditional beliefs about relationships, yet she had made sure she stood firmly by me when my parents threw me out after my pregnancy became public knowledge. She told me right from the start that she wasn't going to let her one and only granddaughter feel isolated, even though, for the most part, I was.

She revealed how she was ashamed of my mother, not me. Mortified by how her own daughter had treated her only child. She was the one who arranged a roof over my head with Catherine and Angus; she was the one who made me believe that everything was going to be all right. And then she died and the baby died and, foolishly, I returned home.

Her death and my miscarriage had happened so close together that I could barely separate my last remaining memories of her from those of my time in the hospital. I hated that, but was thankful that taking on her role as house-keeper as soon as I ducked out of school had kept her close in other ways.

'And, of course,' Angus continued, 'we would have asked about your love of art ourselves, but what with everything else that happened when you first came here, I suppose it just all got forgotten.'

'Well, I'm pleased it did,' I interrupted. 'I wouldn't have wanted to talk about it, even if you had asked.'

Drawing and painting had quickly come to remind me of nothing other than the man who had deserted me and the baby I had lost. Those negative feelings were entirely my own fault, of course. I was the one who had told myself certain things and repeated them out loud so often that I had come to believe them. One day, I would have to face up to that, but for now I was focused on getting over Gavin and quashing my feelings for Gabe. That added heartbreak could wait.

'But, did you really intend to put it all away for ever?' Angus asked, interrupting my emotional thoughts for the second time that morning.

'Yes,' I sighed, pushing open my bedroom door and thinking of more than my sketchbooks. 'That was the general idea.'

I don't think I'd ever known Angus to be speechless before, but as he worked his way through the folder and I stood fiddling with my cuticles, trying to pretend it wasn't all happening, he was completely silent. He lingered longest over the most recent sketches; the ones I had started after Gavin had unwittingly roused the sleeping beast and I hadn't been able to stop myself from picking up a pencil.

'But Hayley,' Angus eventually said, 'I really don't know what to say.'

'Because you can't believe that someone like me could do something like that?' I asked, pointing at the books now spread across the bed.

I instantly regretted my harsh suggestion. He had every right to look hurt.

'Sorry,' I said, 'that didn't come out right.'

'No,' he said, 'I'm sorry because that is partly what I was thinking.'

At least he was honest.

'This is all such a shock,' he continued, looking from me to the books and back again. 'I'm seeing you in a whole new light.'

'Oh god,' I said, theatrically rolling my eyes and planting my hands on my hips, 'you're not going to start going around telling folk I have hidden depths or anything, are you?'

'But you do, my girl,' he beamed. 'You do.'

I could tell he was completely reassessing me; totally re-jigging what he thought he knew and trying to work out where this surprisingly artistic piece of the jigsaw would fit. I wasn't sure it would fit anywhere anymore. I had spent too long trying to squeeze it out.

'Have Anna and Molly always known about this?' he asked, his eyes returning to the bed.

'No,' I told him. 'They found my folder the day I was moving out of the Rose Room. I'd hidden it under the bed and they happened to stumble upon it.'

'Well, thank goodness they did,' Angus cried. 'I can't believe you've been hiding your light under a bushel for so long.'

'Bed, actually,' I quipped.

No matter how serious the situation, I just couldn't seem to stop myself. My make-a-joke-out-of-anything-uncomfortable default button was firmly on and burning brighter than ever.

'Well, whatever,' he went on, ignoring my silliness, 'you, my girl, have been keeping your talent a secret for far too long.'

I shrugged my shoulders and dropped my arms to my sides, unsure as to how I felt about what was happening. Just because everyone now knew about my talent, that didn't mean that I would be properly taking it up again. Sure, I had fiddled about a bit recently, but I had no intention of taking it further than that.

'These are new, aren't they?' Angus asked. 'These have been done quite recently.'

There was no denying it. The pencilled date in the corner of the pages was a giveaway for a start.

'Yes,' I admitted. 'During the last few months, I've been having a quick doodle, as Anna so succinctly put it.'

Angus nodded and carried on flicking through the pages. 'But why?'

'Why what?' I frowned.

'Why did you start again?'

I moved some of the papers to one side and sat on the edge of the bed.

'It was the scorching scaffolder's fault,' I huffed. 'He remembered that I used to carry this folder around at school, along with what was inside it, and that, in turn, got me thinking again.'

'And you felt compelled to draw something?'

I nodded. That had been about the size of it. Once the thought had been planted so firmly back in my head I had been powerless to resist it. I looked at the pictures I had drawn of the hall during the summer and realised that I didn't actually equate them with the painful memories that were tied up with the work I had produced at school at all, but that was probably because they were so different.

My style had changed. A lot.

Apparently, during the time I hadn't been physically exercising my creative muscle, it had still been getting a thorough mental workout, and my eye now focused on different details, quirky little things that stood out, which I had managed to capture. Some of it looked and felt completely alien to me because it was so different, but I liked it. Not having to stick to a curriculum had given me more freedom to develop and explore different subjects. I supposed, without being conscious of it, I had developed my own style.

'And you plan to carry on?'

'Oh, no,' I said, jumping back up and rubbing my hands down my jeans, trying to brush the suggestion away. 'Definitely not.'

Angus looked surprised.

'There's no point,' I went on. 'Maybe one day, in the future, perhaps,' I added, trying to shut him up. 'When I'm retired.'

'But no one retires here,' Angus laughed, 'you know that.'

'Well, whatever.' I shrugged. 'There's no point even thinking about it now, is there? There's always so much to do here that I don't have time for any of this. I should never have started again. It's too difficult. It's all wrapped up with what happened at school and—'

I could hear the words coming out of my mouth, trying to justify my reasons for stopping again, but there was a part of my brain, the same part that had fired up when I was telling Anna why I was packing up my pencils, that was even less willing to accept the old arguments, now. Especially as I had only seconds before acknowledged – mentally at least – that what I had drawn this summer wasn't wrapped up in the past at all. I really didn't associate my new drawings with Gavin, so I could hardly pretend that every time I drew something new my personal life was headed for a man-shaped disaster.

Or could I?

If I could convince Angus that I thought my art was the catalyst behind every bad thing that happened to me, and that, consequently, it always ended up making me feel utterly miserable, then perhaps he'd let me off the hook. Perhaps he'd let me pack it all away and look for someone else to design his precious Winter Wonderland map and posters.

'Hayley, I want you to draw the map for the Winter Wonderland and design the posters and adverts,' he interrupted, cutting across my excuses and not even giving me a chance to lock and load my faux theory.

'But I can't,' I told him, feeling suddenly hot.

'In this style,' he added, picking up one of the new drawings.

'No way. I can't do it. I don't have the time.'

'I'm your boss, I'll give you the time.'

My brain was scrabbling for reasons to turn him down.

'You can't afford me,' I blurted out.

'You aren't going to charge me.'

'But what if something bad happens?' I wheedled. 'It's

always worked out that way in the past. Look at what's just happened with Gavin ...'

'Don't be so ridiculous,' Angus tutted. 'He wasn't unfaithful because you'd been sketching! He did that because he has no morals and even less self-control.'

I bit my lip. He was right. It was ridiculous and Gavin was a guy without principles. My make-believe theory had crashed and burned before it was even launched.

'Well, in that case,' I snapped, losing my temper a little, 'how about, I just don't want to do it?'

'I don't believe you.'

He was right about that as well because, ever since the moment the map and posters had been mentioned down in the kitchen, I had been planning designs out in my head, right down to the last detail. I even had a festive theme in mind.

'Can I at least think about it?' I begged, biting down harder on my lip.

'I'd rather you just got on with it.'

'But it isn't as simple as that.'

'Hayley,' he sighed, 'it's as simple as you want it to be.'

That was Angus's mantra when it came to pretty much any challenge he faced in life. Even those put forward by his patient and long-suffering wife. Perhaps I should tear a leaf out of his book and just get on with it? But, of course, the big question was, had I reached a point where I felt I deserved to take up the one thing in my life that made me really happy again?

And not only that, I had to consider, that if I took this

challenge on I wouldn't just be secretly scribbling away for a few snatched minutes and then hiding the results. This project would be making its way out into the world, possibly travelling even further than the reaches of Wynbridge, and there was every chance that folk would come to know that I was the face behind the drawing board.

'And by the way,' Angus added without a thought for my emotional inner turmoil, 'I'm not sure I should be telling you this right now, but as he's already come up in conversation . . .'

My stomach lurched in fear of what he was going to come out with next.

'Who?'

'The so-called scorching scaffolder.'

'What about him?'

'He came and found me at the bonfire party last night.'

'What?' I choked. 'Why? What the hell did he want?'

'To pay back the money I loaned him.'

'No way!'

I couldn't believe it. Gavin was always skint. Where on earth would he have found the money to do that?

'Way,' said Angus, trying to grasp the youthful vernacular.

I narrowed my eyes, my brain in bits.

'Cash or cheque?' I asked.

If it was a cheque it was bound to bounce.

'Cash,' Angus smiled, 'every last penny, and he asked me to tell you that he was sorry for being such a . . . well, let's just say he said to tell you he was sorry.'

I didn't give two hoots about his apology, especially after

how he had behaved the last time we'd met, when Gabe had to step in, but it was a relief to know he'd paid Angus back in ready notes. Assuming they weren't counterfeit.

'Was he on his own?' I couldn't resist asking, my mind tracking back to the text that had interrupted my moment with Gabe, which I still hadn't read.

'I think so,' Angus shrugged. 'And he didn't stay long.'

Back in the kitchen, Dorothy was still doling out coffee and warm croissants and no one had budged from their seats.

'Is there literally no work to do around here today?' I tutted as I pulled my phone out of my jeans' pocket and plonked back down in my chair.

'Apparently not,' smiled Catherine.

'Well,' said Anna, cutting to the chase. 'Are you going to do it?'

She sounded exasperated and I intended to keep her in that emotional state for as long as possible. Molly, on the other hand, was stirring her coffee and gazing into space, so tormenting her was not an option. There was a lot to be said for living in a dream world.

'Yes,' said Angus, 'she is.'

'No,' I said, 'she isn't.'

'All right,' Angus countered. 'She's going to think about it.'

'Excellent,' beamed Anna, rubbing her hands together and looking thoroughly impressed with herself.

'Which literally means just that,' I told her firmly. 'I'm just going to mull it all over.'

'Well, can you do it by the end of the day?' asked Jamie, looking up from his notepad. 'We need to crack on.'

He carried on staring at me.

'What?' I frowned.

'I just can't believe that you're an artist, Hayley.'

'And yet,' I butted in, 'I have no trouble at all believing that you're a—'

'My goodness,' laughed Dorothy, fanning herself with a tea towel, 'it's just like old times.'

I picked up my phone and opened Gavin's message. My eyes scanned over the lines of text. I wasn't sure what I had been expecting, but his words were as much of a surprise as his loan repayment. There was no boasting about the fact that he had come up with the money to put things right, and no lame attempt to justify his horrid behaviour, either in the gents' loos or when we'd argued outside the pub.

'What's got you so engrossed?' Anna asked when she spotted me scrolling back and shaking my head.

'A text.'

'Stating the obvious,' she tutted, 'who's it from?'

'None of your business,' I said, slipping the phone back into my pocket.

'It's not from Gavin, is it?' suggested Molly.

She really did have an uncanny knack of putting her two pennies worth in when it was least needed.

'Does she look upset?' Anna cut in. 'Is she on the verge of tears?'

'Do you seriously think I'd risk ruining my eyeliner on him?' I blinked back. 'He's hardly worth that, is he?'

'I knew you looked different,' said Dorothy, staring at my face. 'You've totally gone back to your old look.'

'And is that all right with you?' I snapped.

I was getting a bit fed up being the subject of so much attention.

'I think it makes you look a bit hard,' said Molly. 'More like how you used to be.'

'That's because I am how I used to be,' I told her, although now I wasn't so sure that it was possible to completely shrug off something you'd tried on.

From what I could make out, there seemed to be a tiny fragment, an indelible impression, that couldn't be erased, even if you didn't want it. Apparently, I was destined to carry a little of my softer self around, whether I liked it or not.

'I should never have changed or even tried to be any different.'

Had I not blurred my edges I was sure I wouldn't have succumbed to squishy feelings about my new neighbour, and I would certainly have been more able to convince the Connellys that the artist formerly known as Hayley was no longer in residence.

'So, is it from him then?' asked Anna, who was determined to not give up just yet.

'Is what from who?'

'The text,' she reiterated. 'Is it from Gavin? Because if you really are determined not to let him get to you, then we'll never be able to tell if he's been back in touch, will we?'

'But why would that matter?'

'Because we love you,' said Molly. 'And we want to protect you.'

'We don't want to see you get hurt again,' Anna said softly.

'And we need to know if he's going to turn up so Gabe can set Bran on him,' added Molly.

I'd forgotten Gabe was still here, sitting quietly at the end of the table and taking it all in.

'You'd be better off setting Suki on him,' he smiled, affectionately looking down at his gently snoring giant of a dog. 'If it's fire and fury you're aiming for, I'd go for the tiniest dog with the biggest attitude.'

We all laughed at that and I supposed they did have my best interests at heart.

'Well,' I said graciously, 'thank you all. I appreciate your concern and can confirm that, yes, the text is from Gavin, but, no, we don't need to worry about setting any of the dogs on him. He won't be darkening our door again, and even if he did, he wouldn't have any impact on me. He won't be hurting me again because I won't let him – or anyone else for that matter.'

'But don't forget to leave at least a little room in your heart for love, Hayley,' said Molly dreamily.

'Er, no,' I told her. 'I certainly won't be letting my guard down again, thank you very much.'

My thoughts skipped back to the traitorous way dancing

with Gabe had made my heart thump and how I had already entertained the idea that if Mr I'm-not-interested-in-no-strings had an open spot in the serious relationship field then I might have been poised to put myself forward, but god help me if I admitted as much to this lot. Had they even just an inkling that it had crossed my mind, then they would have had Gabe and me tethered for life.

'Are you really planning to stay unattached for ever?' gasped Molly.

'Yes,' I told her lightly, 'like I said before: fun? Yes. Commitment? No. Laughs? Yes. Love? No. Single? Yes. Attached? No.'

Neither Molly nor Dorothy looked particularly impressed by my reinstated mantra, which was fine by me. That was the line I was outwardly sticking with. It was the one I wanted them to believe I was championing, but it was a shame Gabe was there to hear me trotting it out.

'But look at me,' said Anna, reaching for Jamie's hand.

'What about you?'

'Well, not all that long ago I was single, married to my work and carrying around a whole heap of problems, but now, having let love in—'

I had to stop her and her romantic heart right there.

'But you're forgetting,' I said, pushing back my chair and standing up, 'that whole heap of problems you were carrying around had been inflicted on you by circumstances and other people, whereas my bad memories and dubious reputation are all entirely of my own making.'

My knees felt a little wobbly as I realised the carefree me I was so keen to present to the world had turned all solemn again and I was talking about a whole lot more than Gavin dropping his pants in The Mermaid, even if no one else around the table was aware of it.

'And your point is?'

'My point is, the space in my heart that you and Miss Molly over there would like to see filled up with love, unicorns and fluffy kittens is already taken by something I can't even bring myself to think about right now, and there'll never be room to squeeze a significant other in next to it.'

'But you let Gavin in,' Gabe reminded me.

'Exactly,' I said. 'And look how that turned out.'

Chapter 15

Once everyone had eventually tracked back to and then exhausted the will-she-won't-she scenario surrounding the design project for the Winter Wonderland and had gone off to do some work, I hung back to have a word with Catherine.

'I have a favour to ask,' I said to her, trying to convince myself that what I was about to ask wasn't sneaky at all.

'Ask away,' she smiled.

Considering the woman had just given me a permanent home to go with the job I loved and had then added on the possibility that, if I wanted to, I could properly pick up my old passion and do something worthwhile with it, my favour quota should have been all used up, but that was a classic example of Connelly generosity for you.

'Well,' I said, shuffling from one foot to the other, 'I've been thinking that it probably wouldn't be a bad idea for me to take a trip into town this week.'

Truth be told, I hadn't even entertained the idea of

going anywhere near the place until Gavin's text had landed but, I reasoned with myself, the old Hayley wouldn't have shied away from a few wagging tongues, and there was now one unexpected loose end that needed firmly tying up.

'I think that's an excellent idea,' Catherine agreed. 'I know you went back the day you moved your things here, and that your last encounter with Gavin wasn't particularly pleasant, but the longer you leave going out in public, the more difficult it's bound to be for you.'

'Exactly,' I played along, 'and I don't want my absence from Wynbridge to become the focus of even more unwanted attention than it no doubt already is.'

I knew it wouldn't have taken long for tongues to start wagging beyond The Mermaid and I tried to convince both Catherine and myself that stopping them was my sole motivation for going back.

'Quite,' nodded Catherine, reaching for her purse. 'And it will be the perfect opportunity for you to collect some new art supplies.'

'Oh, no,' I said quickly. 'I don't need anything like that.'

'I think you should treat yourself,' she said firmly, thrusting a roll of notes into my hand. Clearly, *she* was going to be the one doing the treating. 'If you decide to take on this project for Angus, and, believe me, it will be a real weight off my mind if you do, then it will be nice to make a fresh start with lovely new things, won't it?'

Now I didn't think I had a choice in the matter. I would

have to take the job on and, knowing the real reason behind my trip into town, I felt like even more of a snake in the grass. I was just about to come clean, but the chance was denied me.

'Ah, Gabe,' said Catherine as the man himself popped in to collect the scarf he had left hanging on the back of his chair. 'Are you still planning to head into Wynbridge this morning?'

'Yes,' he said, looking at the pair of us. 'In about half an hour. Can I pick anything up for either of you?'

'No,' I said, shaking my head, 'no, thank you.'

'But you could give Hayley a lift,' Catherine smiled. 'She's going to buy some new art supplies and hopefully quieten the gossips once and for all. The sooner she's seen getting on with things the better, don't you agree?'

'I couldn't agree more,' Gabe replied.

'So,' said Gabe, when we climbed into his truck, with Bran filling the back seat, 'whose company did I have the pleasure of last night, then?'

'What do you mean?' I frowned, looking over at him as I finished banging out a text that I knew wouldn't have even a remote chance of leaving my outbox until we hit a decent signal hotspot, which would probably be halfway to town. 'We were together last night, weren't we?'

'Well, yes,' he said, 'but was I with the *old* Hayley who you prefer and who everyone recognised around the break-fast table this morning, or the *new* Hayley, who I can't help but think is a bit of a softie and not someone you like very much at all?'

'Which do you think?' I asked, batting my lashes in his direction.

'Given the talk I've overheard this morning,' he announced, 'I would have to say the old fun-loving, no-strings gal.'

'Bingo!' I beamed, wondering if everyone else had been so convinced. 'Give the man a cigar.'

It was on the tip of my tongue to explain that, if I were being totally honest, I didn't think I could have shrugged the newer version of myself completely off even if I wanted to, but I wasn't sure where an admission like that might lead.

I glanced across, expecting to see at least some trace of amusement written on Gabe's face, but he was wearing that semi-serious expression he was becoming known for, in my mind at least.

'What?' I gasped. 'Don't tell me you don't like her. She's a hoot!'

'I don't know,' he shrugged, still not joining in. 'I'm not even sure that *you* really like her, Hayley.'

I could feel my face start to flush and I looked out of the window. This was all I needed. A guy who could equal Molly's prowess at reading minds and seeing into souls.

'You're wrong,' I said lightly. 'She's the best. Every time I'm heading for trouble she steps in, pops up, and reminds me that life is for living, that there's fun to be had and that I need to lighten up.'

That much was true. She was great at helping me persuade Gabe that I had nothing more going for me than my flippant attitude towards men. Perhaps it was time to lay off the sass a little though, especially if I was going to pluck up the courage to ask him what he had meant when he said he liked me.

'Oh, well, in that case,' he shot back, 'she really was the one sitting in the Wynthorpe kitchen this morning.'

'You don't sound very impressed,' I snapped, annoyed that I couldn't easily pull the conversation back to where I wanted it to be going. 'I thought you said you liked me.'

Gabe shrugged and I regretted just blurting it out like that, but, true to form, now I'd started I couldn't seem to stop myself.

'But don't tell me,' I said, feeling further frustrated by his refusal to bite back, 'you don't really like the fun-loving version of me, is that it? Perhaps, as you're not a casual relationship kind of guy, you don't approve of her attitude and antics.'

Gabe shrugged.

'What?' I snapped again.

He was really beginning to annoy me now.

'She's all right, I suppose,' he relented, 'in small doses.'

'Praise indeed,' I said, giving his comment the full eye roll I felt it deserved. 'Anyway, you seemed pretty keen on her last night.'

It was a cheap shot, even by my standards, and one my chauffeur didn't dignify with a response.

'I just think it would be nice to see an amalgamation of both Hayleys,' he said when he had driven a little further.

That was an ironic statement given that only moments ago I had admitted to myself that I didn't think it was possible to completely banish the slightly easier-going version of me.

'Was she the person you were thinking about earlier when you said you liked me?' I asked, my tone softer. 'Because if the right guy happened to come along . . .'

'Don't let Anna hear you say that.'

'I have no intention of letting Anna hear anything, but if the right guy did happen to come along—'

'Then you'd chew them up and spit them out,' he laughed. 'Fun and laughs,' he mimicked, 'not love and commitment.'

'I was going to say,' I said, swallowing away the lump in my throat that had replaced my annoyance, 'that I might give a serious relationship another go.'

'Oh.'

I couldn't believe I'd come out and said that. I had left myself wide open and vulnerable. Traits the old Hayley would have been appalled to even carry in her arsenal, let alone drag them out and put them on display.

'So,' I said, my voice little more than a whisper. 'Do you think it's very likely that I'm going to find the right guy coming along anytime soon?'

Gabe shot me a look, his eyes were filled with a pain it shocked me to see.

'I know I said I wasn't a one-night kind of guy,' he told me.

He sounded flustered suddenly, almost panicked.

'But I'm not on the lookout for anything serious either, Hayley.'

'So why did you say that you liked me then?' I demanded, feeling nettled that I had exposed my emotions only to have him trample all over them and make me feel a fool.

'I'm sorry,' he sighed. 'I didn't mean to imply . . .'

'But what if a relationship could make you happy, enhance your life and generally make everything you have going on so much better?'

My words were straight from Anna's 'why relationships are good' guide, but I didn't care. If ever there was a time for straightforward questioning then this was it. What Gabe said next could well determine my way forward.

'Well, in that case,' he shocked me by saying, 'I'm definitely not looking for one.'

I stared at him for a second.

'You mean, if you knew there was a possibility to grab something that would make you happy then you'd definitely avoid it?'

'Yeah,' he said. 'I'd definitely avoid it.'

That sounded like some extremely sick self-denial, even by my skewwhiff standards.

'That,' I told him as I strengthened my resolve to keep my emotions as far away from him as possible, and as my text unexpectedly shifted to the sent folder, 'was not what I was expecting you to say at all, and thanks for the mixed messages by the way. They've really helped with the hangover.'

'I'm sorry—'

'It's fine.' I smiled brightly as I wondered just how much more of a pummelling my poor heart could take. 'More than fine, actually.'

'The library,' hissed Gavin when he found me sitting at one of the tables tucked behind the shelves of large print editions. 'Why on earth would you want to meet here?'

As far as I was concerned, my suggestion was a no-brainer, but that was the thing with Gavin – he apparently had no brain. Or if he did, it certainly didn't live in his skull.

'You're lucky I agreed to meet you at all,' I reminded him as he looked around in confusion. 'Just sit down. You're making the place look untidy.'

'But why here?' he asked again.

I almost wanted to laugh. He looked absolutely terrified. Clearly it was a long time since Gavin had been acquainted with the pages of a book, and, if his expression was anything to go by, it hadn't been a happy last encounter.

'Firstly,' I said, making sure my voice was quiet enough to match the setting, 'I didn't want to be seen out with you, and don't look like that, you can hardly blame me.'

Gavin shrugged, but banished the pout he had been cultivating.

'And secondly,' I went on, 'the last time we met you were a complete arsehole to me and in here you won't be able to shout. I wasn't going to risk another public confrontation with you yelling the odds and accusing me of being no better than you.'

'I'm sorry about that,' he said, his shoulders slumping as he sat back in his chair.

'And thirdly,' I said, ignoring his apology. 'This has nothing to do with the setting, but I want to know where you got the money to pay Angus back?'

'He told you about that?' He smiled, sounding pleased.

'Of course he did.' I tutted. 'Unlike you, he knows how much I've been worrying about it. I've been trying to work out how I could pay him back because I never expected you to step up.'

'Thanks.'

'Look,' I said, 'the text you sent said that you wanted to meet, and that if I didn't come to you then you'd come to the hall, so here I am. What is it that you want, Gavin? What is it that's so important that you threatened to come down to the hall to say it? As far as I'm concerned, we are done, so why are you dragging things out?'

He sat forward, placed his hands on the table and spread his fingers. I ignored the flashback of just how dextrous he could be with his digits and looked him in his beautiful, blue eyes. He would never stop being stunning to look at, even if he was a total love rat.

'Word around town,' he swallowed, 'is that you didn't go out to get your own back on me with that new guy at the hall after all.'

I could see it was paining him to acknowledge that and I wondered why he was bothering to let me know. I was also wondering who it was who had gone out of their way to set the record straight. Perhaps I had more allies than Jim and Evelyn from The Mermaid.

'If you'd given me the chance,' I told Gavin sharply. 'If you'd have listened, I could have told you that myself.'

'I know,' he nodded, sounding suitably chastened. 'I really had got you all wrong, hadn't I? I just assumed that you wanted to give me a taste of my own medicine because, deep down, you were just the same as me. Just the same as all the other girls I've been with.'

I was furious that he had happily slotted me into a pigeon-hole, and a slutty one at that. For a moment, I regretted meeting him somewhere where I couldn't raise my voice because I would have enjoyed giving him a very vocal dressing down. Not that he was worth raising my blood pressure for.

'You couldn't have been more wrong,' I said, hoping my irritated tone made up for the lack of volume. 'I'm not like that. I thought after all the months of being with me, you would have worked that out for yourself. After all, I now know you gave me more than one opportunity to get my own back, should I have wanted to.'

'I know,' he said, sliding his hand across the table until it reached mine, but this time gently as opposed to the lunging grab he favoured last time we met. 'And I really am sorry. When we first got together, I spent far too long listening to what my mates had to say about you and I based the beginnings of our relationship purely on that.'

'Oh?'

I wasn't sure I could stomach hearing whatever it was they'd said about me behind my back.

'And I believed that you were just like me; someone out looking for some fun.'

'I was,' I told him, pulling my hand away, 'I was happy to have some fun, more than happy, but I was also in love and, unlike you, I've only ever had fun with one person at a time.'

He looked at me and raised his eyebrows.

'And no,' I said sternly, 'this is not the moment to suggest that a threesome would have cured our relationship woes.'

He began to chuckle and I couldn't help but smile.

'And besides,' I reminded him, 'you were the one who took us from fun to serious. You were the one who asked me to marry you and made me fall deeper in love. The night you proposed you said I'd calmed you down and made you grow up, but I hadn't at all, had I?'

At the time, I had been full of hope that I had because I thought Gavin was the perfect partner for me. Two dodgy reputations apiece, similar childhoods and family backgrounds had made us a pretty decent match. We'd both said as much. We didn't have a whirlwind romance like Jamie and Anna, but then, as my father had revelled in reminding me, what did someone like me expect? My relationship with Gavin was as good as I was going to get.

'No,' said Gavin, a little too loudly and making me jump. 'And I hate the fact that I ever said that now, but I was so desperate to believe it. I really wanted to be the bloke who was good enough for you, Hayley, because you're a great girl.

I see now that you're far too good for someone like me, but that night on the beach when I proposed, I wanted to be the bloke who was perfect for you. I wanted to be the fiancé you deserved to have.'

I shook my head, annoyed to find my eyes were filling with tears.

'Well,' I said, swallowing hard and blinking them away. 'You weren't thinking that the night of our engagement party, and anyway, it doesn't matter now, does it?'

'It does to me,' he said. 'And I want you to know that I'm truly sorry. I don't regret a second of the months we spent together, but I do regret the way I treated you. I've never given two hoots about a girl's feelings before.'

'That's nice.' I swallowed again.

'No, it isn't,' he frowned. 'Of course, it isn't, but it is true. And, to be honest, the type of girls I usually go for don't care about my feelings either, but what happened between us has been eating me up. Even though we aren't going to end up together, Hayley, I can't deny that you got through.'

'What do you mean?'

'You found your way into my heart.'

'Wow,' I said, giving myself a sarcastic mini cheer. 'Go me! I had just assumed you didn't actually have one.'

'And I hope,' he carried on, ignoring my derision, 'that at some point you find a man who deserves you and treats you right.'

'Ha, I wouldn't hold your breath,' I cut in, thinking what

a fool I'd just made of myself in front of Gabe. 'I'm not in the market. In fact, I might never venture back in again.'

'You will,' he smiled.

He sounded annoyingly sure about that.

'And promise me that you'll carry on with your art, because you have an amazing talent. You shouldn't waste it.'

'Well,' I said, pushing back my chair. 'I'll keep you posted, but again, don't hold your breath.'

I still hadn't completely made up my mind about Angus's offer so there was no point suggesting that I was going to carry on. My legs were a little shaky as I stood up. Before I even arrived in town I felt like I'd been through an emotional wash cycle, and now Gavin had not only offered me a heart-felt apology, but he'd been unexpectedly honest to boot. It was all a far cry from what I'd been expecting when I woke up this morning with a pounding head.

'You didn't tell me how you'd raised the money to pay Angus back,' I reminded him as we walked back through the library together.

'Doesn't matter,' he shrugged.

'I'd like to know.'

He stopped walking and began fiddling with the van keys he had pulled out of his jeans pocket.

'I sold my gym equipment.'

'What?'

'Shush!' came an outraged voice from behind the enquiries desk. 'Quiet.'

'You're making more noise than she is!' Gavin shot back.

I grabbed him by the sleeve and pulled him out of the door.

'Did you really sell your stuff?'

'I did.'

'But you loved it.'

There wasn't a single day where he didn't spend at least an hour sweating and heaving on the weights bench in front of the mirrors in the garage, which he had converted at his parents' place.

'Yeah, well,' he said. 'I'd borrowed that money and I had to pay it back. If I hadn't then the whole situation would have been even worse, wouldn't it?'

I really didn't think I could cope with any more shocks today.

'Anyway,' he said, turning up his collar from the cold. 'I have to go.'

'OK.'

I let him kiss me on the cheek and I drank in his Paco Rabanne aftershave.

'I really am sorry about everything,' he said. 'I never meant to make such a hash of it all.'

'I know,' I told him as I began to walk away. I was sure he was telling the truth, even though I was shocked to have heard it. 'And thanks for the apology. I really do appreciate it.'

At least now I knew I was safe to come to town without worrying about being the centre of another messy showdown to entertain the locals with.

'And keep your eyes peeled for a decent fella, Hayley Hurren!' he called after me as I spotted Gabe's truck parked on the corner of the market square. 'There's bound to be one around here somewhere.'

'Like I already said,' I called back over my shoulder, 'don't hold your breath.'

Chapter 16

Once Gavin was out of sight, I pulled out my phone. It had almost reached the time Gabe and I had agreed to meet back at the truck, and my meeting with Gavin had seriously eaten into my shopping time, but obviously, I couldn't tell my travelling companion that if I found myself in need of an extension.

In that moment there was nothing I craved more than a marshmallow-topped hot chocolate from the Cherry Tree Café. I was certain the sugar would restore my equilibrium and the thick, creamy elixir would add a soothing layer to my churning stomach, but it was no good. For a start, I still wasn't feeling anywhere near brave enough to meet the eyes of the curious locals, and secondly, my time was almost up. I rushed along the pavement towards Hardy's, the one and only shop in Wynbridge that stocked decent art supplies.

As with most of the stores in town, there was a bell to announce a customer's arrival, and I took a deep breath as I stepped over the threshold into the shop and set it tinkling. The comforting smell of parchment, paint and pencils which hit me as I closed the door sent a surge of memories flooding back.

This had been my refuge at the weekends when I was a teenager, my very first place of work, and I crept past the counter hoping that old Mr Hardy wasn't working. I didn't think I could cope with the kindly old gent's, 'long time, no see' speech.

In the past, when the shop was quiet, he and I had spent entire afternoons trying out the new drawing pens the reps would drop off in the hope that the old man would place an order, as well as comparing the quality of paper in the different brands of sketchbooks he stocked. As first jobs went, I didn't think I could have found a better one, not even one that paid a king's ransom. Every Saturday I was out of the house and working with art supplies – it was the ultimate double-bubble.

'Good morning. Can I help you?'

Thankfully, it was a young woman who popped her head around the end of an aisle, rather than the waistcoat-wearing old gent.

'I'm just browsing,' I told her. 'Thanks.'

'Give me a shout if you need anything.'

'Will do.'

I took my time picking out the few things that I thought would best equip me if I decided to take on Angus and Jamie's Winter Wonderland project. Given what Catherine had said earlier, I really didn't feel as if I had a choice in the matter, but I was determined I would do all I could to keep my name away from the artwork. Anonymity was going to be the key to seeing the plan through.

'Did you find everything you were looking for today?' asked the cheery assistant when I eventually put my few purchases on the old glass-topped counter.

The most exquisite fountain pens and blotters were displayed beneath it, along with the most expensive calligraphy equipment.

'Yes,' I replied wistfully, as I remembered how Mr Hardy would painstakingly polish the glass and regularly update the display, 'thanks.'

The next words to come out of my mouth were something of a surprise, but I simply couldn't resist asking.

'Does old Mr Hardy still come to work here?'

'No,' smiled the woman, 'he's retired now, but he does pop in every now and again to make sure the place isn't falling apart. I'm his granddaughter, Francesca. I've recently taken the business on.'

I was pleased the little empire looked set to continue to thrive in the hands of the very family who had established it. It would be a real tragedy to lose another independent store from the town. The last thing Wynbridge needed was a high street full of phone shops and betting stores, with the odd charity concession thrown in for good measure, like those in some towns I'd had the misfortune of visiting. Us residents, in this part of the Fens at least, prided ourselves on shopping local and supporting family businesses, whether that be out on the farms, in the busy market square, or in the shops that surrounded it.

'Do you know my Grandad?' asked Miss Hardy as she fired up the till.

'Yes,' I smiled, 'yes I do. Well, I did,' I added, my smile faltering because it had been a while. A long while. 'I had my very first job here. I was the Saturday girl for a year or so. Your Grandad and I spent many a wet Saturday afternoon in here looking through new stock and trying to work out what the next Crayola fad would be.'

'Are you an artist?'

'No,' I laughed. 'More of a doodler really, but do please say hello to your Grandad for me. Ask him if he remembers Hayley Hurren.'

'I'm sure he will,' she smiled.

She rang up my total and packed everything carefully into a large brown paper bag, insisting that I took the leaflet and card explaining about the loyalty scheme she was trying to get going.

'I hope you'll be a regular visitor,' she beamed, rushing to open the door to let me out and another customer in. 'It's been lovely to meet you, Hayley.'

'And you,' I smiled back. 'Perhaps I'll see you again soon.'

You certainly couldn't fault her customer service, a skill no doubt passed on from her courteous relative. I hadn't been sure how I was going to feel stepping back into the store, but picking out new supplies and visualising the magic I could potentially create with them had set my heart racing and enthusiasm bubbling to the surface. I hadn't even been this excited when I started sketching over the summer. Apparently, the creative candle still burnt bright in my chest, despite the fact that I had been keeping the wick purposely trimmed for a very long time.

'You're looking pleased with yourself.'

So caught up in the moment, I hadn't noticed Gabe striding towards me with Bran at his heel and his arms weighed down by purchases of his own.

'Are you done?' he asked. 'Have you finished or do you need a while longer?'

'I think I'm sorted,' I said, gripping the bag a little tighter and wondering how long I was going to feel awkward around him.

I should never have pushed him to talk on the journey into town.

'We can head back to Wynthorpe now if you like,' I suggested.

'There's just one more thing I need,' he said, nodding across the square. 'And I'm hoping you'll join me. I'm in need of a mid-morning sugar hit and that looks like just the place to find one.'

'But we could get that back at the hall,' I reminded him, rushing to keep up with his lengthy strides and wishing he would just take me back to my bolthole. 'Dorothy's bound to have baked, and besides, it's nearer lunchtime now than brunch.'

'We won't stop for long,' he promised.

He didn't sound flustered by the thought of being alone in my presence at all. I rather envied him for that.

Given that we were now well into the month of November, Gabe, Bran and I had our pick of the tables, which were still set up outside the Cherry Tree Café.

'Had I known about this place,' said Gabe to Bran, as we installed ourselves in a spot sheltered from the worst of the Wynbridge breeze under a pretty little gazebo, 'I would have left you at home in front of the log burner.'

Bran huffed in apology and curled himself up as best he could, next to our chairs.

'You can go inside to eat if you like,' I told Gabe. 'I don't mind sitting out here with Bran.'

I had seen, as we came through the gate, that the little café was as packed as ever, and I still wasn't sure I much fancied facing the whispers and nudges that my appearance would inevitably set off, but I needn't have worried because Gabe didn't get the chance to force me through the door.

'I thought it was you,' said Lizzie, rushing out to take our order and pulling me up and into a hug. 'I've been hoping to see you. Jemma and I can't believe what happened. We're both really sorry. Are you OK?'

I hugged her harder, appreciative of the fact that she hadn't skirted around the issue or wasted time working her way up to it. If only everyone was as straightforward as Lizzie Dixon, life would be a breeze.

'Thank you,' I said, sitting back down when she finally let me go. 'Yes, I'm fine. Better to have found out now than when I'm walking up the aisle. Knowing my luck, I'd have caught him with his pants down in the vestry.'

I caught sight of Gabe frowning as I retold the old gag. I knew he was weighing up my words and wondering whether I was making a joke because it was what the 'old Hayley' who acted on autopilot did, or whether I really meant it.

'Anyway,' I said, deciding I should drop the comedic comments, 'I'm OK and no harm done.'

'Unless of course you count the damage caused to the cake when Jim shoved Gavin's face in it,' Lizzie laughed.

Gabe cleared his throat and she spun round.

'Oh, hello,' she beamed, her eyes speedily flicking to the hound under the table. 'We haven't met, but you're Gabriel, aren't you? The guy with the gigantic dog who's moved in up at the hall.'

'That's right,' he answered, looking a little nonplussed. 'But most people call me Gabe.'

'Well, Gabe,' she carried on. 'I'm Lizzie Dixon. I help run the Cherry Tree with my best friend, Jemma, who owns it.'

'Pleased to meet you,' he told her while looking over at me in puzzlement.

I tried not to laugh as I felt my awkwardness around him melt away a little. I would have to explain to Gabe that he wouldn't need to introduce himself to anyone in this town because they already knew who he was, and that he would have to behave himself if he didn't want to fall foul of the gossips.

'Right, then,' said Lizzie, pulling out her order pad from her apron pocket, 'do you guys need to see a menu or do you know what you want?'

'Hot chocolate,' Gabe and I said together.

He grinned and unzipped his coat.

'With the works, please, Lizzie,' I added.

'Anything to eat?'

'Better not,' I said wrinkling my nose. 'Woe betide us if we get back and can't manage Dorothy's lunch.'

'I think I'll have something,' said Gabe. 'Could you please just bring me something sweet, Lizzie, and two forks?'

I wasn't going to let him rope me into eating more than my fill. Dorothy could hold a grudge for days.

'You better come in and pick for yourself,' Lizzie said temptingly to Gabe. 'Jemma's just loaded up the sweet trolley.'

I patted Bran's head knowing I wouldn't see my companion for a few minutes now. Lizzie may have lured him inside on the pretence of choosing a cake, but I knew she wanted to show him off. I didn't blame her. It was quite a coup getting first dibs on showing off the newest hottie in town. Not that he was a hottie. Well, he was, but not one I was interested in. Not seriously anyway, especially now he told me he wasn't looking for a relationship, be it casual or serious.

Thankfully, he made his way back out to our table before my inner monologue tied me up in too many knots.

'Had I known what you were ordering when you asked

for hot chocolate with the works,' he said, carefully lowering the two fully loaded mugs on to the table, 'I would have held back on the cake.'

'Oh, I'm sure a strapping lad like yourself will be able to manage it,' said Angela, the other café assistant, who had followed him out with a tray. 'You'll make short work of this little lot, I'm sure.'

Gabe's 'little lot' was far from a light snack, and I laughed as the sweet treats just kept coming.

'Fancied sampling everything on the menu, did you?' I teased.

'Apparently,' he said, when the tray was finally empty and Bran began to stir, no doubt roused by the smell of the sugary delights on offer, 'I can resist everything but temptation.'

Angela looked at me and raised her eyebrows. She didn't say anything, but I knew exactly what she was thinking.

'Don't worry,' she said, heading back inside before the breeze bit through to her bones, 'if there's so much as a crumb left, I'll box it up for you.'

'Just don't let Dorothy see it if you do end up taking any away with you,' I warned him after Angela had gone. 'She loves the cakes from here as much as the rest of us, but she wouldn't appreciate us eating them when she's been slaving over the Aga preparing lunch all morning.'

Gabe winked and sank his teeth into a cherry-topped cupcake, leaving a fine layer of frosting covering his upper lip and the end of his nose.

'Oh my god,' he groaned in ecstasy, the sound making me blush as I handed him a napkin. 'That's so good.'

'Jemma certainly has a way with cake,' I agreed, focusing my attention on spooning up my marshmallows. 'And, hey,' I added, the thought only just occurring, 'I thought you told me you were avoiding stuff that made you happy.'

He shrugged his shoulders and took another bite.

'I also told you I needed to get better at practising the stuff I preached,' he reminded me. 'Consider this a very small bite of happiness.'

We spent the next few minutes eating and drinking in silence, aside from the incredibly erotic yummy noises Gabe couldn't resist making every time he bit into a brand-new bake and, to be honest, I was relieved when he pushed the plate away, the last cake left untouched.

'I take it you enjoyed that little lot then?' I asked, hoping he wasn't going to subject my ears to an encore.

'So much,' he said, 'too much. Thank god I don't live in town. I'd be eating here every day and that would be no good for the old figure at all, would it?'

From what I'd seen of his physique, he didn't have anything to worry about, but the distance to the café was probably a blessing. I mean, it would be a shame to keep putting temptation in the way of perfection, wouldn't it?

'I think you'll be OK,' I told him. 'You'd have to eat a lot of cake to add even a tiny layer of fat over the top of your muscle definition.'

'Oh really,' he nudged.

'Not that I've noticed,' I quickly added, which was a ridiculous thing to say because you couldn't see a person half-naked and not take on board what they looked like. And I'd seen Gabe half-naked twice now.

'Hey now, be careful,' he taunted, 'if you keep on blushing like that, I'll start thinking I'm in the presence of the wrong Hayley.'

'Oh, shut up,' I snapped.

'That's better,' he nudged. 'Don't let your guard down, whatever you do.'

I had no intention of letting my guard down in front of him again. He really was the most infuriating man, but if I let him know how much he was getting to me, I was certain there'd be no end to it.

'We really should be heading back,' I said, determinedly changing the direction the conversation had been heading in.

'What's the rush?' he asked. 'Relax, for goodness sake. We've got plenty of time, we aren't on a clock, you know.'

'I thought you'd be going all out to impress your new boss,' I bit back. 'It doesn't look good if you're swanning about the town all morning when you should be working.'

He looked at me and I shut up again. That was the thing about working at the hall – set hours didn't really exist, but I hadn't realised he'd worked that out quite so soon and, of course, Catherine had told us to take as long as we needed before we left. However, I couldn't help thinking I was pushing my luck. My first proper trip into town had so far been without an embarrassing incident and I wanted to get out before my luck deserted me.

'How are we getting on?'

Angela was back and looking mightily impressed by the amount Gabe had polished off in such a short sitting.

'The woman is a baking goddess,' announced Gabe.

I felt a little stab of jealousy to hear Jemma described in such a passionate tone.

'I'll tell her that,' said Angela, filling her tray back up with the now-empty crockery, 'and I'll box this up for you, shall I?' she added, picking up the one and only cupcake that hadn't found its way into Gabe's sugar-saturated stomach.

'Thanks,' he answered, 'that would be great. A little something to look forward to before bedtime.'

'And can I get you anything else?'

I opened my mouth to ask for the bill but was cut off.

'A pot of tea for two would be great,' said Gabe, 'and can we have it inside if there's a free table?'

'But what about Bran?' I asked as Angela ducked back through the door. 'I'll stay out here with him if you like,' I offered again.

Gabe shook his head.

'Lizzie told me she's taking an early lunch break because she's got a crafting session this afternoon.'

I didn't see how that made any difference.

'She said if we were still here and wanted to move inside she'd take Bran upstairs into her flat for a little while.'

'How kind,' I said, smiling tightly as Lizzie chose that

exact moment to appear around the side of the café and beckon to Gabe.

'I'm going to take him through the back way,' she said obligingly, 'do you want to bring him up and settle him before you have your tea?'

Had I been of a suspicious nature, I would have thought it was all some elaborate set-up to make me go inside.

'You go and pour,' Gabe instructed me, 'and I'll be there in a minute.'

Lizzie looked at me and burst out laughing.

'Gosh, you're brave,' she giggled.

'What?' shrugged Gabe.

'Hayley doesn't appreciate being ordered about,' she told him, pointing out my scowl.

'Oh, she'll get used to it,' he quipped, ducking out of sight under the gazebo and leaving me no chance to bite back and no choice but to go in.

Not that I would have dreamt of telling Gabe, of course, but going inside had turned out to be the right thing to do. The customers sitting in the café, aside from one or two, took little notice of my arrival and it was much warmer inside than out.

'So,' said Jemma, during her one brief appearance from the kitchen as Gabe returned from settling Bran, 'how are things at the hall shaping up for Christmas? Has Angus got anything exciting lined up for us locals yet?'

'Oh, you know Angus,' I reminded her, 'he's always got something spectacular tucked up his sleeve.'

'You mean there is something,' Lizzie tutted, 'but you aren't going to tell us?'

'My lips are sealed,' I told them both.

Jemma turned her attention to Gabe.

'Whatever she says,' he said, pointing at me.

Wise man.

'Well,' said Jemma, 'I hope we'll see you back in town for the switch-on and the Christmas tree auction, Gabe?'

'Oh yes,' added Lizzie, 'we're always on the lookout for some extra muscle the weekend of the tree auction, aren't we, Hayley?'

Once they had gone back to work, I explained to Gabe about the events that made up the town's festive celebrations. Even just talking about the lights going on, the Christmas fair and how we all chipped in to gather the greenery from the hall woods to sell alongside the trees in town, made my pulse race. Add on the tree competition the hall was hosting and the posh party Anna was helping to organise, and I was in danger of overcooking my excitement long before Angus had dragged the advent calendar out from the loft. Fortunately, remembering the potential role I was going to play in setting up the Winter Wonderland was enough to temper my enthusiasm a little.

'I thought you weren't the outdoorsy type,' Gabe reminded me, when I finally drew breath. 'For a minute there you sounded quite taken with the idea of bunching up the holly and mistletoe.'

'Yeah, well,' I shrugged. 'I am willing to get my hands

dirty and make the occasional concession to get into the spirit of the season and all that.'

'Excellent,' he said, pulling a pile of books out of one of the bags he had been lugging about. 'In that case, I shouldn't have too much trouble making you change your mind about helping me with my contribution to the Winter Wonderland, should I?'

'Shush,' I warned him, 'lower your voice. No one's supposed to know.'

'No one's listening,' he said, looking about him.

'You'd be surprised,' I whispered, before adding, 'where on earth did you get all of those?'

'From the library, of course,' he said without looking up.

My heart was suddenly beating far harder and faster than it had been when I let my Christmas excitement get the better of me.

'Oh,' I said, 'right.'

'I went and registered this morning,' he went on, 'it's important to support your local library, you know. The town is lucky to still have one.'

'Of course,' I stammered.

'That is all right with you, isn't it?' he asked.

I couldn't help thinking he sounded a bit peeved all of a sudden and wondered if his change in tone was because he had spotted me and Gavin deep in conversation, hidden behind the large print. Or was my paranoia pushing me to read too much into his words? I knew I had nothing to feel guilty about. I had met my ex with the intention of getting to the bottom of a few things and we had managed to part on civil terms, like proper grown-ups, rather than silly kids squabbling in the street. But for some reason I did feel guilty. For some reason, I was feeling as guilty as hell.

'Of course,' I said again.

'I needed some extra inspiration,' Gabe explained, 'and you'd be surprised what you can pick up in a library.'

I nodded and drank another mouthful of tea.

'I know I might not look the bookish type,' he began.

'No,' I interrupted, 'it's not that.'

'What is it then?' He frowned.

I shook my head.

'Nothing.'

'Look,' he laughed, 'I mentioned the library and you looked like you were going to fall off your chair.'

'It's nothing,' I said again. 'I just thought I'd left some overdue books at my parents', but I haven't. It's fine.'

Gabe nodded and went back to flicking through the pages. I watched him for a few seconds before putting down my cup. He really was dragging our trip into town out now.

'Right,' I announced. 'Come on. We better go and find Bran because we really should be getting back.'

Chapter 17

As it turned out, I had every reason to be wary of Gabe's motives for dragging out our trip to Wynbridge. He may well have enjoyed his sugar hit back in town, but the extended trip to the Cherry Tree Café had really been part of an elaborate ploy to keep me away from Wynthorpe and buy everyone else at the hall as much time as possible.

'We have a surprise for you, Hayley,' said Anna, as she wrenched open the truck door the second Gabe had cut the engine. 'Come with me, and make sure you bring that,' she ordered, when she spotted the bag at my feet stamped with the Hardy's logo.

'What's going on?' I asked Gabe. 'What's all this about?'

'Beats me,' he shrugged, opening the back door to release Bran. 'But you'd better do as you're told.'

I narrowed my eyes and he started to laugh.

'And there was me thinking you were supposed to be able to trust an angel,' I told him with a sniff.

'You can,' he smiled. 'I'm one hundred per cent trustworthy.'

In that moment I wasn't all that sure that I believed him and I had no idea where everyone had got the idea that they could boss me about, either.

'Come on!' called Anna.

'I'm coming,' I yelled back.

This clearly wasn't the time to pick an argument, and the air inside the kitchen seemed to crackle with excitement as soon as I arrived. I didn't feel at all comfortable. I was certain that whatever they had been cooking up would be a good surprise, as opposed to the pretty rotten ones I had recently endured, but that didn't stop me from feeling nervous. I didn't much like being the centre of attention these days, whatever the circumstances.

'Do you think we should blindfold her?' said Jamie, making a grab for a tea towel, 'I think we should.'

'Don't be silly,' tutted Dorothy, snatching the towel from his grasp and hanging it back over the Aga rail. 'You're not kidnapping her. She is allowed to see where she's going, for goodness sake.'

'Look, what's going on?' I asked. 'If you don't tell me where I'm going, I won't be going anywhere because you guys are freaking me out.'

'I thought the old Hayley,' said Gabe, who clearly couldn't resist joining in with the banter, 'was unshakeable. I can't imagine her ever freaking out over anything, or have I been given false information?'

I stuck my tongue out at him and put my bag down on the table just as Catherine walked in and set about unruffling my feathers.

'Wonderful,' she smiled, her cheeks unusually aglow. 'You're back. Come with me, Hayley, please.'

I felt much calmer with her in charge of proceedings and was happy to take her hand and let her lead the way. Everyone else followed on behind, with Anna beaming and clutching my bag of new art supplies.

'Where's Angus?' I asked Catherine.

'You'll see,' she told me, giving my hand a reassuring squeeze.

We made our way past the morning-room door and carried on a few steps further. I always thought of this part of the hall as being very much Catherine's domain. It was the lightest and airiest part, and the rooms were decorated in softer shades than those favoured in the dining hall and along the grand wooden stairway and galleried landing. Angus had a space of his own as well, his very own den, but that was miles away from where we were heading.

'Here we are,' said Catherine, coming to a stop outside the door that I knew belonged to the old conservatory.

The elaborate glass construction had been a late Victorian addition and, no longer in use to showcase the exquisite orchids and other exotic flowers I had seen sepia photographs of, it now had an abandoned and rather unloved air to it. I often secretly slipped inside to read my gossip magazines, admire the architectural flourishes and enjoy the warmth that lingered at the end of the day.

'We hope you like it.'

She turned the handle and stepped aside to let me go in ahead of her.

'Ta-da!' shouted Angus from his precarious position halfway up a very rickety wooden ladder. 'What do you think?'

'Oh, good grief,' said Mick, easing by and rushing to help Angus wobble back down to earth. 'I told you to leave that until we were all here.'

Everyone else filed in and I knew they were holding their breath, waiting to gauge my reaction.

'We know you've always liked this spot,' said Angus, rubbing his hands together and proudly looking about him.

Obviously, my clandestine trips here hadn't been quite so secret after all.

'And the light is wonderful,' added Catherine.

'So, we thought we'd surprise you,' joined in Jamie, 'and turn it into a studio.'

'It's yours for as long as you want it,' Catherine explained, 'with no expectation that you will draw Angus's precious map or anything else he dreams up. This space is simply for you to draw, paint or do whatever you want in.'

'And if you're really lucky,' laughed Jamie, 'I'm sure Gabe here would be up for the odd life-modelling session.'

'Be quiet, Jamie,' said Anna, shoving him aside and walking over to me. 'Do you like it?' she asked.

There were deep lines creasing her brow and I realised I still hadn't said a word, but that was because I didn't know what to say. I looked around, amazed by the transformation. There was a bookcase, an old armchair, a table full of empty pots and an easel, even a pile of clean canvases. I couldn't believe they had put their heads together and come up with all this so quickly!

'You said these would come in handy one day, didn't you?' I said to Angus, nodding at the stack of clean canvases leant against the wall in order of size.

I had spotted him late one afternoon, what must have been getting on for two years ago, cramming them into a cupboard after one of his more eclectic buying sessions in a Peterborough auction house. I wondered if Catherine knew about half of the stuff he had hidden about the place. I was rather grateful for his hoarding habit now, even if it did cut down on cubby holes for my cleaning paraphernalia.

'I did,' he said proudly. 'There's usually a justification for my bidding, even if it isn't always immediately obvious.'

Catherine and Jamie groaned and I started to laugh.

'Sorry,' I apologised, 'I've just vindicated him, haven't I?'

'There'll be no stopping him now,' chuckled Dorothy.

'So,' said Anna, 'you still haven't answered my question – do you like it, Hayley? Do you think you could work here?'

'I think,' I said softly, 'that this is the most beautiful studio I have ever seen and I'm sure I'll be able to work here.'

A cheer went up and I felt tears splash down my face. There was no way of saving my eyeliner, but this gorgeous space, this wonderful, generous gift, was definitely worth crying over and I didn't give a flying fig if my tears were betraying the person I was trying to be.

'Oh, now stop,' said Dorothy, mopping her eyes with the

cotton handkerchief she always had somewhere about her person. 'You'll set me off.'

'Thank you both so much,' I said to Catherine and Angus. 'I don't know what I've done to deserve this or any of the kindness you've shown me—'

As always, when any member of the team made a stab at saying thank you for anything, we found our words were waved away, but Catherine did kiss my cheek and Angus gave me a hug before helping Jamie carefully pop the corks on a couple of bottles of champagne.

'You know, I still haven't got my head around all this,' said Jamie as he handed me a flute filled with fizz.

'It's quite a transformation, isn't it?' I said, admiring the substantial proportions of the room, which I could already imagine filled with the scent of paint and littered with piles of sketches and plans.

'I don't think he's talking about the conservatory,' said Gabe, as he clinked his glass against mine.

'What then?'

'You,' said Jamie, looking down at me. 'My brash, ballsy friend has suddenly turned all soft and arty.'

'Be careful,' warned Gabe. 'I don't think soft is a word the old Hayley allows in her vocabulary.'

I rolled my eyes and took a bubble-filled sip.

'For all you know,' I told Jamie, 'my secret artistic style could be all dark, dramatic skies and raging seascapes.'

'But it isn't,' said Molly, who had just arrived. 'I've seen the contents of her folder.'

She gave me a long hug, helped me rub the worst of my streaming make-up away and then took a tour of the room with me. She was every bit as enraptured as I was.

'Oh, would you look at that?' she gasped, drawing everyone's attention.

The wind had finally driven off the clouds and the sun shone in, coloured light bouncing off the walls as the stained-glass panels came into their own. It was absolutely beautiful. I couldn't wait to get going and I knew exactly what I was going to start with.

'You two really need to get going with this Winter Wonderland project,' I called over to Jamie and Angus, 'because I need to know exactly what it is that I'm supposed to be adding to this map you want me to draw.'

'You mean you'll do it?' asked Jamie, while Angus bounced on his heels in the background. 'You're definitely taking it on?'

'And the adverts and flyers?' Angus added hopefully.

'Yes,' I said, taking a deep breath to calm the butterflies flitting about my stomach, 'I'm definitely taking it on. I'm taking it all on.'

My announcement surprised everyone that day, myself included, but it also properly kickstarted the extra research and planning that was required to turn the Winter Wonderland from Angus and Jamie's fantasy into a reality, and with just over a month to make it all happen, that was no bad thing.

I began my part the next day by sitting down with Catherine and planning out a schedule for my working week that would give me the time to factor in the hours I was going to need to perfect the theme and work on the designs. I hadn't worked on anything like this before and, although nervous, I was certain I could use my new quirky drawing style to capture the essence of the event and combine it with the whimsical eccentricity the hall was locally famous for.

'We need to talk deadlines,' I said to Jamie once Catherine and I were happy with my revised working pattern.

I felt excited by the prospect of working in a timeframe. For the last few years, my daily routine had been pretty laid back and I hadn't realised just how much of a thrilling buzz a deadline could offer. Although, of course, I probably wouldn't be saying that in a couple of weeks' time when I was tearing my hair out and wishing I'd left my art folder hidden in my bedroom back in town.

'Ideally,' said Jamie who was now firmly in charge of scheduling, leaving Angus to the role of dreaming up the more artistic embellishments, 'we need to get the first advert in the local paper on the twenty-third.'

'That's the day before the switch-on, isn't it?' frowned Anna.

'It is,' he confirmed, 'and with the newspaper needing it ahead of publication, the deadline is literally just a couple of weeks away.'

'Crikey,' said Anna, biting her lip. 'That soon?'

'And, if possible, I'd like the flyers and any other promo

bits and pieces ready for then, too,' Jamie continued, 'because that way we can hand them out at the switch-on.'

'And at the tree auction and bake sale the week after,' I chipped in, feeling ever so slightly less confident as my eyes strayed to the calendar on the wall.

'What do you think?' asked Anna. 'Can you do it?'

'Of course,' I said, pushing the beginnings of any niggles away. It was too late to get an attack of the vapours now. 'I'll make drawing up the promo stuff a priority as we're going to need that before the map.'

'Great,' said Jamie.

'Although,' I reminded him, 'my hands are tied until you start confirming what I can include. I don't want to spend an entire afternoon drawing a grotto if you then decide not to have one.'

'That's a good point,' said Jamie, frowning at the paper-work in front of him.

'Are you going to include an illustration of everything on offer, rather than just write a few words and include some sort of festive border?'

'Anna,' I tutted, shaking my head. 'This is a Wynthorpe Hall production,' I told her, 'I think I'm going to have to come up with something rather more exclusive than a sprig of clipart holly in each corner!'

'Sorry,' she mouthed.

'I should think so.'

'But you are right,' Jamie agreed as Angus came stomping into the kitchen. 'We really do need to start firming things up, don't we? Here, Dad, Hayley needs to know what she has to include on the ads and flyers before she can start designing them.'

'I've established the basics,' I told them all, 'the colour palette and font is sorted and I have a theme in mind, but I don't want to start on too many drawings until we've worked out exactly what's going to be on offer.'

'Well, there won't be any reindeer,' said Angus, dumping himself down at the table and looking thoroughly fed up.

I wasn't sure about the others, but I was a little relieved about that. Mick was going to have his hands full looking after the ponies for the sleigh, and I wasn't sure anyone else would have been up to the task of bedding down Dasher and Blitzen, even if they would have looked the part in the woods and drawn the crowds. I supposed Gabe might have taken them on, but he was committed to setting up and running his woodland workshop and probably wouldn't have the time, even if he did have the skills.

'And why not?' Jamie asked his father.

His self-satisfied tone suggested that he already knew what the answer was going to be.

'Because they're all booked up already,' huffed Angus.

'And?' said Jamie.

Clearly more than availability had been an issue.

'They were too expensive.'

'Damn right,' said Jamie, striking the word reindeer from his list with a flourish. 'At well over a grand a day to hire a pair in, I should say so.'

I whistled under my breath and felt a little sorry for Angus who was clearly disappointed, but Jamie was right, that was an awful lot of money.

'Wow,' gasped Anna, 'that's one heck of an outlay.'

'I suppose it is,' Angus pouted, 'but included in that you get the folk who look after them as well. It's not as if they just turn up and hand the beasts over. We wouldn't have had to do anything at all, really.'

'Apart from set up an enclosure for them,' reeled off Jamie. 'Check the insurance and paperwork for DEFRA, house the people travelling with them—'

'We get the idea,' interrupted Anna, 'and it doesn't matter now, does it? Perhaps we can find something a little less expensive, easier to work with, and closer to home.'

'That sounds like a good idea,' I agreed. 'Just don't take too long to find it, if I've got to draw it.'

There were a couple of things that were definitely happening and I could start sketching those straightaway. The snow-covered grotto in the fern garden with Santa's set-up in the summerhouse was one and the sleigh rides were another. I was hoping to include the drawings I used for the advertising on the map as well, to save time, but we were still cutting it fine.

But that, I reminded myself, was how things worked around here, and they always came good in the end. I wouldn't have been at all surprised if we did end up with a reindeer or two kicking about the place, even if they were inflatable or illuminated ones shipped over from the US site Angus favoured when it came to cranking up the festive feeling.

'Don't mind me,' said Dorothy as she squeezed past to get to the Aga.

The smell of fresh bread had been making my stomach growl for at least the last half hour, and the increased aroma she unleashed as she reverently took out the biggest bloomer loaf imaginable did nothing to quell the pangs.

'Thank god I gave in and started eating carbs again when I moved here,' said Anna in an aside to me.

I nodded in agreement.

'Just one slice doesn't hurt, does it?'

I raised my eyebrows.

'I challenge you to eat just one slice,' I taunted her, knowing full well that she was destined to fail. 'If you eat just one teeny tiny slice, I'll . . .'

'You'll what?' she giggled.

'Do anything,' I foolishly blurted out.

'Anything?'

'Yep,' I said, folding my arms, safe in the knowledge that I didn't need to worry about whatever she came up with because I wouldn't have to do it. She couldn't settle for just one slice if her life depended on it.

'All right,' she said, holding out her hand for me to shake. 'You're going to regret that.'

'I very much doubt it,' I yawned. 'So, tell me, what exactly is it that I won't even have to begin worrying about doing because you won't be able to control yourself when the jam and butter comes out?'

Anna looked at me and then out of the window to

where Gabe was fiddling about with something in the courtyard.

'OK,' she said, her eyes shining with mischief, 'if I eat just one slice of this loaf, then you have to kiss gorgeous Gabe under the mistletoe at the greenery gathering.'

'Don't be so ridiculous,' I snapped.

'What, are you scared?'

'No,' I swallowed, 'of course not.'

'What then?'

'It's just a bit childish, isn't it?'

'So?' she shrugged. 'If you're so convinced that you won't have to do it then what are you scared of?'

'I just said I'm not scared,' I reminded her.

'So, shake on it then.'

'But why would you want me to kiss him?' I asked, stalling for time.

'Because I think you *want* to kiss him,' she said, looking straight at me.

'Don't be stupid.'

'And I think he wants to kiss you too.'

'Of course he doesn't,' I hissed, 'and do I need to remind you—'

'That you've just come out of a disastrous relationship,' she cut in. 'No, no reminder necessary. But you told me that you were reprising the old fun-loving Hayley that we all know and love and I thought a bit of mischief like this would be right up her street.'

I didn't think she was being very fair on Gabe, but then

it wasn't going to happen, and I couldn't have her thinking she'd got the better of me, or getting wind of the fact that I liked Gabe rather more than I should.

'Give me your bloody hand,' I snapped, squeezing her fingers perhaps a little too hard. 'There. Happy now?'

'Oh, ever so,' she said, with a grin while she rubbed the blood back into her fingers.

'Anyway, you won't win,' I reminded her as Dorothy nudged between us and laid the luscious loaf on the table. 'You won't be able to resist.'

I watched Anna like a hawk at mealtimes that day and not one crumb more than her allotted single slice passed her lips. Dorothy was desperate to get more down her, but she refused all offers with her eyes laughing and firmly fixed on me.

I refused to acknowledge her restraint and took up the slack. I crammed in far more butter-covered slices than were good for me and sent up a silent prayer to the winter gods that my so-called friend would forget all about our silly bet between now and the annual greenery gathering.

Chapter 18

With so much going on, it wasn't too difficult, most of the time, anyway, to compartmentalise my confused feelings for Gabe, and I also managed to put my silly bet with Anna to the back of my mind, although I made sure I did nothing to remind her about it. I spent a couple of chilly afternoons out in the grounds sketching the fern garden and summer-house, my mind's eye turning them into a snow-encrusted and fairy-lit magical grotto, and next up was the shiny sleigh that Angus kept locked away in a barn for eleven months of the year.

I couldn't resist running my fingers lightly along the glossy red paintwork and giving the sleigh bells a little shake before I settled down to draw. The tinkling attracted the attention of Gabe and Bran who happened to be passing on their way back to their cottage.

'Show yourself, elf!' called Gabe, poking his head around the door.

I popped back up and peeped over the top of where, in a few weeks' time, Santa, aka Angus, would be sitting, resplendent in his fur-edged red suit and massive black boots.

'Hey, Hayley,' said Gabe. 'Long time no see. Have you been avoiding me?'

It had hardly been a long time, but I had been trying to keep out of his way for the last few days. The conversation we had on the way to town kept popping back into my head at inopportune moments, in spite of my efforts not to think about either it or him.

'Oh man,' I said, walking around the sleigh again to make sure I had picked the best angle and opting to brazen Gabe's observation out. 'You sussed me.'

'I thought so.'

'It's been what, three days?'

Thankfully, he decided not to make more of an issue out of it. After all, three days really wasn't all that long, even if we were living and working within spitting distance and could have tripped over each other at every meal time. Had one of us chosen to take her meals at the table with everyone else that is, rather than tucked away in her studio on the pretence of putting in a few extra hours to get her new job underway, instead.

Consequently, Gabe's next question was pretty astute.

'How are things working out in the studio?' he asked. 'Jamie said you've been pretty full-on with the project. I can't wait to see the results.'

I still hadn't shown anyone what I had come up with so far, but I would have to soon in case they didn't like the style I had gone for and I had to start again. I had always been so secretive about my work that it was a hard habit to break, and I had no idea how I would feel seeing the designs launched into the wider world. As long as my name didn't appear on them, and no one other than the few of us at the hall knew they were mine, then I was hopeful I'd be able to handle it.

'The studio's amazing,' I told Gabe. 'I couldn't get anything done to begin with because I just kept wandering about admiring everything.'

'It is a beautiful space,' he agreed. 'Jamie told me you've always loved it. He said you used to read your celebrity magazines in there.'

'I didn't realise anyone knew about that.'

'Apparently there are no secrets here.' He smiled wryly.

He was definitely right about that. I wondered if Jamie had told him anything else about me.

'I've always admired the construction of the place and the intricate work in the stained-glass panels, as well as reading about who was falling out with who on CBB,' I told him a little defensively.

'What's CBB?'

'Never mind.'

'That's what I like about you, Hayley,' he went on.

'What?'

'You're an enigma.'

'An enigma,' I laughed. I wasn't entirely sure what the word meant, but I was fairly certain he wasn't slagging me off. 'Am I?'

'Yes,' he said, 'just when I think I've got you sussed – when any of us thinks we've got you sussed, actually – you pull another surprise out of the bag.'

'Well,' I said, 'I like to keep folk on their toes. There's nothing more boring than being predictable.'

'Well, no one could ever accuse you of that.'

His voice was as thick as treacle and I didn't dare look up at him for fear of what I would see written across his face. So much for his insistence that he was out to avoid anything that made him happy. I was pretty certain that he knew just as well as I did, even if we weren't prepared to admit it, that the pair of us getting together would make us both very happy indeed. Perhaps he had decided to put me in the cream cakes category when it came to working on practising what he preached? Maybe he had come to think of flirting with me as a 'small bite of happiness'?

The memory of Anna's words about him wanting to kiss me quickly joined forces with him tipsily asking me if he could the night we had shared a packet of sparklers, and the realisation that he might still secretly want to began to play havoc with my insides.

I refused to let myself ponder on the fact that my friend had also said that she thought I wanted to kiss him back. God help the pair of us when it came to gathering the greenery and she skipped up with a bunch of mistletoe.

'Good,' I told him bluntly. 'Mission accomplished then. Now, if you don't mind, I really do need to get on.'

'Would you rather we didn't watch?'

'I would love it if you didn't watch. In fact, I'm insisting on it.'

'Fair enough,' he shrugged with a smile as he looked at his watch. 'I suppose I better get on. I'm due in town soon. I'm taking Bran to meet the V-E-T.'

I wasn't sure if it was necessary to spell it out, but then Gabe had been in possession of his huge hound for such a short amount of time, he probably didn't know how he'd react either.

'There isn't anything wrong with him, is there?' I asked, my desire to forge ahead forgotten.

'No,' Gabe quickly explained. 'Not as far as I can tell, anyway. I just thought it was about time he was registered somewhere and had a check-up. He wasn't being very well looked after when I found him. I daresay he'll probably need worming at least.'

'And what about you?' I asked.

'No,' said Gabe, with an amused frown. 'No worms here, as far as I can tell. Well, I haven't had an urge to scrape my backside across the cottage carpets so far if that's what you were getting at.'

'Of course that's not what I meant,' I burst out, laughing. 'What I meant,' I went on, 'although I didn't express it very clearly, was that it probably wouldn't be a bad idea for you to register yourself with a doctor.'

'Right,' he grinned.

'Just in case you do get the urge to drag . . .' I began but stopped as I caught sight of Dorothy heading in our direction.

'You're heading to town aren't you, Gabe?' she asked.

'Yes,' I said, biting the inside of my mouth to stop myself laughing, 'he needs to pick up something to help with the worms.'

'Worms?' frowned Dorothy. 'They can take care of themselves, can't they?'

Gabe and I both started to laugh and Dorothy looked confused and a little annoyed.

'Ignore her, Dorothy,' said Gabe soothingly.

'I do try,' she said, looking at me over the top of her glasses, 'but it's getting harder and harder these days, especially now she's practically living in my pocket.'

'Now, now,' I said, knowing I couldn't possibly let her get away with that, 'sharing the sitting room was your idea. You've only got yourself to blame when you find me pottering about in my underwear every morning.'

'Lucky Dorothy,' said Gabe, looking me up and down.

His efforts at self-denial were failing dismally, but I was determined to neither blush, nor get further drawn into the flirtatious, back and forth banter I usually favoured. Where Gabe was concerned, I reckoned that would be far too dangerous and would quite likely lead somewhere he might tell me he didn't want to visit after all. He had talked about me being full of surprises, but given what he had said in the woodshed about being embarrassed by his forthright behaviour the night of sparkler-gate, he could be quite a match for me when the mood took him.

'That's enough of that,' said Dorothy. 'All I want to know is if you can give me a lift or not, young man?'

'Yes,' said Gabe, smiling over the top of her head at me. 'Sorry, Dorothy. Give me five minutes and it will be my pleasure to escort you into town.'

'Well, that's all right then,' she said, transferring her shopping basket from one arm to the other. 'I'm off to see the girls in the Cherry Tree Café to ask them if they'd like the catering spot next to the ticket kiosk during the Winter Wonderland weekend.'

I was certain Jemma would be delighted to finally discover what Wynthorpe was planning, if nothing else.

'That sounds like a good idea,' Gabe enthusiastically agreed. 'Although probably not for my waistline.'

He could have been skating on thin ice openly admiring Jemma's baking prowess, but fortunately Dorothy wasn't one to take umbrage when it came to her young friend's baking skills.

'But won't it be a bit chilly?' he asked. 'Serving tea and cake under a gazebo in the middle of winter. They'll freeze and who will run the café while they're here?'

'Don't worry about that,' I told him as I quickly scrolled through the photos on my phone. 'They've got a pretty big team and this little beauty for outside catering.'

'Oh wow,' said Gabe as he squinted at the screen, 'that's quite something.'

Dorothy leant in to take a look too.

'It's wonderful, isn't it?' she smiled. 'Reminds me of the caravans I used to see on the roads when I was growing up.'

The converted vintage van and bespoke awning had proved a popular choice for all sorts of outdoor events in and around Wynbridge and even further afield. It would make an ideal addition to the Winter Wonderland and would be great to include on the map and in the promo material.

With Lizzie's creative crafting skills, I knew it would be beautifully styled for the occasion and would definitely add a quirky, but sophisticated, wow factor to the courtyard area for when visitors arrived. However, I hoped I could sketch it from the photos on my phone. If Jemma agreed to come onboard I didn't much fancy having to ask for a private viewing. Turning up with my sketchbook and pens would soon blow my cover.

'A young lass up the road converted it,' Dorothy explained to Gabe. 'She's got a whole field of these that folk come and take their holidays in. It's a really thriving little business.'

'Glamping in the Fens,' smiled Gabe. 'Who'd have thought it?'

'Her name's Lottie Foster,' I told him. 'She goes out with the V-E-T you're supposed to be seeing this afternoon.'

'Crikey,' he said, whistling for Bran. 'At this rate I really will be late. Come on lad, let's go and get you MOT'd.'

'And while you're about it,' I called after him, 'ask Dorothy to give you directions to the doctors. Worms or no worms you should have registered by now.'

Dorothy looked disapprovingly from one of us to the other but thought better than to ask.

The conversation at dinner that evening was abuzz with talk of Winter Wonderland plans and I decided to forgo eating in isolation in favour of joining in with the fun. Dorothy was the first to share her news.

'I spoke to Jemma,' she told us as she served up and passed around plates of fragrant korma resting on soft pillows of fluffy rice, 'and she was very keen to come onboard.'

A look passed between Angus and Jamie and they both breathed a sigh of relief.

'Thank goodness for that,' said Jamie. 'I thought they might be too busy, what with their Christmas-bakes-and-makes stall on the market.'

'That had crossed my mind,' nodded Dorothy, 'but apparently Ruby and Steve are going to be back in Wynbridge for Christmas and Jemma has a new lad working in the café who's happy to help out, so she was confident they'll be able to cover everything.'

The Cherry Tree Café empire had been steadily growing since Ruby, another Wynbridge local, had made such a success of the festive market stall, and what with that and the mobile tea room, I was certain Jemma's cupcakes were poised to take over the world. Well, a large part of East Anglia, at least.

'I wonder if they'll have a theme this year?' Anna mused.

'Reindeer would have been wonderful,' sighed Angus wistfully.

Clearly, he still hadn't come to terms with missing out on the opportunity to personally welcome Rudolph to Wynthorpe.

'She could have baked reindeer-shaped cookies with red sweets for the nose,' he carried morosely on.

'Have you thought about what you'll be making yet, Dorothy?' I asked in an attempt to distract him with the sweet treats his own cook would be conjuring up.

'Well,' she said, finally taking her seat at the table, 'there'll be the usual, of course, but I rather fancied having a go at making some old-fashioned sweet things this year.'

'Such as?' asked Gabe.

'Sugar mice,' she said dreamily.

'Now they're a real blast from the past,' piped up Catherine.

'With real cotton tails,' Dorothy continued.

'Health and safety,' Jamie mumbled, but no one took any notice.

'Sugar plums,' Dorothy went on, 'ginger snaps and perhaps some sort of candy cane. That kind of thing. Things that will really appeal to the kiddies, as well as plenty of pastry swirls, laced with cinnamon for that extra festive flavour.'

'That all sounds wonderful,' said Mick.

'And not just for the younger visitors,' Angus beamed, suitably mollified by talk of excessive sugar.

'But for the child in all of us,' agreed his wife, sounding every bit as delighted as her husband.

'So, that's the eats all sorted,' I said, thinking how I could incorporate some of what Dorothy was suggesting on the adverts and flyers. Perhaps candy cane bunting would work around the edges.

'Yep,' said Jamie, consulting the notepad he seemed to have permanently glued to his hand these days. 'We're really getting there, now.'

'And I have a proposal,' said Gabe, sounding unusually apprehensive. 'If you're still looking for an attraction with a wildlife sort of twist.'

We all turned to look at him and I was surprised to see him looking, well, choked would be the best way to describe it. I wasn't sure if anyone else noticed, so I might have been wrong. After all, talk of childish sweet treats wouldn't usually stir up so much emotion, unless you were Angus of course, but to my eyes, Gabe looked just a little too bright-eyed.

'Always,' said Angus, rubbing his hands together and everyone else nodded in agreement.

I joined in when no one else asked if he was all right. Clearly I was reading too much into it. Perhaps he had just choked on a grain of rice or something.

'Well,' he began, 'I took Bran to the vets this afternoon.'

'And given that you said the word rather than spelt it out, I'm guessing he got on OK?' I asked.

'More than OK,' said Gabe fondly. 'He was as good as gold.'

'Of course he was,' said Dorothy indulgently.

'And no worms?' I couldn't resist asking.

'Not a worm in sight,' laughed Gabe, looking more like himself, 'for either of us.'

The others were clearly confused by our private joke and Dorothy tutted loudly. I looked at Gabe and smiled and he smiled back. It was the silliest of shared moments, over in a second, but it warmed me to the tips of my toes and I couldn't help wondering if my pupils were as dilated as his.

'You mentioned wildlife,' I reminded him, clearing my throat and pulling myself back together.

'Hmm,' he said, still gazing at me.

'Wildlife, via the V-E-T,' I prompted.

'Yes,' he said, suddenly coming to his senses, 'sorry, wildlife.'

'Was it Will you saw?' asked Anna. 'He's dreamy, isn't he?'

'Hey!' said Jamie.

'Yes,' Gabe said, 'it was Will, but I'm not sure about the dreamy part. He's not really my type, to be honest, but he did have a potential idea for the Winter Wonderland. I hope it was OK to mention what we're planning?' he added, looking to Angus.

'Absolutely OK, my dear chap,' said Angus. 'It's definitely happening now so we can't keep it a secret much longer otherwise we won't have any visitors!'

'That's all right then,' said Gabe, 'because I happened to tell Will how disappointed you were feeling about not having reindeer in attendance and he suggested owls.'

'Owls?' said the rest of us all together.

'Yes,' Gabe continued. 'Apparently, there's a sort of sanctuary around here somewhere and they have a few owls, which they take around to schools and that sort of thing.'

'I remember reading something about that in the paper this summer,' said Mick, 'but I've heard nothing since.'

'According to Will, it's been a quiet start for them, but they're looking for ways to raise their profile.'

'Did he happen to mention who runs it?' asked Catherine.

'A young friend of his was responsible for setting it up. A lad called Ed, I think, and his mum. It sounds very much a family affair from what I can make out.'

'Oh, we've heard all about Ed,' said Angus. 'There's nothing that boy doesn't know about the local landscape and the birds and animals living in it.'

'He's our very own little Durrell,' smiled Catherine.

'Well, there you are then,' said Gabe, sounding pleased. 'The sanctuary should be right up your street, and potentially far less problematic than reindeer.'

'And owls will look great on the artwork,' I beamed. 'Well done, Gabe.'

'I've got a contact number back at the cottage,' he happily added. 'You'll have to give them a ring, Jamie, to see which owl species they could bring and then you can pencil them in, Hayley.'

'Pun intended,' I laughed.

'Absolutely,' he laughed back.

Chapter 19

The next couple of weeks flashed by, confirming the old adage that time really does fly when you're having fun. Not that I had been expecting fun. Truth be told, having fun had been pretty low on the agenda when the Connelly father and son duo had first coerced me into taking responsibility for the artistic flourishes of the Winter Wonderland.

Something else I hadn't been expecting was another shift in my relationship with Gabe. It might have only been a fleeting moment, a silly private joke shared across the Wynthorpe table, but those few seconds smiling at one another over our korma-filled plates had set something in motion.

I couldn't be sure what exactly, but our friendship flourished and slipped back to what it had been before our post-bonfire heart to heart, and he and Bran had taken to joining me in the studio in the evenings while I quietly worked on the promotional materials and made a start on drawing the map of the Wynthorpe woods.

When Gabe visited he made a point of slipping in and out of the conservatory door, which led to the garden, so no one else was aware of his coming and going, and that suited both of us, but especially me. Anna already had a bee in her bonnet about pushing the pair of us together and I didn't want her getting the wrong idea if she found out we were spending so much time alone. If she thought there was even the remotest chance of the two of us developing deeper feelings I wouldn't have put it past her to have Molly on standby at the greenery gathering to perform some kind of hand-tying pagan rite, binding us for life.

Gabe and I didn't talk all that much. I worked mostly at the table and he sat and read or dozed with Bran asleep at his feet. I found it impossible to get a great deal of work done when he was absorbed in a book because his face, serene and still, was simply too captivating. I had started to sketch both him and the hound, but that was something else I had chosen to keep to myself. I would probably share the drawings with him at some point, but this deep, developing friendship with a man was the first of its kind for me, and its easy-going, no-fuss, quiet manner was taking some getting used to.

Thanks to Gabe and Bran's calming company in the evenings, it wasn't until the afternoon before the advert was due to be submitted to the newspaper that my nerves really decided it was time to put in an appearance and, as a result of a last minute addition from Angus, they were quickly cranked into overdrive.

'But are you sure that bit,' I said, reaching over Jamie's shoulder and pointing at the area of concern with a pencil, 'doesn't look too cramped?'

'It's fine,' he said again, trying to reassure me.

'And the text isn't too small?'

'It's perfect,' added Anna.

'And you like the snowflake theme?'

I had opted to draw snowflake bunting, rather than candy canes, and had dotted the flakes about the page to tie the different elements together. It was hopefully going to work well with the snowflake ink pads Jamie had bought to include around the woodland trail. Now, appropriately named, The Snowflake Trail.

'We love the snowflake theme,' Anna reiterated.

In the early days I had been all for ripping up and starting again a hundred times over, but gradually, thanks to Gabe's subtle suggestions and encouragement to let the others have a look as I went along, I had got used to them adding their opinions and ideas and I was delighted with the results. I had managed to include everything that would be on offer during the Winter Wonderland weekend, from the crafts in the woods with Gabe, to Dorothy's sugary and cinnamon delights, along with drawings of the hall, sleigh, owls, grotto and the Cherry Tree caravan to add a festive flourish and, hopefully, even more appeal.

'Although,' said Jamie.

'Although what?' I jumped in, my eyes frantically search-ing the page for mistakes.

'Although, I would like to know why Dad wanted this particular addition,' he said, pointing at the recently added line that had given my arrangement so much trouble. 'I don't suppose he told you what the "surprise" element of the weekend was all about, did he?'

'No, he didn't,' said the man himself as he wandered in. 'Because I haven't decided yet.'

'So why put it in?' Anna asked suspiciously.

'To add intrigue,' said Angus innocently. 'Folk love anything that's value added, and if they think they're going to get something extra on top of what we're already offering, they'll flock down the drive to see what it is.'

I was sure he was right, and as long as that 'something extra' didn't involve me making a spectacle of myself in stripy elf tights and pointy plastic ears, then it was fine by me.

'I better go and get this scanned in,' said Jamie, pushing back his chair and picking up the design I had sweated over for so long. 'Are you sure you don't want to come with us, Hayley?'

I shook my head.

'We're going to the printers to sort the flyers as well,' he said. 'You don't fancy watching your handiwork being prepared to fly off the press.'

I wasn't sure that would have really been possible, but even if it were, it was the last thing I wanted to see.

'Please come,' said Anna, tugging at my sleeve. 'It'll be fun.'

'No,' I said firmly. 'I've done what you asked, and please don't think I'm being rude, but I don't want to even think about it anymore and please, please remember not to mention my name if anyone happens to ask you who drew it all.'

I might have got used to my Wynthorpe family knowing about the talent I had started to use again, but I certainly didn't want the news spreading further than the end of the drive.

As adamant as I was that I didn't want to think about either the advert or the flyers now they were finished, my head wasn't going to let me off the hook that easily. I spent a restless night tossing and turning and was up extra early the morning the paper was due to be delivered, even though I knew it wouldn't be with us until late in the afternoon.

'Come over to the cottage this afternoon,' said Gabe when he popped into the hall for his mid-morning coffee break. 'I've got something that will keep your mind off things.'

I looked at him and raised my eyebrows.

'Nothing like that,' he tutted. 'I just want your opinion on something I've been putting together for the Winter Wonderland myself.'

'I thought you were all for asking everyone their opinion,' I reminded him. 'You made me share my design before I was ready to.'

'Well,' he said, shifting in his seat, 'this is a very basic prototype and I was hoping you would consider adding an artistic flourish or two before I present it to the masses.'

'So really, you're only interested in me for my skills with a paint palette?'

'Something like that,' he grinned.

'Marvellous,' I tutted, pretending to be offended.

I made sure I had caught up with my work before I headed over to Gabe's that afternoon. If ever I had been worried that working and living at the hall was going to be too stifling I needn't have. The way my life had picked up apace since I had permanently moved in had ensured that I didn't have a spare second in which to even ponder on that. If anything, I was thinking it was a miracle that I had ever had time to go back to town every evening when I was living with my parents.

'Come on then!' I called to Gabe, when Bran eventually shifted far enough to let me over the threshold. 'What have you got that has the power to stop me obsessing and listening out for the paper guy?'

Back in the hall I had turned the vacuum on and off at least half a dozen times during my last stint on the stairs, convinced that I had heard a van on the drive. I hadn't of course.

'I'm in here,' Gabe called back from the sitting room.

I found him sitting in front of the fire, the carpet covered in a vast plastic sheet and surrounded by what looked like piles of sawn logs. Closer inspection confirmed that was exactly what he was sitting amongst.

'What on earth?' I frowned.

'I know,' he said, biting his lip. 'But bear with me.'

'And all will be revealed?'

'Don't start,' he said, indicating a tiny spot next to him

where he wanted me to sit, 'or you might end up getting more than you bargained for.'

I laughed and sat where I was told. It felt good, being able to spar like this again. Packing away my growing feelings for Gabe had definitely been the right thing to do. There was a comfortable and straightforward flow to our relationship now and I was enjoying getting used to it.

'You know, you really have a knack for bringing out the worst in me,' Gabe tutted.

'It's a gift,' I told him with a cheeky grin, 'and besides, I don't think you're half as shy as you made out after our firework celebration.'

'No?'

'Nope. You were just covering your embarrassment because I turned you down.'

'Better luck next time, perhaps,' he smiled, reaching for the nearest log.

'Perhaps,' I sniffed. 'We'll just have to wait and see about that, won't we?'

I wasn't sure it was me bringing out the worst in him because he was pretty good himself when it came to turning the tables, but that was fine. The opportunity to stretch my innuendo-bingo skills was fun and, given everything I'd been through recently, some innocent entertainment was very much appreciated.

'So,' I said, clearing my throat and picking up a log. 'What have we got here then? A pixie-sized burn-out or something more impressive?'

What Gabe had put together turned out to be far more impressive than a pint-sized bonfire.

'These are perfect,' I told him, rocking back on my heels to get the circulation flowing back in my legs.

'Do you really think so?' Gabe asked, spinning his creation around to check it from all angles.

'Absolutely,' I said, popping my slightly smaller version down next to his, 'and they'll cheer Angus up no end.'

'Well, I hope so,' said Gabe thoughtfully. 'But do you really think they're good enough to be the woodland craft activity?'

'Definitely,' I nodded.

Dotted around the floor were half a dozen wooden reindeer, all carefully constructed from pre-cut kits, which Gabe had been working on putting together. The largest log, with four holes drilled into the underside, formed the body which the legs slotted into. There was another hole on top for the neck which then held the head, complete with branchy antlers and a red nose made from a tiny painted bauble and glued into place. Gabe had tied a red scarf around the neck of his and added a pine cone for a tail. For something so simple, they oozed personality and charm.

'Now that I've got into the swing of it,' he explained, 'I can put together a kit in a matter of minutes.'

'That's just as well,' I laughed, 'because you're going to need plenty.'

'Really?' He frowned. 'You really think so?'

'Really, Gabe,' I told him. 'Families will stand in line to make one of these.'

I watched as his shoulders started to relax and realised that he had been genuinely worried that I wouldn't think they were any good, when actually they were exactly what the Winter Wonderland needed. No tools were required, which would be a relief to Mr Health and Safety, aka Jamie, and they would appeal to all ages and be a long-lasting reminder of the fun the visitors had.

'Have you costed them out yet?' I asked.

I knew that Jamie would be keen to establish outlay as well as safety.

'Roughly,' said Gabe, 'but don't worry, now you've given them your artistic seal of approval I'm going to talk to Jamie about all that.'

I nodded, pleased that he had taken every aspect of the venture into account.

'And I thought,' he went on, 'if everyone thinks it would be worth the effort, that I might make a couple of really big ones, which you could add to the map for The Snowflake Trail.'

'That's a brilliant idea,' I agreed, thinking how excited the younger visitors would be to come across a reindeer hidden amongst the trees, 'and I know you wanted me to add some extra paint to them,' I told him, 'but I think they're perfect just as they are.'

'Me too,' he grinned slyly. 'I didn't want you to paint them at all. I just thought that thinking about it might take your mind off . . .'

I didn't give him a chance to remind me what I had in fact

forgotten all about for the last hour or so, but leant over and shoved him hard on the shoulder.

'You manipulative sod,' I laughed as he shoved me back and I tried to stand up.

The pins and needles in my feet didn't help and before I knew what was happening he had pulled me over, pinned me down and was hovering over me. It wasn't at all the kind of behaviour I had come to expect from my new-found friend and chivalrous guardian angel, but I couldn't bring myself to complain.

'I had your best interests at heart,' he told me huskily, 'you were tying yourself up in knots over at the hall.'

'That's as may be,' I told him, trying not to giggle as I attempted to wriggle myself free, 'but when I get up, I'm going to tie *you* in knots.'

'Promises, promises,' we laughed together and then he lowered his body on to mine.

'Gabe,' I gasped, 'I think I can hear an engine outside.'

'No, you can't,' he said, his lips almost touching mine, 'that's just my heart pounding.'

I didn't think it was, but I couldn't be sure. My own essential organ was going like the clappers so it was hard to tell. He let go of my hands, pushed my hair out of my face and looked longingly into my eyes before finally kissing me.

His tongue teased my teeth apart, the tip of it sending a pulse of pleasure through my entire body. Unbidden, my arms wrapped around his back and I pulled him down harder on to me, but he wouldn't be rushed.

When he eventually pulled away I gasped for breath, my mind confused and my body yearning for more. Every man I'd ever been with would have wasted no time in taking the kiss further – much further – but Gabe, in spite of the very green light I was sending him, was putting the brakes on after just a kiss.

Not that his kiss was just any old kiss. This one had been like nothing I had ever experienced before. His firm caress had reached all the way to my toes, stopping en route to play a few enticing tricks of its own, so it was hardly surprising that he had left me wanting to sample whatever other sensuous skills he had tucked up his sleeve – and down his trousers.

'Are you all right?' I asked him.

'I'm not sure,' he said uncertainly, gently drawing me back up to sit next to him.

I was surprised to see he was frowning. I couldn't believe he hadn't enjoyed what had just happened. As far as I was concerned, that all too brief embrace was off the kiss-o-meter and I refused to imagine that he felt differently. But perhaps he was thinking it was too big a bite of happiness for him to cope with? After all, he had made it perfectly clear that he wasn't looking for a quick fling or a serious relationship, hadn't he? But for someone who had inferred they were currently living a monk-like existence, he had just failed pretty spectacularly.

'Oh,' I said. 'OK. Right.'

Still he didn't say anything and I began to wonder if perhaps he really had done more for me than I had for him.

How embarrassing. Not only had I crossed the line we had so carefully drawn and gone too far with a colleague, I'd been a disappointment to boot.

'That kiss was amazing, Hayley,' he eventually said.

Well, that was something, but he still didn't sound exactly thrilled about it, and given that I had been going out of my way to get used to the platonic delights of our friendship, I knew I shouldn't have been as turned on as I was, either, but I couldn't help myself.

'Far better than I ever imagined it would be,' he added.

'Have you been imagining it for long?' I nudged.

'Ever so long,' he groaned.

'I suppose it wasn't a bad effort for someone who recently told me they're not interested in having any sort of a relationship,' I carried on, trying to keep my tone light, 'especially one that might make them happy.'

Gabe nodded and took a deep breath before running his hands through his hair.

'Why is it,' I asked, 'that every time we seem to be getting somewhere you back off? One minute you're happy to settle for friends, which is fine by me by the way, but the next you're pinning me down and—'

'I'm sorry,' he whispered.

'Just tell me what it is that you want,' I pleaded.

More than anything, and in spite of the fact that I had been trying to convince myself otherwise, I wanted to hear him say that he wanted us to be together, but I knew he wasn't going to. From the look on his face I could see that he was feeling even more confused than I was, but for some reason he couldn't bring himself to explain why.

One thing I did know, however, was that those feelings in me that he had aroused so soon after his arrival hadn't been set aside at all. They had been sitting just under the surface and now Gabe had thrown a stone at them, they'd started to ripple all over again. I should have been annoyed, the old me would have been furious, but, to be honest, the man sitting next to me didn't look as if he was messing me about on purpose. If anything, he looked every bit as confused by it all as I was beginning to feel.

'I want you, Hayley,' he said simply. 'I really do.'

My heart leapt.

'But I can't have you,' he swallowed, 'because—'

I didn't get to find out what came after, as Gabe's words were lost in the din Bran started making in response to the sound of a vehicle pulling up outside.

'Now that really is the paper,' said Gabe, quickly standing up and then pulling me to my feet.

'Can we carry on with this conversation?' I begged him, feeling certain that he hadn't only kissed me to stop me worrying about the imminent arrival of the newspaper. 'Please. Later on, once we've looked at the ad with the others?'

'Perhaps,' he shrugged. 'Maybe. I'm so sorry if you think I took advantage of you again, Hayley, but sometimes when we're alone I just can't seem to help myself. When I'm around you . . .' his words trailed off again. 'Look, I know I said to you when I arrived here that I had a handle on my baggage, but I don't. I thought I did, I thought I was doing really well and would be able to get by without giving my happiness a second thought, but then you came along and now I'm just so confused. About everything.'

I should have taken that as my cue to tell him that he didn't have a monopoly on that particular emotion, but my attention was pulled back to Bran who came trotting in with the paper clamped firmly in his jaws. How he managed to still look like he was smiling with a mouthful of newsprint was beyond me, but he did.

'Come on,' said Gabe, relieving the dog of his quarry and consequently putting an end to his unfathomable monologue, 'let's go up to the hall and look at this all together.'

With me sitting in my usual spot at the table and everyone crowded around, I tentatively opened the paper and began turning the pages. Between us we had three copies, but everyone was waiting to see my reaction before they started thumbing through the others.

A collective gasp filled the air as I finally found the page. I slowly took it all in and, as my eyes filled with tears, I looked up and sought out where Jamie was standing.

'You never said you were going to make it a full page,' I croaked. 'It must have cost a fortune.'

'I got a special rate,' he shrugged, looking pleased.

'And besides,' said Catherine, laying a hand on my shoulder, 'this is a very special occasion.'

'And you aren't just talking about the Winter

Wonderland,' said Angus, his eyes shining as bright as mine, 'are you my dear?'

The sight of something I had been solely responsible for creating filling a whole sheet of newsprint like that literally took my breath away. I don't think I had ever felt happier with anything in my entire life.

'I can't wait to see how the flyers are going to look,' beamed Molly. 'This is spectacular, Hayley. Absolutely stunning.'

I nodded in agreement but didn't say anything for fear of coming across as big-headed, but she was right. It was truly spectacular.

'We've gone for a high-gloss finish on the flyers,' said Jamie, 'and it's going to be all hands on deck to get them distributed.'

'Starting with the switch-on tomorrow night,' Anna confirmed.

Given everything that had been going on during the last couple of weeks, and in spite of the hours I had been putting in at the drawing board, I hadn't really taken in just how quickly Christmas was creeping up on us. In just one more month it would be Christmas Eve and the weekend we were all so focused on would be done and dusted.

'There,' said Gabe, moving closer as the others picked up the spare papers. 'I told you you had nothing to worry about. This looks amazing. You must be over the moon.'

'I am,' I swallowed as I felt his fingers become lightly entwined in my hair. 'What are you doing?' I whispered.

'Hiding the evidence,' he said, showing me a piece of twig, which had taken root, 'before your eagle-eyed friends spot it.'

'Too late,' I sighed, as we looked up to find both Anna and Molly beaming in our direction.

Chapter 20

'I'll give him five more minutes,' said Jamie late the following afternoon as we all gathered in the kitchen to head into Wynbridge for the switch-on, 'and then we'll have to go without him.'

'If we don't leave soon,' said Mick, glancing up at the clock, 'we'll never get parked.'

'Are you sure he said he was coming?' asked Dorothy. 'He gave the fireworks a miss because he was worried about Bran.'

'Perhaps he's going to drive himself in,' suggested Angus.

'What do you think, Hayley?' Anna asked, turning to me.

'Yes,' said Molly. 'You're the one he talks to most. Did he mention anything about his plans to you?'

I felt myself turning annoyingly red as everyone turned their attention to me.

'Don't ask me,' I snapped. 'I don't know any more than the rest of you.'

I was certain Gabe wouldn't have forgotten about the

traditional Christmas lights switch-on in town because we had talked about it in the Cherry Tree, but I genuinely couldn't remember if he had said he would be attending or not. I was hoping so as it would give us the perfect opportunity to spend some time together, among our friends, and hopefully distance ourselves from the searing embrace I hadn't been able to put out of my mind all day. Although, perhaps the fact that he hadn't rushed back over to the hall to find me and explain his behaviour further, meant that he had forgotten about it already.

'Well, I'm going to get the Land Rover warmed up,' said Mick, pulling on his coat. 'I'm still not convinced the battery on it is all it should be.'

'Why don't you nip over to the cottage, Hayley?' suggested Jamie. 'Find out if Gabe's coming or not.'

I didn't think it was worth protesting. Whether I went to chase Gabe up or made a point of refusing, my friends were going to waste their time reading too much into my actions, and so I reached for my coat and headed out into the rapidly descending darkness.

I could hear Mick revving the engine in the stable yard, keen to make sure the Land Rover wasn't going to let him down on this occasion, so it would have been useless calling across to Gabe at the cottage, even though the front door was wide open. Not even my best impression of a hollering fishwife would have carried that far.

It was far colder than I initially realised and I stopped for a second to quickly pull on my coat. By the time I had finished fiddling with the buttons and looked back up, I saw a woman walking down the path towards the cottage's open door. There was a blasting bark from Bran and then Gabe rushed out to meet her. The way he lifted her off her feet and spun her around suggested she wasn't a speculative double-glazing sales person or a Jehovah's Witness, and before I had even thought of my next move they disappeared into the cottage slamming the door behind them.

'He's got company,' said Mick, making me jump almost right out of my skin.

'Looks like it,' I shrugged, trying to convey that it meant nothing to me.

'I take it he's not coming then.'

'I guess not,' I said, heading back to the kitchen door to help hurry everyone along. 'We better get on or we'll be late.'

'You think he would have said something though, wouldn't you?' Mick persisted.

'Not really,' I snapped, even though I didn't mean to. 'It's the weekend, so, officially speaking, no one's beholden to the hall.'

Mick didn't comment further.

'What did he say?' shouted Jamie from the doorway as everyone wandered out and he started fiddling with his massive bunch of keys.

'Nothing,' I said bluntly.

'She didn't get a chance to ask him,' said Mick, keen to elaborate. 'Because he's got company.'

'So, I thought it best not to disturb him,' I cut in. 'Now

come on,' I goaded, before Mick told everyone that the Wynthorpe woodsman was holed up with a beautiful woman for what would I imagined be a weekend of cosy fun and romantic frolics. 'Or it won't be worth going.'

As no one could decide when exactly we would want to return to the hall that evening, we decided to take two vehicles. This would mean that those of us who were in the mood could hang about in town, while those in favour of an early night could head back.

Anna insisted on driving in with Jamie, Molly and me as passengers. If it had been her intention to quiz me about who our neighbour was entertaining, I didn't give her a chance as I immediately got Jamie chatting about the plans for the Winter Wonderland and he thankfully didn't draw breath until we parked up in Wynbridge.

The little market town was heaving by the time we arrived and I resolved to put all thoughts of Gabe and his visitor out of my mind and enjoy what was always one of my favourite evenings of the year. But who was she?

Gabe had never given any indication that he had a girlfriend tucked away or, heaven forbid, a wife. Perhaps this woman – who I had already convinced myself was as sophisticated as she was tall, and as beautiful as she was willowy – was some part of the baggage from his past. If that were the case, what right had he to kiss me and go about awakening all manner of tumultuous feelings I hadn't realised I was capable of?

'Right,' said Jamie as he thrust a pile of papers into my hand. 'Let's see how many of these we can shift between us.'

I looked down at the bundle and then held one of the flyers up into the light.

'They look even better than the ad in the paper,' gasped Molly. 'I bet you're pleased we found that art folder of yours now, aren't you, Hayley?'

'That Suki found, you mean,' Anna quickly added.

'Yes,' said Molly, 'that's what I meant.'

I couldn't help but laugh at Molly's flushed face and was about to comment when someone made a grab for her from behind causing her to drop her flyers, which the rest of us set about speedily retrieving. Jamie was swearing about the cost and how we couldn't afford to waste a single one, but when he stood back up the complaints died in his throat as he found his brother, Archie, kissing Molly keenly on the lips.

'Good god,' he laughed, passing Molly's dropped bundle to me and pulling his brother away from our friend and into a hug. 'What are you doing here?'

'Archie,' beamed Anna. 'What a surprise!'

'A good one, I hope,' he said, smiling sheepishly as he took his place once again at Molly's side.

'Of course it's a good one,' Jamie laughed. 'A bloody brilliant one, actually.'

'I thought you said you wouldn't be back until nearer to Yule,' said Molly, her cheeks glowing even brighter as Archie reached for her hand and kissed it.

'I couldn't stay away any longer,' he told her. 'Africa was wonderful, but it didn't have the hold on my heart that the Fens has claimed.'

'Is there something the pair of you would like to share with the rest of us?' Anna asked.

'Oh, I don't think that's necessary,' I said with a wink, 'I think we can all work out what's going on here, don't you?'

'Well, yes,' said Anna, 'but what I want to know is, how long has it been going on and why haven't you told us before?'

'We wanted it to be a surprise,' said Archie, taking the pile of flyers Molly had dropped from me and passing it back to her.

'Well, I for one am not surprised in the slightest,' I told him.

'Me neither,' said Anna.

'Nor me,' added Jamie and we all laughed.

'And what's all this?' asked Archie, as he took in the details of the Winter Wonderland his family were putting on this year. 'I know you said Dad was planning something, Moll, but this looks far more spectacular than the usual sleigh rides.'

'It's all right,' said Jamie, 'we're all on board and, actually, your arrival couldn't be better timed. We're a man down tonight so you can pick up the slack.'

I refused to allow myself to think about the man he was referring to or start wondering whether his guest was succumbing to his heavenly kisses.

'We better go and find Mum and Dad first,' said Archie. 'They've got no idea I'm back. Perhaps our long-distance love affair will surprise them,' he said to Molly.

'I wouldn't bank on it,' she smiled up at him. 'Your parents have always been pretty intuitive when it comes to matters of the heart.'

I hoped they hadn't sussed out my shifting feelings towards Gabe, especially now they had shifted a long way back again.

'Are you coming?' asked Anna, turning to me as they all headed off to find Angus, Catherine and the others.

'No,' I said, shaking my head.

'Sure?'

'Yes,' I nodded. 'I'm fine. I'm going to have a mooch around and hand out some of these. I'll meet you outside The Mermaid in time for the switch-on.'

'As long as you're sure?'

'Absolutely,' I insisted, 'now go on before you lose sight of them.'

Thanks to my previous successful and relatively stress-free trip into town to clear the air with Gavin, I felt fine on my own and enjoyed wandering through the market, handing out the flyers and making a start on some Christmas shopping. The Cherry Tree Café stall had drawn quite a crowd, but given the pretty crafts on sale and the wafting scent of Jemma's irresistible iced and festively spiced buns, that was no surprise.

'Just the person I was hoping to see!' cried out the lady herself as she spotted me picking out some pretty presents for my girlfriends.

She waited until I had paid, then steered me by the elbow to a slightly quieter spot. I had no idea what she wanted, but hadn't forgotten my commitment to the Winter Wonderland.

'Before you say anything,' I told her, 'I must give you a couple of these. I know you guys are coming along with the caravan, but would you mind putting these up on the café community board, or even in the window?'

'Of course,' she grinned, looking at them with a more interested eye than I was expecting. 'They're what I wanted to talk to you about, actually.'

'What do you mean?' I asked, looking about me to see if anyone else was close enough to overhear our conversation.

'What do you mean, *what do I mean*?' she mimicked. 'You designed these didn't you, Hayley?'

I swallowed hard and gripped the handles on my shopping bags a little tighter as my palms began to sweat.

'Designed them, drew them up and painted them,' she went on. 'That is right, isn't it?' she added with a frown when I still didn't say anything.

'Yes,' I said, my voice barely louder than a mouse's squeak. 'Yes,' I tried again, a little louder, 'I did, but how did you find out?'

'That's for me to know,' she said mysteriously, 'and you not to find out.'

'Bloody Anna,' I muttered, thinking I was really going to take her to task over this, especially as she knew how desperate I was to keep it all under wraps.

'Not Anna, actually,' said Jemma, looking back at the flyer again. 'But what I really want to know is, why would you not want anyone to know that you can do this?'

252

'Because,' I bristled, 'it isn't something I do very often. Something I haven't done for years, in fact, and I have no intention of making a habit out of it. Not a public one, anyway,' I quickly added, as my thoughts tracked back to the conservatory studio I was in no hurry to abandon, even if Gabe wouldn't be joining me in the evenings from now on. Not unless he came up with some quick and competent answers to the hundred plus questions that were whizzing about my brain, refusing to be silenced.

'But that's absurd, Hayley.' Jemma laughed. 'Don't tell me you don't enjoy it?'

I couldn't tell her that because I didn't go in for telling lies. Not anymore.

'I do enjoy it,' I said instead, 'I just choose not to do it publicly.'

'Well, I hope you change your mind about that pretty sharpish.'

'Why would I?'

'Because I would love it if you came up with some designs, in exactly the same sort of style as these,' she said, waving the flyer under my nose, 'to print on cards, stationery, mugs and cushions, all sorts of things. I want to stock and sell them in the café.'

'Be serious!' I blurted out, drawing the attention of the couple with a pushchair standing nearest.

'I am being serious,' she said, looking at me as if she really meant business. 'You have a phenomenal talent, Hayley, and more than that, a great eye for detail. The town is crying out for more local artists and craftspeople to represent the area, and I think your work would more than happily sit side by side with those who are already here. It's certainly good enough.'

I really didn't know what to say. It wasn't often that I was at a loss for words, but this was right up there with my top floored moments.

'Think about it, please,' she said, 'and in the meantime, stop hiding your light and let folk congratulate you on a beautiful job very well done.'

'Does that mean that everyone knows?' I squeaked.

My stomach squirmed as I took in the crowds and the number of people carrying flyers. Flyers designed by me, which were now out in the public arena. I mentally crossed my fingers in the hope that they would be more focused on the details of the Winter Wonderland than the person who had worked so hard to try to depict it.

'Pretty much,' she smiled, waving to Tom and her two children. 'You think about what I've said, OK?'

'OK,' I promised, 'I'll certainly give it all some thought.'

Having tucked the rest of the flyers into one of my bags, I decided against biting into my bun, despite the tempting scent of spices, now that my appetite had been well and truly curbed. I made my way over to The Mermaid, where I had agreed to meet the others for the countdown to the switch-on.

'Are you all right?' asked Anna, herself the picture of rosy-cheeked health as she tucked into a hog roast roll from Skylark Farm. 'You look a bit peaky.'

'I'm all right,' I nodded, feeling guilty for assuming that she was the one who had let my artistic cat out of the bag. 'Where are the others?'

'Jamie, Catherine and Angus are chatting to Ed, the lad from the owl sanctuary, and his mum, Mags. Apparently,' she explained, 'the boy is the brains behind the whole thing. He has a real passion for wildlife and has taken in injured and abandoned birds ever since he was a young lad.'

'I bet that's made for an interesting home life,' I smiled.

There had been a girl at school who had been mad keen on saving hedgehogs. She was always in the paper appealing for pet food. I bet birds made far more mess than the hedgehogs.

'And what about Molly and Archie? Where are they?'

'Where do you think?'

'Don't tell me they've gone back to the hall?'

'No,' said Anna, grinning. 'A taxi back to Molly's place. Apparently, that's where Archie's going to be staying over Christmas.'

'Well I never,' I laughed as I tried to imagine Archie Connelly living in Molly's incense-filled little cottage. 'I bet he heads back to the hall for his dinners though.'

Anna gave me a sideways glance and I felt a little panicked.

'Did that sound bitchy?' I gabbled. 'Because I didn't mean it to, I just meant—'

'That Molly can't cook for toffee,' said Anna, finishing my sentence. 'I know that, we all know that, even Molly, so no, you didn't sound bitchy at all.'

'What then?'

'Well,' she said, linking arms as the local radio presenter took to the stage in front of the town hall for the official Wynbridge Christmas lights switch-on, 'I was just thinking that with Jamie and I loved up and Molly and Archie tucked up in the woods, all that's left to do now is to find a man for you.'

'You know full well that I'm not in the market,' I reminded her.

'That's as may be,' she said, pulling me into her side, 'but let's see if you're still of the same opinion after the greenery gathering, shall we?'

So much for her forgetting all about our stupid bread-based bet.

After the town and trees were lit and the smoke from the fireworks had finally cleared, everyone either headed home or into the pub. As ever, The Mermaid was packed but I didn't have to worry about joining the queue because I had barely crossed the threshold before half a pint of cider was thrust into my hand.

'I saw you outside earlier,' said Gavin, 'and I had a feeling you'd end up in here.'

'You've got a bloody cheek,' said Anna, stepping between us, trying to prise the glass from my hand.

She looked absolutely furious, as well she might, given that I hadn't let her or anyone else at the hall know that I had met Gavin in secret and set a few things straight. Had I relinquished my grip on the glass, I was certain my ex would have ended up wearing its contents.

Gavin looked at me and shrugged his shoulders.

'It's fine,' I told Anna, putting down my bags and pulling the glass free. 'We're fine,' I added. 'I should have told you before, but we've sorted things out. Well, enough to be civil to one another at least.'

'Why didn't you say anything?' she frowned.

'Because I didn't think it would matter,' I said simply.

'And it's nothing to do with you,' muttered Gavin as he followed me away from the queuing hordes.

'That's not fair,' I said over my shoulder. 'She's my friend and she cares about me, so really it's everything to do with her.'

I felt bad for Anna and knew that I would have to apologise before bedtime.

'So why didn't you tell her we were talking again?' asked Gavin as we wedged ourselves into a corner.

I didn't feel comfortable being in such close proximity to him, especially with so many pairs of curious eyes trained on us, but there was barely room to breathe let alone cordon off any personal space.

'None of your business,' I shot back and Gavin laughed.

'Seen much of your mum and dad since you moved?'

'I haven't seen them at all,' I told him, 'I've been too busy at the hall.'

Gavin nodded, took a pull at his pint then reached down and lifted one of the flyers out of my bag.

'Good this, isn't it?' he said, his eyes scanning the information.

'Should be,' I agreed, trying not to think of him and his mates rocking up to see Santa and finding me in the dreaded elf outfit I just knew Angus had tucked away somewhere for me.

'I meant this,' said Gavin, waving the paper, 'although the weekend sounds like fun too.'

I narrowed my eyes and wondered if he had been the one to spill the beans. Surely not.

'Can we expect the pleasure of your company at the Winter Wonderland then?' asked Anna, who had managed to get served and fight her way through the crowd to us in record time.

Her tone was just bordering on the right side of civil, which I was sure was for my benefit rather than Gavin's.

'Perhaps,' he smiled, turning his blue eyes on her. 'I know my sister's little 'uns would love it.'

That was a marked improvement on the thought of him descending with his scaffolding crew.

Anna looked at me and raised her eyebrows.

'Don't look so surprised,' said Gavin, giving her a nudge when he spotted the look. 'I'm a great uncle. I often take the girls out. I'll have you know, I take my family responsibilities very seriously.'

Anna didn't look all that convinced.

'Well,' she said primly, 'it's good to know there are some things in life that you take seriously.'

Gavin's hand flew to his heart.

'Ouch,' he yelped, 'you got me.'

A smile tugged at the corners of Anna's mouth as I rolled my eyes.

'Hayley knows that I'm sorry, Anna,' Gavin went on, sensing her frostiness towards him was melting a little. 'So can we at least try to get along?'

'Gavin,' said Jamie, catching us up before Anna had a chance to answer. 'I thought I heard your voice.'

That was an outright lie. It was so noisy in the pub it was impossible to distinguish one voice from another. My friend's eyes flicked to me and I did my best to let him know that the situation was fine. No fisticuffs required.

'I just wanted to congratulate Hayley on a job well done,' Gavin said. 'I'll be off in a minute.'

'What's that supposed to mean?' I asked.

'This,' he said, waving the flyer about again. 'It's one of your designs, isn't it?'

I stood rooted to the spot, opening and closing my mouth like a fish out of water. Anna burst out laughing.

'My god,' she said, 'you should see the look on your face, Hayley.'

'It is yours, isn't it?' Gavin asked me again.

'She tried to tell us,' said Anna, when it became clear that I was keeping my lips sealed, 'that she wasn't going to do it anymore because every time she did, something in her life went wrong.'

'But you convinced her to change her mind?' smiled Gavin, making Anna blush.

'I was part of the posse who cajoled her into having another go after the pair of you parted company, yes,' she confirmed, bobbing her head.

How did he do that? Not ten minutes ago she had been all set to drown him in cider and now she was sounding almost coquettish. It was one heck of a skill.

'But I'm done,' I said, finally finding my voice. 'I don't think I'll carry on.'

'You need to go and find Jemma,' said Gavin with a grin. 'If you have a chat with her, you might just find yourself being cajoled all over again!'

There was no way I was going to tell him in front of the others that I'd already seen her, but at least I now knew who had let my artistic cat out of the bag.

Chapter 21

I was pulled out of my slumber ridiculously early the next morning, ridiculously early for a Sunday, anyway.

'Hayley,' came Dorothy's voice through my bedroom door. 'Are you awake?'

I ignored her, hoping she would go away, but it was no good. My manners got the better of me.

'A bit,' I groaned, pulling the eiderdown further up the bed and over my head.

The Sunday lie-in was sacrosanct as far as I was concerned, but apparently my roommate hadn't received the memo. I heard the door knob being turned and knew that I was done for. There was no way I would be able to go back to sleep now.

'You haven't forgotten, have you?'

'I think I might have,' I replied, peeping over the top of the covers and squinting as the light from the sitting room shone like a beacon across my bed.

I had no idea what it was that I was supposed to have remembered, but that was probably because of the amount of local cider I'd drunk at the post switch-on celebration in the pub.

'It's stir-up Sunday,' said Dorothy. 'Today's the day I make the puddings and everyone has a hand in giving them a stir and making a wish.'

'Oh, yeah,' I croaked, wondering why she had to start so early. 'Of course.'

Not surprisingly, stir-up Sunday wasn't a tradition kept in my childhood home. My mother had been all about the microwave when it came to heating the sweet post-turkey pud.

'Well, come on then,' said Dorothy, tugging at the corner of the blankets, 'up and at 'em or you'll miss your turn.'

'Don't wait for me,' I told her as I turned over and hunkered back down. 'I haven't got anything to wish for this year.'

'Now, I don't believe that,' she laughed, flicking on my bedside lamp before she left, 'I don't believe that at all.'

I wasn't the only one looking a little bleary-eyed around the breakfast table, but the heady aroma wafting from the huge bowl of brandy-infused mixed fruit Dorothy was attending to was enough to make me feel tipsy all over again.

'I know I haven't been here for all that many switch-ons,' said Anna, bouncing into her seat and handing her other half a box of paracetamol and a glass of water, 'but that was definitely my favourite so far.'

It had been a good night, you only had to look at Jamie's bloodshot eyes to see that, but Little Miss Designated Driver was rather too perky for my liking.

'How's your head this morning, Hayley?' She beamed, taking back the box from Jamie, popping out two pills for him and then sliding the packet over to me.

'Fine,' I said, pushing the box back. 'Nothing a cup of tea and a bacon butty won't set to rights, anyway.'

'I'm afraid you'll have to wait for the bacon,' said Dorothy, 'but the pot's fresh.'

'I'll do breakfast this morning,' said Anna, jumping back up and pecking Dorothy on the cheek, 'you concentrate on the puds.'

To my amazement our beloved cook didn't object, and in no time at all Anna set down platefuls of fried breakfast for us to feast on.

'I have to say I was surprised to see you three drinking with Gavin of all people last night,' said Mick, who had also been tempted from his bed to join us.

'Yes,' said Jamie, who appeared to be feeling ever so slightly more human now he had a plate of food in front of him, 'how did that happen, Hayley? Have you really made up with him?'

Dorothy tutted and shook her grey head.

'It wasn't some playground spat they had,' she reminded him. 'The blaggard broke her heart.'

'You make him sound like some love rat from a Jane Austen novel,' frowned Anna as she thoughtfully buttered her toast. 'Which is exactly what he is, isn't he?' She gasped, as if only remembering the truth now. 'So yes, Hayley, how exactly did we end up spending the evening with him?'

She knew that Gavin and I had met and cleared the air, but she was obviously as puzzled about his unique ability to make a woman forgive and forget as I was, although, in my case, I wasn't going to forget what he had done in a hurry. His abhorrent behaviour had ensured I was sworn off all serious relationships with men. Or at least I was supposed to be. The unforgettable kiss with Gabe and the feelings the mere thought of him aroused had made my new plan tough to stick to.

'Although,' she went on before I attempted to frame an answer, 'I can't help but notice how he has made some sort of effort to make amends for his behaviour.'

Jamie nodded in agreement and attacked his chipolatas with gusto.

'And how do you work that one out?' scowled Mick.

'Well, if it wasn't for him,' chewed Jamie, pointing his loaded fork towards one of the flyers we hadn't handed out, 'then no one would be any the wiser that it was Hayley who'd designed these.'

'But she didn't want anyone to know,' said Mick exasperatedly, 'so I fail to see how him letting it slip has led to his redemption.'

'Because he happened to tell Jemma,' I explained, picking up the thread, 'and now she's got it in her head that I can come up with some unique designs to print on mugs and cushions to sell at the café.'

Mick raised his eyebrows and looked at the flyer again.

'And stationery,' chipped in Anna. 'You said she mentioned stationery as well.'

'She's completely bonkers,' I continued, shaking my head.

I didn't add that I had spent half the night staring at the ceiling imagining what it would actually feel like to create something shop-worthy and then seeing it sitting on the café shelf, before being selected, paid for and taken away to be displayed and treasured.

To say it was the stuff of dreams didn't even come close. But it was just a pipe dream, wasn't it? Something to be fantasised about in the wee hours and then set aside when it was time to get up and start vacuuming again.

'So, you aren't going to do it, then?' asked Jamie, sounding disappointed.

'You could start really small,' said Anna. 'Just a couple of designs on one sort of product to begin with to see how they go.'

'That's a good idea in theory, but you all seem to be forgetting,' I reminded them, 'that I already have a job. One that I'm really rather fond of.'

'But that doesn't mean that you can't combine it with another,' said Catherine.

I hadn't heard her enter the kitchen. The last thing I wanted was for her to think I was planning to hand in my notice, especially after I had only just moved in. I wasn't going to do anything that would jeopardise living at Wynthorpe Hall.

'I've just been reading an article about women who manage to combine day jobs with bespoke craft businesses,' she said, laying the most recent issue of *Country Living* magazine down on the table.

I looked at the competent women smiling out of the pages. Women with style, substance and business acumen, all proudly showing off their accomplishments.

'But what you're *also* forgetting,' I sighed, 'is that I'm Hayley Hurren from Wynbridge. The woman who put her life on hold because of her teenage mistake. How would my tight tops and skinny jeans look amongst this lot? These women are in a different league to me.'

'Nonsense,' said Catherine. 'It doesn't matter what sort of clothes you wear. And I can't see a single paragraph on any of these pages that spells out the mistakes these women may or may not have made in their lives. What happened in their pasts may even define their current successes, but we don't need to know that, do we? This feature is all about utilising skills, seeking out opportunities and biting the bullet.'

'And half of that is done for you already,' said Anna. 'Here are the skills,' she said, pointing at the flyer.

'And Jemma's giving you the opportunity,' said Jamie.

'Now all you have to do,' added Mick, with a grin, 'is bite the bullet.'

He seemed to have forgotten his loathing of my ex-fiancé and, as one, they all began to laugh, but I wasn't sure I could see the funny side of this particular situation.

'Christmas has come early for you this year, my dear,' chuckled Dorothy.

They all looked and sounded so sure and I found myself almost wishing that my ambition for myself could match theirs. I wondered what I looked like through their eyes, because I couldn't be the scared and vulnerable version of myself that I envisaged.

'Now,' Dorothy continued, thrusting her favourite wooden spoon in my direction. 'I know you said you have absolutely nothing to wish for, but you can have the first stir, Hayley. Dig deep,' she added, with a wink, 'and see if you can think of something after all.'

If there was only one good thing to come out of my morning spent daydreaming about the possibilities of what Jemma had suggested, it was that it took my mind off wondering what Gabe and his mystery visitor were up to in Gatekeeper's Cottage. Ordinarily, when faced with a conundrum I couldn't puzzle out for myself, I would have headed to see Molly, but as neither she nor Archie had put in an appearance during breakfast, I thought it best to leave them to it. Gooseberry had never been my favourite fruit.

After helping Dorothy with the puddings, which had put us all very definitely in the mood for Christmas, and tidying my room, I gravitated towards the conservatory and flicked through my sketchbooks wondering if I already had something suitable I could use to turn into a design, should

I choose to take Jemma up on her offer, which I probably wouldn't.

'Nothing,' I muttered out loud, piling them all back up again.

'Perhaps you should come up with something brand new,' suggested Angus, who happened to be passing.

'Angus,' I gasped, 'you made me jump.'

'Sorry,' he smiled. 'You'd think that would be impossible with my bulk, but it happens quite a lot.'

'That's because you're always up to mischief,' I told him. 'You've learned how to tread lightly so you don't get caught.'

His eyes crinkled at the corners as he grinned and came further into the room.

'It's worked out all right in here for you, hasn't it?' he said, looking about him.

'More than all right,' I told him. 'I absolutely love it.'

He crossed the room and looked out of the window into the wintery garden.

'I had once thought about using this space myself,' he told me, 'I thought it would make an ideal hidey hole, but I hadn't bargained on Catherine being able to keep an eye on me through all this glass. So, I moved my stuff upstairs.'

Given the amount of 'stuff' he had snaffled away over the years it was a miracle the floor hadn't given way.

'Anna told me about Jemma's suggestion,' he continued, making himself comfortable in the chair I had consigned to Gabe. 'And that it was Gavin who got the ball rolling.'

'I know,' I said. 'His bad behaviour seems to be as

inexhaustible as yours, Angus. Although, on a completely different level, of course,' I quickly added.

'Actually, I rather thought this was one of his more enlightened misdemeanours,' said Angus. 'I hope you're going to give the matter some serious thought, Hayley. This could be the beginning of a whole new career for you.'

'But I love working here,' I told him. 'I love my job at the hall, working with the antiques and looking after the paintings.'

'So, do both,' he said, clapping his hands together as if the suggestion was a *fait accompli* rather than something that warranted months of careful consideration. 'What are you so afraid of?'

'Nothing,' I pouted, 'other than failing and making a fool of myself.'

'Oh, well,' he said, levering himself back out of the chair, 'if that's all that's stopping you.'

'I'm being serious,' I swallowed. 'I've made mistakes before – very public ones – and I have no desire to repeat the experience.'

'Well, in that case,' he said, 'you better work your butt off to make sure you get this right, hadn't you?'

I didn't answer. Was it really possible that it could be as simple as he was suggesting?

'You know,' he continued, 'there's absolutely nothing more infuriating than those folks who stumble through life wondering "what if". Don't become one of those people, will you, Hayley? Your job here is safe, the hall is your home and if you're wondering what to draw then take inspiration from the things around you. The hall and the grounds are at your disposal, my dear.'

'Thank you, Angus,' I swallowed as the distant sound of Dorothy banging the dinner gong reached my ears. 'For everything.'

There was even more food than usual to go around that dinnertime, which was wonderful if you were a fan of Dorothy's mouth-watering Yorkshire puddings and melt-in-the-mouth beef brisket, but I can't say I liked seeing empty chairs around the table. Archie and Molly were no-shows and there was no sign of Gabe or Bran either. I guessed their absence was even more notable because of the amount of space the pair of them took up, and it made me realise just how quickly I had got used to having them around.

'I thought Gabe might join us this evening,' said Dorothy, looking at the empty spots herself. 'I'll have to put his dinner on a plate in the warming oven.'

Unlike my mother, Dorothy didn't believe in microwaves.

'I wouldn't bother,' I told her. 'He's probably still got company, so I doubt he'll be over at all.'

'No,' corrected Mick, helping himself to more roast potatoes from the 'extras' dish in the middle of the table. 'He *had* company. That fancy car has gone, so I'm guessing his visitor has gone with it.'

'Do we know who the visitor was?' asked Anna.

I shrugged and kept my eyes focused on my plate.

'Some woman or other,' said Mick. 'She turned up when we were heading to town Saturday night.'

'A woman?' said Anna, her eyebrows shooting up. 'You never said it was a woman. Before you just said he had company, Mick.'

'Does it matter?' Mick shrugged. 'Man, woman, whatever.'

'Well, no,' said Anna, her eyes flicking to me the second I dared to look up. 'I suppose not.'

'Do you know who this mystery visitor of Gabe's was?' Anna asked me as we joined forces to clear away the dishes after pudding.

'No,' I said lightly, 'of course not. Why would I?'

'Well, you two seem pretty thick these days,' she went on in a loaded undertone, 'I thought he might have mentioned something about her to you.'

'No,' I told her. 'Not a word.'

I didn't add that he had been too busy kissing me and turning my emotions to mush to explain anything, just hours before he was ushering her in.

'Well,' said Anna again, 'not to worry. You'll just have to give it all you've got at the greenery gathering. I'm sure you'll kick this rival for his affections into touch.'

'Anna,' I said sternly, 'I don't know what you think is going on between me and Gabe, but you've got it all wrong.'

It had to be worth a shot even if she didn't look convinced.

'Honestly,' I told her, 'we've got a bit pally because we moved in at the same time, but he's no friendlier to me than he is to you or Molly or even Jamie. Surely you've seen that for yourself?'

'Perhaps,' she shrugged, 'but you're forgetting one important thing.'

'Which is?'

'Molly, Jamie and I are spoken for, and you most definitely are not.'

Chapter 22

The weather took a wintery turn during the last week of November, and even though it wasn't yet time to hang the massive advent calendar that Angus had imported from the US a couple of Christmases before, that didn't stop him from humming carols and quoting Dickens at every opportunity.

There had been an unprecedented amount of interest in the Winter Wonderland as word spread like wildfire through Wynbridge, and Jamie had already made a return trip to town to distribute more flyers to various businesses as well as the local schools and the library.

The week felt very much like the calm before the storm and we all took advantage of the lull to write out our cards, shop online and even start wrapping. If experience had taught us anything, it was that, once December dawned, it would be all hands to the pumps and full steam ahead.

The only person on the team who seemed immune to the sudden upsurge in festivity was Gabe. His noticeable absence from both the kitchen and my studio in the evenings meant that we were all a little concerned about him. But Jamie assured us he was just getting his work done, and Molly, when she could tear herself away from Archie, was certain he was fine, even though she refused to disclose what the pair of them had been discussing the morning I walked in on their cosy chat. I was sure it had a bearing on the situation, but she refused to elaborate.

When I wasn't sorting out Christmas presents, polishing the hall to perfection or helping Dorothy come up with sweet treat ideas for the Winter Wonderland, I took the time to think about some designs I could present to Jemma.

I was under no illusion that combining my work and my passion would be anywhere near as straightforward as the Connelly clan had suggested, and I knew I would probably never even get around to showing Jemma what I had come up with. Nonetheless, it was fun to imagine myself in the role of a bona fide artist, and I took pride in designing things I thought she might like.

A bolshie robin proved the perfect first subject and he was soon joined by a quirky blue tit. Emphasising the more interesting aspects of their personalities gave them added character, and as I quietly worked away I could easily imagine the drawings gracing mugs and egg cups and adorning a breakfast table or two.

Following on from the designs I had used on the Winter Wonderland advertising and map – complete with Snowflake Trail – my style was ever-changing, and although the subjects were nothing like those that had inspired me at school, I very much liked this new direction.

'Anyone at home?'

I hurriedly stuffed my papers together and grabbed the magazine closest to hand.

'Gavin,' I gulped, 'what on earth are you doing here?'

He was the last person I expected to slip into the conservatory via the door that accessed the garden. Gabe was the only person who used that particular entrance as a rule and I can't deny there was a definite flicker of disappointment that it wasn't him. My evenings, although productive, just weren't the same without him and Bran, and my sketches of the pair were as yet unfinished.

'Don't worry,' smiled Gavin. 'I'm not trespassing. Jamie asked me to come and pick up a couple of scaffolding brackets that the lads missed when they came to take away the tower.'

'Right,' I said, flicking through the pages of the latest issue of *Heat*, but not really taking in what I was looking at. 'I see.'

'And Angus said I'd find you in here,' Gavin elaborated. 'This is a bit of all right, isn't it?' he added, looking around and taking in the space I had been slowly converting into my own.

I saw him eyeing up the fairy lights around the book case. Gabe had helped me set those up. He hadn't even needed to stand on tip toe to tuck them over the top.

'I suppose you could say that,' I replied.

'No wonder you produced something so magnificent for the flyers,' he smiled. 'With a space like this to work in I'm sure you can't help but feel creative.'

He was right, of course. Even when the weather was too gloomy to venture out, the studio provided inspiration enough, and the view into and across the gardens was a definite bonus.

'Was there any reason in particular why Angus told you where to find me?'

I hoped he wasn't going to make a habit of popping up when I least expected him. I was willing to be civil when our paths happened to cross, but I wasn't looking to entwine them on purpose.

'There was, actually,' he nodded. 'I have a message for you, but what's all this?'

Without asking, he started tugging at the papers under my magazine and unearthed the characterful bird designs I had been working on.

'Never you mind,' I said, slapping his hand away and moving the papers out of his reach.

'Are they the ideas for Jemma?' He grinned.

'No,' I lied, turning beetroot.

'Well, you better get a move on with some,' he said, suddenly serious, 'because that's who the message is from. She wants to know when you'll have something ready for her to look at.'

I didn't say anything, but I could feel my internal thermostat reacting.

'You aren't going to be able to wriggle out of this one, you know, Hayley. She means business.'

'And it's all your fault,' I snapped, annoyed that he seemed to have adopted the role of artist's agent. 'Had you not blabbed she never would have known.'

'And that would have been a good thing, would it?' he questioned.

'Yes,' I glowered, 'that would have been perfect.'

I came out from behind the table and dumped myself down in Gabe's chair. I had a horrible feeling that I might burst into tears.

'I know you think we're all being pushy,' Gavin said, his tone softer, 'but it's only because we care about you.'

'Well, you certainly had a funny way of showing it when we were a couple,' I reminded him.

'Oh, no,' he said, shaking his head. 'I'm not letting you get away with that.'

'But it's true!'

'Of course, it's true,' he shot back, 'but what I mean is I'm not going to let you turn this conversation into an argument about what an arsehole I was to you, just so you can avoid talking about . . .'

'All right, all right,' I conceded.

The clever sod had seen straight through my ruse and I found myself starting to smile.

'So,' he said, again tugging at the pile of papers on the table. 'Are these some new designs or not?'

Resignedly, I got up and went to show him.

'They are,' I admitted, 'but they're not very good. Just doodles, really. I haven't got anything anywhere near decent enough to even think about showing Jemma.'

Gavin looked with interest at my collection of distinctive birds, including the outline of a plump little wren that I had spotted bobbing along the top of the moss-covered wall just outside the conservatory door earlier that afternoon.

'You know,' he said, smiling as he took in the aloof expression I had given the mighty round robin, 'that day in the spring when you came out to me and the lads with a tray of drinks and toast, the first thing I remembered about you was that you were the girl who had been so good at art at school.'

'Not that I'd ended up pregnant?' I swallowed.

'No,' he said vehemently, 'that was the others, not me. What I remembered was that you were a really cracking artist, and I just wish there was a way of proving to you that you still are. Why is it that you refuse to see the value in what you can do, Hayley?'

'I don't know,' I told him. 'I really don't, but part of me is beginning to wish that I could see what you guys see.'

'If only you could believe in yourself, you'd be all set.'

I nodded and sighed and he gave me a nudge.

'This one,' he said, holding up the robin who really did think he was cock of the hoop, 'is my favourite.'

I wasn't at all surprised.

'I want you to promise me that when you come to town to show Jemma these—'

I started to protest, but he just carried on.

'When you get to this one,' he grinned, 'you'll tell her that he's called Gavin, OK?'

We both laughed and carried on looking at the others, trying to come up with names that would best fit the rest of the gang.

We were still looking when there was a knock on the garden door.

'Come in!' I called without turning around, assuming it was Angus, coming to see if his directions had led Gavin to me. 'It's open.'

Gavin looked up and grinned.

'All right?' he asked.

That wasn't how he would address Angus.

'Gabe,' I faltered, 'come in.'

'No,' he said, backing off before he was even properly over the threshold and confusing Bran, who had headed straight for his familiar spot on the mat, in the process. 'You're all right. I didn't realise you had company.'

'I haven't,' I stammered. 'He isn't.'

Gavin looked at me and raised his eyebrows, and Gabe's expression was thunderous. He looked very Heathcliff-like, in full menace mode.

'Gavin was just leaving,' I tried again.

'Was I?' Gavin frowned. 'What, right this instant?'

'He had a message for me from Jemma, and yes,' I added, shoving my ex towards the door that would take him back through the hall and swiftly away from Gabe, 'you were.'

'Well, looks like I'm off then,' he laughed. 'What do you want me to tell Jemma?'

'Anything,' I said, 'whatever you like.'

'Great!' he gushed. 'In that case, I'll tell her to expect you by the end of the week.'

'No,' I said, grabbing his arm and pulling him back, 'I didn't mean that.'

'Look,' said Gabe, 'you two clearly have stuff to discuss, so I'll go.'

'No,' I said, spinning around to face him again and cursing the fact that he had the worst possible timing in the world. Yes, I might have been feeling miffed about his mystery female visitor, but I still wanted to be his friend, and his reaction to finding me cosied up in the conservatory, with Gavin of all people, was clearly jeopardising that. 'Please don't go,' I insisted, but he had already left.

Gavin knew his behaviour hadn't been the best, again, and made a point of calling the hall to apologise the very next day.

'I've told Jemma all about your little flock,' he told me, 'and she's really keen to meet them. She asked if you could go around after she closes the café on Saturday. Is that all right?'

I was fairly certain he was trying to make amends, but, for the life of me, I still couldn't remember when I had appointed Gavin Garford as my agent. That said, if he hadn't stepped in and made a nuisance of himself I probably would have never done anything about Jemma's request.

'I suppose,' I said uncertainly.

'I'll come and pick you up if you like,' he carried on. 'Then we could go for a drink in the pub afterwards.'

'No,' I quickly cut in. That really was a step too far. 'Thanks, but you're all right. I can get myself to town.'

'Sure?'

'Sure.'

'OK then,' he said, 'but if you have a minute after, do come to the pub and tell me how it went, won't you?'

'If I have time,' I replied, feeling fairly certain that I wouldn't.

'See you Saturday, then.'

'Before you go,' I said hurriedly.

'Yeah?'

'Tell me, why hasn't Jemma called to set this up herself?'

'She said she felt bad about pressurising you at the switch-on,' he explained, 'and I don't think she wants to push her luck. When she found out we were speaking again she asked if I'd act as a sort of go-between.'

I still couldn't really believe that we were talking again and I wouldn't have put it past him somehow to ensure he was down to receive a percentage of any future profits. Not that there were going to be any, because nothing was really going to come of the venture. Jemma would look at my portfolio of little birds and realise she was barking up the wrong tree, and that would be the end of it.

'Because you have absolutely no reservations about exerting a bit of pressure, do you?' I responded.

'Oh, Hayley,' Gavin laughed, 'you know me so well.'

Chapter 23

It wasn't usual for the dinner gong to echo through the hall to announce breakfast, but then December the first wasn't a usual day, and actually it wasn't ringing to summon us to our cereal bowls at all.

'Come on, come on!' cried Angus, ushering us all into the kitchen.

'Morning, Molly,' I yawned. 'I wasn't expecting to see you here so bright and early.'

Truth be told, I wasn't expecting to see her at all. She and Archie were still proving hard to track down. Apparently, they had a lot of catching up to do and plenty of ground to make up, what with him having been away for so long.

'I stayed over,' she whispered, tucking her wild hair behind her ears and readjusting the neckline of her rainbow-patterned kaftan.

'I insisted,' said Angus. 'I wanted everyone together this morning.'

Not satisfied with a simple advent calendar of the chocolate variety, Angus, no doubt ably assisted by Mick, had
re-hung the elaborate wooden affair he favoured, which had
a roomy drawer for every day, and which he took great pains
to fill with unique gifts for us all.

'Morning,' rumbled a deep voice, making us all jump.

'Gabe,' beamed Angus, 'I'm so pleased you could make it.
We've missed you around the table this week.'

'Yes, I'm sorry about that,' he awkwardly began to explain,
but Jamie cut him off.

'No need to apologise, mate,' he said, slapping his
friend firmly on the back, making him wince. 'You're
here now.'

I wondered if Gabe had been unwell. He certainly looked
under the weather, with dark circles beneath his eyes and his
beard, which clearly hadn't seen a brush in days, was rather
unkempt. It had never been the sort of glossy, groomed affair
favoured by the hipster types in town, but it wasn't usually
quite so Wildman of Wynthorpe, either.

I couldn't decide whether it was more likely that his untidy
appearance had anything to do with the fallout after our kiss
and his subsequent annoyance at finding me in the studio
with Gavin, or if it was the after effects of entertaining his
mystery lady caller?

'So,' said Angus, clapping his hands together and refocus-
ing our attention, mine included. 'Most of you know how
this works, don't you?'

'Yes,' we all chorused.

'It's an advent calendar, Dad,' said Archie, who would clearly rather have been back in bed, 'not rocket science.'

'I know, I know,' grinned Angus, 'so let's see who's first up, shall we?'

I couldn't believe it when he pointed to Gabe and then me.

'I thought it only fair that we should start with the two newest housemates,' he said, beckoning us forward.

'I wasn't expecting this,' Gabe began, looking uncertain. 'I don't even live in the hall.'

'Just go with it,' I told him. 'In case you hadn't worked it out yet, everyone is treated like family, here. We're all included and if you take the time to join in, you might find you actually enjoy it.'

He looked at me and nodded, and I hoped he had the sense to realise that I wasn't just talking about the advent calendar. He had made a great start when he moved in, *we* had made a great start, but since his mystery visitor and my unexpected one, things had gone decidedly downhill.

'Point taken,' he smiled, suddenly looking far more like the Gabe I had gotten to know.

'OK,' said Angus impatiently, 'that's enough faffing. Just open the drawer.'

Some of the drawers were larger than others and the one Gabe and I had been assigned was one of the biggest. There was a parcel and envelope for me and a parcel for Gabe, with another in a bag that Angus whipped out from under the table.

'Technically this is cheating,' Angus told us as he handed

Gabe the bag, 'because the presents should all fit in the drawer, but it's my game, so I'm making an exception.'

We all laughed and everyone crowded around to see what Gabe and I had got. I opened my envelope first and found a voucher inside for Hardy's in town.

'I know vouchers aren't that exciting,' Angus said uncertainly, 'but I would imagine you've probably got lots of odd bits and pieces for the studio you need to stock up on, so is that all right?'

'Hardy's is my favourite place to shop,' I said, jumping up to plant a kiss on his whiskery cheek, 'thank you so much, Angus. I know exactly what I'm going to buy with this.'

'Well,' he chuckled, 'before you decide, you better open your present. I'm fairly certain you didn't buy anything like these when you were last there, but the lovely Francesca told me she would be happy to exchange them for something else if they aren't quite right.'

I sat back down and picked up the present that accompanied the voucher. It was very light and I turned it over in my hands wondering what could be inside.

'Come on,' encouraged Archie, 'just get on with it.'

I tore into the paper and felt my breath catch in my throat.

'Oh, Angus,' I gasped as everyone crowded closer again, 'this is too much.'

'My game, remember,' he beamed, looking well pleased. 'So, I get to choose what to give.'

'But—'

'The special case will keep them safe if you want to paint

outside,' he interrupted. 'That's why I went for this particular set.'

I carefully turned them over in my hands. They were beautiful watercolour brushes in a variety of sizes. The brand name wasn't lost on me and I knew they would have cost a small fortune. If I needed confirmation that he thought my talents were worth investing in, then my generous employer had just supplied it.

'Thank you,' I nodded, 'thank you so much, Angus.'

'Brushes?' questioned Mick, sounding as puzzled as everyone else looked. 'I thought you had brushes.'

'I have,' I swallowed, 'dozens, but absolutely none of them are anything like these.'

Next it was Gabe's turn. His face turned bright red as he tore into his own parcel. Clearly, he wasn't used to this kind of pre-breakfast ceremony, but he'd soon settle into it.

'Crikey,' he gasped, when he finally worked his way through the wrapping and a thick layer of bubble wrap. 'Wow.'

'What are they?' I asked.

'Chisels,' he croaked. 'Wood-carving chisels.'

'They belonged to my great grandfather,' said Angus as he watched Gabe running his hands over the handles. 'I thought I might learn how to use them myself one day so I hung on to them. However, my skills are still woefully lacking and as we now have such a talented woodsman in our midst, I thought I'd pass them on.'

'They're beautiful, Angus, but I can't accept them,' said Gabe softly. 'Surely they should stay in the family.'

'You still don't get it, do you?' said Anna kindly. 'You are family, Gabe. We all are.'

He didn't say anything else, but began opening the other parcel, which was a leather pouch, worn and soft with age, with a little pocket for each of the chisels.

'These are truly wonderful,' he eventually said, 'thank you so much, Angus. I really don't know what else to say.'

'Just promise me you'll make use of them,' said Angus. 'That's all I ask.'

'I certainly will,' smiled Gabe, still looking at the set.

I couldn't help wishing he'd look at me like that.

'They all need sharpening and some rubber hose will protect the blades when they're not in use,' he said to no one in particular.

Clearly, he knew his stuff when it came to chisel maintenance. Angus looked thrilled.

'I wonder whose turn it will be tomorrow,' said Dorothy, wistfully looking at the calendar and no doubt imagining the delights hidden in its drawers.

'No peeking,' said Angus sternly. 'I'll know if anyone's been having a crafty look.'

We all laughed and settled down together for breakfast.

Before Gabe headed back to Gatekeeper's Cottage, he mentioned that he would be driving into Wynbridge in the afternoon and asked if anyone needed anything picking up. I told him I wasn't in need of a collection service, but if he wouldn't mind giving me a lift in I'd very much appreciate it.

'Off to spend that voucher, are you?' he smiled, sounding very much like his old self.

'Something like that,' I played along, trying to match his comfortable tone and not think about the last time we were alone together.

What a godsend that timely gift from Angus was. Popping to town on the pretence of spending it was the perfect cover for my meeting with Jemma, not that having a cover story was going to stop me getting the jitters, but it definitely helped.

'Are you still decided on what you're going to spend it on?' Gabe asked as we set off and I tucked my envelope full of drawings into the footwell, hoping he wouldn't offer to post them.

'Pretty much,' I nodded. 'And I thought I might pop into the electrical store and pick up a radio for the studio.'

It was a cunning way in, but provided an opening into the potentially awkward conversation nonetheless.

'I thought you preferred to keep things quiet when you're working.'

'I do,' I agreed, 'but there's quiet and then there's complete silence.'

He nodded, but kept his eyes fixed on negotiating the potholes along the drive.

'I'd kind of got used to Bran snoring next to me in the evenings and—'

'Yeah,' he cut in, 'I'm sorry I haven't been around much.'

'Much?'

'All right, at all.'

'One searing fireside encounter,' I went on, trying to sound more like the old Hayley than I felt and not mention his other cottage companion, 'and then I don't see you for dust. None of us have,' I added, so that he didn't think this was all about *me* missing him. The others had, after all, commented on his absences as well.

'I know,' he said, 'I'm sorry. I've had a lot on my mind this week.'

'Such as?'

'Just stuff,' he said, looking both ways before he pulled out on to the road.

'Stuff?'

'Yeah, you know, stuff. Things to mull over.'

'Would you care to elaborate?'

'No,' he said, sounding as gruff as a Billy goat, 'not really, but how about you? I have to say I was rather surprised to find you with Gavin.'

'Were you?' I gasped, 'you didn't let it show!'

'All right, Little Miss Sarky,' he tutted. 'Let's talk about something else, shall we?'

Clearly our kiss wasn't up for discussion and neither was the visitor that I was now sure he didn't realise I knew existed, and I certainly wasn't going to talk about Gavin and me because there was nothing to say.

'How are your reindeer kits coming on?' I asked instead.

We spent the rest of the journey avoiding intimate chat and talked about the Winter Wonderland and the events in town that would precede it. I couldn't help thinking Gabe sounded a little hesitant when I reminded him about the more family orientated events that would soon be happening, but we both agreed that we needed to join forces to set up The Snowflake Trail so that, I suppose, was a reconciliation of sorts. Not that we'd really been properly estranged, but things had gotten awkward for a while and it felt good to be back on a more even keel.

'I can hang about to give you a lift home if you like?' he offered once he had parked in town.

'No, don't worry,' I told him. 'I can manage to get back. I might pop into the Cherry Tree Café for an early dinner so I'll make my own way home after that, but thanks.'

'Fair enough,' he smiled, looking pointedly at the envelope now tucked under my arm.

I wondered if he knew what I had really come to town to do, but I didn't risk asking. I was nervous enough already without the pressure of anyone else, other than Gavin that is, knowing why I was really heading to the café.

'I'll see you later then,' he said, turning tail and heading towards the hardware store, Bran, as ever, hot on his heels.

'Does that mean you'll come to the studio tonight?'

'Maybe,' he grinned. 'I'll see how I feel.'

'Right,' said Jemma as she switched the café sign from open to closed. 'Let's see what you've got.'

'And don't look so worried,' added Lizzie, who I hadn't been expecting to hang about. 'You look like you're going to throw up.'

'I *feel* like I'm going to throw up,' I told her.

'Well, take a moment,' said Jemma, 'and I'll be back in a sec.'

My hands were shaking as I tore open the top of the envelope and slid the few sheets of paper out on to the table. This afternoon had been the longest of my life. I had spent my voucher from Angus, listening to Francesca as I wandered around Hardy's aisles, selecting the things I wanted, and she had told me how excited Angus had been to pick out the brushes. I then took a trip to the library, before milling about the market until it was time to call at the café. I'd gone to call a taxi to take me home at least half a dozen times, but here I was, about to do what I had thought was the impossible and show Jemma the designs I had come up with.

'Here,' said Jemma, putting down a plate and pulling out a chair. 'Sit and eat this. You'll feel better for it.'

'What is it?' I asked, gratefully sitting down.

'Cinnamon toast,' smiled Lizzie. 'It's back on the menu for December.'

'It's delicious,' I said, taking a tentative bite and discovering it tasted familiar.

'Thanks,' said Jemma. 'Dorothy gave me the recipe.'

I spluttered, almost spraying my work with half-chewed crumbs.

'Good god,' I gasped.

'I know,' Jemma laughed.

Not that I really needed confirmation, I realised, as I took a sip of the water Lizzie had rushed off to get when I had started choking, but I was certainly talking to the right person if I did want to do something with my designs. It was unheard of for Dorothy to share any of her recipes with anyone, so she must have considered Jemma trustworthy in the extreme.

'So,' she said again, 'let's see what you've got.'

I forced down another half a round of the subtly spiced toast as the two friends silently scrutinised my collection of feathered friends.

'I wouldn't have had you down as a garden bird kind of gal, Hayley,' smiled Lizzie.

'Wynthorpe garden birds actually,' I found myself explaining. 'These guys have been flitting about the garden outside my studio at the hall, and you're right, I wouldn't have categorised myself as a twitcher either.'

Jemma wasn't saying a word so I guessed these little fellas weren't the sort of thing she had in mind after all.

'I know they're probably not the right subject,' I carried on, 'but the style is the same as I used for the Winter Wonderland advert.'

'They're exactly the right subject,' Jemma suddenly burst out. 'They're gorgeous! How on earth have you managed to pack them all so full of personality?'

'Well,' I said, completely taken aback, 'they've done that themselves, I suppose. I've just watched them and then tried to emphasise it a bit.'

'And succeeded,' she beamed. 'I love them.'

'Do you?'

'Of course,' she laughed, 'what did you think?'

I looked at the robin named Gavin and shrugged my shoulders.

'I don't really know what I thought.'

'Have you got more?' asked Lizzie.

'No,' I said, 'although I've made a couple of preliminary sketches of a blackbird and there's been a flock of fussy long-tailed tits flitting about, who I think might be fun to draw.'

Jemma was looking thoughtful again.

'Jemma, I know you said you wanted to see them on mugs and cushions and things and then sell them in the café,' I said meekly, 'but I have absolutely no idea how to go about sorting that out and, to be honest, I didn't think you'd know either, isn't it Lizzie who's the crafty one?'

'You're right, I don't know,' Jemma nodded, 'and yes, she is,' she said turning to Lizzie. 'And I know I said I wanted to sell them here in the café . . .'

She'd changed her mind, then. I hadn't thought the café was big enough to stock anything else to sell. It was already packed to the gunnels. She had made the offer without thinking it through and was now trying to find a way of letting me down gently. I was surprised to feel a twinge of disappointment that it wasn't going to happen, because I had fully expected to feel relieved. Perhaps I had come around to the idea of taking my talent seriously far sooner than I thought possible.

'But there just isn't the room,' she continued.

'I see,' I said, piling the papers back together. 'I understand.'

'And this has taken a lot of thinking about.'

She was certainly going out of her way to try to save my feelings.

'And it isn't common knowledge,' Lizzie confused me by adding. 'It won't be for a good while yet. Another couple of months, at least.'

'But we're extending the business,' said Jemma excitedly.

'And diversifying,' chimed in Lizzie.

I looked from one to the other but still couldn't fathom what it was they were trying to tell me.

'We're taking up the lease for the shop next door,' Jemma gushed. 'The place has been empty for ages so the council have offered it to us at a reduced rate.'

'With a fortuitous stipulation or two,' said Lizzie with a smile, 'so I'm moving my crafting side of the business into there—'

'And the café will extend into the crafting area in here, but still cater to folk coming to Lizzie's classes. I might even offer baking classes of my own,' Jemma wistfully added.

It all sounded incredibly exciting, but I couldn't see how it was going to have any impact on me and my little flock.

'So, where do I fit into all this?' I frowned.

'Well,' said Jemma, 'the council are keen to promote the work of local artists and craftspeople, and one of their stipulations is that we support and sell their work in the shop.'

'We have a few folk interested, including another designer, but wanted someone younger to come onboard,' Lizzie continued, 'and that's where we hoped you would come in. I'm taking responsibility for getting the designs printed on to the mugs, cushions and so on, so you wouldn't have to worry about any of that.'

'And then we'd sell them in the arts and crafts shop, along with everyone else's stuff.'

It was a lot to take in.

'Crikey,' I said, 'you guys really are spreading your wings, what with this and the outside catering business.'

'I know,' said Jemma, 'and that's why it's taken us a long time to work it all out. There was no way I was going to even consider it if we couldn't extend our team to make it a sensible proposition. However, the numbers have been crunched and now we're going full steam ahead. What do you think?'

I don't think I had ever come across anyone with quite so much ambition and vision as this pair of hardworking friends. They were truly inspirational.

'There won't be anything happening until early spring on the shop front,' Lizzie added, 'but, ideally, we need to know soon if you think there might be a possibility that you would like to join us. It's going to be a wonderfully supportive environment to work in.'

'And you never know,' said Jemma with a winning smile. 'Before long you might be drinking tea in the café here from a mug sporting one of your own designs!'

Was this really happening? I was pleased I was sitting down because just the thought of that was enough to make me feel giddy. All of a sudden, I was feeling rather grateful that Gavin, Anna and Molly had found me out and given me a shove in the right artistic direction.

'And don't worry about the nuts and bolts of the business side of things,' said Lizzie, 'because we can help you with all of that. Can't we, Jem?'

'Absolutely,' said Jemma, picking up the sheet again and smiling at my little plump wren. 'For now, you just focus on coming up with more of these delightful characters.'

I left the café and walked around to The Mermaid. Well, I say I walked, I'm not actually sure that my feet touched the ground, but the clouds beneath them definitely had the number nine firmly stamped all over them.

'Are you all right?' asked Evelyn when I requested a large double brandy. 'You look a bit flushed.'

'I'm fine, Evelyn, thanks.' I nodded dreamily. 'It's just the Wynbridge wind.'

'It's not like you to go for brandy though, is it?' she persisted. 'Have you had a shock?'

'No,' I told her. 'I just want warming up, and in the absence of a Saint Bernard I thought I better sort myself out.'

I found myself a table and sat down wondering how on earth it was possible that finding my then-fiancé in a compromising position in the pub loos could lead to so many wonderful things. A new home and now, potentially, a new career was knocking on my door, and all within a matter of weeks of crying over a lost relationship, a wasted buffet and one very squashed cake.

'How'd you get on?'

It was Mr Life Changer himself. I'd forgotten all about his insistence that I should join him for a drink after the meeting.

'Have you been to see Jemma? Please tell me you have.'

I looked up and offered him my most grateful smile.

'I have,' I nodded, 'and I got on very well, thank you.'

Chapter 24

I have to admit, I can't remember an awful lot about the evening after Gavin shelled out for my third celebratory double brandy. However, I do know that we spent quite a lot of time talking about what might have happened to me had I not given up on my art when I left school. Gavin was also keen to talk about what had really occurred around that time, and in my unusually unguarded state, I ended up explaining rather more than I bargained for. But as he was the person who had reignited my passion and helped me secure a potential outlet for it, I figured that I could trust him with a little more of my sad story. Well, that was what my brandy-soaked brain thought, anyway.

I began to feel rather worse for wear on the drive back to Wynthorpe and by the time we reached the top of Lovers Lane I was begging him to stop the van so I could jump out and grab a lungful of air.

'It wasn't all that many weeks ago that you were dragging

me down here for a different reason,' he reminded me with a cheeky wink as he rushed around and opened the passenger door to help me out.

That was true enough. There had been more than one sweet seduction atop a pile of work coats in the back when we had been dating, but those days were well and truly over.

'Yes,' I said, feeling slightly less queasy as the cold winter air sharpened my senses, 'and given what I know now, I daresay I wasn't the only one.'

I didn't give him an opportunity to elaborate and we drove the rest of the way back to the hall in silence.

'Thanks for the lift,' I whispered as I slid out of my seat, relieved that my legs were just about capable of bearing my weight. 'And for pushing me to go to see Jemma.'

'You're welcome,' Gavin smiled and then added more seriously, 'If you can find a way to let go of the past, Hayley, I'm pretty certain you've got a great future ahead of you.'

I didn't dare risk climbing the stairs up to bed and woke with a very crooked neck, having spent what was left of the night passed out in Gabe's chair in the conservatory. The fact that the throw I had wrapped myself in still smelt of him did nothing to relieve the guilt I felt about spending the evening with my ex, and when I spotted the bottle of wine and note Gabe had left, it was elevated a few floors higher.

In my excitement after my meeting with Jemma and Lizzie, I had completely forgotten that Gabe had hinted he might drop by. I didn't allow myself to think about how much nicer my evening would have been had I elected to come straight home. Still, at least I hadn't been foolish enough to take a trip down Lovers Lane for all the wrong reasons, and no one had seen Gavin dropping me off. That would have made the situation ten times worse.

'Evelyn called here last night and said you left the pub with Gavin,' Dorothy informed me over breakfast.

Oh, for heaven's sake, my luck really had deserted me.

'Did she, Dorothy?' I said through gritted teeth. 'How considerate of her.'

'She said you were a little wobbly on your feet, actually,' added Mick.

'That you'd been knocking back the brandy,' joined in Jamie. 'I don't think I've ever known you to drink brandy.'

So, pretty much everyone knew about my chaperone home, then. I was surprised they hadn't all waited up to see me safely tucked into bed.

'It was only a few weeks ago,' I reminded him tersely, 'that you'd never known me to be an arty type either, but you've managed to assimilate that without too much pain, so this shouldn't prove a problem, should it?'

My tone left him in no doubt that the question was of the rhetorical variety, and in the silence that followed I grabbed a slice of toast and escaped up to my room.

During the next few days, in the lead-up to the greenery gathering, I followed Gabe's lead, kept my head down and got on with my work. Thankfully, there was no word from Gavin. I had been worried that he might have read too much into my willingness to spend an evening with him, but all appeared quiet on the Western front.

I happily immersed myself in both scrubbing the hall and drawing some new designs for Jemma, which went some way towards helping purge the memories of the extra information about my school days that I had shared with my ex, of all people. I was desperate to tell Anna and Molly what the latest Cherry Tree plans were, but kept my promise and my lips zipped.

The plans for the Winter Wonderland were all but finalised and bits and pieces for the grotto and The Snowflake Trail were arriving every day. Angus had been most excited when the collection of inkpads and snowflake-patterned stamps arrived for the maps, and even I was looking forward to seeing Catherine's beloved summerhouse turned into Santa's grotto, assuming I could avoid donning the stripy tights to complete the tableau, of course.

'You all set for tomorrow, then?' asked Anna the night before the gathering in the woods.

The way she suggestively raised her eyebrows left me in no doubt that she still hadn't forgotten about our foolish bet.

'I saw Gabe earlier,' said Molly, who was gracing us with her presence and staying over at the hall again, 'and he said there's a bumper crop of mistletoe ready to harvest, and the holly is packed full of berries this year.'

She sounded as innocent and ethereal as ever, so it was impossible to work out whether Anna had enlightened her as to what she hoped would happen, but I wouldn't have put it past her.

'That really is wonderful news,' Anna beamed mischievously, 'you can never have too much mistletoe!'

The weather decided to play nice on the day of the gathering, and by the time I'd headed out to join the clan, the clouds were thinning and the sun was trying to peep through. We set off, with Gabe and Bran leading. Gabe sounded in great spirits so I didn't go to the trouble of apologising for not being around to share his wine for fear of quashing it, and Molly's pale cheeks were unusually bright. The pair were literally in their element, and before we started pairing off, they took a moment to remind us of the need to harvest sympathetically and not take everything in sight.

'These woods are a refuge and a haven as well as a food source,' Gabe said seriously, 'so let's make sure we only take our share and not a leaf or berry more.'

Molly then backed up his words with a sort of pagan prayer and the harvesting began. I couldn't help but be reminded of the commotion I had caused at a previous gathering when I had brazenly kissed Jamie in front of everyone – including Anna. I had only done it to prove that she was in love with him, but I hoped she wasn't going to go out of her way to give me a taste of my own medicine this time around.

'Why don't you pair up with Gabe?' she suggested, once everyone else had gathered tools, baskets and bags from the quad trailer and set off. 'I'm sure he would be safer doing the trickier bits with someone to help him.'

'Excellent idea,' he agreed, plonking a bright orange hard hat on my head and handing me some safety glasses, 'you'll need these.'

It turned out that Gabe had volunteered to harvest some of the biggest bunches of mistletoe, which were growing on a few of the trees usually out of reach to the rest of us. Even Angus.

'We'll get the biggest bunches down and gathered first,' he told me, 'and then see how much more we need. Up there it all looks like it's been growing untouched for a while. Some of the clusters are vast.'

'And how are you planning on reaching them?' I asked, squinting up into the branches to where the mistletoe looked to be thickest. 'You aren't climbing up, are you?'

I didn't much fancy being responsible for seeing him safely up and down or fiddling about with climbing ropes. That was all far more up Angus's street than mine.

'No,' Gabe smiled. 'Not today. I'm going to be using this.'

This turned out to be an extendable pruner, which reached high up into the branches and cut through the stems almost as easily as a knife through butter.

'Don't look up!' Gabe yelled as the bunches began to fall, and I was grateful for the headgear even if I did look a plank.

Within minutes the woodland floor was covered, and we gathered the bunches together and hauled them back to the trailer. It was hot, hard work and by mid-morning I was grateful to see Dorothy on standby with flasks, fruit, and syrupy flapjacks.

'You were right, Gabe,' said Archie who had been helping Molly. 'The woods are packed this year.'

'Do you think that means we're in for a hard winter?' I asked.

That was what my nan always reckoned when there were plenty of berries about.

'Fingers crossed,' beamed Angus, 'real snow for the Winter Wonderland would be so much nicer than the synthetic stuff.'

'And cheaper,' added Jamie.

'I wouldn't be surprised if we had a harsh winter,' said Gabe looking around.

'The portents are all suggesting it,' added Molly mysteriously.

Gabe nodded in agreement.

'Talking of signs,' said Anna, 'there's an unusual abundance of mistletoe this year, isn't there?'

'Yes,' laughed Archie, giving Molly a squeeze, 'and plenty of romance around here to go with it.'

'Exactly,' Anna enthusiastically joined in, giving me a knowing look.

'Although, according to Norse mythology,' Molly began, but Anna was not to be diverted from her course and cut across her.

'I think,' she said, pulling out her secateurs and snipping away, 'in the spirit of the season, we should all carry a piece with us this afternoon.'

'Are you sure?' laughed Jamie. 'The last time I bran-
dished mistletoe berries in these woods I caught a smacker
from Hayley.'

'What a surprise,' Gabe muttered sarcastically behind me.

His tone was just loud enough for me to hear and far from
funny. He sounded nothing like the happy and enthusiastic
chap I had been working with all morning. I felt my hackles
rise in response.

'What's that supposed to mean?' I snapped, spinning round.

He had made me feel nettled and defensive and I wanted
an answer, but he'd already headed off.

'Oops,' said Jamie, looking embarrassed as Anna scowled
at him. 'I didn't catch that. Was it something I said?'

'No,' I flushed.

'Is there something going on between you two?' he asked
suspiciously.

'Hardly,' huffed Anna, standing with her hands on her
hips, her quest to see her forfeit fulfilled possibly ruined. 'And
especially not if you go around saying stupid things like that.'

'What?' said Jamie looking thoroughly confused. 'What
have I done?'

'Here,' I said throwing him my hard hat and glasses, 'you
can work with the Gruffalo this afternoon. I've had enough
of his split personality for one day.'

I really wanted to head back to the sanctuary of my studio,
but thought it would be better all round if I stayed to keep
an eye on Anna. Goodness knows what she would say if I
wasn't there to keep her in check.

'I'll stick with you, Anna,' I told her firmly. 'Gabe said it would be a good idea to take some strands and shorter pieces of ivy to town along with this lot. Apparently, it's all but strangling the trees, so we'll be doing them a favour by pulling it off.'

Although at that moment I would have liked to strangle *her*.

'All right,' she agreed, abandoning the mistletoe she had hoped would bring Gabe and me together, 'perhaps that would be a better idea.'

She tried every trick in the book to get me to tell her what Gabe had said, but after the third refusal she let it drop and we worked in silence, steadily filling bags and dragging them back to the trailer, which Mick had been towing backwards and forwards to the courtyard.

By the end of the afternoon we were all exhausted but fresh faced, and our moods had lifted back to where they should have been on what was one of the busiest days in the hall calendar. I had tracked the fluttering of the little long-tailed tits I was so keen to capture on paper, and enjoyed the company of another equally bolshie robin who hopped in and out of the leaf litter looking for tasty morsels to supplement his winter diet.

'Everyone all right?' Jamie asked as we all prepared to set off back to the hall to whatever delights Dorothy had spent the afternoon cooking up.

'Yes,' we all chorused.

Looking around at the tired but happy faces of my friends, I could see that a day out in the fresh air had done us all the world of good. Even Gabe was looking less churlish and more charming.

'Sorry about earlier,' he said in a low tone as he dropped back and fell into step with me.

'Don't worry about it,' I shrugged, even though I was having to bite my tongue to stop from asking what he had been getting at.

During the afternoon, as I mulled Gabe's cutting comment over, I had started to entertain the idea that he had somehow spotted Gavin dropping me off and jumped to the wrong conclusion, but I knew he hadn't. Gatekeeper's Cottage had been in complete darkness. I had made a point of looking to check.

'I only meant that, given what Jamie said, that sounded very much like something the *old* Hayley would have got up to and, as you know, I've always been rather keen on the *new* Hayley, even if you haven't.'

'Oh,' I swallowed. 'Right.'

I wasn't sure if that was what he had actually meant, but his explanation was far more palatable than what I had assumed, so I decided to accept it.

'Although,' I added, 'to be fair, even though it was the old Hayley who kissed Jamie, she did have the best of intentions for doing it.'

'Oh?' He smiled. 'She wasn't making a play for the youngest Connelly son, then.'

'Absolutely not,' I gasped, pretending to be hurt that he would even suggest such a thing. 'It was actually a brazen wake-up call for Anna, to make her realise that she had fallen for him.'

'And did it work?'

I pointed ahead, to the spot where Anna and Jamie had stopped walking and were wrapped in each other's arms.

'Like a charm,' I grinned.

When I looked back at Gabe, he had stopped walking too and was holding a small sprig of mistletoe over my head.

'I'm not sure that's a good idea,' I swallowed, my voice thick in my throat.

The last thing I wanted was for Anna to turn around and catch sight of us in a clinch, no matter how brief or chaste.

'Me neither,' he said, tossing it aside and pulling me into his arms. 'Who needs it?'

It was another swoon-worthy kiss, which soon made me forget that Anna was even anywhere in the vicinity. Gabe's full lips pressed firmly against mine sent heat coursing through my body, reaching even as far as my chilled fingertips and toes.

'Gabe,' I eventually gasped, as I began to register the dull ache in the back of my neck that signified I had been kissing someone significantly taller than me for quite an extraordinary length of time. 'Gabe.'

'No,' he said, refusing to break away. 'I don't want to stop.'

I put aside all thoughts of how he wasn't looking for either a brief encounter or something serious, or indeed anything that had the remotest chance of making him happy, along with memories of his recent house guest, and instead focused on giving the kiss my full and undivided attention.

It was a passionate effort on both sides and I couldn't help hoping that it meant he had finally unpacked and sorted through the baggage that was pulling him back every time we got close. If this was the all-clear I had been secretly hoping for, then I was ready to run with it.

'You can stop now!' called a voice somewhere ahead of us. 'You've made your point.'

Anna's laughter cut through the unexpected but most marvellous moment.

'Good god, Hayley,' laughed Jamie as he and Anna walked back to where Gabe and I were about to fall to the floor and get even better acquainted. 'You're insatiable, do you know that? Next year I'm not allowing you within a fifty-metre radius of anything that even resembles mistletoe. But at least you got something positive out of losing!'

'What are you talking about?' said Gabe, as he finally came to his senses.

I looked at Anna and shook my head. Disaster was heading in my direction and I had no idea how to avert it.

'Anna just told me,' said Jamie, looking from one of us to the other.

Anna looked panic stricken but, like me, was unable to shut Jamie up.

'Told you what?' asked Gabe, bending to pick up his long-reach pruner.

'Nothing,' Anna blurted out, 'I didn't tell you any-thing, Jamie.'

'Yes, you did,' Jamie teased, thinking it was some game

and that he was having the last laugh by dropping his beloved, and me, very firmly in it. 'It's too late to deny it now. She told me that she had a bet with Hayley here, and as the loser, she had to kiss you under the mistletoe by the end of today.'

'Is that right?' said Gabe, nodding his head and forcing himself to sound as unaffected as possible. 'Well, there you go.'

'No,' I began to say, but he didn't give me the chance to remind him that he was the one who had instigated the kiss, and that I had had very little say in the matter.

'Well, I'm sorry to say you haven't won on this occasion, Anna,' he rallied with as much dignity as he could muster, 'because, as you can see, there's not so much as a single berry of mistletoe in sight.'

'Gabe,' I swallowed.

Anna didn't say anything, but she looked thoroughly ashamed and very aware of what her blabbing had done.

'So, I guess you do win this one, Hayley,' Gabe shrugged, striding off in the opposite direction from the hall before I had the opportunity to make him see sense.

Chapter 25

On Saturday morning we woke early to discover that it had been steadily snowing for a few hours. As a result, we knew that the festive feeling in town would be cranked up a notch and the tree auction and bake sale were bound to be a roaring success. The gardens looked beautiful as I opened my bedroom curtains and when I pushed open the window for a second or two, I discovered it was eerily quiet. Not even my bolshie robin was in the mood for making his presence felt on this particularly chilly morning.

I hadn't put my name down as a volunteer for the auction or the sale, but I was heading to Wynbridge nonetheless as I had folk to see and a rather large hamper from Dorothy to drop off at the town hall.

'Don't leave the basket with Jemma in the hall,' Dorothy told me for what must have been the hundredth time, 'because it will get muddled with all the others.'

'Empty on arrival into a cardboard box,' I cut in, paraphrasing the speech I now knew by heart, 'and then put the basket straight back in the Land Rover.'

'Thank you, Miss Clever-Clogs,' Dorothy tutted. 'And tell Jemma—'

'That you'll be there as soon as Anna's ready to drive you in.'

She nodded curtly and I went to find Mick who would be driving me in and helping with the auction. Gabe had set off far earlier to deliver the greenery in the trailer that was hooked up to his truck rather than the Land Rover, and I wondered if Mick was feeling a little redundant.

'You must be joking,' he laughed, when I asked him. 'Having Gabe here feels like Christmas has come early for me.'

I felt exactly the same way, but for very different reasons.

'Although,' he frowned, looking concerned, 'I can't help wondering if the lad has taken all this on and is working so hard because he's running away from something.'

I had discovered enough about Mick to understand that he had endured tough times after leaving the armed forces, so he knew what he was talking about when it came to picking up on problems. He didn't necessarily say much, but he was the kind of man who took things in, and given what Gabe had told me about trying to practise what he preached when it came to his own baggage, I thought that perhaps Mick was right.

'Well, he's in the best place if he needs a shoulder or three to cry on, isn't he?' I smiled.

'That he is,' said Mick, 'but Christmas can be a tough time of year, even when you are living at Wynthorpe Hall.'

'What makes you think his troubles, if he has any, are wrapped up with Christmas? You don't think we've got another Anna on our hands, do you?'

Anna had arrived at the hall with an extreme aversion to December and all its trimmings having lost her mum to cancer on Christmas Day when she was a little girl. Thankfully, meeting the Connelly clan and falling in love with Jamie had gone some way to helping recover her seasonal spirit.

Mick shrugged.

'I don't know about that,' he told me, 'but I get the impression that there's something about this time of year that Gabe doesn't like.'

As predicted, Wynbridge was awash with folk all keen to embrace the Christmas cheer and many were talking about the Winter Wonderland, which was now, unbelievably, just one week away. Having emptied Dorothy's beloved basket and stowed it away as instructed, I stood and surreptitiously watched Gabe getting stuck into sectioning off the wonderful array of trees that would soon be going on sale. To my eyes he looked as if he had a healthy handle on Christmas, but Mick had given me food for thought nonetheless.

Gabe didn't so much as glance in my direction and I felt

grateful that there was a full-on, manic week of preparation ahead because it would stop me worrying too much about what had happened, wondering how I could put it right.

'Hello, Hayley,' smiled Francesca as I made my way back through the crowds to her art store again. 'This is a lovely surprise.'

'Morning, Fran,' I smiled back.

She had insisted I call her that when I spent my advent voucher, and had also told me that her grandfather had sung my praises when she'd mentioned I'd been in.

'What can I do for you today?' she asked.

'I need a frame,' I told her, 'something plain for this.'

I reached into my bag and pulled out a small bubble-wrapped picture which I had already mounted.

'My goodness, did you do this?' Fran asked, wide eyed. 'It's very good.'

'Yes,' I swallowed, looking at the simple painting I had created from a sketch I had taken of Mum in a rare quiet moment as she was reading a magazine at the kitchen table at home, 'but it's years old.'

'It's beautiful,' said Fran, taking in every detail.

'Thank you,' I blushed. Acknowledging my artistic efforts without turning as red as Santa's suit was going to take some getting used to. 'Thank you very much.'

'And I have just the frame to suit it,' added Fran, not noticing my colour.

Together we slotted the painting into place and then she kindly wrapped it, ready for me to pass on.

'So, how's it looking out there?' she asked with a nod to the market square.

'Busy,' I told her. 'Which is why I'm having an early lunch in the pub.'

'I don't blame you,' she laughed, 'it'll be standing room only in there soon. I'm staying open all day to make sure I catch any passing trade, but I've no chance of being as busy as the bar.'

'Well, you never know,' I told her as I buttoned up my coat. 'Folk are filling their bags and getting into the festive spirit, so I can't imagine you're in for a quiet day. I'll see you soon.'

'Next weekend,' she reminded me. 'We're coming to the Winter Wonderland.'

'In that case, wrap up warm,' I advised her, 'and set aside the whole day because there's going to be loads to see and do.'

The pub was already getting busy by the time I had made a quick lap of the market, including another stop at the Cherry Tree Makes and Bakes stall, but I managed to grab a table after ordering Skylark ham, eggs and chips and a coffee at the bar. It was far too early in the day to be drinking alcohol, and I needed to thaw out.

I had just finished my rather large lunch and was getting ready to deliver my artistic parcel when Gavin walked in with a couple of mates. He sent them off to order and then came and plonked himself on the stool opposite me.

'All right,' he said, his grin as wide as ever.

I tried to ignore the nudges I could see working their way

along the line of lads buying drinks, but Gavin turned and spotted them.

'I haven't told a soul about what happened,' he whispered to me, 'not a dicky bird to anyone.'

I was rather taken aback that he thought there had been anything to tell. Unless he was referring to the details surrounding my departure from school. I have to admit, I had been feeling rather regretful about disclosing that.

'Scouts honour,' he promised when I didn't say anything.

'I'm not sure what you're talking about, Gavin,' I frowned.

'In the van on the way home,' he winked. 'You know.'

'I know that absolutely nothing happened on the way home,' I told him sternly, 'so don't even think about suggesting otherwise.'

'All right,' he laughed, 'don't get your knickers in a knot. I was only going to tease you about having too much to drink, but I'm guessing we're not quite there yet.'

'Believe me,' I said, 'we will never be there again.'

He couldn't resist pulling out his cheekiest grin and my heart sank as I spotted Mick and Gabe walk in. There was no way they wouldn't see us so there was no point trying to pretend I was invisible.

'Well,' said Gavin, reaching under the table and giving my knee a playful squeeze, 'I better get back to the lads.'

'Off you go then,' I said, sitting further back in my seat so I was out of reach. 'And if I hear so much as a whisper that you've been telling folk something happened between us, I swear to god I'll … well, I won't be responsible for my very violent actions.'

'I didn't realise that even just the suggestion of sleeping with me again would be that bad,' he pouted. 'I know I have a few faults.'

'You have more than a few,' I told him with a shudder.

How was it possible that he, along with practically everyone else, had already forgotten that not all that long ago he had been prepared to promise himself to me for life? Come to think of it, how was it possible that I had ever thought that was an appealing proposition? At the time I thought his cheating had put me off relationships for good, but now I wasn't so sure. The feelings I had for Gabe had made me question a lot of what I thought I knew, and my experiences of being in love was one of them.

'God knows where you've been,' I spitefully added.

Gavin bit his lip but didn't argue back. I got the sudden impression that there was plenty more he would have liked to have said, now he realised that I wasn't interested in indulging in some no-strings fun in the back of his van. I bitterly regretted knocking back those brandies and letting my guard down. He might have got my artistic ball rolling again, but I had ended up paying a high price for it.

'I'll see you around, then,' he said, standing back up and adjusting the waistband on his trousers, 'and by the way, if you happened to be thinking of popping round to visit your mum this afternoon, I've just seen your old man in the bookies. Timing couldn't be better.'

The house looked just the same as it did on the day I left. It was a shame, really. The little row of nineteen-fifties council houses were far from the prettiest in Wynbridge, but the abandoned furniture, broken down cars and beer cans that graced the gardens of two or three, my parents' place included, made me feel sorry for those in between struggling to make the best of what they had while living next door to the neighbours from hell.

It didn't feel right to just walk in, so I knocked on the back door and waited. When there was no reply I tried the handle, but it was locked. I didn't particularly want to leave the parcel for just anyone to find so I would have to psych myself up all over again and come back another time.

'Hayley,' came a voice from above. 'Is that you?'

'Yes,' I said, squinting up and spotting Mum leaning out of the upstairs hall window.

'Give me a minute.'

'I don't want to interrupt you if you're busy,' I called up, showing her the bag, 'I can just leave this on the step.'

Before I had time to put the bag down she had unlocked the door and pulled me in.

'Are you on your own?' she asked, looking towards the road.

'Yes,' I said, 'of course. What's going on?'

'Nothing,' she shrugged, looking more furtive than ever.

For a mad moment I wondered if she had another man upstairs. Thinking of my father, I wouldn't have blamed her.

'Mum?'

'Give me a minute,' she said, rushing back up the stairs. 'Stick the kettle on, love, and I'll fill you in on what's happened.'

I had made the tea and filled a plate with biscuits, from the stash she kept hidden from Dad, before she came back down.

'Sorry about that,' she apologised. 'I had to put the floorboards back.'

'You had to *what*?'

'The floorboards under the rug in the bedroom,' she elaborated, 'that's where I've been hiding the money I've managed to squirrel away for when I leave your father.'

Her face was aglow and, despite usually being on the skinny side, I thought she looked as if she'd gained a few pounds. We looked at one another and then burst out laughing. I was amazed by her cunning and her determination to see it through.

'When I didn't hear from you,' I told her, 'I thought you'd changed your mind.'

'You must be joking,' she laughed, biting into a biscuit. 'Even just the thought of it has changed me.'

'I can see that,' I agreed, 'you look amazing. You want to be careful. If he notices—'

Mum let out another laugh, almost choking on her biscuit.

'Since when has your father noticed anything beyond his betting slips?'

'And his belly,' I joined in.

I drank a mouthful of tea and looked at her over the rim of my mug.

'So, have you found anything yet?' I asked.

I hated the thought of her wanting to get out but not being able to find somewhere to go. I knew that if I asked them, Catherine and Angus would take her in, in spite of the differences they'd had in the past, but I wasn't sure that would be a good idea.

'Yep,' she grinned. 'I'll be off straight after Christmas.'

'Really?'

'Really,' she breathed. 'I've got myself a job like yours that comes with board and lodging.'

I couldn't believe what I was hearing.

'Where?' I gasped, 'doing what?'

'Housekeeping,' she giggled, 'in a boarding school down south.'

'But when? How?'

She refused to tell me any more for fear of jinxing her good fortune, but she did explain that she was hiding more than money away upstairs, getting ready for the day she'd go. The person in charge of the school was sympathetic to Mum's situation and everything was all arranged. Mum looked and sounded like a completely different person. She *was* a different person.

'I'm not telling you any more,' she said, 'because it's best if you don't know anything when your dad comes calling. You better get off, he'll be back soon.'

I left her with the present, made her promise not to open it until she was settled, and to call me at the hall as soon as she was on her way.

'It's going to be an adventure,' she told me, 'and it's all down to you, love. I hope you're every bit as happy as you deserve to be.'

Given everything that had happened since I moved out, I wasn't sure if I was, but there was hopefully still time to make it all right.

Chapter 26

With so many other things happening in my life, it would have been all too easy to let the situation with Gabe just carry on drifting, but I wasn't prepared to let that happen. I didn't want anything to dull the excitement of the Winter Wonderland and I reckoned that if I could clear the air between us, curb his passionate outbursts and convince my heart to take a break, then settling for friends would be a halfway decent compromise.

I was still astounded that the last thing I thought about at night was what a serious relationship with Gabe might look and feel like. I had been adamant that quick flings were the way forward and yet, within days of catching Gavin with his trousers around his ankles, I had made a complete U-turn and fallen for a man I hardly knew, who was nothing like my usual type.

'Right, folks,' boomed Angus early on the Monday morning as we began preparations for the Winter Wonderland, 'this is it.'

'From today,' joined in Jamie as he consulted his bulging clipboard, 'it's all hands on deck. The trees for the competition will be going up in the hall and groups will be popping in and out all week to decorate them. Dad and I are going to oversee the positioning and check everyone is happy with their spot, and then we'll leave them to it.'

'I'll check up on things when I can,' Dorothy offered, 'and if there's a problem I'll give you a shout on this contraption.'

The 'contraption' was an ancient walkie-talkie. Angus had dug half a dozen out of his man cave and set them up, again proving that not all of his hoarding was without merit.

'Thanks, Dorothy,' said Jamie, before turning to address his brother. 'Archie and Molly, we were wondering if you would be happy to make a start on converting the fern garden into Santa's grotto? I've already put the boxes of lights and decorations in the summerhouse.'

'Sounds good to me,' beamed Archie.

That was a huge relief. Molly would look far better in stripy tights than I would.

'Mick, you're in charge of sorting the ponies and sleigh, and Gabe and Hayley,' he said, finally turning to us, 'as you've worked together on planning The Snowflake Trail, we're hoping you two can set it up and double-check the features on the map match up with the path the visitors will take. There'll be extra manpower to help erect the tarp for the crafting area and so on, but do you think you can handle the rest?'

Given that he had been largely responsible for the

argument and witnessed the fallout after the greenery gathering, he didn't sound sure that we'd be up for pulling together, but I was game if Gabe was.

'I don't see why not,' I said keenly.

I didn't much fancy spending the week freezing my bits off in the woods, but if it meant I would have the chance to make my peace with the Wynthorpe woodsman, then so be it.

Jamie looked relieved.

'Whoever finishes first will be assigned to help those with the most left to do,' he went on, 'but if we all knuckle down then we should finish ahead of time, which will save a lot of stress all round.'

'Who's stressed?' shrugged Angus.

'Catherine and I will be putting the finishing touches to the party plans,' Anna reminded us, 'and decorating anything in the hall that isn't already bedecked in baubles, but after that we'll muck in with everyone else.'

Thanks to Jamie's organisational skills balancing out his father's exuberance, everything was set to run like a well-oiled machine. Well, in theory, at least.

'Oh,' piped up the mischief maker himself, 'and there is just one more little job that will need sorting, but I've got some chaps coming from town to help, so if you see a couple of strangers milling about, don't panic.'

'What is it, Angus?' Catherine was the only one who dared to ask.

'Reindeer,' he beamed, his excitement shining as brightly as the Christmas star. 'One of the places I talked to originally has had a cancellation, so they're setting up here, next to the owls, hopefully, for practically nothing. They're bringing three adults and one calf and have gone through all of the formalities on our behalf!'

'Was it just my take on the situation,' I said to Gabe in a friendly tone as we loaded up the trailer with all the things we would need to create The Snowflake Trail, 'or was no one surprised that Angus has managed to bag himself a Blitzen or two?'

'You're right,' he agreed with a smile, 'I know I haven't been living here long, but I've already worked out that Angus is pretty good at getting his own way.'

'He's not selfish though,' I was keen to point out. 'The things he wants are always ultimately for everyone's benefit and enjoyment.'

'I know that,' Gabe snapped. 'I wasn't suggesting he was.'

There was a sharp and defensive edge to his tone, which I was determined to soften.

'Gabe,' I said, biting my lip.

'What?'

'About that kiss,' I said, 'the one in the woods,' I added to stave off any confusion.

'Do we have to talk about it?'

'Yes,' I swallowed, 'I think we do.'

He pulled on his quad helmet, passed the spare to me and fired up the engine, which made it impossible to carry on talking. He jumped aboard and patted the seat for me to join him.

'Let's find somewhere without an audience then,' he shouted.

The snow in the woods had all but gone, and Gabe drove carefully to the clearing we had allocated for his wood-crafting area. Fortunately, his steady driving meant I didn't have to hang on to him, which was a relief. Wrapping my arms around his strong body would have done nothing to strengthen my determination that I was happy settling for friendship.

'So,' he said as he cut the engine again, 'what about it?'

Now I finally had the opportunity to sort things out, I was too afraid to speak for fear of messing it all up again. Perhaps I had hung on to more of the new Hayley than I realised, because the old one would have simply charged ahead like a bull in a china shop.

'Well,' I eventually began, pulling the helmet off again and ruffling my flattened hair, 'Anna and I did have a bet. I lost and the forfeit was to kiss you under the mistletoe at the greenery gathering.'

'I know that,' he said, sounding sullen.

'But if you remember,' I reminded him, 'it was actually *you* who kissed *me*.'

Gabe frowned but didn't say anything.

'I was going out of my way to avoid having to do it.'

'Thanks.'

'But not because I didn't want to.'

'Why then?'

'Well,' I stammered, 'because . . .'

'Look,' said Gabe, 'let me say something before you tie yourself up in an even tighter knot.'

I scuffed the sodden leaves with the toe of my boot and waited.

'Hayley,' he said, 'I know I've done nothing but make a fool of myself over you since the moment we met, and I've sent you so many mixed messages you've probably lost count by now.'

He was right about that.

'But given that you've banged on about not wanting anything heavier than a quick fling I can't see why you're all that bothered about it all. I would have thought the old Hayley would be able to brush all this off without a moment's hesitation.'

He was obviously still determined to wear his hair shirt, even though I didn't know why, and it was glaringly apparent that he hadn't believed I had changed at all since those first few post-Gavin days.

'But I said I'd be willing to change, if the right person came along,' I reminded him. 'What is it that's made you think I was lying about that?' I asked.

He shook his head, refusing to answer.

'Come on,' I goaded, 'tell me.'

He looked right at me, biting his lower lip so hard that I thought it was going to bleed.

'I saw you climbing out of Gavin's van down Lovers Lane,' he croaked. 'And I heard what he was suggesting to his mates in The Mermaid after the tree auction.'

I felt my face start to burn. That was the last thing I had been expecting him to say.

'I know I told you I'm not looking for a relationship, Hayley, and I'm not, but if I was I wouldn't be thinking about having one with you now. As far as love is concerned, I know that we're poles apart—'

How dare he judge me on an assumption and a smutty suggestion. He hadn't even bothered to ask for an explanation before making up his mind.

'Well, I know that you had some woman staying at the cottage the weekend of the switch-on,' I blurted out, my upset getting the better of me. 'So how can you stand there and tell me our expectations are so different when actually, if what appearances suggest are true of both of us, then you're no better than I am.'

I was so angry that my sole motive was to hurt him, give back exactly as good as he was giving me, and see how it made him feel.

'Oh, Hayley,' he sighed, 'if only you knew.'

Exasperatingly, he sounded resigned rather than cross. My cutting comments hadn't had the desired impact at all. If anything, they had made me feel worse than Gabe, and that hadn't been my intention at all.

'So, tell me then.'

'I can't,' he shrugged.

'You won't, you mean.'

Apparently, we had reached an impasse. I knew about his house guest and he had believed Gavin's laddish innuendo. My ex had promised he had just been winding me up when we last met in pub, but apparently the temptation to further embellish his reputation had proved too much. I didn't think he would ever grow up, but at least his cheeky charm had put me on the path to Jemma and furthering my artistic ambitions.

'Right,' I said, pulling off my glove and holding out my hand to Gabe before my annoyance with Gavin caused an even bigger rift between us. 'I'm sick of this. It's ridiculous, we're just going around in circles. Can we just forget everything that's happened during the last few weeks and start again?'

'As friends?'

'Yes,' I said, swallowing down my disappointment. 'As friends. Let's see if we can get through Christmas without you kissing me whenever the mood takes you, and I can convince Molly to come up with a spell to shrivel Gavin's balls to the size of sultanas because, believe it or not, Gabe, whatever he was saying about what happened that night was a lie.'

Gabe grabbed my hand and pulled me in for a hug, which did nothing to strengthen my resolve that, from now on, I was going to resist him and his manly charms.

'Now, come on,' I said, breathing him in before I pulled away, 'let's get on. We've got work to do.'

Chapter 27

Wynthorpe Hall was the perfect setting for a Winter Wonderland. That was what I, and everyone else, hoped would be the headline the press went with, because the entire event was truly spectacular. We had all worked our butts off to make it happen, but it was worth every gruelling hour, and the gently falling snowflakes, which made a return appearance just as the reindeer were being installed, was the prettiest icing imaginable.

Before we opened the gates and Catherine cut the ribbon to officially get the weekend underway, we took a collective walk around to check everything was perfect. We started in the festively decorated hall, which was aglow with dozens of extra strings of twinkling lights and an unusual array of decorated trees that formed the community group's competition.

'I'm pleased we don't have to pick a winner,' sighed Angus, who was clearly in love with them all, 'these sticker sheets are a far easier option than heaping the responsibility on one person's head.'

The idea was that everyone would take a sheet, which listed all the trees, and put stickers next to their top three choices. At the end of the weekend, the tree with the most stickers would be announced as the winner.

In the area directly in front of the hall, which marked the access point to the festive fun, Angus's beloved sleigh shone and the ponies in the paddock were whickering in anticipation. Clearly, they were as excited as the rest of us. The Cherry Tree Caravan also looked the part; bedecked in festive snowflake bunting and bathed in the subtle sounds of Mr Bublé, it matched the similarly decorated ticket kiosk beautifully.

'Morning, Angus!' called one of the WI ladies who had been drafted in by Dorothy to help out. 'Morning, everyone! Are we all set?'

'I think so, Mrs Harris,' Angus called back. 'And if we aren't now, we never will be.'

I took the momentary interruption to have a quick word with Jemma. I wanted to warn her that Gavin was, in spite of his promise not to, gossiping behind my back.

'Don't you worry,' she said patting my arm. 'I soon sent him packing once I heard what he'd got to say.'

'Well,' I told her. 'I'm relieved about that, even if I am embarrassed.'

'There's nothing to be embarrassed about,' she said, rushing away to help Lizzie string up yet more bunting, 'it's all in the past now and is no one else's business. There was no real harm done so it's all best forgotten. It won't make any difference to our little venture.'

I went to call after her, but there was no time as Angus was ushering the troops together again. Clearly Jemma and I weren't talking about the same thing, but there wasn't time to get to the bottom of it. It would have to keep for now.

'What was that about?' frowned Anna.

'I haven't the faintest idea,' I shrugged, deciding to put it to the back of my mind for the next forty-eight hours at least.

We set off into the woods, the path indicated by dozens of red and white striped wooden candy cane markers that had taken Gabe and I hours to paint, but were certainly worth the effort. The snowflake stamps for the maps were all in boxes to protect them, should the weather turn inclement, and Gabe's reindeer kits were lined up and ready to go under the large tarp that had been lashed between the trees and would provide the perfect dry spot for any woodwork enthusiasts who came along.

'Do you think we've set out too many?' he asked anxiously, frowning at me. 'Looking at it all now, there seems to be an awful lot.'

'I wouldn't worry about that,' said Jamie before I had a chance. 'If anything, you might find you end up needing more.'

'Really?'

'Really,' said Angus. 'We're expecting hundreds of visitors rather than dozens, you know.'

'Well, I do have enough wood to make more,' said Gabe, sounding far from relieved.

His hands looked as raw as mine felt, so I hoped we wouldn't have too many more to prepare.

'Listen,' said Molly. 'Can you hear that?'

A few more steps along the path led us to the source of the screeching and the spot where Ed and his mum, Mags, had set up their beloved owls. Ed, his curls dampened by the snow, which was falling thicker by the second, was checking things out with what appeared to be a crow sitting on his shoulder, pirate-style, but with a twist.

'How's it all looking, Ed?' Gabe asked, striding up to him and shaking his hand.

Clearly, they were peas in a pod.

'Wonderful,' beamed Ed before turning to Angus. 'Thank you so much for letting us come, Mr Connelly.'

'I do wish you'd call me Angus,' Angus laughed. 'Is every-one happy here? Have you got everything you need?'

'Yes,' said Mags, 'but I'm pleased we decided to bring the canopy. I didn't think we were forecast snow.'

I looked at the array of owls on display. The barn owls were beautiful. One had been rescued after a collision with a car and was still happily recuperating in Ed's care, and the other had been hand-reared by someone but then abandoned because the responsibility of looking after it had proved too much. They were both very calm and I imagined the young lad as some modern-day Dr Doolittle. The little owl was obviously the comic of the group, with his furrowed brow and haughty looks, but it was the plump tawny with the large dark brown eyes that melted my heart.

'You can hold her if you like,' said Ed as if it was the most natural thing in the world. 'She's very friendly.'

She stared up at me and slowly blinked, her behaviour conveying just how unflappable she was.

'Maybe later,' I said, 'thanks, Ed.'

I wasn't sure if I was brave enough to do more than just look.

'She won't bite,' said Gabe, who had competently taken charge of the hand-reared barn owl.

Suddenly there was a flapping of wings, but not from the little tawny. The owl Gabe was holding thought Bran looked like a far more comfortable perch than Gabe's hand and had quickly made himself very much at home, wrapping his talons around the dog's wide leather collar.

'Kindred spirits,' said Molly dreamily when Bran didn't so much as flinch.

'Actually,' smiled Mags, nodding at the owl now nestling companionably in Bran's wiry coat, 'we're looking for a home for him.'

Looking at the rapt expression on Gabe's face I didn't think she would have to look much further.

'Come on, troops,' rallied Anna, having just noticed the time, 'we better keep moving otherwise we're going to find the hordes descending before Santa makes it into his grotto.'

'I'll come back,' I heard Gabe say to Mags as she gently

lifted the owl, who was named Jareth, from Bran's back. 'I'll come and talk to you about him later.'

The reindeer paddock was next and the sight of them standing in the snow-flecked woods, sleigh bells on their head collars tinkling every time they moved, was breathtaking.

'Oh, Angus,' gasped Catherine as we all turned into seven-year-olds again. 'You clever man!'

Angus proudly puffed out his chest and introduced us to the owners. I couldn't tell you what any of them were called, though, because once I had spotted the little calf, which was about the same size as Bran, I seemed to come over all soft, but I wasn't the only one.

'What an absolute sweetie,' said Anna, clicking her tongue.

'Do you think I'll be able to talk Angus into letting me have a reindeer as well as a barn owl?' Gabe laughed.

'Without a doubt,' I laughed back as the little thing ventured closer to the fence before skittering off again. 'He'll probably let you have two.'

Last, but by no means least, the path finally led us through the snowy gardens and into Santa's grotto. Molly and Archie had done a wonderful job and Angus had managed to borrow a life-size penguin and polar bear family from the local garden centre and had strategically placed them in the borders so that the walled space looked more like the North Pole than I would have thought possible.

'Wow,' gasped Anna, who, like the rest of us, was taking it all in for the first time, 'this is amazing.'

'And it'll be even better this afternoon,' giggled Molly.

'When the light starts to fade,' explained Archie, 'you'll see what we mean.'

'Right!' shouted Jamie, bringing us all back to earth with a bump. 'Forty-five minutes until showtime. Let's grab a hot drink and get to our stations folks, it's time for the Winter Wonderland to open!'

The visitors came in their droves and we barely had time to draw breath, let alone sample the cinnamon swirls and snow-flake biscuits Dorothy and Jemma had been baking. Angus had certainly been right to predict such high numbers and Gabe and I worked long into the night preparing more of his bespoke reindeer kits for the next day. They had proved so popular that we had less than a dozen left when the final visitors headed off on Saturday evening.

Not that anyone had been in a rush to leave, because once the lights around the grotto had sprung to life, the place looked even more magical, and the final few families hung on for as long as they possibly could. Truth be told, we really could have done with double the number of volunteers so we could have kept the place open right through the night. Something I had overheard Angus discussing the possibility of, when he escorted the reindeer owners to their quarters in the stable block.

'Well, I had been going to suggest we all headed to town to celebrate the day's success,' yawned Jamie as we finally finished devouring a very late supper, 'but the pub will be shut by the time we get up there.'

'How about tomorrow, instead?' I suggested. 'We won't

have anything to prepare for the next day and I'm sure the boss won't make us take everything apart the second the gates close.'

'That sounds like an excellent idea,' Anna agreed. 'We'll help Jemma and Lizzie pack up and see the wildlife teams are all set, then reward ourselves with a wild night on the tiles.'

'Or, in this case,' I grinned, 'a quiet evening propping up the bar in the sleepy Mermaid.'

Sunday was every bit as thrilling as the day before and I knew I would never tire of hearing the excited squeals from the children and gasps of pleasure from the adults as they ventured around The Snowflake Trail, discovering something new around every corner as they filled up their maps with the appropriate stamps, ready to collect their gifts from Santa at the end.

Every aspect of the venture had been a huge success, and Angus and Jamie had every right to look proud. Wynthorpe Hall was a beautiful place, made all the more special by the Connelly family's willingness to share it with the world. The only person who occasionally looked subdued during it all was Gabe, and I put that down to him being worn out from all the extra hours he had been putting in to help get everything ready. Being built like The Rock was all very well, but more often than not, with a venture like this, that meant you were doubly in demand when it came to the lugging and lifting.

'I can't believe you actually live here,' sighed Fran

when she spotted me helping Gabe in the woods. 'How lucky are you?'

'Very,' I beamed, knowing that I didn't have enough words in my vocabulary to express how truly blessed I felt to be a part of such an amazing family.

'This has made Christmas for me,' she said. 'I feel like I've been to Lapland, but for a fraction of the price. Will you pass on my congratulations to everyone?'

I was happy to and plenty of other visitors had said the same. It was a very merry Connelly clan who drove into Wynbridge that night. We were greeted like heroes in the pub, and for once Evelyn didn't seem to mind that the takings had been down because the locals had ventured further afield for their weekend entertainment.

'So, what's the deal with you and Gabe, then?' asked Archie when we headed to the bar for another round of drinks.

'What do you mean?'

'Well, you two are together, right?'

'No,' I flushed, 'absolutely not.'

I didn't add that we may well have been, had the pair of us met when we were further along our complicated paths through life, and I decided not to remind Archie that Gabe had another woman tucked away somewhere.

'But you like him?'

'About as much as I like you,' I told him, 'which right now . . .'

'Well, he likes you,' he laughed, whipping up the refilled

tray and heading back to the table. 'And as more than a workmate,' he threw in for good measure.

I didn't have a chance to tell him I already knew that, but being aware of the situation didn't guarantee anything was going to happen. In fact, knowing how Gabe felt about me was making the situation all the harder to deal with, because for some inexplicable reason, he refused still to act on those feelings.

What was it about loved-up couples, I thought, as I watched Archie stoop to kiss Molly. They always wanted to get everyone else paired up. I couldn't help feeling bad for Gabe. Obviously, I knew he liked me, we'd discussed that often enough, but I bet he had no idea that his feelings had been observed by everyone else.

'Where's Gabe gone?' Jamie asked, as I joined the others and helped Archie hand out the glasses.

'Don't ask me,' I snapped. 'I'm not his keeper.'

He was another one who seemed to assume we kept track of each other's movements. I was all set to take him to task over it when the glass panelled doors, which separated the bar from the corridor and led down to the infamous loos, burst open and Gavin fell flat on his back with blood pouring out of his nose. Gabe strode forward, towering over him and looking as if he was about to pick him up and hit him again. That is, assuming his fists had been responsible for the first blow.

'What the fuck?' said Jamie and Archie together, leaping out of their seats and upsetting our drinks in the process.

'Out!' bellowed Evelyn from behind the bar, as Jim raced around the tables and roughly dragged Gavin to his feet.

'Why is it,' Jim shouted, ramming a tea towel up Gavin's freely-flowing bloody nostrils, 'that if there's ever any trouble in this place, you're always involved?'

'But *he* hit *me*!' Gavin exclaimed, pointing an accusatory finger at Gabe who was rubbing what looked like a bruised right hand.

Standing in the doorway, he appeared more like the devil himself than a kind guardian angel.

'Don't throw him out on my account,' Gabe growled at Jim. 'I'm going.'

'Gabe!' Jamie called after him, but he didn't look back.

'He's mental!' shouted Gavin, now the threat was out of sight. 'Completely off his head!'

I might not have been all that enamoured with my ex right now, given that he had been suggesting to everyone that we'd settled our differences in a far too friendly manner, but a part of me did wonder if he was right. Gavin might have been a jack the lad who would always resort to any number of half-truths to enhance his randy reputation, but what about Gabe? Suddenly it seemed to me that there was an awful lot more to the wild man of Wynthorpe woods than any of us knew.

Chapter 28

Had I been at all concerned that when the Winter Wonderland was over I would let my excitement about the Cherry Tree expansion and Mum's amazing news get the better of me, then I needn't have worried. Thanks to Gabe and Gavin's antics in the pub, blabbing about my news was the last thing I felt like doing.

'I'm not going to mention any of this at home,' Jamie had said as we all bundled back into the Land Rover after deciding to cut our celebration short. 'I know Mum and Dad aren't the types to judge, but I also know that Gabe has his own way of dealing with things.'

With his fists, I thought, but I didn't say as much.

'I think we should just leave him alone for the time being,' Jamie concluded. 'He's not the type of guy who would appreciate a fuss being made, and I know he's had a lot on his mind recently.'

He didn't explain what that lot was.

'I agree,' said Anna and the rest of us nodded in approval. 'If Gabe saw fit to punch Gavin then it must have been for a good reason. I never was completely convinced when he turned into Mr Nice Guy, Hayley.'

I nodded again but didn't comment. It was obvious to all of us now that Gavin would never give up the Wynbridge Wide Boy crown. When surrounded by his mates, with a drink or two in him, he would always resort to laddish behaviour, even if he was almost able to pull off the saintly act when alone. I was just waiting for one of them to suggest that, in spite of what Jamie had just said, I should go over to Gatekeeper's Cottage and ask Gabe for an explanation, but fortunately no one piped up.

Jamie's plan to keep his pal out of further trouble soon hit a snag, however, as we had forgotten that lots of people would be turning up at the hall to help tidy up, and all any of them wanted to talk about during the next few days was the brawl in the bar.

Not that it had been a brawl, of course, but the rumours had escalated to Gavin being in hospital, the police having cautioned Gabe, and Evelyn threatening to close the pub to emigrate to Australia because she felt threatened by the town's increasing antisocial behaviour.

'I understand,' said Angus, 'that there was a bit of bother in town on Sunday night.'

'Only a little bit,' shrugged Archie, shooting his brother a look. 'Hardly worth mentioning, really.'

There was no point denying it.

'And has anyone seen Gabe since?' asked Catherine.

'He's not answering his door,' said Mick, 'but he's still here. Or at least his truck is.'

I didn't think I could bear it any longer. The time since the incident had dragged by and I didn't want to care quite so much, but I couldn't seem to help myself. Gabe may have decided to cling on to his conviction that, even though he had feelings for me, he wasn't going to act on them, and he may well have dug his heels in when it came to telling me about his other woman, but none of that stopped me caring for and worrying about him.

'Gabe!' I shouted, hammering on his cottage door. 'It's me. Open up!'

The front rooms were in darkness and all the curtains were closed, but I could hear Bran scrabbling about inside so I knew Gabe was home, and as far as I was concerned, forty-eight hours after a brief bout of fisticuffs was plenty long enough to wallow. Any longer would have been indulgent.

'I'm not leaving!' I told him, 'so you might as well open the door before everyone else traipses out here.'

I was just about to start knocking again when I heard the key turn in the lock and the bolt slide across.

'What do you want, Hayley?' he growled, turning his back before I had a chance to look at him.

'To find out what the hell's wrong with you,' I said, following him inside. 'We've all been . . .'

The words died in my throat as I caught sight of the sitting room in the light coming from the kitchen. It was covered in photos, newspapers and empty bottles. The cottage was freezing and Gabe winced as I pushed past and flicked on the table lamp. I gasped when I turned and saw his face.

'What is all this?' I asked, 'and what happened to your face?'

His right eye was almost closed and it was embellished with bruises from every colour of the spectrum.

'Gavin,' he shrugged, dumping himself down on the sofa and reaching for the nearest bottle, 'he threw the first punch, but its impact wasn't immediately obvious.'

'Gavin hit you,' I frowned, 'but why?'

He gave me a look, through his one good eye.

'Because,' he sighed, 'he was in the gents mouthing off to his mates about whether he'd have the pleasure of escorting you back to the hall again and, if so, he was hoping you'd be up for another trip down Lovers Lane. I decided to take him to task over it and got thumped for my trouble.'

'Oh, Gabe,' I groaned. 'You should have just ignored him.'

If only he'd known my ex as well as the rest of the Wynthorpe clan he would have realised what a prize dick he could still be when the mood took him. I daresay Gavin only lashed out because he knew Gabe was about to set his mates straight about what had *really* happened. Not that that justified him resorting to violence.

'And let him get away with what he was saying?'

'Yes,' I told Gabe. 'He can't help himself when it comes to playing Jack the lad. He's a completely different person when he's sober and on his own. Still a wind-up merchant, mind you, but nowhere near as bad as when he's with the others.'

Gabe didn't look convinced.

'Look,' I said, 'I'm sorry he thumped you, but can we just forget about him?'

I really didn't want to talk about my ex anymore. There were still parts of our brandy-enhanced conversation that were a little on the hazy side, but for now, I needed to focus on what was going on with Gabe because, given the state of the cottage, something obviously was.

'So, what's all this then?' I asked, as I carefully stepped over the mess and set about lighting the wood burner.

'Just some stuff I look at every now and again,' Gabe mumbled. 'Please don't move it,' he added as I began to push it all together, waiting for the fire to take.

'This is the woman who came to stay here, isn't it?' I said, picking up one of the photos.

I couldn't be certain it was her, of course, but it was worth a shot. I looked at the rest of the scattered images, my heart suddenly thumping harder in my chest.

'She must be someone pretty special,' I swallowed, 'you've got enough pictures of her.'

There were also dozens of shots of a pretty little girl with a headful of dark curls and Gabe's eyes.

'Jeez, Hayley,' he snapped, leaning quickly forward and snatching the photo from my grasp. 'What does it matter? Will you just leave it?'

'All right,' I said, hoisting up my jeans and taking a deep

breath. 'I'll go. At least I can tell the others you aren't dead and haven't deserted us. I'll see you around.'

'The others?'

'Yes, the others,' I snapped back. 'Your friends, your work-mates, who are all over at the hall worried sick about you.'

'I didn't realise.'

'Well, you should have. You've been here long enough to know how things work. Jamie said you'd probably want to be left alone, but this has gone on long enough. We look out for each other here, Gabe. We might not be blood, but we're family nonetheless.'

I had almost made it out to the gate before he called after me.

'So was she!' he shouted.

'Who?'

He didn't answer and I walked back into the cottage.

'Penny,' he whispered, pointing at the photo. 'She's my sister. That's who came to stay.'

The admission didn't cheer him in the slightest, but suddenly I was on top of the world. Not a mystery wife then, not a secret lover, just a sister. So much for keeping my feelings for him on the right side of friendly. There was nothing platonic at all about the way my body and brain had reacted to his revelation.

'But why didn't you just tell me that before?' I frowned, suppressing the urge to indulge in a quick happy dance around the room. 'Why the cloak and dagger?'

He reached down the side of the sofa for another beer and tossed the bottle to me.

'It's a long story,' he said, hanging his head.

'I've got all night,' I told him, sitting in the chair.

I might have been perched on cloud nine but my companion still sounded in the depths of misery. I needed to be there for him, I needed to get to the bottom of whatever it was that had turned him into such a wreck.

'I have a date with the vacuum at eight sharp tomorrow morning,' I smiled, 'but until then, I'm at your disposal.'

'I need to use the bathroom,' he muttered, standing up and swaying slightly.

Bran came over and rested his head on my knee. He looked utterly miserable. Not even so much as a hint of a smile on his usually cheery face.

'I'll make tea,' I told him as I abandoned the beer and headed for the kitchen, 'and I daresay you'd like some dinner.'

Gabe gratefully drank the sweet tea and devoured the thick wedges of toast I had spread with generous curls of salted butter.

'Hungry?' I smiled.

'Apparently,' he smiled back, looking slightly less ropey. 'I hadn't realised.'

I waited for him to finish then cleared everything away, and when he didn't object, gathered the papers and photos together and set them on the sofa next to him. The room was much warmer already, and to the untrained eye, it all appeared to be back to normal, but there was something gnawing away at my friend. There was the biggest elephant marauding about the room and I hoped he was finally feeling ready to turf it out into the night, or at least share it so it didn't weigh him down quite so much.

'So,' I began, when it was obvious he wasn't going to or didn't know how. 'You were saying about your sister, Penny.'

'She came to stay for the weekend.'

'The weekend of the switch-on, I know.'

'It was actually the wrong date,' he said sadly, reaching for the photo on top of the pile. He stared at it intently and stroked it with his thumb, 'but she couldn't make it any closer because she's had to go to Paris for a work thing.'

He still wasn't making much sense.

'What was the wrong date?' I frowned.

'She should have been here for yesterday,' he swallowed.

'Why?' I shrugged. 'What's so special about December seventeenth?'

His face crumpled, pain twisting and contorting his handsome features as he struggled to get the words out. It was a torturous sight.

'It's the day my baby died,' he sobbed. 'The day my girl was taken from me for ever.'

It was leukaemia that had stolen Gabe's seven-year-old daughter, Hannah, and grief that was the main contributor to the subsequent breakdown of his marriage to Hannah's mum, Rebecca.

'She lives in Colorado now,' Gabe explained, 'she's married and has a son. We don't keep in touch.'

'But Penny looks out for you,' I nodded, moving the

things next to him on the sofa so I could sit closer. 'She spends Hannah's anniversary with you.'

'And her birthday,' he whispered, 'we always go to my baby's grave on her birthday.'

I didn't know what to say. The details were too dreadful to get a handle on. I knew that no words would do justice to the tragedy my friend had been through, must still be going through. I had no idea that he had this burden to bear. None of us did. Or did we?

My mind flitted back to the conversation I overheard between him and Jamie. Jamie had been concerned that Gabe wouldn't be able to cope with the grieving children who came to stay with us, but actually, there were few among us who could understand them any better.

'Does Jamie know?' I asked, just to be sure.

'Yes,' he nodded, 'he knows about Hannah, but not the specifics.'

'You mean, he doesn't know the significance of this week?'

'No.'

I knew he mustn't have because there was no way Jamie would have left his friend to suffer if he had worked out the real reason behind his outburst in the pub and subsequent low profile.

'He's asked me more about it all since I've been here, but I don't want him or anyone to know.'

'But why not? We could support you, try to help you through it.'

'No,' said Gabe firmly, 'thanks, but no. I couldn't stand the scrutiny and the sympathy every time the dates roll around. I'm better left to my own devices.'

'I'm truly sorry,' I said, taking hold of his hand as a few more pieces of the puzzle that made up his personality slotted into place. 'The bonfire party,' I started to say, remembering the way Gabe had written what looked like a name over and over again with his sparkler.

'I just couldn't face going into town,' he swallowed. 'Hannah loved fireworks and she would have loved the sweets and pastries Dorothy made for the Winter Wonderland. Rebecca was always nagging me not to spoil her, but now I wish I'd given her the world and everything in it.'

I nodded and tried to blink back my tears. My heart felt like a lump of lead in my chest, all excitement about Gabe's sister being the mystery visitor forgotten.

'I'd give anything to fill her up on sweets and take her to watch the fireworks again. She used to be scared, hanging on to my hand until I lifted her up. I should have been able to keep her safe from everything, but I couldn't.'

I nodded again, choked to think how hard it must have been for Gabe to watch the families all working together and enjoying the run-up to the Christmas he had played such an important part in creating. It must have been the same on the day of the tree auction in town, and yet he'd never said a word. How had he managed to get through all of those things, take part so wholeheartedly, without breaking down? My own heart contracted further still and I sent it out to him.

'I can't imagine how difficult the last few weeks here must

have been for you,' I whispered, knowing that throwing our rocky relationship into the mix couldn't have helped at all. 'I shouldn't have kept pushing you to tell me all this. I'm sorry.'

'I don't mind you knowing, Hayley,' he said, lacing his fingers through mine.

'You said you didn't want anyone to know.'

'Yes, but you aren't just anyone, are you?'

I could feel the heat between us beginning to build and it had nothing to do with how high I had stoked the wood burner. It seemed to me that, even though Gabe wouldn't act on his feelings for me again, there was no way he could deny their existence. I took a deep breath to help strengthen my resolve. I couldn't give in to temptation now. If Gabe did suddenly change his mind and make a move it would only be because he was seeking comfort, and as much as I wanted to help him, a one-off wouldn't ultimately be the answer for either of us.

'You know,' I said, although I had never willingly uttered the words to anyone, 'I lost a baby. Not in the same way that you did. Mine was an early miscarriage, but it never goes away, does it? The pain I mean.'

Gabe looked at me and shook his head.

'No, no it doesn't. In the early days I thought it was going to kill me. I wanted it to. It consumed me completely and I thought, why should I live when my girl . . .'

I squeezed his hand tighter.

'I'm sorry about your baby,' he whispered when he had recovered.

'And I'm sorry about your daughter,' I whispered back.

'And I'm sorry Gavin let you down,' he added.

'Actually,' I told him, 'I'm not too bothered about that.'

'No?'

'No, in fact, I think his continuing stupidity might have done me a favour.'

'How did you work that out?'

'Well,' I said, 'had he not been mouthing off in the gents, we wouldn't have ever had this conversation, and I think it's important that we have, don't you?'

Gabe was quiet for a minute, his fingers still wrapped around mine.

'Yes,' he said, cracking the first smile I'd seen since I'd arrived, but given the circumstances, that was hardly surprising. 'Yes, I suppose it is.'

I smiled back at him.

'And, you know,' he said, edging closer, 'I appreciate your friendship more than anything, Hayley.'

'I know you do,' I said, backing off before I gave in and lost myself in the moment. 'And I would hate for us to get carried away and do something that might jeopardise it, wouldn't you?'

Gabe might have readily admitted on more than one occasion that he found me attractive, but he had also said that he wasn't in the market for a relationship, and given how deeply I felt for him, I couldn't risk my heart. Not again. I might have shouted about my fun and frolics theory, but where Gabe was concerned, that simply wasn't true. If I gave in now there was no telling how I would feel afterwards.

'I would,' he said, 'but I really don't think we're in any danger of that. If anything, I think this would make it stronger.'

I allowed myself one glance at his beautiful eyes; eyes now filled with longing, the pupils dangerously dilated. Was he suggesting that taking things further would be good for our friendship? Because if he was looking for some sort of friends-with-benefits set-up then that wasn't enough for me.

'Gabe,' I gasped, groaning with pleasure as he quickly pulled me close and began to kiss my neck while tracing his fingers lightly along my collarbone and then down to unbutton my shirt. 'I really don't think this would be a good idea. I mean . . . you said . . .'

My back arched in response and my resistance melted away as his hands slowly parted the fabric. His kisses travelled further south and my resolve not to offer the ultimate comfort flew out of the window.

My gut feeling that I would be risking my heart turned out to be the right one, so it was a shame that I hadn't dug my heels in and resisted Gabe's sweet seduction. I had soon realised as he pushed me to the heavenly precipice and then over it, not once or twice, but three times, that I had enjoyed sex before, but I had never made love with any man, and I had never truly been in love before, either.

When I eventually woke, I lay for a moment or two, the soft light from the landing spilling across the bed as I watched the steady rise and fall of Gabe's broad chest and the way his lips parted as he exhaled. Then I slipped out of bed, dressed and took the shortest, but chilliest, walk of shame ever back to the hall under the clear starlit December sky.

I didn't manage to take everything back to the hall with me, though. My heart was left wrapped in Gabe's strong arms and I had a feeling I wasn't going to be able to recover it anytime soon. If only he wasn't so determined to deny himself what had the potential to make him happy. If only he could open up just the tiniest bit, then I was certain we could have something special.

'What happened to you last night?' asked Anna, an hour or so later when I bumped into her in the kitchen as she was getting ready for her morning run.

'What do you mean?'

'You went over to Gabe's and you didn't come back. Was he OK?'

'Not really,' I replied, busying myself with the kettle, 'but I promised him I wouldn't say anything.'

'About what?'

I looked at her and sighed.

'Sorry,' she giggled, 'that was a cheap shot.'

I ignored her and splashed milk into my mug. I wasn't much in the mood for giggly girl chat.

'But you know, you guys really would make a great couple,' she began.

'We really wouldn't,' I said, more out of habit and with far less conviction than every other time she happened to have mentioned it.

'Why not?'

'Well,' I began, 'for a start, from what I can make out, Gabe isn't looking for a relationship right now and I still have a hangover from my last one. I simply haven't got the headspace or the inclination to be thinking about starting something new. I'll probably never have the heart for a serious relationship again, to be honest.'

Not when the heart in question was so firmly clasped in Gabe's grasp.

'Rubbish,' Jamie unhelpfully blurted out as he joined Anna and began stretching to stave off a yawn.

'Which bit?' smiled Anna.

Why did she persist in thinking this was all some sort of joke?

'You know full well which bit.'

'None of it is rubbish, actually,' I butted in, frustration beginning to bubble like a witch's cauldron on a rolling boil. 'But even if it were, the way I feel about relationships now is all down to you anyway,' I ranted, pointing an accusatory finger in Anna's face.

'What did I do?' she said, looking genuinely upset by my sudden spark of temper.

'You and Mr Perfect, here,' I said, carelessly pouring boiling water into my mug and splashing it about in the process. 'You made me see just how good relationships can be and that's probably part of the reason why I couldn't keep my mouth shut and settle for Gavin. If I'd shut up and put up then I'd be planning my wedding right now.'

'And that would be a good thing, would it?' Anna frowned. 'You think you would have been better off sticking with a bloke who would always do whatever he felt necessary to impress his mates?'

Of course I didn't, but I was too angry to admit it.

'Well, it would be a far more preferable situation than you trying to pair me off with Gabe every hour of the bloody day,' I snapped.

'But Gabe's not Gavin,' Jamie pointlessly reminded me as he began mopping up the mess I had made with Dorothy's best tea towel.

'I'm well aware of that!' I shouted back, my voice catching in my throat. 'I'm not suggesting that he is, but neither of us need anyone interfering in our lives right now. You,' I said pointing at Jamie, 'should be more aware of that than anyone else as far as Gabe's concerned.'

'I just thought—' he began, turning red.

'But you didn't think, did you?' I accused. 'I thought you were supposed to be his friend.'

'I am.'

I knew I was taking my temper out on the wrong people, but there was no one else I could shout at. I could hardly go back and shout at Gabe, could I? It wasn't his fault that, unlike him, I wanted more from our night together than a fortified friendship.

How was it possible that I had managed to fall for a man who liked me but was so determined not to have me? If this was the last of the karma I had been expecting to come and kick me up the backside one day, then it had certainly taken a long run-up to achieve maximum effect.

'Then you should know better than anyone else that the last thing he—'

'What do you think you're doing with my best tea towel?' Dorothy interrupted, snatching it from Jamie's grasp, 'and will you all keep your voices down, it's far too early for amateur dramatics!'

I stormed out of the kitchen and up to my room without a backwards glance. I didn't even hang out of my window to try to work out if Gabe was up yet. I downed the contents of my scalding mug and dived under the duvet, resolving to put in an appearance after some scientist had worked out how to turn back time.

Chapter 29

My resolve didn't last, of course. It was Anna's birthday on the 21st of December, along with the solstice celebration that Molly was organising, so I had no choice but to get out of bed and make peace with my best friend. I still had no idea what I was going to say to Gabe when I saw him, but I would cross that bridge when I came to it.

'Happy birthday,' I said to Anna, shoving a parcel on to her lap when I joined them all for breakfast. 'Sorry for being a bitch,' I added in my trademark brusque style.

'I should think so, too,' she beamed tearing into the paper. 'And I know you probably think I should apologise for everything I've been saying and what I've been making you feel,' she added with emphasis, 'but I'm not going to.'

Had it been any other day I wouldn't have let her get away with that.

'Let's just agree to disagree,' I said, 'and leave it at that, shall we?'

'Oh my god, Hayley!' she squealed, making Suki and Floss jump out of their beds, and thankfully forgetting all about our disagreement, 'this is amazing. Thank you so much.'

That was just the reaction I had been hoping for. Apparently, my artistic talents could make friends discard arguments *and* cry at the same time. Perfect.

'I was hoping you'd like it,' I said, bending across to look at the little pen and ink sketch and wondering if, when I presented Gabe with his, it would make him feel as good as Anna.

'Let's see, then,' said Dorothy, as keen as everyone else to get a look.

'Oh my,' said Catherine. 'You've captured her beautifully, Hayley.'

The sketch was of Anna sitting cross-legged on one of the squashy sofas in the family room with a book open on her lap.

'Fortunately,' I smiled, 'you're quite the daydreamer, Anna, so I was able to get most of this down while you were staring out of the window.'

I didn't add that I had finished it while sulking in my room, but I was amazed to think that I could now sit so comfortably and discuss the moment my creativity had taken hold. For years I'd been hiding my work – from myself as much as anyone else – refusing to give in to the desire to even so much as pick up a pencil, and yet here I was, ready to share it all with my friends, and if the Cherry Tree plans came to fruition, then even with the wider world. If it all fell into place, then next year I'd be able to dish out presents featuring my own designs. How thrilling was that?

'I'll treasure it always,' said Anna, hugging it to her chest. 'It's one of the most beautiful presents I've ever been given.'

One of her other beautiful presents was pinned to her blouse. A cameo, identical to the one her mother had had, but which Anna had lost. This new one was given to her by Angus the Christmas she decided to make Wynthorpe her home, and she always wore it on high days and holidays.

'I'm so pleased you like it,' I smiled, looking again at the picture.

'I love it,' she beamed. 'Look, Molly. Look what Hayley's given me for my birthday.'

Molly and Archie arrived together, of course, flushed from the chilly walk from the cottage in the woods.

'So, are we all set then?' Mick asked, after everyone had finished admiring my handiwork. 'How's the weather look-ing this year? Any chance of actually seeing the sun on this particular solstice?'

'Everything's ready,' sniffed Molly, as she first peeled off her chunky handknitted scarf, then her coat and then her thick cardigan, also of her own creation. Archie pulled the felt hat off her head, releasing her abundant, wild hair.

No wonder she had a rosy glow.

'And yes, there's definitely a good chance of seeing the sun,' she added. 'It's going to be a perfect day.'

'That's what I like to hear,' said Anna.

During the last couple of years, I realised, we had both reclaimed something we had lost. Whilst I had been push-ing away my art, ever since the death of Anna's mother at

Christmas, she had been denying herself any sort of birthday or seasonal celebration, but since arriving at Wynthorpe she was embracing both with gusto. I put it down to the magic within the hall walls and I hoped Gabe would someday soon benefit from its healing embrace.

'Is Gabe going to be joining us?' Molly asked when I looked up and caught her staring at me.

She had an uncanny and somewhat unnerving knack of doing that. Clearly there was more magic around the breakfast table than that wrapped up in the fabric of the hall.

'Hopefully,' said Jamie, his gaze also flicking to me. 'He's been keeping himself to himself for a few days, but fingers crossed he'll put in an appearance.'

There was something in his look that suggested he now had more of an idea about why Gabe had been staying away. I hoped his knowledge didn't include the part I had played in his friend's absence from the hall. Gabe had told me that he thought us being together would strengthen our friendship, but considering his continued absenteeism it appeared that the opposite was in fact true.

'He's no doubt worn out after all his hard work at the Winter Wonderland,' said Angus. 'His efforts, ably assisted by Hayley, of course, made more profit than the rest of us put together.'

'Yes,' said Catherine, 'we must thank him properly for that.'

'And as the newest recruit,' Molly chimed in, 'I'm rather hoping he'll agree to seek out the hall yule log. Although, thinking about the strength of him, we might have to remind him not to go for something too big,' she added and every-one laughed.

Having been carried up the narrow stairs in Gatekeeper's Cottage with ease, I could vouch for Gabe's strength, but thought it best to keep the details of that to myself.

I was disappointed when Gabe didn't show up for the sol-stice ceremony, but I wasn't completely surprised. I had been hoping to get our first post-coital conversation underway amidst the other yule log gatherers from town and the rest of the family. Yes, it was a thoroughly selfish and cowardly idea, but as the week had worn on I had felt more and more ashamed of myself for running out on him, especially given everything he had shared with me.

I was hardly being the supportive friend I had promised to be and I wanted to rectify that, but I wasn't quite sure how. I just hoped it wasn't too late to make amends. I might have left my heart in Gabe's embrace, but that wasn't his fault. I had no intention of burdening him with my feelings, especially now I knew just how much his own heart had to deal with. I might have still wanted more from him than friendship, but I needed to just let it go and be there for him.

'I was hoping to see Gabe here this afternoon,' Mags from the owl sanctuary said as she fell into step beside me.

'Me too,' I told her.

'The last time we spoke after the Winter Wonderland he seemed really keen to take on our barn owl, Jareth.'

In my mind's eye, I could picture Gabe striding out across the misty early-morning Fenland landscape, Jareth on his arm and Bran at his heels, but I wasn't sure how I felt about the image. Bran had seemed every bit as smitten with the mysterious beauty as his master, but Gabe's desire to make the owl his own didn't quite tally with his resolve to deny himself anything that made him happy. Perhaps his ethos only included people like me, the woman who had loved and promptly left.

'But I don't think it's going to happen now,' Mags shrugged.

'Why not?' I frowned, the image disappearing with a pop as I tuned back into what she was saying.

'Jamie says Gabe's gone away for a bit. We couldn't let him take Jareth if that's something he's going to make a habit of.'

'I see,' I said, my head spinning.

'He's a creature with a damaged past, who needs some constancy in his life.'

I wasn't sure if she was referring to Jareth or Gabe, but I knew exactly how whoever it was felt.

'Well, I'm sure Gabe will be back soon,' I said, striding ahead to catch up with Jamie. 'And I'm certain he really would be the perfect person for Jareth.'

Once Molly and her coven – although she preferred me to call them her friends – had selected Mick in lieu of Gabe to search for the yule log and had said a few words, I took the opportunity to ask Jamie what was going on.

'Why didn't you say earlier that Gabe had gone away?'

I didn't want to sound confrontational or cause another upset, but I was feeling floored. What if our night together, and my early departure after it, was the reason Gabe had decided to do a runner? I had promised him that friendship and comfort were on offer to all at Wynthorpe Hall and I hated the thought that my actions might have denied him access to both when he needed them most.

'Because I didn't know,' Jamie said simply. 'He rang my mobile just before we came out to say he had stopped in town, was phoning from the Cherry Tree, and was going on to visit family. He said he'd be back after Christmas, ready to start work in the New Year.'

As far as I knew, aside from Penny who was in Paris, he had no family. I let out a sob as I imagined him spending Christmas camped out next to his daughter's grave.

'Are you all right?' Jamie asked. 'Has something happened between you two?'

'No,' I swallowed, 'nothing. Of course not.'

'That's what I was afraid of,' he said, sounding suitably unimpressed. 'What a pair of idiots you are.'

I didn't comment and Jamie wandered off to see how Mick was getting on.

I stood rooted to the spot, my feet becoming more and more frozen to the woodland floor. I should have felt relieved that Gabe had gone away and left me to take back possession of my heart in peace, but actually I was gutted. Just as I had predicted, the fleeting comfort our night together provided had ruined our friendship rather than strengthened it. I had been weak and now I was paying the ultimate price, and so was Gabe.

'Hayley,' said Anna, laying her hand on my arm. 'Are you all right?'

'You look frozen stiff,' said Molly, standing the other side of me.

'I'm fine,' I told them, taking a deep breath and shrugging them off.

They looked doubtful, and a little hurt at being given the brush off.

'Honestly,' I told them both, flashing what I hoped was a reassuring smile, 'I was just miles away. Come on,' I rallied, 'let's go and catch the others up.'

The last thing I felt like doing was traipsing through the trees all afternoon and chanting as the sun began to set, but I joined in nonetheless. I answered when I was spoken to, I helped Molly fill her jute bag with leaves to make a seasonal collage and I posed for the obligatory photographs when Mick declared he had found the Wynthorpe yule log, but through it all my heart wept.

I didn't much care about myself anymore, but poor Gabe. How could I have let him down so badly when he had always been there for me? Literally from the moment we had met he had protected me with his mighty wings. Surely now it was time for me to do the same for him, and not only by offering him physical comfort.

It was up to me to make him see sense, I realised. I needed to convince him that denying himself any chance of happiness was not the way forward. If anything, his determination to be alone would only prolong his grieving, and I was certain his daughter wouldn't have wanted to see her father suffering any more than he already had.

I had to get through to him. Even if he did decide he didn't want to be with me, we could still be friends, helping each other along life's rocky path. It was a thrilling prospect, tempered only by the fact that he had sprouted wings and taken flight just hours before I had worked out what I could do to really help him.

Chapter 30

Having gone to so much trouble to tell Jamie that nothing had happened between Gabe and me, it felt impossible to quiz him further about where he thought our woodsman might have gone. However, given the fact that Jamie seemed so unconcerned about his disappearance, I could only conclude that perhaps Gabe did have more family than he had mentioned to me and was subsequently safely nestled in the warm and festive embrace of kith and kin. But it didn't feel like that. Deep down in my bones there was something niggling away at me, telling me that wasn't the case at all.

'I was rather hoping,' said Anna as, between us, we measured out the space in the main hall, trying to work out the very best fit for the tables, chairs and things for the party, 'that the menfolk would be on hand to help out with all this.'

I gave a loud tut at her suggestion.

'Are you suggesting that we aren't capable of wielding a measuring tape?' I frowned.

'No,' she said primly, 'not at all, but we might have a job trying to move the long table and set up the stage on our own.'

She had a point; the table was solid oak and the stage was unwieldy for two to manage.

'I don't suppose you've heard anything from Gabe, have you?' she asked innocently. 'He's the sort of hefty chap we need to help us lug all this stuff about.'

I wondered how long she had been working her way up to bringing the conversation round to him.

'There does seem to be rather a lot to sort out,' I said with a nod to the most recent delivery of large cardboard boxes.

'I think these are the snowflakes for the ceiling,' she said, abandoning the tape measure, and, thankfully, her questioning of my lack of info about Gabe's current whereabouts.

She whipped a small penknife out of her pocket.

'Where on earth did you get that?' I gasped, feeling slightly taken aback as I watched her competently slit open one of the boxes and plunge her hands inside.

'Angus, of course,' she beamed. 'It was my advent calendar gift the day you were sulking in your room.'

'I wasn't sulking—' I started, but she carried on talking over me.

'He thought it would come in handy,' she said, 'and he was right. Oh now, these are perfect.'

She pulled open a large bag and tipped out a variety of different sized snowflakes cut out of ice blue coloured card. Some were covered in sparkly silver glitter while others were plain. Lots were strung together garland style. She passed me one end and together we spread it the length of the entire floor.

'It's snowflake bunting,' she told me. 'To carry on your clever theme from the Winter Wonderland. Pretty isn't it? And these,' she added, picking up the sets that were joined together in shorter lengths, 'are for hanging from the ceiling.'

'Lovely,' I told her.

I couldn't help thinking that if she wasn't careful the party would end up looking like a scene straight out of *Frozen*, but I was sure she knew what she was doing.

'How have the guests responded to you including a colour scheme for their outfits?' I asked.

There hadn't been time for me to design the invitations myself, but Anna had said she would definitely be securing my services for the next party.

'Everyone's really excited,' she told me warmly. 'Although, as you know, we've had to concede a little for the gents, because finding white suits was almost impossible.'

'I should imagine so,' I said with a wry smile.

The guests had all been asked, if possible, to wear white, in keeping with the snowy theme, but the colour palette had subsequently been enlarged to include blue.

'My goodness,' she laughed, 'can you imagine Angus in a white suit? He'd look like a snowman. And what about Gabe? He really would look like an angel, wouldn't he?'

Thankfully, my mobile began to ring just at that moment and I was saved from having to answer. As I pulled it out of my jeans pocket I hoped it was Gabe, but of course having no phone of his own I'd never bothered to pass my number on to him.

'Hayley?'

'Yes?'

'It's Evelyn, from The Mermaid.'

'Hello, Evelyn, is everything all right?'

I had no idea why the landlady of my local would be calling me.

'Yes, love,' she said. 'Sort of.'

I was somewhat knocked off-guard by her use of an endearment. Clearly something wasn't right at all.

'Is this a convenient time to talk?' she asked. 'I don't want to interrupt your work.'

'It's fine,' I said, waving at Anna to indicate that I'd come back after I'd finished the call. 'It's not Dad, is it?' I gasped, thinking the worst. 'He hasn't run up a bar bill again, has he?'

'After last time,' sniffed Evelyn, sounding more like her usual self, 'you must be joking. He's the last person I'd offer credit to. No, this is about the other bane of your life.'

'Gavin?'

'Gavin.'

'What's he done now?' I groaned.

Surely it was about time that folk stopped associating him with me. At least I wished it was.

'It's nothing he's done,' she said, sounding jittery again, 'more something he's said.'

'If he's still suggesting we had a quickie down Lovers Lane—'

'No,' she interrupted, 'it's not that.'

'What then?'

'Well,' she said, clearing her throat and cranking my paranoia up a notch, 'he'd had a drink or two last night and started rattling on about . . . about the bit of bother you had when you left school.'

'About me getting pregnant, you mean?'

There was no point in beating about the bush. If I was heading for further trouble then I needed to be in possession of the plain facts, even if hearing them said out loud did leave me reeling.

'That's it,' she said with a heavy sigh. 'Last night he was telling everyone how your art teacher wasn't actually the father, even though you always maintained he was.'

I felt my internal temperature soar and my knees wobble as I dumped myself down on the stairs. Clearly Gavin had decided that he needed to spout off to a wider audience. He couldn't have picked a better subject if he was hoping to draw everyone's attention.

'Oh?' I croaked.

I couldn't deny that Gavin was right. Mr Ridley wasn't the father. There was never any question that he could be, but when I found out that he was leaving school for another job, right when I needed him the most, I saw to it that everyone thought otherwise. He had nurtured my talent, fed my confidence, explained to me a future I could never have even imagined living under my parents' uncultured roof, let alone had the courage to grasp. And then he left.

I was devastated.

I was also bitter, spiteful and seven weeks pregnant. There was to be no sweet sixteen for me.

'Right,' I swallowed.

This confirmed everything I feared I had talked to Gavin about on the night of the numerous brandies. Whatever must everyone in town be thinking about me now? I would never be able to show my face in Wynbridge again.

'I just thought you ought to know,' said Evelyn, 'forewarned and all that,' she added stoutly.

'Thanks, Evelyn.'

'But, of course, no one cared,' she went on. 'He wasn't telling us anything we hadn't already worked out for ourselves, and he certainly didn't gain any fans with his tittle tattle.'

'Sorry?'

'Well, it was obvious,' she went on, 'we all knew right from the start. About the teacher, I mean.'

'I don't understand.'

'We guessed that you'd made it up,' she said softly. 'Everyone knew that if the authorities had thought there was even a whiff of truth behind what you were telling folk then they would have investigated, wouldn't they? A teacher getting a student pregnant would have been headline news.'

She was right, of course. It sounded very much as if I was the only person still living with the web of lies I had spun. For years I had been feeling ashamed and guilty about it all, but everyone else had worked out the truth right from the start. I had made a silly mistake. I had been an emotional teenager who told a lie and then hadn't had the sense to either retract it or notice that no one had believed it in the first place. What a prize plank.

'So, what do you think Gavin was hoping to get out of all this?' I asked.

'A bit of attention,' she told me, 'but it didn't work. No one cared. If anything, they felt sorry for you, sad about what you'd been through. Everyone knows it hasn't been easy living where you did, with a father like you unfortunately have, and then you'd fallen for this twit, Gavin to boot.'

That was something, I supposed, knowing folk understood, and to be honest it was a relief to have it all out in the open. I'd never meant to hurt anyone, especially Mr Ridley, but once my temper was tamed and I had realised what I'd done I didn't know how to make amends. I should have come clean at the time, but I hadn't and I had always felt ashamed about that.

'I'm going to have to talk to Gavin, aren't I?' I said as I realised that this was what Jemma had been referring to when she was setting up for the Winter Wonderland.

I knew we'd been talking about different things, but we'd been so busy I hadn't had a chance to quiz her further. From what I could deduce, Gavin had been gossiping to her without the assistance of a few pints. This was fast becoming a nasty habit he needed to drop, otherwise he'd soon find he had no audience to crow in front of at all.

'There's no need,' said Evelyn firmly. 'Besides, you won't be able to find him now. He's gone.'

'What do you mean?'

'He's just left the pub with his tail firmly between his legs.'

'You mean he was there all night?'

'No,' she tutted. 'Hardly. He came back here first thing looking like death warmed up to ask if his behaviour had been as bad as he thought it had been.'

'I hope you told him it had.'

'Of course I did,' she continued. 'I thought he was going to be sick. He said he'd also told Jemma about it all and that he couldn't blame alcohol on that occasion as he'd been stone cold sober.'

'Sounds to me like he's got the taste for sharing secrets as well as drinking lager.'

'You're right,' she agreed, 'but he did look genuinely upset and sounded pretty sorry.'

'Sorry for himself,' I butted in.

I hoped Evelyn hadn't fallen for his puppy dog act.

'Well,' she said, 'perhaps. Anyway, he had a rucksack with him and when I asked him if he was going somewhere, he said he was off to stay with a cousin up north. He said last night made him realise that, even though he had been trying to mend his ways, he was turning into someone he didn't like. He thought time away from here might not be a bad idea while he sorted himself out.'

'That's something I suppose,' I conceded. 'Although I can't deny I would have liked the opportunity to sound him out about what he's done.'

'I don't think that would help either of you,' said Evelyn,

who usually relished a verbal back and forth. 'It's time to draw a line, my love. Let him go and move on.'

I went back to help Anna with mixed emotions, knowing that I was going to have to come clean to my friend. I had told her the same lie when she first moved to the hall and I wanted her to hear the truth from my own lips, rather than through talk in town.

'I kind of guessed,' she said, once I had finished explaining. 'I didn't think a teacher would get away with something like that, to be honest, but I was hardly in a position to cross-examine you, was I? Plus,' she added, 'it wasn't my business, any more than it was Gavin's, so I thought it was best left forgotten.'

I nodded and swallowed, determined not to cry.

'Which is what you should do,' she said, rubbing my back, 'forget all about it.'

'I will,' I told her, knowing I would do exactly that but not until I had sought out Mr Ridley's address and written to him or sent him an email. I wanted to explain and apologise. I owed him that.

'Now who could that be?' Anna frowned as someone began beating a tattoo on the main door. 'Everyone knows to go around to the kitchen.'

'I'll go and see,' I told her, 'everyone else seems to have disappeared this morning.'

My thoughts strayed back to Gabe and how he had disappeared before I had a chance to apologise. I wondered if

Gavin had been spouting off about my lie in the gents, as well as our non-existent tryst. No wonder Gabe knocked him on his back, if that were the case.

'Hayley, hi. How are you?' It was Will, the wonderful Wynbridge vet. 'I tried the back but there was no one about,' he explained. 'I've come to have a look at one of the ponies.'

I had no idea where everyone had gone, but I quickly grabbed my coat and led him out to the paddock. It was freezing outside, but I was happy to leave Anna to her snow-flakes and my thoughts about our missing angel behind for a few minutes.

'Do you know which one?' I sniffed, rubbing my hands together and blowing on them as we approached the paddock.

The two of them had been responsible for pulling the sleigh throughout the Winter Wonderland and, according to Mick, one was now a little lame. I couldn't say I was all that surprised given the number of visitors we'd had. The ponies were strong, sturdy little souls, but if Angus and Jamie had plans to repeat the experience they would have to call in more equine help and set up some sort of tag team scenario to help share the load.

'I'd say that one,' suggested Will, pointing as one of them approached looking decidedly down in the dumps. 'Wouldn't you?'

'Yes,' I said, feeling a little foolish given that she had a pronounced limp. 'Yes, I think you're right.'

The pair were easy enough to tempt into the stable with a bucket of pony nuts, and I closed the door hoping Will wasn't going to need an assistant. They were pretty to look at, but I'd never been hands on with them before.

'Would you mind holding her head?' he asked, before I had even finished thinking the thought. 'Just keep her steady while I have a quick look. She might be a bit tender. But if you whisper sweet nothings into her ear,' he grinned, 'I'm sure she'll be fine.'

I tentatively held Peppermint by her bridle and tried my best not to convey my fear on to her. Fortunately, she stood stock still, stoic as she faced her fate. I have no idea what Will did to her back hoof, but the little pony whinnied once and then there was a quick squirt from an aerosol and it was all over.

'That's all done,' he said, patting her rump and giving her a friendly rub. 'Who was a brave girl?'

'Thank you,' I grinned, 'but if it's all the same with you, I won't make a habit out of it.'

I could cope with the dogs, but the equestrian side of the estate was very much Mick's territory.

'I've time for a cuppa, I should think,' Will laughed, looking pointedly at his watch.

As we walked back to the hall he explained that Peppermint had nothing more vexing than a thorn embedded in a tender spot between her hoof and the fleshy part on her foot. Apparently, manoeuvring the sleigh hadn't been responsible at all.

'The spray's antibiotic,' he told me, 'so she should be fine now, but if you could just ask Mick to keep an eye on her.

I can't imagine there'll be any complications, but with his experience he'll be able to spot anything untoward.'

The man himself was waiting for us at the back door and the pair went into the kitchen together, chatting amiably and I went to meet the postman whose van I had spotted weaving its way along the potholed drive.

'I'll take it if you like,' I called to him, 'save your suspension from the final stretch.'

'Thanks,' he said, handing over the pile, which was bound together with an elastic band. 'Much obliged.'

I pulled off the band as I walked back and flicked through the various envelopes. The hall always had plenty of post, but it was rare to find anything for me. That particular morning, however, there was an envelope, written in a hand I didn't recognise.

I collected a mug of tea from the table and headed up to my room to open the mystery missive. I had a feeling deep in my gut that this wouldn't be something I should open in company.

'I'll be back in a sec,' I said to Anna, 'nice to see you, Will.'

My hands were shaking as I tore open the envelope and pulled out the letter within. It was from Gabe. Knowing him as I now did, it felt fitting that he should write rather than call. I took a few deep breaths and braced myself to read what it was he had to say. The controlled intake of air did nothing to tame the wild fluttering in my chest.

His words were sad, resigned and defeated and they tore my heart in two. I would have been more able to cope had he ranted, raved and accused, after all, that was nothing less than I deserved after running out on him, but his tone throughout was devastatingly sad.

I know that when I first came to the hall you couldn't comprehend why I always felt so bad about relaxing and enjoying myself, and that you thought that telling you I liked you then backing off was some sort of sick self-denial, but I'm hoping you can understand now. I hope that you can see why I can't allow myself even a moment of happiness or the promise of a better future when my darling daughter can have neither.

How can I possibly smile and laugh, sing and dance when those basic delights have been denied to Hannah? I should be helping her to learn and grow; I should be watching her perform in school plays, taking part in sports day, helping with her homework and tucking her in at night. In short, I should be being her daddy, but all I am is a visitor to her grave. It would be wrong for me to even consider living more of a life than the one I have now.

During my time in Africa, I had settled all this in my head, Hayley. I was getting on with my life, being helpful to others, making a difference to their lives without letting my efforts improve my own, but meeting you was like being struck by a thunderbolt.

You forced your way into my truck and then into my life, and suddenly the world started to shine again. You made me feel things, feel better, laugh and dance, participate in everything I knew I had no right to, and I foolishly allowed myself to be pulled along. I was compliant, enthusiastic even, and that wasn't fair on either of us. I can only apologise for my behaviour towards you during what I know has been a difficult time in your own life, even though you try to pretend otherwise.

I know you aren't as tough as you make out, Hayley. The old you really doesn't hold sway anymore, does she? I could tell that when we spent the night together. For those few hours, you helped me to forget my pain, but I'm not sure that I should have.

I admit that I was relieved to wake and find you gone, because I don't know what I would have said to you then any more than I do now. I'm terrified to ask you to be mine, because that will mean a fresh start and a new life and I don't feel I am entitled to either, but at the same time I feel sick to my stomach when I try to imagine my life without you in it.

The thing is, I'm in love with you, Hayley. I think I have been from the very moment we collided in the corridor in The Mermaid, and I don't know what I'm supposed to do about it. This isn't how I imagined my time at Wynthorpe would work out, but I don't think I'm going to be able to come back.

I'm so sorry.

I fell back on to the bed, exhausted and emotionally wrung-out. Gabe had finally admitted that he was in love with me and he had left. Why had I not stayed at the cottage and made him talk things through? Why had I jumped to conclusions rather than realising that he was clinging to the misguided, grief-driven belief that he should never know a moment's happiness again because he had lost Hannah?

If there was one thing my phone call from Evelyn had made me realise, it was that holding on to past hurts was fruitless. There was nothing to be gained from it, nothing positive, anyway. I had spent too many years clinging to something that held me back, and while I had no intention of suggesting that Gabe should let Hannah go, I knew that he needed to be guided by his grief when it came to forging a future for himself, not ruled by it.

I had to find him. I had to make him understand.

I snatched the envelope back up and studied the postmark. The letter had been sent in Wynbridge. It had certainly taken its time to find me if he had posted it on the day he left. Given the strain on the festive postal service, that was hardly surprising, but it wasn't franked on the day he left. Was it possible that he hadn't ventured that far after all?

I raced back down to the kitchen, drying my eyes on my sleeves and not caring at all about the impact my tears had had on my kohl liner.

'Hayley,' gasped Dorothy as I burst in, 'what on earth's the matter?'

'You've been crying,' frowned Anna. 'What's going on?'

'It's Gabe,' I said, swallowing down the lump in my throat and refusing to sob again. 'I need to find him, but I don't know where to start.'

The women looked blankly at one another and then back to me.

'He's at Cuckoo Cottage,' said Will, who I hadn't noticed was still drinking tea at the table.

'What?' I gasped.

He looked from me to the others and then shook his head.

'Oh, crikey,' he said, his eyes wide in panic as he no doubt remembered his former military training. 'I can't believe I told you that. I'm not supposed to crack under interrogation.'

I had hardly been cross-examining him.

'Just forget I said it,' he rushed on. 'I'm probably wrong, actually. I mean, it might be him,' he stammered, 'it might not . . .'

'Will!' I shouted. 'If you know something then please tell me.'

'I can't,' he said, 'I'm not supposed to . . .'

'Will, please,' I pleaded. 'This is important.'

'Oh, all right,' he sighed. 'I suppose I've let the cat out of the bag now, anyway, haven't I? He's rented out one of the caravans from Lottie,' he went on.

'Go on,' I encouraged.

'Well,' he said, shifting in his seat. 'She usually shuts down the glamping site over the winter, but Gabe turned up and asked if there was any chance he could stay for a couple of weeks.'

The rest of us looked blankly at one another.

'I thought it was a bit strange that he wasn't going to be here over Christmas,' said Will, scratching his head, 'but he said he would prefer it if no one knew where he was, and that he was going to keep a low profile until the New Year. He said he just fancied a bit of peace and quiet. He isn't in trouble, is he?'

'No,' said Mick, 'of course not.'

'Although you might be,' said Anna to Will, 'when he finds out that you've given him away.'

'Oh, bugger,' said Will, 'he's not the sort of guy you'd want to cross, is he?'

And this from a bloke who once served in the highest ranks of the British army and was built like a ... well, he was fit.

'It's fine,' I told him, feeling far better and knowing exactly what I had to do. 'This time tomorrow he'll be shaking your hand and thanking you.'

Will didn't look so sure.

'I better go and warn Lottie that I've compromised Gabe's mission,' he said, standing up and brushing biscuit crumbs on to the floor.

'Good idea,' I said, snatching up my coat. 'And as you're heading that way, you can give me a lift. I don't much fancy getting the bike out in this weather.'

Chapter 31

Will wasn't too keen on giving me a lift to Cuckoo Cottage, but the thought of me risking life and limb on two wheels along the icy roads was enough to make him relent. We drove in silence to the vintage glamping site Lottie Foster had created from her inherited legacy of some very lovely old caravans, a collection of barns and an obliging field.

'Which van?' I asked as we slowly drove through the gate and Will pulled up outside the pretty cottage. 'You might as well tell me,' I said when he refused to be drawn, 'I'm going to check them all anyway.'

'The furthest one,' he said, pointing.

'I can't see his truck.'

'It's parked up in one of the barns,' he explained. 'He really didn't want to be found, you see.'

I nodded.

'Well,' I sighed, 'you've rather blown his cover now, haven't you? But I promise I won't mention your name if he asks.'

'Thanks,' said Will, 'and good luck. I don't think you'll find him in the best of tempers.'

'That's all right,' I said with a smile, 'I'm not expecting the warmest of welcomes.'

It was easy to approach the caravan in silent stealth mode on foot, and as I made my way across the frosty field I tried to think about exactly what I was going to say. I was sorrier than I could possibly hope to convey for being the cause of so much angst and confusion, but at the same time determined to make Gabe find a way to come to terms with everything that had happened to him, and prove that his past shouldn't blight his future. I truly hoped his way forward would include me, but I knew that if I failed to find the right words, if I made a mess of the next few minutes, it would be more than my own happiness that would be scuppered.

I sent up a silent prayer as I approached the van, swallowed hard and took a deep breath before knocking on the door. The curtains were all drawn and it was deathly quiet. I had an overwhelming sense of déjà vu. This was exactly how Gatekeeper's looked the night I found him drunk and inconsolable.

'Gabe,' I said, my voice cracking as it caught in my throat. When there was no answer I tried again.

'Gabe! It's me, Hayley. Please let me in.'

I wasn't the type of girl who resorted to turning on the waterworks when she wasn't getting her own way, but my eyes filled with tears that refused to be blinked away, and they spilled down my cheeks, painful in the bitter breeze, taking with them the last of my already-smudged liner.

'I'm so sorry about everything,' I sobbed. 'I should never have run out on you the other night. I should have stayed. I should have realised what was wrong and found a way to help you see that you don't have to spend the rest of your life punishing yourself for what happened to Hannah. None of it was your fault, Gabe, and you won't gain anything from torturing yourself. I'm sure she wouldn't have wanted you to do that.'

Still nothing.

'The thing is,' I choked, 'I know what it's like to try and live your life with something hanging around your neck pulling you down.'

My own experience was nowhere near as traumatic as Gabe's, but I was fast approaching the point where I would do, say or admit to anything to make him see.

'It's all too easy to get things twisted in your head when you're in so deep, and you end up believing them, unsure how to find a way forward without taking them with you. I'm not saying you should move on and leave Hannah behind, because she's a part of you and she always will be, she *should* be, but you do deserve to be happy, Gabe. You aren't going to be letting her down by looking out for yourself.'

Still nothing.

I pulled a crumpled tissue out of my pocket and violently blew my nose. It didn't help much and the tears continued to flow.

'I got your letter,' I said, rubbing my hand over the pocket where I had put it, 'and I know you blame me for waking you up, but you've woken me up, too. I thought I'd been in love before, but until you came along I didn't know the meaning of the word. We've both made each other think and feel new things. We've both been responsible for changing each other and I can't help thinking that's a good thing.'

I began to realise that nothing was going to work. I would walk over to the cottage and ask Lottie if I could wait there until Anna could come and pick me up. At least I could go back to the hall knowing that I'd tried.

'I'm leaving now,' I sniffed, the cold air so sharp it tickled my nose, 'but please, *please* don't sacrifice your home and job at the hall because of me. Those children need you, Gabe,' I sobbed again as I thought of what they would be missing out on if he left, 'every bit as much as I think you need them.'

I had barely taken two steps before I heard the caravan door creak open and was spun around from behind and pulled into Gabe's strong embrace.

'I'm so sorry,' I said again, as his lips met mine.

'I know,' he said, when he eventually pulled away and, holding me by the tops of my arms, stared down into my tear-streaked face, 'I know you are and so am I. I love you, Hayley, but I don't know how I can possibly move forward when I'm still not sure that I should.'

At least now he sounded slightly more inclined to consider that he might.

'Well, what about if we take really tiny steps,' I suggested.

'We'll talk about things and take our time and not expect to be able to run before we've barely fallen into step.'

'But I'm so scared of getting it wrong,' Gabe croaked. 'I don't think I could bear it if I couldn't keep up with you emotionally and ended up losing you, too.'

'I'm not going to rush off anywhere,' I told him, 'emotionally or otherwise. You don't have to worry about that.'

Gabe stifled a sob of his own and nodded and we stayed, locked in each other's arms until the cold eventually forced its way into our embrace.

'Could we go inside, do you think?' I sniffed, looking towards the caravan and beautiful, big Bran framed in the doorway.

'No,' said Gabe, as he wiped a hand over his eyes. 'I'm sorry, Hayley, but I don't think that would be a good idea.'

I couldn't believe it. From the strength of his hold on me I thought we were going to be OK. I had dared to believe that everything was going to be all right. I dropped my hands to my sides and pulled away from the arm he still had wrapped around me.

'There's no room,' he smiled, banishing my fears in a heartbeat and pulling me close again, 'the two of us have been going stir crazy tripping over each other. I don't think we can squeeze another thing in there, not even a little pain in the backside like you!'

I shoved him hard in the chest and rolled my eyes.

'So why have you stayed then?' I laughed, pointing at the van. 'Why didn't you just pack up your truck and find somewhere bigger?'

'Because I knew as soon as I posted that letter that I'd made a mistake,' he said gruffly, 'I knew I wasn't going to be able to let you go and I hoped—'

'Yes?'

'I guess I hoped that you would come and find me.'

'Really?'

'Even though I still wasn't completely sure it would be the right thing, I wanted you to rescue me.'

I snuggled back into his arms. I had no idea that sometimes angels needed us every bit as much as we needed them.

Chapter 32

The Wynthorpe Hall snowflake-inspired Christmas party was every bit as exquisite as you could imagine. The frosty theme was elegant and not at all overdone, and Anna and Catherine were thrilled with the results. The yule log burnt brightly in the magnificent grate, ensuring the guests wore a rosy glow in spite of the snowy seasonal decorations. The air was filled with the spicy scent of mulled wine and the festive fare Dorothy had made, including yet more cinnamon swirls, which filled the packed buffet tables. The Christmas tree decoration competition winner – the book club and library this year – had been left in situ along with the family's own magnificent tree, and everyone dressed as the invitations requested, thrilled to be a part of another Wynthorpe celebration.

Gabe and I were a little late in arriving, even though we had the shortest journey to make. But that was not, as Archie suggested, because we couldn't be bothered to get out of bed, but because we had been talking to Mags and making arrangements for when Jareth, the barn owl, would be joining us in the New Year.

Fortunately, it hadn't taken too much effort on my part to convince Gabe that coming back to the hall for Christmas was going to be a far better option than staying in Lottie's caravan, as pretty as it was, and we had been holed up in Gatekeeper's Cottage together pretty much ever since. He had even admitted to me that, when he first arrived at the hall, Molly had assured him how she envisaged his year was going to end, but he hadn't believed her. He thought it was impossible for so much to change in such a short space of time.

I couldn't recall a time in my life when I had been happier, and it was a feeling I knew I would enjoy getting used to now that I had finally convinced Gabe that we had a happy future ahead of us.

I'd been through a lot during the last few months, not all of it good, but had settled in my new home with the love of a wonderful man to keep me warm and a new career on the horizon. I couldn't possibly wish for more.

I had no intention of giving up my work at the hall, but the thought of combining my old job with something new was thrilling and I was looking forward to building stronger bridges with Mum, who I wished every happiness in her new venture as she planned to escape my father's lazy clutches. The new year was going to hold a great deal of joy for both the Hurren girls.

'Hayley,' smiled Jamie, when Gabe and I finally arrived at the party, 'crikey, you scrub up all right, don't you?'

'What a charmer!' I laughed, as he took in my navy dress with a more appreciative eye.

It was a girlie frock for me – strapless with a full skirt, white net petticoats and a white ribbon around the waist. I had expected to feel trussed up in it and completely out of my comfort zone, but actually it was all right. With my hair pinned up and pretty drop pearl earrings demurely dangling, I was almost elegant. *Almost.*

'But isn't that—?' Jamie frowned as Molly and Anna skipped into view and he took the three of us in.

'Yes,' I smiled, linking arms with my two friends, 'it is.'

We looked at one another and laughed. Anna and Molly's dresses were exactly the same as mine, only Anna had gone for white and Molly was in ice blue, which set off her almost tamed red hair beautifully.

'I told you it would work,' said Anna, with a wink. 'Didn't I say it would be fun?'

I had thought she was mad when she suggested the three of us went for the same frock, but she was right, it worked well, and Anna, almost bride-like, was radiant. Jamie held out his hand for her and I took a step forward.

'If you don't ask her to marry you, tonight,' I whispered in his ear, 'then you're even more of a fool than I am.'

He looked at me and smiled and I just knew that a proposal was right at the top of his agenda. I looked at Archie, his fingers lightly touching Molly's creamy shoulders, and wondered if he was thinking the same thing.

'Hayley Hurren,' tutted Gabe, as we watched the others

walk away and he pulled me towards where everyone was dancing, 'I seriously hope you weren't interfering in matters of the heart?'

'I wouldn't dream of it,' I laughed up at him. 'I'm hardly qualified, am I?'

'Oh, I don't know about that,' he smiled as we began to gently sway in time with the music, 'I don't know about that at all.'

The evening passed by in a happy blur and the only time the hall was quiet was when Angus made his trademark speech. He thanked the guests for coming and for contributing so generously to swelling the charity funds, as well as for the part everyone had played in helping with the Winter Wonderland, which he hoped would become a regular feature in the Wynthorpe calendar from now on.

'I would also like to properly welcome our two new residents,' he added, pointing to where Gabe and I were standing, trying to melt into the background, 'and finally,' he beamed, raising his glass and looking as if he were about to burst out of his waistcoat with pride, 'I would like to hand over to my youngest son, Jamie, who has something he would like to say.'

'Thanks, Dad,' Jamie grinned, pulling Anna along with him. 'I won't keep you long everyone, I just have something I would like to ask Anna.'

Everyone, Anna included, gasped as he turned and went down on one knee.

'Anna,' he beamed, pulling something large and glittering out of his jacket pocket, 'you know I love you more than Dorothy's Sunday dinners, don't you?'

She laughed and rolled her eyes, her cheeks glowing as she shook her head.

'Even the chicken one with the special gravy?' she giggled.

'Even that one,' he swallowed, suddenly looking more serious. 'Will you make me the happiest man in the world? Will you promise to eat Sunday dinner with me always? Will you marry me?'

You could have heard a pin drop as everyone held their breath and leant in, desperate to hear her answer.

'Of course I will!' she beamed. 'Yes!'

Jamie slipped the ring on her finger and then jumped to his feet, swept her into his arms and kissed her tenderly. The room erupted in cheers, claps and whoops.

'Would you all, please,' cried Angus, with Catherine now close to his side, 'join us in raising our glasses to toast Jamie and our future daughter-in-law, Anna.'

'To Jamie and Anna!' the guests chorused, before their voices were drowned out with yet more claps and cheers as the happy couple were swallowed up by well-wishers all wanting to offer their own congratulations.

'You knew, didn't you?' laughed Anna, when I finally found my way through to her.

'I had an inkling,' I smiled, kissing her cheek. 'But I had no idea he was going to bring Dorothy's beloved roast dinners into it! I know you will both be very happy,' I told her, determined not to get all teary again as Archie filled the gap between us. 'Come on,' I said to Gabe, pulling him towards the door while everyone else was preoccupied with the happy couple. 'Come with me. I have something for you.'

'Oh, Hayley,' he laughed, 'I don't think I have the energy. Not again.'

'It's not that,' I burst out laughing.

I laughed even louder when I saw the look of disappointment on his face.

'I do have a present for you,' I explained, 'but it's not me. You can unwrap me later, though, if you like.'

'I like the sound of that,' he said with a glint in his eye, shrugging off his jacket and wrapping it around my shoulders.

Not surprisingly, we didn't make it back to the party and Gabe didn't unwrap his present before he'd unwrapped me either. Lying in his bed in Gatekeeper's Cottage, our clothes in an abandoned pile on the floor, I reached over the side and picked up the gift I had taken so much time over.

'I hope you like it,' I said, hardly able to watch as he tore at the paper with every bit as much enthusiasm as Anna had shown on her birthday.

I peeped over the duvet as he slowly took it all in. My heart began to panic when he didn't say anything and I hoped I hadn't crossed the line. Perhaps I should have concentrated on the sketch I had almost finished of him and Bran instead.

'I thought you could put it up above the fire,' I suggested, feeling worried that my true intentions were about to be misconstrued. 'These few months,' I went on, 'being here and being with you, have made me realise that there are some things you should face up to rather than shy away from. There are some experiences in life that are too important to pack away and try to pretend never happened, even if they didn't end how you hoped they would.'

He nodded, but still didn't say anything.

'Life's too short not to acknowledge the good bits,' I tried again.

Gabe put the painting down on the bed and pulled me to him.

'It's absolutely beautiful,' he said, 'thank you.'

I felt the tension that had been building in my shoulders slip away.

'And you're right,' he whispered, 'I've been running long enough. I do need to acknowledge the good times, every bit as much as you need to accept that, deep down, you're a bit of a softie, Hayley Hurren.'

There was no arguing with that. I reached out and tilted the frame just enough so I could see it. Gabe and his daughter were on the beach, heads bent together as they explored a rock pool on a sunny day. I had taken the inspiration from a photograph I saw the night we first ended up in bed together. I knew he needed to remember the good times he had shared with his daughter and I wanted to create something new that would enable him to do that.

'I'm afraid,' he said, kissing the top of my head, 'that I still haven't got a Christmas present for you.'

'I shouldn't worry about that,' I told him, melting back down into the bed, 'you've given me the greatest gift of all, my guardian angel, and I'll never want for anything more.'

'I thought,' he said, laying the painting carefully to one side so he could join me under the duvet, 'you were the sort of girl who maintained that she wasn't looking for love?'

I was delighted that he knew what I was talking about.

'No,' I giggled, 'that wasn't me. That was some other girl who used to hang around here, but she's gone now,' I told him. 'I'm a champion for true love and I always will be.'

Acknowledgements

A little over a year ago I had the pleasure of writing the acknowledgements for *Sleigh Rides and Silver Bells*. At the time I had no idea how Anna, the Connelly family and Wynthorpe Hall would be received, but I was soon to find out. To my delight, the entire Wynthorpe clan was awarded the warmest welcome into the world, my dreams of becoming a *Sunday Times* bestseller were realised and the opportunity to make a return visit to the hall was guaranteed. Last Christmas was, without doubt, one of the best ever and I am full of hope that the festive magic sprinkled throughout the pages of this new book will weave its way into your hearts and enhance your seasonal spirit yet again!

As always, I have had the assistance of a professional and dedicated team to help me tell this tale. My agent, Amanda Preston, my editor, Emma Capron, along with Rebecca Farrell, Gemma Conley-Smith, Pip Watkins, Harriett Collins, Hayley McMullan, Alice Rodgers and S-J Virtue, in fact the entire Books and the City Team, have all been on hand. Thank you all so much. You all go above and beyond and the opportunity to work alongside you makes me one very happy author.

And talking of going above and beyond . . .

The fabulous book blogging community have also, yet again, had a helping hand in spreading the word about this book by way of tweets and Facebook posts, by signing up to take part in blog tours, coming along to events, sharing covers online and organising giveaways. Thank you all for making this year even more thrilling than the last.

The same of course can be said for my author chums, especially those close to home, who provide friendship, support and most importantly human contact! Writing can be a solitary business so thank you Jen, Clare, Rosie *et al* for dragging me away from the screen when time allows.

And where would I be without you wonderful readers? Please do keep messaging, mailing and sending those brilliant #shelfies. Each and every one is appreciated and reminds me that the world of Wynbridge and Nightingale Square extends much further than the meanderings of my imagination. There is no greater reward for the hours at the keyboard than discovering that the words have hit the spot, inspired someone to take up a new hobby, get in touch with old friends or perhaps even celebrate the festive season again.

And last, but by absolutely no means least, sits the family. There they are, patiently waiting with the cat, for the end of another writing day and, if I'm lucky, a reviving cup of tea, to help ease the transition from my fictional world back into the real one. I'm certain that living with an author can't be easy but you all pull it off with aplomb. Thank you.

All that remains is for me to wish you all a very merry Christmas. May your bookshelves – be they virtual or real – always be filled with fabulous fiction!

H x

Curl up with Heidi Swain for cupcakes, crafting and love at *The Cherry Tree Café*

Lizzie Dixon's life feels as though it's fallen apart. Instead of the marriage proposal she was hoping for from her boyfriend, she is unceremoniously dumped, and her job is about to go the same way. So, there's only one option: to go back home to the village she grew up in and try to start again.

Her best friend Jemma is delighted Lizzie has come back home. She has just bought a little café and needs help in getting it ready for the grand opening. And Lizzie's sewing skills are just what she needs.

With a new venture and a new home, things are looking much brighter for Lizzie. But can she get over her broken heart, and will an old flame reignite a love from long ago . . .?

'Fans of Jenny Colgan and Carole Matthews will enjoy this warm and funny story'
Katie Oliver, author of the bestselling
'Marrying Mr Darcy' series

Available now in paperback, eBook and eAudio

**Escape the winter blues and fall
in love with country living . . .**

Amber is a city girl at heart. So when her
boyfriend Jake Somerville suggests they move
to the countryside to help out at his family
farm, she doesn't quite know how to react. But
work has been hectic and she needs a break, so
she decides to grasp the opportunity.

Dreaming of organic orchards, paddling in streams
and frolicking in fields, Amber packs up her things
and moves to Skylark Farm. But life is not quite
how she imagined – it's cold and dirty and the farm
buildings are dilapidated and crumbling . . .

Even so, Amber is determined to make the
best of it and throws herself into farm life.
But can she really fit in here? And can she and
Jake stay together when they are so different?

Summer at Skylark Farm

Available now in paperback, eBook and eAudio

Christmas has arrived in the town of Wynbridge and it promises mince pies, mistletoe and a whole host of seasonal joy

Ruby has finished with university and is heading home for the holidays. She takes on a stall at the local market, and sets about making it the best Christmas market stall ever. There'll be bunting and mistletoe and maybe even a bit of mulled wine.

But with a new retail park just opened, the market is under threat. So together with all the other stallholders, Ruby devises a plan to make sure the market is the first port of call for everyone's Christmas shopping needs.

The only thing standing in her way is her ex, Steve. It's pretty hard to concentrate when he works on the stall opposite, especially when she realises that her feelings are still there . . .

This Christmas make time for some winter sparkle – and see who might be under the mistletoe this year . . .

Mince Pies and Mistletoe at the Christmas Market

Available now in paperback, eBook and eAudio

Curl up with this glorious treat of
glamping, vintage tearooms and love . . .

When Lottie Foster's grandmother's
best friend Gwen dies, she leaves Lottie her
lovely home, Cuckoo Cottage.

Lottie loves the cottage but Matt, a charming local
builder, points out that beneath its charm it is falling
apart. Luckily he is always on hand to help with the
problems that somehow seem to keep cropping up.
But is he just a bit too good to be true? Certainly
Will, Lottie's closest neighbour, seems to think so.

Lottie plans to set up her own business renovating
vintage caravans. She hasn't told anyone about the
project she has cooked up with Jemma from
The Cherry Tree Café to repurpose Gwen's old
caravan and turn it into a gorgeous tearoom.

But before she can finally enjoy living with her
legacy she must uncover who she can trust, and
who to avoid. And with two men vying for
her attention, will she also find love?

Coming Home to Cuckoo Cottage

Available now in paperback, eBook and eAudio

The *Sunday Times* Christmas bestseller!

When Anna takes on the role of companion to
the owner of Wynthorpe Hall, on the outskirts of
Wynbridge, she has no idea that her life is
set to change beyond all recognition.

A confirmed 'bah humbug' when it comes
to Christmas, Anna is amazed to find herself
quickly immersed in the eccentric household, and
when youngest son Jamie unexpectedly arrives
home it soon becomes obvious that her personal
feelings are going all out to compromise her
professional persona.

Jamie, struggling to come to terms with life back in
the Fens, makes a pact with Anna – she has
to teach him to fall back in love with
Wynthorpe Hall, while he helps her fall
back in love with Christmas. But will it all
prove too much for Anna, or can the family of
Wynthorpe Hall warm her heart once and for all . . . ?

*Sleigh Rides and Silver Bells at
the Christmas Fair*

Available now in paperback, eBook and eAudio

'Pour out the Pimm's, pull out the deckchair and lose yourself in this lovely, sweet, summery story!' Milly Johnson

Kate is on the run from her soon-to-be ex-husband, who still desperately wants her back, when she stumbles across a cosy nook in Norwich – Nightingale Square.

What Kate doesn't count on is being pulled out of her perfect little hiding place and into a community that won't take no for an answer. Before long, Kate finds herself surrounded by friends. But when developers move in on the magnificent Victorian mansion on the other side of the square, the preservation of their community's history is challenged.

As all hope seems lost, will the arrival of a handsome stranger turn things around for both Kate and Nightingale Square? Or have their chances for a happy-ever-after finally run out . . .?

Sunshine and Sweet Peas in Nightingale Square

Available now in paperback, eBook and eAudio

booksandthecity.co.uk
the home of female fiction

BOOKS | NEWS & EVENTS | FEATURES | AUTHOR PODCASTS | COMPETITIONS

Follow us online to be the first to hear from
your favourite authors

booksandthecity.co.uk   **books and the city**   **@TeamBATC**

Join our mailing list for the latest news, events and
exclusive competitions

Sign up at
booksandthecity.co.uk